DEATH
ON TAP

ELLIE ALEXANDER

St. Martin's Paperbacks

This is a work of fiction. All of the characters, organizations, and events portrayed in this novel are either products of the author's imagination or are used fictitiously.

DEATH ON TAP

Copyright © 2017 by Kate Dyer-Seeley.
Excerpt from *The Pint of No Return* copyright © 2018 by Kate Dyer-Seeley.

For information address St. Martin's Press, 120 Broadway, New York, NY 10271.

ISBN: 978-1-250-19070-3

Our books may be purchased in bulk for promotional, educational, or business use. Please contact your local bookseller or the Macmillan Corporate and Premium Sales Department at 1-800-221-7945, ext. 5442, or by e-mail at MacmillanSpecialMarkets@macmillan.com.

Printed in the United States of America

Minotaur hardcover edition / October 2017
St. Martin's Paperbacks edition / September 2018

St. Martin's Paperbacks are published by St. Martin's Press, 120 Broadway, New York, NY 10271.

10 9 8 7 6 5

To my root brewmaster, Luke, and craft brewmaster, Gordy, cheers to you.

ACKNOWLEDGMENTS

Many thanks to the town and people of Leavenworth, Washington, for inviting me in, answering endless questions, sharing insider secrets, and capturing me in your charms. I've enjoyed every minute I've spent in the Pacific Northwest's Bavaria, and hope that my fictional creation pays homage to the real-life inspiration.

To my crew of early readers, Erin, Beth, Elaine, Malinda, and Pam, I can't thank you enough for reading drafts and offering your input and advice. I owe you a pint! I'm equally grateful to the authors who took time out of their busy writing schedules to read and blurb the book, including Kate, Shelia, Barbara, Leslie, Meg, and Cindy. Next mystery convention, drinks are on me.

Lastly, I'd like to raise a glass to the team at St. Martin's Press for their incredible support. Prost!

CHAPTER
ONE

IT WASN'T SO MUCH THE sight of my husband's bare ass that would become permanently etched in my memory, but rather the rhythmic sounds of the German brass band oompah-ing in the background, coupled with the strong, but delicious smell of grains steeping in the mash tun.

I shouldn't have been in the pub anyway. It was my day off, but instead of spending it in the late summer sun, I had opted to tinker with a new recipe I'd been working on. A few minutes into the brewing process, I realized I'd forgotten cinnamon. Mac, my husband and brewmaster for Der Keller (the Cellar if you don't *sprechen sie Deutsch*, as my mother-in-law likes to say), was nowhere to be found. Typical.

"Otto," I called to my father-in-law, the patriarch of our family and an award-winning brewmaster. "I'm running to grab some cinnamon. Can you watch the wort? I'll be back in a few."

"*Ja,* Sloan," Otto replied from behind an eight-foot copper kettle. "I will wait with ze beer."

I grabbed a twenty from the register, tucked it into my pocket, and weaved through the crowd of regulars kicking back with midafternoon pints. Country air greeted me outside on the cobblestone streets. I hurried along Front Street for two blocks, passing flowerpots and window boxes stuffed with red geraniums, an authentic fifteen-foot-tall cuckoo clock in the town square, and rows of antique streetlights. A-frame rooftops lined the thoroughfare like gingerbread cottages. The sound of Steller's jays squawking greetings to each other overhead made me pause and look up.

Gently sloping peaks rose around me in every direction. The nearby mountains sheltering our village stood at five to eight thousand feet, like gentle guardians watching over us. I smiled at the thought and noticed how the first signs of fall were beginning to creep in. A scattering of yellow and orange leaves dotted the otherwise dark green mountainside.

Continuing up Front Street, I saw that more preparations for fall were under way. Workers were installing crimson Oktoberfest banners, and shopkeepers were adorning their front windows with garlands of gorgeous foliage and yellow twinkle lights. Oktoberfest was right around the corner, which meant that soon our sidewalks would be packed with merry revelers toasting with overflowing beer steins and dancing to accordion music. Even the grocery store, with its brocade façade, looked like it should be nestled in the German Alps, not the Pacific Northwest. Like everything else in our small town, it was fashioned after a Bavarian village.

I stepped inside and weaved my way through aisles of imported chocolates, gummy bears, and sauerkraut until I found the cinnamon. Then I paid quickly and hightailed it back to the pub. Beer making is an art and a science. Timing is everything. I knew that Otto would keep his eye on my new creation, but this batch was the result of months of experimenting, and I wanted to make sure nothing went wrong.

"What's your rush, Sloan?" the owner of The Nutcracker called as I hurried by. She positioned a miniature nutcracker wearing forest-green lederhosen and holding a stein in the window.

"The beer won't wait." I grinned and continued on.

As promised, Otto was dutifully watching my batch when I returned. His wiry gray hair stuck out in all directions. He looked more like a mad scientist than a jovial beer-loving grandpa (or *Opa*). Ursula, his wife, stood shoulder to shoulder with him.

"Sloan, we must go." She pressed a timer into my hand. "Your beer is smelling good."

She had to stand on her toes to kiss my cheek. In her prime, she'd stood not much taller than five feet. With age, her shoulders had started to slump and her walk had turned to a shuffle. She was the only mother I'd ever known, and watching her get older was sometimes more than I could bear. No tourist would ever have thought we were a family. Otto and Ursula, with their fair German skin, short stature, and matching gray hair; me with full lips, huge pores, and jet black hair. One of my foster moms once told me that my mother was Greek. It would fit. The sun loves my skin. Fifteen minutes outside, and my skin looks like a nut brown ale. Mac, on the other hand, is burnt to a crisp and glowing like a pint of amber in five minutes.

His ass certainly hasn't seen the sun—that was the first thought that flashed through my mind when I walked to the back office to grab my notes and swung the door open, and there stood Mac with jeans slouched around his ankles and the twenty-three-year-old barmaid we had just hired sprawled on my desk.

My hand flew to my mouth. I dropped the spice jar on the floor. It broke and sent shattered pieces of cinnamon stick in all directions.

"Sloan!" Mac jumped and whirled around. "This isn't what you think." He yanked up his jeans and coughed.

Yeah, right. I couldn't think of what to do next, so I pointed to the cinnamon shards on the epoxy floor, dusted off my shirt, and said, "You're going to need to clean this up."

I turned and tried to keep my composure as I walked away. The smell of wort enveloped me as I sprinted toward the fermenting tank. Usually the scent was comforting, but at the moment, it made me want to vomit. My hands shook. My knees felt like they were about to give way. I clutched the ladder at the base of the copper kettle.

Don't make a scene, I told myself while trying to ignore the woozy feeling working its way up the back of my neck.

Years in the foster care system had taught me that making a scene gets you sent to bed without dinner or sent

4

packing. I wouldn't give Mac the satisfaction. I sunk onto the ladder. What an ass—literally.

I'd suspected for a while that Mac had been fooling around, but I'd never been able to prove it. The twenty-three-year-old barmaid, in *my* office? That, I never saw coming.

CHAPTER

TWO

ADRENALINE PUMPED THROUGH MY TREMBLING body. How could he have done this to me? Fifteen years of marriage down the drain.

The room felt hot, and not because of the hundred-gallon copper tanks heating my malty blend of organic grains. Sweat beaded on my forehead and dripped down my face. I wiped my brow with the back of my hand.

What was I going to do?

At that moment, I heard a door slam and caught a glimpse of the beer wench scurrying toward the pub. Her long blond locks swung to the middle of her back, and her jeans looked as if she'd painted them on.

God, she was young.

Probably as young as I was when I married the scoundrel.

I couldn't entirely blame her. Mac exudes an intense attraction. Wherever we went, women let their eyes linger a little too long on his baby face and flirtatious eyes. Over the years I'd gotten used to it, but that didn't mean that I enjoyed watching women ogle my husband.

Mac and his family of German brewmasters had taught me everything I knew. Otto, Mac's dad, had brought his German techniques with him to Leavenworth, Washington, in the early 1970s and formed one of the city's first breweries and pubs. He and his wife, Ursula, had started a tiny tasting room in the midst of a full-scale town remodel. The dingy five-hundred-square-foot space was all they could afford when they uprooted their two young children, Mac and Hans, from Germany and transplanted to Leavenworth. It had been a family affair ever since, and Der Keller had grown into one of the largest breweries in the state, with a bevy of international clients and accolades to boot.

Beer aficionados credited the Krause family with putting Leavenworth on the map for its now globally famous microbrew culture. Times had changed dramatically since the Krauses began brewing. The villagers had poured everything they had into creating a destination town, and their bet had paid off. Our little town was now a beer travel destination with over a million visitors roaming our quaint streets each year.

Learning the beer business wasn't something I ever aspired to. Nor was falling for Mac. It happened all at once. When I graduated from high school, I left the foster care system behind and took every job I could to pay the bills while attending community college. Being broke was infinitely better than being a foster kid.

My high school home economics teacher had seen potential in my ability in the kitchen—I think in part because the group of obnoxious football players I was paired with intentionally tried to burn everything we were tasked with baking. She recommended me for a scholarship in the cooking and restaurant management program at the college. Having my tuition covered was more than I could have wished for, but it still left me struggling to pay rent and buy groceries. I worked as a waitress in the evenings and managed a booth at Leavenworth's farmers' market on the weekends. That was when I met the Krauses. They were regulars at the market, where they would source fresh fruits and herbs for the brewery.

"Sloan, how is the schooling going for you?" Otto asked with a jovial smile, examining a bundle of pineapple sage. "Tell us about your newest cooking creations."

"Otto!" Ursula hit him gently. "She's working. Don't bother her."

The market stall owner had agreed to let me sell small batches of cookies and bars. Cooking had been an escape for me and a handy skill to have when I was hopping between foster homes.

I handed the Krauses a German chocolate cookie bar.

Ursula grinned as she took a bite. "Sloan, zis is wonderful. It is funny zey call zis German because it is an American recipe. Our Mac is coming home from his beer tour in Germany next week. We bring him to meet you, *ja*?"

"Sure." I laughed, tucking a wavy curl behind my ear. The Krauses had been trying to set me up with their oldest son since the first day they stopped by my booth. "I'd love to meet him." I don't remember, but I'm sure I blushed. I hadn't dated much, mainly because I never stayed in one place long enough.

The way the Krauses spoke about their children made my lonely apartment feel even more empty and cold than usual. Never having known my parents or any kind of stability as a child left me with a tender wound that I didn't even know existed until I met the Krauses.

True to their word, they brought Mac the next week. My fellow market vendors called him the golden boy. His blond hair seemed to shimmer in the morning light. He towered over his parents at nearly six feet and captivated the busy market with his presence. His muscular body oozed sensuality and confidence. It was easy to fall for the golden boy. Although, in hindsight, I think really I fell for his family. One date led to another. Within four months, I was pregnant.

Fifteen years later, I didn't regret marrying Mac. I knew I was biased, but Alex, our son, was the coolest kid I knew. When I felt generous, I had to credit Mac for being a good dad. However, with the scent of cinnamon searing on my burning cheeks, I didn't feel an ounce of warmth toward the father of my only child. I had to get out of the brewery—now.

CHAPTER

THREE

I DUG MY HAND INTO the back pocket of my jeans and pulled out my cell phone. There was only one person I could call—Hans. *I'll call Hans,* I told myself. *He'll know what to do.* My fingers shook so violently I didn't think I could punch in my passcode. I held my wrist with my left hand to steady the tremors and dialed Hans's number.

It seemed to ring forever.

Pick up, pick up.

"Hey there, sis. What's up? Having trouble with the mash tun again?"

"Hans," I whispered into the phone, "you have to get over here—now! Mac, I just found Mac . . ."

"Wait, Sloan. Speak up. I can't hear you."

I whispered louder. "I need you. Can you come to the brewery, now?"

"Hang on a sec."

I heard Hans shout to his crew to turn off their power tools.

"Okay, sorry. That's better. Couldn't hear a thing over the circular saw. What's up?"

"Hans." I fought back tears. "I found Mac with the new barmaid."

"What?"

I froze as Mac stepped out of the office. He smoothed the front of his white tailored shirt with the Der Keller logo on the breast and scanned the brewery. I crouched lower behind the kettle.

"Sloan, Sloan, are you there?" Hans's voice blared in my ear.

"Shhhh! One sec. I think Mac's looking for me."

I could see Mac's blond head craning to see if anyone was around. My body felt like it would betray me. The aluminum ladder I was perched on led to an access hatch at the top of one of Der Keller's four fermenting tanks. An extensive network of platforms and scaffolding ran between each of the tanks. While most of the system was automated, the access hatches were used to add dry hops to the fermenter. The ladder felt stable, but I was worried that if I couldn't stop trembling, it might crash into the expensive copper tank.

Mac gave the room one last glance and walked away.

"Okay, he's gone," I said to Hans.

"Sloan, where are you?"

"Hiding behind the fermenting tank." I glanced at the filtered light streaming in through the tinted skylights. Ursula had insisted on adding skylights to the industrial space a few years ago. The simple act of allowing light into the brewery had transformed the previously dark and cold warehouse into a warm and radiant workplace.

"You're what?"

"Please, come over here."

"Don't move. I'll come find you."

I had no intention of moving a muscle. The echoing space smelled like Grape-Nuts. So much for my new batch. It had to be ruined by now.

Thank goodness it was bottling day. The brewery staff were across the street at the bottling plant. Der Keller's operations took up fifty thousand square feet of warehouse space in three buildings. The building I was hiding in housed our brewery and pub. We bottled and distributed the beer across the street.

The brewery's brick-red epoxy floors reflected the sun overhead. I studied the rows and rows of medals and awards lining the opposite wall. Der Keller had won nearly every national and international brewing competition over the years. The collection of gold, silver, and bronze medals hanging from the wall was proof that the brewery was esteemed in the world of craft beer.

"Sloan!" I heard Hans's voice. "Where are you?"

"Back here," I called, not releasing my grip on the ladder.

It didn't take long for Hans to find me. He reached a tanned arm out and pulled me to my feet. "Come on, Sloan. Let's get you a pint."

I froze and shook my head. "I can't. No way. I can't see anyone right now."

Hans tightened his grip. "No one's here. Mac just left. The

pub's pretty empty. Only a handful of regulars too focused on their beers to notice you." He shifted the tool belt resting on his waist and reached into the pocket of his faded Carhartt pants. Brushing sawdust off a handkerchief, he handed it to me and focused his golden brown eyes on mine. "Take this. I'll meet you in the beer garden in two minutes."

Did he think I'd been crying? I clutched the handkerchief and pushed my shoulders upright. We navigated past twenty-foot copper kettles imported from Europe. When I hosted brewery tours, the copper kettles were always one of the highlights. Beer lovers would ooh and ahh when I explained that the kettles weren't just for show. The type of metal, the way it was welded together, and its shape could greatly influence the taste of beer.

Hans led me to the pub. He was right. The lunch crowd had cleared out. A couple of regulars sat at the bar debating the IBUs (that's International Bittering Units, or the measurement of hop bitterness in the beer, for non–beer geeks), but otherwise the place was empty except for two barmaids, who were restocking gleaming pint glasses behind the bar. They both were outfitted in matching red dirndl dresses tied with black, yellow, and white checkered aprons. German memorabilia of all kinds, from flags and banners to the Krauses' collection of vintage beer steins, were displayed throughout the old world pub. The bartender, who also wore our standard red checkered *Trachten* shirt and black suspenders, caught my eye and waved as I rushed past.

Der Keller's *Biergarten* sits off to the side of the pub. I opened the patio doors and sighed with relief that the picnic tables were empty as well. Despite the sunny skies, the air held a crispness. I could almost smell the changing season. Leavenworth boasts three hundred days of sun each year. We keep the beer garden open as long as the weather will allow. It's one of my favorite spots in the spring and summertime, with hop vines snaking along the picket fence that encloses the space from the street. Last summer Hans built a lattice for the hops. They braided themselves in tight spirals up hemp strings, stretching toward the sun. The dappled light they let in gave the space a dreamy vibe.

I picked the table farthest from the door and squeezed my long legs under the bench.

Hans returned with two pewter beer steins engraved with the Der Keller family logo. Placing a stein in front of me, he paused for a second and stared at a cedar hop lattice that needed mending. I recognized the warm red color of the beer as our award-winning Doppelbock.

Doppelbock is the strongest beer style we brew. For such a hearty beer, it's very drinkable, with heavy malt and almost no bitterness. Most beers weigh in with 5 to 6 percent alcohol content. Our Doppelbock has an alcohol content of 10 percent. One pint of this baby, and most newbies would start to spin. But I was no newbie and was more than ready for a stiff drink.

"Thanks, good choice," I said, forcing a smile.

Hans removed his tool belt and rested it on the table. He adjusted the dull navy baseball cap on his head and tilted it toward my stein. "Drink slow. It's good for your soul."

Hans is eight years younger than Mac. You'd never know it based on their work ethic and maturity. Hans was a scrawny teenager when Mac and I married. Ever since, he's been the kid brother I never had.

I stuck my nose in the custom stein with the Der Keller logo (two lions waving German flags) before taking a sip. Old habits die hard. I'd tasted this beer a thousand times. The recipe hadn't changed, but I every time I drank it, I ended up catching a hint of something different. Today I picked up a full-bodied, roasted flavor with a hint of toffee. One sip confirmed Hans knew exactly what I needed. The dark amber malt felt like liquid gold on my throat. Hopefully the alcohol would kick in soon and make me forget what I'd seen.

"Are you going to spill, or am I going to have to extract information out of you like usual?" Hans hadn't touched his beer.

"What's that supposed to mean?"

He picked up his stein and set it on the table again, as if he'd had second thoughts about drinking. "You know, you're not the most forthcoming person, Sloan. I love you, and I understand why, but . . ." He trailed off.

I took another swig of the beer, but despite my best efforts to keep my shaky hands steady, I managed to spill it on the table. Hans noticed, but didn't say a word. Instead, he dabbed the table with a napkin and waited for me.

"I don't even know where to start," I said, clutching the frosty pewter pint.

"How about the beginning?" Hans pushed the beer-soaked cloth napkin to the edge of the table.

It didn't take long to fill Hans in on the gory details of

catching his brother shagging the beer wench, as she would forevermore be known.

When I finished relaying the scene to Hans, he sat without responding for a minute. My beer was nearly empty. Hans's stein was full. I can't stand the bottom quarter of a pint. Beer should be ice-cold and full of carbonation. There's no way to avoid the warm dregs of the last of a pint. I grabbed my stein and dumped the warm beer on the hop vines.

"Are you going to drink that?" asked Hans.

He shook his head and offered me his full glass.

"And are you up for driving me home?"

He reached over and picked a few hops from the vine. Fingering one, he nodded again and tossed it to me. I breathed in the scent. The smell of hops returned my heart rate to normal. Hops are a known relaxant. I often sleep with a stash under my pillow to help unwind at night.

Hans crushed the hops in his hand and threw the shreds on the ground. "Sometimes I can't believe Mac is my brother." Then he yanked another hop cone from the vine and rubbed it between his hands. "Don't take this the wrong way, because I'm not condoning his behavior, but I know that he loves you."

I followed suit and ran my fingers over the hop. "He has a funny way of showing it." The oil from the hops coated my fingers.

"What are you going to do?"

"I don't know. Change the locks? If he's so enamored with the beer wench, he can go shack up with her."

Hans started to respond, but I cut him off in midstream.

"Oh no! Alex. What am I going to say to Alex? This will

crush him. And—your parents? The town? Oh my God! I'm going to be the laughingstock of the entire village, aren't I? Or am I already? Does everyone already know that Mac's been cheating on me?"

Hans reached his arm across the table and rested it on my hand. "Slow down. Breathe."

I took a deep breath.

"That's it." He took a screwdriver out of his tool belt and tightened a loose bolt on the picnic table. "No one in town knows, and we'll make sure we keep it that way."

After I drained Hans's beer, I allowed him to lead me out to where he'd parked his Jeep. I didn't believe him. In a town this size, everyone was going to be talking about one thing—me.

CHAPTER

FOUR

THREE WEEKS LATER, MY ANGER at Mac hadn't subsided. In fact, if anything it was worse. After kicking him out and hiding in my bedroom for longer than I wanted to admit, I finally decided that I wasn't going to give him the satisfaction of making me feel humiliated. If anyone should have been ashamed, it was him. So when Hans called to check in and mentioned that a new nanobrewery was looking for help, I jumped at the chance, not caring what anyone in town might think.

For the next few days, I researched everything I could about Nitro, Leavenworth's newest taproom and my new temporary place of employment. I'd been working with the Krause family at Der Keller for my entire adult life. The idea of branching out was equally exhilarating and terrifying. As was evident by the queasy feeling in my stomach the morning of my first day. I barely touched my morning coffee and changed outfits at least five times.

Relax, Sloan, I told myself as I finally decided on a black pencil skirt and a charcoal gray blouse. I pulled my hair into a tight ponytail and was relieved that at least for the moment my natural waves were cooperating. My hair is so thick that it has a tendency to frizz and escape from attempts to tie it back.

Glancing at the cuckoo clock mounted above the fireplace, I called down the hallway, "Alex, grab your stuff. We've got to get moving."

When Mac and I purchased our farmhouse ten years ago, he fell in love with the rambling yard. The house was situated on several acres of land a few minutes from the town square. Mac had needed to wipe drool off his chin when our real estate agent had opened the doors to the wraparound back porch to showcase the acreage. To me the giant space, with overgrown blackberry bushes and ivy vines, looked like a major project. Not to Mac.

"Think of the hops, baby," he said, squeezing my shoulder. "We'll level this all out and run rows and rows of Smaragd hops." Turning to flash his signature smile at our agent, he gasped, "Full sun!"

While they explored the weed-infested yard, I wandered through the interior of the house on my own. Mac could have the backyard. I claimed the kitchen—with its high exposed-beam ceilings, clapboard walls, brick fireplace, and wood-burning bread oven. I fell in love with the cozy vibe of the inviting space and the idea that I'd serve my family from the same kitchen that had dished up warm meals to hungry farmhands and family members for decades.

Over the next few years, I made the kitchen my own by

painting the walls a warm buttercream and decorating with rustic farm accents like old tin milk pails, barnwood frames, and vintage wicker baskets filled with hand-pressed tea towels and sacks of flour. Transforming the space to its original roots became my mission.

The sound of Alex's footsteps racing along the reclaimed hardwood floors pulled me from my memory. What was I going to do with this place now? A mini hop farm and nearly four thousand square feet of farmhouse were more than I needed or wanted for just Alex and me.

No time to think about that now. I had to get Alex to school and myself to my new job. I grabbed a yogurt from the fridge and an apple from the bowl on the kitchen island.

"You ready?" I asked, ruffling Alex's shaggy auburn waves as he came into the kitchen.

He playfully tossed my hand away and adjusted the athletic bag hanging from his shoulder. A pair of muddy soccer cleats banged against the counter. "When are you going to stop doing that, Mom? I'm not a kid anymore, you know."

"I know." I tucked the yogurt and apple into my purse and opened the front door. "After you, big man."

In the last few months, Alex had shot up. It was strange to have to look up to meet my son's eyes. "We have to hurry; I don't want to be late on my first day."

"When have you ever been late?" Alex said, and then sprinted outside to our black Mercedes, an anniversary present from Mac (more like a guilt present). Fancy cars aren't my thing—the Mercedes was Mac's style. He had thrown a huge party for our anniversary last year, invited the entire town, and surprised me with the Mercedes tied with a big red bow. I would have preferred Hans's beat-up Jeep.

Alex threw his backpack and athletic bag on the back seat of the car and stuffed his long legs into the front. He'd definitely inherited his leanness from me. "Mom, I don't want you to worry about being late. Drop me off at Carly's. I'll walk from there."

"You sure? I thought you two were on a break."

I busied myself fiddling with the mirrors and clicking on the radio. As long as we didn't make eye contact, Alex would divulge details about school, friends, and his emerging world of girlfriends. The car was like a traveling therapy office.

"Yeah, it's cool. We're kind of hanging a little." He didn't notice me check his appearance in the side mirror.

He's so beautiful, I thought, trying to fight the lump forming in my throat. He'd been graced with Mac's full frame and my olive skin. His pale blue eyes were flecked with gold. I could still see the outline of the baby I'd rocked in my arms in his maturing face, but it was beginning to firm into adulthood. Time was a fickle beast. I wouldn't have traded the wisecracking kid sitting next to me, but there were moments when I ached for the memory of his baby skin and pudgy little legs.

Nothing about his laid-back teenage body revealed that he was upset about Mac and me. But I knew better. I watched him twist a strand of hair on the back of his neck, a nervous habit left over from his toddler days. Getting him to talk to me was going to take a slow and deliberate effort. There was no need to rush him.

We pulled into Carly's driveway, and Alex leaned over to give me a kiss on the cheek. "Love you, Mom. Good luck today. I know you're going to be great."

I hoped he was right.

CHAPTER

FIVE

I STEERED THE MERCEDES ONTO the one-lane highway that led into town. Nitro was conveniently located near the town square. The sun cast a flaxen glow on the mountains. It wouldn't be too long before they were capped with snow and bustling with backcountry adventurers. Skiers and snow-shoers flocked to our Cascadian Alps every winter. In true European spirit, Leavenworth welcomed the cold weather visitors with spicy mugs of hot mulled wine, outdoor bon-fires, sleigh rides, and holiday markets. Kids would sled and sip hot cocoa under a canopy of festive lights and decora-tions while their parents played the part of der Weihnachts-mann (Father Christmas) and filled bags with handmade toys and chocolates. The village would truly become a winter wonderland soon, but for the moment I drank in Leavenworth's beauty as I passed acres of organic farmland, ripe apple and pear orchards, and small family vineyards where rows and rows of cluster-laden grapevines stretched along the ridge.

On the drive I reviewed everything I'd learned about Nitro. The new taproom, dining area, and brew operation would be Leavenworth's first nanobrewery.

The distinction between brewery sizes is all about production. Nanobreweries have been spreading like wildfire across the Pacific Northwest. There's a big debate in the brewing community about who fits or doesn't fit within the nano criteria.

At Der Keller, we produced about fifteen thousand barrels of beer each year, giving us the title of microbrewery. To give you some perspective, the big guys—those national watered-down brands sold in cans in grocery stores across the country—produce upwards of two million barrels of beer annually. Nanos produce much smaller quantities of beer, which gives them the freedom to experiment with flavors and grains.

The word around Leavenworth was that everyone wanted what Nitro's owner, Garrett Strong, was brewing.

Garrett had hired me sight unseen, thanks to Hans. I'd learned that Garrett had spent ten years home brewing in Seattle while working as an engineer. When his great-aunt Tess died last fall, she'd left him a historic building off Front Street that he'd been refurbishing for the past few months. I'd heard rumors about him, but he'd been keeping to himself since he arrived in town, which only fueled local speculation.

"I think you'll really like him, Sloan," Hans had said as he cracked open a bottle of session ale on my back porch. "He needs someone to help him with marketing, food, and the tasting room. He's kind of in his head, but he has the nose."

"Having the nose" was a constant topic of discussion in the Krause family. Otto had the nose, but neither of his sons did. That didn't bother Hans, as his preferred art form involved a hammer and chisel, but Mac had tried desperately to develop his palate. From beer classes to tours in Germany, he'd spent years trying to find his nose. Nothing worked.

Don't get me wrong—the Krause men knew beer. Both brothers could have offered a college-level course on the brewing process, but having the ability to smell each unique ingredient and hop variety in a single mug was a skill you either had or didn't. It couldn't be taught.

"You know a little something about that, don't you?" Hans had teased.

Since neither of Otto's offspring had inherited his discerning sniffer, he had set his sights on me. Convinced I had magic nostrils, he'd taken me under his wing. "Sloan, *ja,* you have it. You have the nose." I wasn't sure that he was right, but I had enjoyed working under his direction.

Now that is all changing, I thought as I navigated through downtown and turned off Front Street onto Ninth. Nitro was located two blocks from the main village on Commercial Street, near Waterfront Park, with its lush walking trails that wound along the Wenatchee River and onto Blackbird Island. I pulled into an empty parking space and took a minute to listen to the calming sound of the rushing river and watch fish fly from its banks. On the hill opposite the river, mountain goats noshed on grass at Leavenworth's outdoor mini-golf course.

Here goes nothing, I thought as I sucked air through my "special" nose and strolled through the front doors of Nitro.

"Hello?" I called as I entered the building. My voice echoed off the stark white walls, and my heels clicked on the cement floor.

I studied the space. Comparing Nitro to Der Keller would have been unfair. The original tasting room and small cellar where Otto and Ursula started had grown into a two-block conglomerate with warehouses, bottling plants, grain storage silos, loading docks, and a restaurant and tasting room.

At first glance, Nitro appeared to be more like the Krause family's humble roots. I'd have guessed the space to be about five thousand square feet with twenty-five-foot-high ceilings and cement walls painted in a glaring white. Everything was white, from floor to ceiling. The only things breaking the monotony were a few beer charts and posters of chemistry tables and formulas for fermenting.

This guy really has a thing for science, I thought.

An assortment of barstools and tables were arranged in the front of a bar that divided the tasting room from the brewery equipment in the back. Shrink-wrapped boxes of pint glasses sat unpacked on the bar. I walked past the twenty-foot bar carved from distressed wood and into the brewery.

Garrett scored points on the cleanliness scale. From mash tuns to the clarifying tanks, the stainless steel sparkled. That was good. Nothing turned me off more than a brewer who skimped on sanitation. Any reputable brewmaster knew that cleaning was half the equation when it came to producing high-quality craft beer.

The sound of someone clearing his voice behind me made

me jump. "You must be Sloan." Garrett Strong approached me from a small walled-in office in the farthest corner of the brewery. He stood at over six feet with the physique of a basketball player and professor rolled into one. His dark hair fell over one of his hickory-colored eyes.

He brushed the hair behind chemistry goggles resting on his forehead and extended his hand. "I've never met anyone named Sloan."

I shook his hand. "And I've never met anyone named Garrett." Shrugging, I gave him a wink. "I guess that makes us even."

He tossed his head back in a laugh that transformed his face. Dropping my hand, he stuck his hands in his jeans pockets. "You look like someone I know. Have we met before?"

"I don't think so." I felt overdressed in my skirt and tailored shirt.

Readjusting his goggles, he appraised me with a frown. "Are you sure? There's something really familiar about you. Really familiar."

I shrugged. "I don't think we've met, but maybe you saw my picture on Der Keller's Web site or something?"

He tapped his index finger on his chin and thought for a second. I got the sense that he wasn't convinced, but he dropped it and motioned toward the brewery. "Yeah, that could be it. So what do you think? Did you ever see the place when my aunt Tess owned it?"

"Yeah." I swallowed and managed a nod. Was it just me, or had there been a tiny spark of electricity when we touched? It was probably my nerves. Kicking Mac out had left me feeling unsettled and unsteady, even though I knew it was the right choice.

"Different, isn't it?" Garrett extended his arms out to showcase the blindingly white warehouse.

"It doesn't look anything like the old inn." The last time I'd been inside the restaurant, it had looked completely different, with vinyl booths, wainscoting, and lace curtains. Garrett must have spent a small fortune demoing the space. And he must have gotten a deal on white paint.

"I'm sure it's not the operation you've been used to," he said with a sheepish smile. "But you want a tour?"

"Sure." I gave him a thumbs-up and followed him to the office. He pulled a set of keys from his pocket and unlocked the door.

"You really are from Seattle, aren't you?" I joked. "No one locks up around here."

Leavenworth is the kind of town where no one locks their doors. Break-ins are unheard of. The only robbery I've experienced is when one of my neighbors "borrowed" some of my overgrown rhubarb, then she "broke in" and left two fresh pies on our kitchen counter.

Garrett raised his eyebrow. "Huh. Well, I do."

I couldn't read him. My ability to size up people is like a sixth sense, a survival strategy I sharpened over years of carefully observing a rotation of foster parents, but Garrett wasn't giving anything away.

The office wasn't much bigger than my broom closet at home. He'd managed to squeeze two desks and rolling chairs, along with a filing cabinet and desktop printer, into the tight space. The white walls were covered in writing—recipes, formulas, and mathematical equations I couldn't understand.

I pointed to the pens hanging from strings tied above the doorframe. "Writing on the walls? I thought they taught us not to do that in school."

He licked his finger and wiped a small section of orange pen off the wall. "Dry-erase paint. One of the only tricks from the corporate world that I held on to. It's easy for me to work things out in a big space."

Profound. That philosophy could have applied to my life. I needed a big space to work out what had happened with Mac.

To Garrett I said, "Genius. I like it."

"Feel free to use anything you want in here. I know it's kind of tight, but we probably won't be in here at the same time much." His eyes landed on three open bags of Doritos on the desk. He blushed slightly and moved them to the top of the filing cabinet. "Sorry, I like to snack while I'm doing research and development on new recipes."

"Don't apologize, but don't leave those lying around—I have a serious addiction to Doritos. I can't promise that I won't devour an entire bag." *Especially now,* I thought to myself. *I might need more than Doritos to get through the next few days.* One thing about life in a small town was that everyone was sure to come out for Garrett's grand opening. Since I had found Mac with the beer wench, I'd been successful at staying underground. I wasn't sure I was ready to face the entire town and the Krause family.

"Hans told me that you and I had a lot in common. You

can't go wrong with Doritos." Then his lips tensed and his brow furrowed. "Do what you want with Doritos, but in all seriousness, whatever you do, be sure to lock the door anytime you leave. Even if you're coming out to the brewery. This is my working lab, and I don't want anyone else wandering in here."

"You got it." I nodded, hoping my face shared his solemn attitude.

"Ready for the rest of the tour?" He held the door open for me.

As I followed him out of the office, I glanced at the recipes on the walls behind me. I knew brewmasters were protective of their creations, but this seemed borderline obsessive. Keeping your office on total lockdown in a building that no one else had access to, in our tiny town of two thousand residents?

I tagged behind Garrett with an equal mix of excitement over starting something new and a stomach queasy with worry that I was leaving behind the safety of the only family I'd ever known.

CHAPTER

SIX

"WE'RE DOING THE SOFT OPENING tomorrow?" I asked as I siphoned a taster from the clarifying tank. The liquid in the long turkey baster shimmered against the stainless steel tank. I took a sip, swirling the golden-colored ale in my mouth before swallowing. "Did you dry hop this?"

Garrett let out a low whistle. "I'm impressed. Hans told me you have an extraordinary nose." He waved me over to the side of the tank and opened a viewing window. "Check it out." Hops floated on the top of the beer, bobbing like sea lions on the ocean.

Typically, hops are added during the boiling process. Dry hopping is a unique way to infuse a beer with extra hop flavor and aroma. Instead of hopping during the brewing process, in dry hopping, fresh hops are added in after the beer's been fermenting for several days. The taste is unmistakable.

"This really has a bite," I said, handing Garrett the taster so I could get a closer look at the floating hops.

"Not too bitter, is it?" Garrett asked. "I've been working on how long to leave them in. The last batch I left in too long, and I wasn't thrilled with the flavor profile. I mean, I drank it, but it wasn't my best effort."

Garrett had spoken a universal truth among brewers—no matter the taste or flavor, there's an unspoken code that if you pour a pint, you finish it. Over the years, I had put up with my fair share of undrinkable beers, thanks to the code. I shut the hatch and stepped off the ladder. "Can I have another taste?"

Garrett handed me the taster.

Taking another sip, I let the beer settle on my tongue. When I led brewery tours at Der Keller, this was always my favorite part. I quizzed guests on what they tasted. Usually the first thing that people noticed was that the beer wasn't carbonated. Carbonation is the final step in the brewing process. Even without a frothy head or bubbles, once a beer has been clarified, it's remarkably drinkable. Farm-style beers from England and France are often served uncarbonated.

The first pass of Garrett's beer left my tongue tingling from intense citrus flavors like grapefruit and oranges. The beer had a nice hoppy finish without being too bitter.

"It's so clean," I said to Garrett. "Tons of fruit on the front, but no aftertaste. Very nice."

Garrett hid a smile. "Thanks. I've been perfecting this recipe for a couple years. I still have one more batch of hops to throw in."

"You've done a great job. This is one of the better beers I've tasted in a long time. And that's saying a lot. What are you calling it?"

"Citrus IPA."

"Really?" I raised my eyebrows.

"Yeah." Garrett looked confused. "Why?"

No wonder Hans said that Garrett needed my help.

"A beer this good deserves a name worthy of it." I twisted the wedding ring on my finger. For some reason, I hadn't been able to take it off yet.

"I never thought of that." Garrett removed his chemistry goggles and cleaned them on his shirt.

"That's why you hired me. We'll come up with something."

Returning the goggles to his face, Garrett climbed to the top of the shiny silver tank and peeked inside the access window. "One more round of hops, and we should be ready to keg."

"What's the plan for food?"

"Food?" Garrett looked at me as if I were speaking a foreign language.

"You know, food for the pub. What are we serving with the beer?"

Garrett climbed off the ladder and pushed the goggles back on his forehead. His dark hair had a slight curl. "I'm glad you brought that up. I hear that you're a culinary star, so I'm going to leave food up to you. My idea of bar food is pretzels, nuts, and a few bowls of chips, but I know that's not going to cut it or meet the state regulations for serving alcohol."

Pretzels and nuts were fine at a sports bar, but launching a new brewery definitely called for something more refined, and Garrett was right: our liquor license required us to offer small plates. I knew that Garrett had hired me for my brewing and culinary skills, but Hans hadn't made it clear whether Garrett wanted me to manage the kitchen or provide ideas. I decided to tread carefully for the moment. "What do you think about a menu revolving around the beer?"

"Like what?"

"I'm thinking simple pub fare—nothing extravagant. I sketched out a few ideas at home, but wanted to sample the product first. That way I can create recipes that complement each beer."

Garrett pushed his hair from his eye again. "That sounds awesome, and way better than bowls of Doritos."

"Oh, there will be Doritos." I smiled and looked at the brewery. The cavernous space with its stark white walls reminded me more of a clean lab than a cheery pub. Nitro's outdoor façade blended in with Leavenworth's pastoral vibe. Garrett had left the chocolate brown balcony, spires, and carved lion's head crest intact. City code demanded that every building in the town square had to adhere to German aesthetics. However, what business owners did inside was completely up to them. Garrett had obviously decided not to embrace German heritage in his redesign. I appreciated the fact that there wasn't baroque music playing or that the walls weren't plastered with coats of arms and nutcrackers, but the cold space was too severe.

I chose my words carefully, not wanting to offend Garrett. "It might be nice to add some warmth in here. What if we wrap those beams with string lights? I get that you're deviating from the German theme, and trust me, I've seen enough lederhosen in my years here to last a lifetime, but I think it needs a little splash of color."

He scratched his head. "Do you think people are going to be mad that I took down my aunt's dusty tchotchkes? Every square inch of wall was covered with German kitsch."

"Welcome to Leavenworth." I winked. "But, no, I don't think you should worry. In fact I think it's good to set yourself apart, especially since you're not on Front Street. I mean, there are a few crazies around who think that everyone should dress the part to please tourists, but I'm not worried about that. A few lights and prints on the walls should make it feel a tad more welcoming."

Garrett nodded. "Right."

"Did you happen to save any photographs of the inn or family pictures? I could create a display to pay homage to your aunt."

"Great idea." Garrett's eyes brightened. "I have stacks of framed photos upstairs. I'll bring them down." He bit his bottom lip. "Are you sure this isn't going be too much work?"

"No work at all. I love doing projects like this." That was true, but I hoped that I hadn't oversold my capabilities. I had less than twenty-four hours to create an upscale beer menu and transform Nitro for opening night.

Time to get to work.

CHAPTER

SEVEN

GARRETT SPENT THE REST OF the morning and early afternoon walking me through Nitro's operations. His long-term plans included expanding the tasting room into a full-scale pub and bottling plant.

After lunch he suggested we take a break, so I decided to head home and start on a menu. The drive up Front Street was particularly gorgeous. I passed the wooden gazebo in the center of town. Beer barrels flanked each side and had been draped with red and white flower garlands. Every storefront boasted rounded arches, turrets, or rooftop gardens. White stucco three-story A-frames were trimmed with dark brown wood and bursting with lush flower boxes. German and American flags hung from windows and lined the street.

I took the long route, past the orchards and vineyards. The sky was alive with color and a handful of wispy clouds. I turned onto Mountain Home Road and wound up the hill

"Garrett, I'm back," I called as I thrust open the front door with a confidence I didn't feel.

The sound of angry voices came from the back room.

"Suit yourself. This is the best offer you're going to see," I heard Mac holler. "You might want to reconsider. That's a ton of money. If I walk out of here, you're not getting another offer from me or anyone else in this town. That I can guarantee."

I couldn't hear Garrett's response.

Whatever he said must not have gone over well. The office door slammed, and Mac stormed toward me.

He stopped in midstride. "Sloan, baby, what are you doing here?" He smoothed his tailored pale blue dress shirt and took a step closer.

I took a step back. "I work here now."

With a glance over his shoulder, he said, "So I heard." He rolled his eyes and moved closer to me. I could smell his expensive cologne and stale beer on his breath. "Listen, Sloan, you don't want to work for that amateur. He's nothing more than a glorified home brewer. Trust me, he has no idea what he's doing."

"Stop there." I blocked him with my free hand and waved the empty growler at him with my other hand. "He happens to have some of the best beer I've ever tasted. Better than yours. I think he knows exactly what he's doing."

Mac's face flushed with anger, but he kept his eyes neutral. "One good beer isn't enough to support this entire operation." The third button on his shirt looked like it was about to burst open. I wasn't sure if it was because he was fuming or had been imbibing too much.

I wondered what the beer wench saw in his expanding belly. "Look. I'm not doing this," I said, clutching the growler in my hand. "I don't know why you're trying to spy on me, but you need to leave—now!"

"Spying?" Mac sputtered. "I wasn't spying. I'm here on business."

"I don't care. You're clearly done with whatever business you had. Time to go." I pointed to the door.

"Can we talk?" He inched closer to me and opened his baby blue eyes in a puppy-dog stare. "I miss you."

Every muscle in my body tensed. "Get out."

"Okay, okay, I'm going, but I'm not giving up on us. We had a good thing going, baby."

I wanted to scream. I wanted to remind him that he threw everything we'd had out the window when he decided to shag the beer wench. Instead, I inhaled through my nostrils and remained silent.

Mac hung his head on the way to the door. He glanced down at my feet. "You're wearing my favorite polish."

I'm not a girly girl. The whole makeup thing doesn't appeal to me. And let's face it, when you're hanging out in a brewpub all day, it isn't really worth the effort. The one vice I afford myself is well-manicured toes. I have an entire bathroom drawer dedicated to nail polish. As Mac slammed the door, I looked at the polish adorning my toes. The slate gray polish had been one of my favorites, too. Not anymore. I planned to dump the bottle in the trash the second I got home.

"Sloan, is everything okay?" Garrett's deep voice disrupted the silence.

How long had he been standing there?

"Yeah." I held the growler under my arm and tried to twist the cap off. "I'm going to grab some IPA. I think I figured out a menu."

The cap wouldn't budge.

"Sorry, about my hus . . . about Mac." I didn't meet his eyes. "I don't know what he's trying to stir up, but I promise I'm not into drama. That won't happen again."

Garrett reached for the growler and twisted off the cap in one move. "He wasn't here about you."

We moved toward the bar.

"Nice shirt," Garrett commented. "We should sell those. Maybe, like, 'Real Women Drink Nitro.' What do you think?"

"I like it. Let's add it to the list." I twirled my wedding ring. It was coming off with the toenail polish tonight. "What did Mac want?"

Garrett busied himself filling the growler. When he finished, he sealed the cap tightly and handed it to me. "He wants the recipe for this. I made it clear that it's not for sale."

"He wants to *buy* your recipe?"

Garrett shrugged and fiddled with the tap handle. "It's not for sale."

Most brewers are protective of their recipes, especially when trying to establish themselves. "Out of curiosity, what did he offer you?"

Mac was frugal about all the wrong things. He would throw money around for his souped-up Hummer and designer shirts, but when it came to spending money on quality ingredients and equipment for Der Keller, his purse strings cinched tight.

"It doesn't matter. Like I told him, the recipe's not for sale."

Condensation formed on the glass growler. I wiped my hand on my shirt. "Smart move." I'd have given anything to know what Mac had offered Garrett for his recipe, but his quick redirection made it clear he wasn't about to reveal anything more.

"Thanks for the beer." I looped my finger through the handle. "I'm off to finish cooking. See you tomorrow."

Garrett positioned his goggles over his eyes. "Back to the chem lab for me. By the way, I brought down stacks of old photos for you. They're in a box on the bar."

"Perfect! I'll see what I can do with them tomorrow."

He gave me a two-fingered wave.

At home the first thing I did was tug off my wedding ring and hide it in my sock drawer. Then I blasted Bach in the kitchen while I diced red onions and chopped cilantro. After carefully cutting chicken breasts into long, thin strips, I poked holes in them with a fork and then dropped them into a bath of citrus IPA, onion, cilantro, olive oil, and a dash of salt and pepper. I'd let them soak overnight. Hopefully, the meat would become infused with the beer marinade.

Next I began mixing a cupcake base of butter, eggs, and buttermilk. I couldn't shake Mac from my head. What was he really doing at Nitro? Could he really have been interested in buying Garrett's recipe, or was he spying on me?

I refused to let him get under my skin. This was my gig, and I wasn't about to let him ruin it for me. He needed to back off. Cooking unleashed my anger. I took a swig of the citrus IPA and then poured the rest into the batter. It foamed nicely. I swirled the froth by hand and gave the batter a taste with my finger.

Beer cupcakes. Yum. I grated fresh orange and lemon peel into the mixture, cut the fruits in half, and squeezed in the juice. I was counting on them to pull out the citrus flavor of the beer. My lips puckered when I inadvertently licked my fingertips, soaked in lemon. *Pucker Up, that's it,* I thought. Pucker Up IPA.

After adding a touch of Mexican vanilla, I dipped my pinky into the batter for a taste. The tang of Pucker Up (I hoped Garrett would like that name) and fresh orange and lemon balanced beautifully with the buttery base.

I wondered what Garrett's story was. Hans hadn't told me much about him. I got the impression today that he wasn't the kind of guy to throw out personal information. Not that I could blame him. I knew how it felt to want to keep my emotions closely guarded.

According to Hans, Garrett had left his software engineering position immediately when he inherited Nitro's building from his great-aunt Tess. Tess Strong, one of the original founders of Leavenworth, had passed away last spring. She died, sharp as a tack, at age ninety-seven, leaving her entire fortune to Garrett. Rumor had it that he'd never even visited Leavenworth when he decided to ditch his corporate career and turn his inheritance into a brewery. I wondered if he had any other family.

Over the years, I'd learned that the easiest way to deflect attention from yourself was to focus on someone else. I'd mastered the art of deflecting questions. Whenever anyone asked questions about me, I would quickly steer the conversation back to them. Working side by side with Garrett should provide an opportunity for me to figure out if he planned to be around for the long haul or was looking to make a quick buck. Brewing wasn't a get-rich-quick scheme; in fact, many of the smaller breweries pulled in just enough profit to pay their staff and cover their overhead. It was a lifestyle, and I couldn't decide yet if Garrett was cut out for it or not.

CHAPTER

EIGHT

THE NEXT MORNING, THE SOUND of finches chattering outside my window woke me before the sun. I liked to sleep with the windows open year-round. The fresh air and the calming sound of Icicle Creek helped me relax. For the first time in recent memory, I awoke with eager anticipation. *This must be how Alex feels on the first day of school,* I thought as I mentally reviewed everything that needed to be done. Before we officially opened Nitro's doors to the public, I needed to finish preparing and assembling the food, pick up tables and chairs, bring the space to life with festive lights and candles, make sure we had enough barware, learn Garrett's system for billing and payments, continue to familiarize myself with the space and brewing equipment, and brainstorm witty names for each of Garrett's beers.

Sometime in my insane day, I also had to carve out a few minutes to talk to Hans. I had a singular mission for him—to keep Mac away from Nitro. Far away.

I threw the covers off and rolled out of bed. Mac's side of the mattress, untouched for weeks, served as a physical reminder of the deadweight in my life. I sighed and pulled a sweatshirt over my head. After scrunching my feet into fuzzy slippers, I padded down the hallway to the kitchen, instinctively stopping at Alex's bedroom door to check on him. It took me a minute to register that he wasn't there. He had slept at the hotel where Mac was staying last night, and as mad as I was at Mac, I knew that for Alex's sake I had to preserve their relationship, even if that meant sharing custody. I didn't think I could ever get used to the idea of sharing my son.

The house had an empty ache without Alex. Every creak in the hardwood floors seemed amplified as I made my way down the hall. Even my naked ring finger served as a reminder that everything I had worked so hard for had been turned upside down. It was a good thing that there was a lengthy to-do list to prepare for Nitro's soft opening. Staying busy was going to be the only way I was going to stay sane.

In the kitchen I flipped on the coffeepot and dug through the refrigerator for butter and cream cheese. My beer cupcakes had cooled on the counter overnight.

"Time to taste my creation," I said to no one as I peeled off a wrapper and popped a bite into my mouth. To my surprise, the beer flavor really came through, and the cupcakes left a tiny hint of tanginess on my tongue.

Pleased with my results, I whipped together butter and cream cheese with a splash of beer and more freshly grated orange rind. The ivory-colored frosting blended into firm peaks. Sneaking a taste, I grinned and admired my whimsical creation. Beer cupcakes and frosting, perfect for a tap-room launch. Hopefully Garrett would like them, too.

I poured a cup of black coffee and got to work frosting the cupcakes. Once the cupcakes were assembled on silver serving platters, I shifted my focus. I pulled the marinated chicken from the refrigerator and carefully skewered it on wooden sticks. We would serve the skewers warm, so I covered them in plastic wrap and put them in the fridge to grill later.

I'd reserved some of the marinade to use as a base for a salad dressing. I chopped lettuce, tomatoes, onions, and cucumbers into a large wooden bowl. Then I sprinkled feta and olives over the top. I removed the lid from the container of extra marinade. It smelled heavenly. I added a splash of olive oil and balsamic vinegar. Giving it a vigorous shake, I watched the oil and vinegar emulsify and then took a taste. Delicious.

Breakfast wasn't really my thing, despite Alex's constant nagging. I surveyed the kitchen counter and settled on a banana. *That should please my son. Maybe I should text him, and let him know that I'm starting my morning out right.* I looked at the cuckoo clock. He should be awake and getting ready for school.

I took a photo of my half-eaten banana with my cell phone and shot Alex a message. "Proud? I'm eating breakfast before work."

A minute later my phone dinged. "Nice, Mom. How much coffee u had?"

"Never enough! Are you coming tonight?" Pubs in Leavenworth, as in Germany, were designed with families in mind.

Kids could often be found noshing on warm German pretzels and drinking frothy root beer floats while their parents
sipped stouts. Washington State law allowed for minors to
be present as long as food was served and there was some
sort of wall or barrier between the bar and the dining area.
Garrett had wisely licensed Nitro as a family-friendly pub.

"Yep."

"See you later. Love you. Have a great day!"

"Luv u 2. Bye."

Having Alex at the party would give me an anchor; so
would having Hans. I sent him a text too.

"Are you coming tonight? Hope so. Be sure your brother
doesn't show, okay?"

He texted back a few minutes later. "Wouldn't miss it. Tonight's about you. I'll take care of Mac."

With that settled I jumped in the shower. Working at Der
Keller meant that I hadn't had to think about my wardrobe
for years. My closet was stuffed with Der Keller sweatshirts,
T-shirts, and baseball hats. I figured that Nitro's soft opening called for something a little nicer than jeans.

I found my red cocktail dress in the back of the closet.
There was no way I was working all day at the brewery in
that sucker, so I tugged on a pair of jeans and opted for an
eggplant scoop-neck T-shirt. The purple brought out the
bronze color in my skin, which had tanned naturally over
the summer. I twisted my hair into a ponytail and tucked a
pair of black sandals into my gym bag. Later I could change
into my cocktail dress, but for the time being, I was all about
comfort over fashion.

I loaded my car with the food and headed into town.

"Hey, Sloan! You moving in?" the town librarian yelled as I passed the library, designed to look like an alpine ski lodge, with boxes of party food and my red dress.

"We're doing a soft opening of the new pub tonight. Come by!"

"I'll be there, along with everyone else in town!" She waved and returned to watering the vivid red geraniums blooming in the window boxes.

Living in Leavenworth sometimes felt a bit like stepping back in time, without the wagons and outdoor bathrooms, of course. It was impossible not to be swept up by the village's charm. From the intricate details in each building's Bavarian architecture to the soaring mountains and the Pacific Northwest's friendly attitude, the village invited everyone in.

In the mining and logging days, the Nitro building had housed a brothel. Like everything else in the village, it had been converted to a German-style chalet in the 1960s. Garrett's great-aunt had run a successful restaurant on the ground floor and a bed-and-breakfast upstairs until about five years ago, when her health began to fail. The building had been empty ever since.

Getting the space ready to reopen meant that Garrett had sunk a chunk of change into ground floor renovations. As far as I knew, he hadn't touched the upstairs guest rooms yet. He'd moved into one of the larger guest suites, but otherwise the rambling building was empty. And I thought sleeping in the farmhouse was lonely.

"Good morning," I called out as I unlocked the door with my free hand and balanced the boxes of food with the other.

Unlocking doors was going to take some getting used to.

The door slammed behind me. "It's me—Sloan. I'm here early!"

No response. Garrett was probably still asleep.

The muscles in my forearms started to spasm from the weight of the supplies. I hurried to the office and set the boxes on the concrete floor. As I bent over to retrieve my keys from a box, I accidentally kicked the base of the door. To my surprise, it swung open. Garrett had been so adamant about locking it that I couldn't believe it was unlocked.

Maybe he was right, I thought as I caught sight of the office space. Papers were strewn all over the floor. The filing cabinet was covered in scratch marks, as if someone had taken a key to it. The place had been trashed.

Out of nowhere I heard a loud crash.

I ran out to the brewery. "Garrett?"

"Sloan?"

I whirled around to find Garrett standing behind me. His hair was disheveled, and his shirt was untucked. He looked like he had just crawled out of bed, and his pants looked suspiciously like pajama bottoms.

"Your office," I sputtered. "Someone went through the office." I pointed to the open door.

Garrett perked up. "What?" He rushed to the office.

I watched his shoulders sag as he stopped at the door.

"Can you tell if anything's missing?" I asked.

He dropped to his knees and began picking up papers with notes, charts, and indecipherable scribbles on them. "No." He shook his head. "But I can guess."

"Your recipes?" I stooped over to help him.

Handing me a stack of papers, he nodded. "I thought this might happen."

Something didn't add up. Why would someone ransack Garrett's office for a beer recipe? "Don't you have the recipe on your computer?" I asked.

He cracked his knuckles. "Of course, but now someone else has it. What's going to stop them from brewing my beer?"

"Should we call the police?" I asked, setting paper on the desk. I'd never had to call the police. The biggest excitement in recent memory was last year's hunt for the mayor's missing cat.

"No, don't bother."

Why didn't he want to call the police? After being so insistent about locking up, his reaction confused me. To him I said, "Okay. If you're sure?"

"I'm sure." He sounded dejected.

"I'll clean up. Should I put the food for the party in the kitchen?"

Garrett abandoned the clutter on the floor and stood. "Right, food. Yeah. What did you bring?"

I showed him the boxes.

"That looks like enough food to feed the entire town."

"That's the plan."

He effortlessly grabbed the boxes and carried them to the out-of-date kitchen. I followed after him.

He placed the boxes on the brown Formica countertop. "Something smells amazing. What did you make?"

After I relayed the evening's menu, Garrett let out a whistle.

"Damn. That beats my pretzels. I hope you didn't go to too much trouble."

"No problem." I brushed him off. "I love to cook."

I wasn't sure how to frame my question about his files. I pretended to check on the salad dressing, removing the lid from the container and swirling the liquid in its plastic tub. "Hey, about your recipes. Doesn't it seem weird—"

Before I could finish, there was the sound of shrill voice calling, "Yoo-hoo! Anyone home?"

I'd have recognized that voice anywhere—April Ablin. Oh no, not April Ablin.

"Back here," Garrett answered, before I had a chance to shush him. He strolled to the brewery.

I shook my head frantically and looked for a place to hide. April ran Leavenworth's tourism association and was notorious for ferreting out every detail of gossip she could. I hadn't seen her since Mac and I split. April was the last person I wanted to see. Short of climbing into one of the fermenting tanks, there was no place for me to hide. I'd have to suck it up. Her heels clicked on the concrete floor as I walked as slowly as I could out toward the beer equipment.

"Guten Morgen!" She plastered on a smile to match her caked-on makeup. "I'm April. You must be Garrett." She curtseyed and lifted the sides of her frilly pink and green checkered German dress. "You are even more handsome in person."

Garrett looked uncomfortable.

I rolled my eyes. April was the only person in town who thought she was living in a real German village. None of the rest of us (including my in-laws, who actually *were* German) dressed in full barmaid attire unless it was for one of the festivals or special events.

April moved closer to me and put her thin, freckled arm around my shoulder. Her voice was laced with fake sympathy as she squeezed me into a half hug. "Sloan, hon, how are you doing? I heard about Mac." She whispered so loudly that Garrett turned away.

"You need anything, hon, you know where to come. I mean, imagine all this time, I thought his flirting with me was harmless. I should have warned you." She fanned her face.

Resisting the urge to punch her, I grimaced and removed her hand from my shoulder. "Thanks, April."

"Now, Garrett, back to you." April turned on the charm, batting her long, fake eyelashes and leaning forward so that her ample breasts, squeezed into a dress one size too small, were on full display. "You've been avoiding my calls. I've been trying to get ahold of you for weeks. I had to pop in before the grand *Partei*—that's German for party, as I'm sure you know—tonight."

Her teeth were coated like a candy apple in red lipstick. I didn't say anything. April was on the wrong side of forty, and her attempt to hang on to her vanishing youth included applying hideous amounts of makeup and poorly done hair extensions. I also didn't mention the fact that *Partei* in German referred to a political party, not a celebration.

She babbled on. "You are simply the talk of the town. As the village liaison, I must know what prompted you to move from the big city and open this . . . this pub. You are planning to keep it in the German tradition, I hope?" She stopped and fixed her eyes on the bare white walls. "Oh dear, this is worse than I thought. I had heard a mumble or two that things had changed, but we're going to have to help you get this looking like Beervaria, aren't we?"

Garrett couldn't get a word in. April paused long enough to take breath and launched back in. "Word has it you're out to give Mac Krause a run for his money. Opening a new beer hall and stealing his wife. I imagine you've ruffled a few feathers." Her nasal laugh made me want to plug my ears.

As much as I wanted to stick around and hear how Garrett handled April, I had work to do. "Well, I'll leave you two to it," I said as I backed away. "Nice to see you, April."

"Oh"—April put her hand to her heart—"you take care, hon. Everyone, I mean *everyone* in town is talking about you. I mean, how terrible we feel for you."

Swearing April's name under my breath, I turned and made a beeline for the office.

It didn't take long to put everything back in order. I lost track of time as I sorted through files. Garrett's system of organization appeared to be cramming loose notes into file folders until they exploded. Ransacking the space must have been a fairly easy gig.

Who would have done this? And why didn't Garrett want me to call the police?

I used the opportunity to systematically file Garrett's notes, recipes, and invoices in the filing cabinet. Once the room looked presentable, I went to work rearranging the pub for the party. Despite the fact that Garrett seemed to be the kind of guy who spent a lot of time in his head, I was impressed by what he'd done with the space.

Upon entering Nitro's front doors, customers would be greeted with exposed industrial ceilings and concrete floors. The dated vinyl booths and benches from his aunt's restaurant had been replaced with dining tables in the front and then a collection of high-top bar tables and stools. A half wall ran the length of the room, dividing the dining area, where minors were allowed, from the bar.

I strung twinkle lights from the top of the bar to the front windows and placed votive candles on each table. The box of photos that Garrett had left on the bar was a treasure trove. I didn't take the time to look through all of them, but there were photos of Garrett as a boy with his aunt Tess, black-and-white photos of the inn in its original glory, and tons of pictures of parties and events that had been hosted in the space throughout the years. Positioning framed photos in the bar anchored the room and offered a nod to Nitro's roots.

He had installed a ten-foot whiteboard behind the bar that would serve as a menu for our rotating beers. Since we were launching with only three beer options, there was plenty of extra space. I wrote descriptions of each beer and our food menu on the board. Then in a stroke of luck, I discovered a photo of Icicle Creek at the bottom of the box. Icicle Creek originates at Lake Josephine and flows from the Cascade Mountains until it meets the Wenatchee River here in Leavenworth. I mounted the photo on the board with two magnets and wrote a quote that I'd heard Hans repeat many times beneath it: HISTORY FLOWS FORWARD ON A RIVER OF BEER.

Stepping back, I appraised my work. It felt like a blend of the old with the new. I hoped that Garrett would like the end result.

With that complete, I focused my attention outside, where a small patio enclosed by a wrought-iron gate sat at the front of the building. I found some patio chairs in the storage area next to the kitchen and dragged them out. After a good wipe-down, they looked like new.

A man's voice startled me as I plugged in the lights and stood to survey my work. "Is Garrett around?"

I turned to see a man wearing dirt-caked boots that came to his knees and overalls covered in dust.

"He's in the back. Can I help you with something? I'm Sloan, Garrett's new brewer and one and only employee."

"Van Gieger, hop supplier." He shifted a box of hops in his arms. "I'd shake your hand, but mine are kind of tied up at the moment."

"I see that. You want to set them down?" I pointed to an empty bistro table.

He set down the box he was carrying. "Sorry, I'm kind of dirty." He brushed off his shirtsleeve. "I guess these are for you, then. Special delivery."

I opened the box. It was filled with fragrant green hops. I caught a whiff of lemon and tangerine under the intense bitterness. "I'm picking up a lot of citrus, but this isn't a hop I know. Is it a hybrid?"

"Yeah. How did you know?"

"Der Keller," I replied. "I learned everything I know about beer from Leavenworth's orginal brewmaster."

He gave his head a half shake. "I don't know what that means."

"You don't know Der Keller?" I was shocked. Everyone in the hop business knew Der Keller.

"Oh yeah, maybe. Did I work with them in Wenatchee?"

"Huh?" I frowned. "They're the biggest brewer here in town. You must be new to Leavenworth."

"Oh right, sure, Der Keller. Yeah, I know those guys, but they already have hop suppliers. I'm starting small, like you guys."

"That's great." I rubbed a hop cone between my fingers and breathed in the lemony scent. "Is your farm nearby?"

"Yep, and no one else in town has these." He motioned to the box. "Garrett has a contract for exclusive rights. These are an experimental vine project. Can you give them to him? I've got a load of deliveries in the truck."

"Sure, but I can go grab him if you need to talk to him. We're getting ready for the big launch tonight. You should come."

"Yeah, I'll try. Don't bug Garrett. Tell him I'll catch him tomorrow with the contract. Good luck tonight if I don't see you."

With a wave, he walked away. I made room for the box of citrus hops in the fridge under the bar. To preserve their freshness and flavors, hops needed to be refrigerated. With that task complete, I returned my focus to the party. I arranged the IPA cupcakes on a long folding table lined with a white tablecloth, covered them with plastic wrap, and then hurried to the kitchen and fired up the grill. The scent of cilantro quickly filled the kitchen. If the citrus skewers tasted as good as they smelled, we'd have happy customers. Once the chicken had been grilled to perfection, I found warming trays amongst the stack of kitchen equipment. Note to self: *organize the kitchen next.*

Back in the bar, I set the skewers and salad next to the cupcakes and surveyed the room. Not half bad. The room glittered to life with the lights and smelled like a real pub.

My watch read quarter to four. I needed to change and put my game face on. Time to meet the masses. "Hey, Garrett," I said as I knocked on the office door. "Everything's ready. Want to come check it out?"

He removed his goggles and rubbed his eyes. "Sure, yeah."

I noticed him quickly close his laptop and place it in the bottom desk drawer along with a spiral notebook. He locked the drawer and followed me to the front room.

"Wow!" He scanned the pub. "Is this the same place?"

"You bet. If you're satisfied, I'm going to change before we open the doors in a few."

"Satisfied? I had no idea something I owned could ever look like this."

"Just a few touches to bring it to life. That's why you hired me, right?"

"Right." Garrett nodded, looking slightly dazed. "I love the pictures. You are a genius. They totally bring everything together. And the beer names and that quote—brilliant!"

"You like it?" I bit my bottom lip.

He pursed his lips. "Well, there is one thing missing."

"What?"

His dark eyes gleamed. "Doritos."

I laughed. "Right. I'll get on that, but first I have to change. Meet you back here in five to greet our first customers."

CHAPTER

NINE

I CHANGED INTO MY RED dress in the bathroom. As a kid, I could fit everything I owned into a suitcase. Some habits die hard. Nowadays, I tended to shop for timeless pieces like the red dress. Despite the fact that I had purchased it years ago, it didn't look dated. It hugged my narrow waist and hit just above the knee. Appraising my reflection, I sighed as I studied my appearance. The mirror showed lines creeping around my eyes and finely etched on my forehead. Maybe it was time for a makeover. I ran a coat of red lip gloss over my lips and let my dark curls fall loose on my shoulders. Why did Mac have to cheat on me with a twentysomething? It was such a cliché, but it made the thin lines in my forehead feel like ruts.

Tonight would be my first time interacting with the entire town since I had discovered Mac cheating. I knew, thanks in part to April Ablin, that while no one would say anything outright, they'd all be acutely aware of the situation.

Suck it up, I told myself as I stuffed my bag of clothes in the office and headed to the front. The sound of voices greeted me as I entered the tasting room. That was another thing about this town—everyone was always early.

Happily, the first guests were familiar faces. The Krause family—Otto, Ursula, Hans, and Alex—stood gathered around the bar. My heart leapt with pleasure, and I could feel my cheeks warm. I wasn't surprised that they had come. Otto and Ursula were steadfast in their support of Leavenworth's brewing community, and always the first people to welcome new brewers to the scene. But given the situation between me and Mac, having them here meant even more.

Ursula greeted me with a squeeze. "You look so beautiful. You are practically glowing, my dear." She was dressed for the shifting weather in an ankle-length black skirt and cable knit sweater. Due to Leavenworth's proximity to the Cascade Mountains, evenings tended to cool rapidly once the sun sunk on the horizon, especially with fall approaching. "And it smells so wonderful in here. I think you must be cooking today."

Otto patted me on the shoulder. "She is right. Ze beer it must be good for you." The age spots on his cheeks scrunched together when he smiled. "We are very happy for you to try something new, but you return to ze pub soon, *ja*?"

Hans caught my eye. I wondered how much he'd told them.

"Of course." I hugged them both. "Thanks for being here. You're going to love Garrett's beer. It's very different from Bavarian beers."

Ursula walked to get a better look at the wall of photos. "Sloan, did you do zis? It is so wonderful."

"Aren't they great? I bet you'll recognize many faces up there. They are all old photos from Tess's collection."

She smiled, but as she continued to examine the photos, a look of nostalgia washed over her. Was she upset that I had left Der Keller, or just reflecting on her past? She placed the reading glasses that hung from a chain around her neck on the tip of her nose and stepped closer. One photo had caught her eye. She ran her finger around its frame and then turned to me. For a moment, I thought she might cry, but instead she removed her reading glasses and moved on to the next photo.

Alex punched me gently in the shoulder. "Yeah, Mom, you look good, for someone soooo old." His eyes twinkled with impish delight and matched his pale blue shirt. He had dressed for the occasion. "Nice place. Not German, that's for sure. You going to show us around?"

"You know it, kid." I reached to ruffle his hair. He ducked away as I led them toward the fermenting tanks. Hans matched my stride and leaned close. I could smell the faint hint of wood polish on his skin, even though he had showered and changed into jeans, rafting shoes, and a khaki shirt. "Nice move, Sloan."

"What do you mean?"

One side of his lip curled into a smile. "You look amazing. If my brother could see you now, he'd really be kicking himself."

"He's not coming, is he?" I could hear the shrill tone in my voice. "You promised you would keep him away."

"Chill." Hans squeezed my shoulder and brushed a loose strand of hair from my face. "He's not coming. I meant that you look great, and what better way to show everyone in town that you're fine?"

"Right." I sighed. "I guess I'm slightly on edge."

"I know," he replied with an understanding smile. "Here's a tip. If you start to think about Mac and Hayley, remember the old saying: beauty is in the eye of the beer holder." Winking, he continued. "You, Sloan, exude real beauty inside and out."

"You're the best," I bantered back with a laugh, but caught a glimpse of a wistful look in his eyes.

When I returned from giving the Krause family the tour, Garrett looked at me with wild eyes from behind the bar. I weaved between masses of locals lining up for pints. The place was hopping, and Garrett's deer-in-the-headlights gaze made me chuckle.

"Need a hand?" I scooted behind the bar to help him pour.

"Why is everyone so *early*?" he whispered.

I shrugged and grabbed a pint glass. "It's our thing." With a population of right around two thousand residents, whenever something—or someone—new arrived on the scene, the entire town showed up.

Garrett scowled and then seemed to notice me for the first time. "You look amazing, Sloan." His voice cracked slightly.

"Thanks." I could feel my cheeks start to warm. "You look nice, too." He had changed as well. He wore a crisp white dress shirt, which brought out his dark hair and dusty brown eyes. Pointing to the overflowing pint Garrett was holding, I said, "I think that's good."

Removing his gaze from me, Garrett yanked the tap handle back and shook foam from his hands while I waited on the next person in line. "What can I get you?" I asked the customer. "We're pouring three tonight: Pucker Up, a fresh IPA infused with citrus fruits and big hops, Cherry Cordial, a black cherry stout that's dense and sweet, and Bottle Blonde, a light summer ale."

"Which one is your favorite?"

I recommended Pucker Up, but all of Garrett's beers were award-worthy. An impressive feat for a new brewer.

The secret to pouring a perfect pint was how you held the glass: I angled the pint glass to avoid too much foam and positioned it underneath the tap. Beer should also be poured slowly. I poured it halfway, then let it settle for a minute before topping it with a creamy head.

As I handed the customer her pint, the front door swung open and in barged Eddie Deluga, brewmaster at Bruin's Brewing, one of Leavenworth's original beer halls located on the outskirts of town.

Eddie elbowed his way to the front of the bar and slapped a scrawny tattooed arm on the counter. "Gimme one of each."

I turned to Garrett. "Have you met Eddie yet?"

Garrett shook his head. He rolled his sleeves and extended his hand. "Garrett Strong."

"I heard." Eddie ignored Garrett's outstretched arm. "Whatcha waiting for, Sloan? I want to taste a cold one."

"Knock it off, Eddie," a jovial voice called out. A burly, graying man with a teddy-bear-like beer belly came up behind Eddie and rubbed his shoulders. He wore a forest green felt hat with a German flag tucked on the side.

Eddie snarled. I handed him a pint of Pucker Up.

He stuck his nose in the glass.

"Sloan, so nice to see you! You look great!" Bruin, the teddy bear and Eddie's boss, grabbed my hand and crushed it so hard my fingertips blanched. He turned to Garrett. "You must be the whiz kid I keep hearing about. Bruin Masterson, of Bruin's Brewing—nice to meet you."

He shook Garrett's hand with gusto. Garrett looked at me, dumbfounded.

I poured Bruin a pint of Pucker Up and filled Garrett in. "Bruin owns Bruin's Brewing on the other side of town, and Eddie is his head brewmaster. They've been a fixture around here for years."

"We've had a friendly little rivalry for a while now, haven't we, Sloan?" Bruin chugged his Pucker Up.

Eddie examined his. He held the pint up to the Edison-style lightbulbs hanging on individual wires above the bar and swirled the sunglow ale in the air. They were quite the pair—Bruin with his portly body and rosy red cheeks and Eddie with his skeletal rock star body and tattoos.

"Now, that's a nice hoppy finish you've got going here," Bruin said to Garrett, then he turned to me. "Bet Mac's pretty pissed you're working with the competition, huh?" Bruin laughed and gulped the rest of his pint with a giant swig that caused his hat to fall off.

I didn't respond, but picked up Bruin's hat. He tipped it in thanks and repositioned it on his head.

"So, Eddie, what do you think?" Bruin watched as Eddie finally took a sip.

Eddie swished the beer around in his mouth. "Not bad,"

he said, setting his full pint glass on the bar. "I've had better."

Bruin snatched his glass. "If you're not finishing that, I will." His swollen cheeks glowed crimson.

"You dry hop that?" Eddie asked, cracking his knuckles. He wore fat rings on all of his fingers. His ribbed white tank top displayed a buxom woman in a Bettie Page dress, and his black skinny jeans had chains hanging from the pockets and belt loops.

Garrett looked unsure how to respond. I gave him a little nod to let him know that Eddie was harmless.

"Yeah, a little," Garrett said, offering Eddie a taster of the cherry stout. "Not on this one, though."

While Eddie and Garrett cautiously talked shop, Bruin leaned over the bar. Slightly slurring his words, he patted my hand. "You know, Sloan, if this doesn't work out, I'll always have a spot for you my way. You remember that."

He must have had a couple before coming to Nitro.

Regardless, the moment of beer-induced tenderness struck me. "Thanks, Bruin."

He downed the last drops of beer in his pint glass and handed it to me. "I'll take another, Sloan."

My jaw tightened. "Sorry, Bruin, I can't serve you now." I caught Garrett's eye. There was no way we could continue to serve Bruin, who was obviously already inebriated. Garrett frowned. I gave him a look to let him know that I had the situation under control. Years of working the front at Der Keller had trained my eyes to spot someone who had had one too many. There was no room for error when it came to overserving, and I had no problem cutting Bruin off.

Bruin waved his empty pint glass at me. "Come on, Sloan. I'm fine. Just one more pint."

I was about to offer Bruin a cup of coffee, but at that moment, Van, the hop guy, squeezed his way to the bar. His overalls were still dusty from harvesting hops.

"Hey, you made it," I said.

He glanced at Bruin and then read the whiteboard menu behind me. "Wouldn't miss it. Sloan, right? What should I try?"

"They're all good, but since Garrett used your hops in the Pucker Up, you have to taste that first." I tucked my hair behind my ears. I wasn't used to wearing it down, and it kept falling in front of my face.

"Your hops!" Eddie dropped the conversation he had been having with Garrett and interrupted. "What does she mean *your hops,* man?"

I wondered why Eddie was reacting so strongly. Had Van promised him proprietary hops, too?

Before Van could answer, I made the mistake of looking up. Mac was headed straight toward me, with the beer wench tagging behind.

CHAPTER

TEN

GARRETT, CONSUMED WITH SERVING THE lengthy line of customers, didn't notice as I swayed. What was Mac doing here? Where was Hans? This couldn't be happening. Not tonight.

I tapped Garrett's shoulder. "I need to grab something in the kitchen. Be right back."

He flashed me a thumbs-up, but before I could escape, Mac's eyes had locked on mine.

Oh no.

Bruin, plenty of pints in, was oblivious to the panic that was surely evident on my face. Eddie, on the other hand, focused his black, eagle-like eyes on mine and then turned slowly to see what I was looking at.

He swiveled around with force and puffed his chest. "What's that hussy doing here?" he said loud enough for the entire bar to hear.

Mac stopped in midstride and glanced around the room

to see if Eddie was referring to him. Eddie kept his gaze locked on the beer wench.

I felt like I was in some sort of waking nightmare where nothing made sense. Why was Eddie standing up for me? I'd met him a number of times over the years when we'd gathered as local brewers to promote tourism and at festivals and fairs, but we'd never had a connection beyond that.

The buzzing room became eerily quiet. Conversations hushed, and glasses stopped clinking. Eddie's beady eyes remained locked on the beer wench. "God, I hate that cheating little witch."

Garrett gave me a look as if to ask what was going on. I waved him off and made my way to the front of the bar. Keeping my gaze away from the beer wench, I marched over to Mac and pulled him by the expensive shirtsleeve to the hallway.

"What do you think you're doing here?" I hissed at Mac. Spit flew from my lips, landing on his immaculately groomed face.

"Easy, easy, baby." Mac held his hands in the air, motioning like he was petting a cat. "I came by to wish you and the competition well."

"With *her*?"

"With who?"

"Mac. Don't do this." I put my hands on my hips. "You know exactly who I'm talking about. I can't believe you would bring *her* here—tonight. That's low. Even for you."

"Who, Hayley?" He pulled a silver lighter with his initials monogrammed on the front from his back pocket and flicked it on and off. "You look smoking hot tonight, Sloan."

"Don't use her name." I folded my arms over my chest. "You're smoking again?"

"No!" Mac flipped the lighter off and stuffed it back into his pocket. He moved closer and lowered his voice. "I didn't bring her. She followed me here. I made a mistake, but I promise I didn't bring her. I'm trying to shake her."

We both turned as Eddie's voice became louder in the bar. "You've got some nerve, showing your face here, you little cheat."

I brushed past Mac into the doorway to see what was going on.

Garrett and a staggering Bruin were holding Eddie. He reminded me of an overly carbonated bottle of beer about to blow its cap.

Hayley, the beer wench, chewed on an unlit cigarette. Eddie puffed out his chest like he was about to break free. She cowered and inched her way toward the door.

"That's right, keep backing up. No one wants you here." Eddie heckled her. His posture, like a boxer waiting to throw the first punch, baffled me. Why was he suddenly my protector? Or was there more to it? Could he have had a fling with her, too? There had to be something else between them.

As Hayley backed her way out of the pub, Bruin tried to pull Eddie away, but Eddie threw him off. The motion made Bruin lose his footing. He swayed. The crowd gasped. Garrett caught him with his free hand. This was more drama

than Leavenworth had seen in years. Everyone was captivated.

"Don't you start with me either, old man. I'm done with
your crap." He shot Garrett a nasty look and stalked out the
door.

"You better go after your girlfriend," I said to Mac. "You
wouldn't want Eddie catching up with her. He seems pretty
fired up."

Mac started to say something and stopped. As he raced out
the door, he yelled, "She's not my girlfriend."

So much for a low-key opening night.

I took a minute to catch my breath. "I'm so sorry about
that," I said to Garrett, returning to the bar and smoothing
my dress.

The crowd resumed conversation, but the tone had
changed. People gushed with nervous excitement. They'd
talk about this for weeks to come. Why did I have to be in
the middle of it?

"Why would you be sorry?" Garrett asked.

"I think that was about me."

Bruin, who rested his head on his hand and swayed to
music no one else could hear, gave a cackle. "You? What are
you talking about, Sloan?" He raised his hand as if to swat a
fly and almost fell off his barstool.

Garrett reached over the wooden counter to steady him.
"Easy there, man."

Bruin winked at Garrett and rose on shaky feet. "You remember what we talked about. Don't worry about Eddie.
I'll take care of him."

As Bruin started to fall forward, a local grabbed him and

guided him toward the door. Bruin's hat tipped to one side, and he teetered out of the bar.

"What was that all about?" I asked, returning my attention to Garrett.

"Nothing." Garrett didn't look up as he poured a frothy pint.

The rest of the evening passed without incident. Sometime after midnight, we finally ushered our last guest out and closed the door. I collapsed on a chair. Garrett joined me with two mugs.

"Cheers!" He offered me a raised glass.

"Not sure if we should be celebrating," I said, taking the glass from him and breathing in the scent of the hops. I took a long sip.

"We survived, didn't we?"

"I guess." I laughed. "Look at this mess."

Empty pint glasses and paper plates littered the tables and the bar. The food station had been wiped clean, and the candles had burned out.

"Leave it," Garrett said. "Let's deal with it tomorrow, okay?"

"Sounds good to me." I savored the IPA. "Listen, I want to thank you for giving me this opportunity, and I completely understand if you want to let me go."

"Why would I want to let you go?" He stretched his long legs onto an empty chair and rolled up his shirtsleeves. I hadn't noticed how freckled his arms were before.

"You know, because of Mac." I twirled a strand of hair. "I'm sorry he made a scene. People are going to be talking about it for weeks."

"Exactly." Garrett grinned. "And they'll want to keep coming here to talk about it."

I gave him a weak smile.

His tone became serious. "Sloan, don't sweat it. I couldn't have done this without you. For a soft opening, I would say that was a success. Go home and get some sleep."

Easy for him to say. The entire town wasn't talking about him.

CHAPTER

ELEVEN

I SLEPT THROUGH THE SOUND of the birds chattering the next morning, waking to my alarm clock blaring. I should have turned it off. Garrett had told me not to come in before ten, but once I was awake, the odds of sleeping again were slim to none. I figured I might as well get a jump on the cleaning.

After a cup of strong coffee and a long shower, I tugged on a pair of jeans, a thin flannel shirt, and my rubber boots. No self-respecting brewer would brew without boots. The process involved constantly hosing down the brewery floor. During my early years at Der Keller, I'd quickly learned why brewers wore waders and boots. Without a solid pair of waterproof boots, my jeans would be soaked. I twisted my hair into two braids and drove to Nitro brimming with energy. I couldn't wait to actually brew this morning.

The sun threaded through wispy clouds. The streets were deserted, except for the maintenance crew, who woke before dawn to water the hanging baskets and tidy up the cobblestone streets. I didn't bother to rouse Garrett when I entered Nitro. He must have crashed as hard as I had last night. He'd forgotten to lock the front door.

My eyes adjusted to the dim light inside. It smelled like spilled beer and leftover food, probably what the aftermath of a fraternity party must look like. Something about the space felt off. I tugged the wooden mini blinds. Light filtered in through the slats, casting a hazy luminosity and revealing dust particles floating in the air.

I carted dirty dishes and empty beer glasses to the kitchen. The industrial dishwasher looked like a relic. It took me a half hour to figure out where to put the soap. When it finally chugged and clanged to life, the sound was so loud that I was sure it would wake Garrett. Next, I wiped down the countertop and organized the dishes I'd brought from home.

All of a sudden, something crashed. I jumped and let out a little scream. Had a pot fallen off the rack?

I opened the dishwasher and was assaulted with hot steam. Hey, at least it was working.

Wiping steam from my face, I peered inside. Everything looked to be intact. Crossing my fingers, I closed it and hit start.

Thud! There was the sound again. Was it coming from the tasting room?

I raced to the front to see. My boots squeaked on the floors. The doors were wide open. Early morning light seeped in like a spotlight. How had that happened? I knew I'd shut them behind me when I had come in. Was Garrett awake? I hadn't heard any movement upstairs.

"Garrett?" I called, looking over my shoulder.

Nothing.

After securing the front door and locking it, I went to work putting the taproom back together. As I wiped the bar with a mixture of water and bleach, I opened the glass door to the refrigerator under the bar and found the box of hops that Van had delivered the day before.

Oh no! I'd forgotten to tell Garrett that they'd arrived. He'd wanted them in the fermenter yesterday. There was a small window for dry hopping, and I didn't want to be the cause of him missing it. With the pub smelling fresh, I grabbed the hops and headed to the brewing tanks.

As I scurried toward the back, I kicked something with my foot. Hoisting the box of hops under my arm, I bent over to see what it was.

What is this doing here? I thought as I picked up Mac's lighter with my free hand. There was no mistaking the initials MK etched in the expensive lighter. Had Mac been snooping around Garrett's beer tanks?

Dropping the lighter, I shifted the box of hops and climbed the ladder leading to the landing for the access hatch. Placing the box on the platform, I tugged on the stainless steel circular window that opened at the top. It wouldn't budge.

Odd.

I checked the latch. It looked like it had been pounded with a hammer. Huge dents and scratch marks marred the side of the brand-new tank. *Garrett should get this replaced,* I thought. The tank had to be under warranty. Throwing my full body weight into it, I yanked the silver latch with one hand and held tight to the ladder with the other. After my third attempt, the lock finally came loose, nearly knocking me off my feet. I stooped over to pick up the box of hops resting at my feet.

A blast of aromatic citrus hit my nose. I took in the scent of clover, honey, fruit, and a hint of spice. How Van had managed to infuse such a bountiful array of flavors into his hybrid hop was amazing to me.

I scooped a handful of the tangy hops into one hand and took another whiff. The scent triggered memories of last night. Leave it to Mac to find a way to mess up my first night. Between him prancing around with the beer wench and Eddie's weird behavior, I was sure that everyone in Leavenworth would be buzzing with gossip about Nitro's grand opening. Garrett seemed to think that any chatter was good for business, but I wasn't sure that was true. If he couldn't get the local community behind him from the start, Garrett was going to face an upward struggle to carve out his place in Beervaria. The fact that he'd decided to bulldoze any trace of his aunt Tess's German inn and go with a sterile beer lab vibe wasn't going to attract tourists. Our beer was going to have to be the best in town if we wanted to compete.

The sound of a door slamming upstairs spooked me. I dropped a few of the hops on the landing.

Focus, Sloan, I told myself as I reached into the fermenter to dump in the hops.

To my horror, I spotted something in the tank. What was that? I blinked twice and leaned closer. Once my mind caught up with what my eyes were seeing, I let out a scream that rivaled Alex's night terrors as a young child. There was more than beer in the tank. Eddie's face, bloated with beer and death, bobbed on the top.

CHAPTER

TWELVE

I NEARLY FELL OVER BACKWARD. Clutching the handrail that ran the length of the platform, I tried to steady my breath. Had I had one pint too many last night? I didn't feel the slightest bit hungover, and internally I knew that I wasn't imagining what I had just seen, but at the same time, my brain couldn't comprehend how Eddie's body had ended up in the fermenter.

As much as I wanted to flee, I grasped the hatch again and double-checked. That was definitely Eddie, and he was definitely dead. My stomach sank and the smell of hops suddenly made me queasy.

Now what? This couldn't be happening. Was I in some kind of a waking nightmare?

With one eye open, I peered into the tank again to triple-check. Yep. He was dead.

Move, Sloan, I commanded my wobbly legs and started down the ladder. As soon as I made it to solid flooring, I raced into the office to call 911. The operator who answered seemed to be having as much difficulty as I was grasping the fact that someone was floating in our fermenter. Things like this didn't happen in Leavenworth.

The operator told me to stay put and wait for the police to arrive. I paced back and forth in the small office. Who could have done this? There was no way that Eddie had ended up in the tank without help. Was there? I thought back to everything that happened last night. Had Eddie come back after Garrett and I closed up? Why? Could any of this be connected to yesterday's break-in? Maybe Garrett was hiding more than a recipe in here.

Should I wake Garrett? This was his pub after all. He deserved to know.

Before I had a chance to consider whether I should wake him, I heard the sound of someone yelling, "Police," in the front. I shut the office door and hurried to the bar.

"Sloan, what are you doing here?" Police Chief Meyers greeted me with a surprised expression. Her khaki uniform and brown tie made her look more like a forest ranger than an officer of the law. However, the gold star badge pinned to her chest said otherwise.

"I found Eddie!" I blurted out, wondering if I sounded as crazed as I felt. "He—well, his body is in the tank."

"Show me." She didn't waste any time trying to console me, which I appreciated. Her bulky frame moved with purpose as I led the way to the back of the brew house and pointed to the ladder.

"He's in there," I said, keeping my boots planted firmly on the concrete floor.

Despite the fact that Police Chief Meyer's belt was cinched so tight it must have been cutting off circulation to her waist, she climbed the ladder with ease and muttered under her breath after opening the hatch and getting a glimpse of Eddie's body. "Well, that's a body, all right." She adjusted her pants and tugged a walkie-talkie free from her belt buckle. "Dispatch, I'm gonna need you to call Chelan County and have them send the coroner."

She stuck the walkie-talkie back in her belt, reached for a spiral notebook in her pocket, and focused her steely eyes on me. "I'm gonna need you to walk me through what happened here, Sloan."

I explained how I'd arrived to find the door unlocked.

She held up a finger to stop me. "And that's different than usual."

"Yeah, Garrett is new to Leavenworth and insists on locking everything up."

"Mmm-hmm." She made a note and waited for me to continue.

After I told her everything that had happened since I arrived this morning, she frowned and asked, "When was the last time that you saw the deceased?"

I knew that she knew Eddie as well as me. Police Chief Meyers was what we called a "lifer." She'd grown up in Leavenworth and had been in charge of the town's small police force for the last fifteen years. Usually, her duties involved issuing citations for illegal parking and urinating in public, especially when busloads of drunk frat brothers rolled into town for Oktoberfest.

"He was here last night for the grand opening," I said, pointing toward the front.

She must have picked up on my hesitation, because she followed my gaze and asked, "Anything out of the ordinary?"

"He was in rare form." I told her about how he had verbally assaulted Hayley and how Bruin had tried to calm him down.

As she finished asking me questions, Garrett appeared from upstairs. If possible, he looked more disheveled than he had yesterday. I wondered if he had slept in his clothes from last night. Had he had more to drink after I left?

"What's going on?" he mumbled, rubbing his bloodshot eyes.

"Garrett, this is Police Chief Meyers," I said. "She's here because there's been an accident."

He rubbed his eyes harder and straightened his back. "Right, hi, Chief. Accident? What kind of accident?"

Police Chief Meyers stepped forward and pointed behind her. "There's a dead body in your fermenter."

"What?" He ran his hands through his disheveled hair and stared at me. "Is this like some kind of practical joke? Welcome to Leavenworth, you've been pranked?"

I shook my head.

Garrett's face turned ashen. "What? A body?" He moved toward the fermenter.

Police Chief Meyers held out a beefy arm to stop him. "Back up. I'm gonna need you to step back. This is a crime scene."

Giving me an incredulous look, Garrett ran his fingers

through his unruly hair, again. "Wait, a crime scene. I thought you said this was an accident."

"The last time I checked, I don't think many people accidentally find their way into a tank this size." Police Chief Meyers scowled. "Walk me through what happened last night."

Garrett repeated what I had told her almost verbatim. She made a couple of notes and then asked, "Did you hear anything last night?"

"No. Nothing. I crashed after Sloan left and I closed up. It's been a stressful few weeks getting everything off the ground, so I took a sleeping pill and was out cold."

That explained his sloppy appearance and bloodshot eyes. Somehow, Garrett didn't strike me as the sleeping pill type.

"What time was that?" Police Chief Meyers asked.

"Maybe around one."

"And did either of you check this equipment before you left last night?"

I looked at Garrett and shrugged. "Not me."

"Me neither," he seconded.

"Why don't you both wait right here. I'm gonna take a better look around while I wait for the coroner to get here."

We nodded and watched as Police Chief Meyers carefully scanned the brewery. My breath caught in my chest when I noticed her bend over and pick up Mac's lighter. Why hadn't I kept it?

"This belong to either of you?" she asked over her shoulder.

Garrett and I both shook our heads. I debated whether or not I should tell her it was Mac's.

She held it out in front of her. "I know these initials." She turned to me. "Was Mac here last night?"

"He was," I replied. "Up at the bar anyway. He wasn't back here last night, although he was yesterday afternoon."

She mumbled something I couldn't make out and stuck the lighter into a plastic evidence bag. "Word is that he's not very happy you're working here. Leaving Der Keller for the enemy."

I wasn't sure what she was getting at. She couldn't possibly think that Mac had something to do with Eddie's death, could she? Mac was a cheating scoundrel, no doubt about that, but he wasn't a killer. Or was he? How well did I know my husband? After what he'd done, I was beginning to wonder if I knew him at all.

"Mac can be as angry as he wants," I said. "And you know how things work around here. Everyone freaks out when something—or someone—new comes to town, and then two minutes later, it's like they've always been here. Plus, I'd hardly call us the enemy. Our operation is a sliver of what Der Keller is producing."

She raised a bushy eyebrow and stared at me with her quick eyes. "Not an unwelcome coincidence that his new competitor is gonna be shut down for a while right after opening, is it?"

"Shut down?" Garrett chimed in. "You're shutting us down?"

Police Chief Meyers nodded at the stainless steel tank. "Don't think many folks around here are going to be interested in drinking that beer. As soon as the coroner arrives, we'll remove the body, but I don't know when I can let you open up again. Could be later today. Could be a day or two. It depends on what the coroner has to say, what our window for time of death is, and how long it takes my guys to sweep the scene."

"Understood." Garrett let out a long sigh. I couldn't blame him. Last night had gone so well, and the entire town was buzzing over his new beer. Having to close for any extended period of time would put a damper on the energy we'd built. Of course Eddie's death would cast an even darker gloom on Nitro.

"It'll be okay," I tried to reassure him. "Everyone loved your beer. No one is going to give up on us just because they have to wait a few days for another pint."

He gave me a halfhearted smile. "Yeah, I hope you're right, but we're going to have to dump that entire batch. That's going to take a while to brew again." His pupils went wide with disbelief. "What am I saying? A man was killed in one of my tanks. How are we going to recover from that?"

He was right. Replacing the entire tank of beer would take a couple of weeks. Not to mention the cleaning. Would we even be able to use the fermenter? How much would it cost, and what would the delay be in getting a new one installed? I could tell that Garrett's head was swirling with the same questions. When word got out that Eddie had been found at Nitro, that wouldn't be good for business. Were we sunk before we'd even begun?

CHAPTER

THIRTEEN

THE CORONER ARRIVED SHORTLY. POLICE Chief Meyers gave us permission to wait at the bar so that we didn't have to witness the removal of Eddie's body. I let out a small sigh of relief as I followed Garrett to the front of the building.

"This is insane," he said, pulling out a barstool for me. Bags had formed under his eyes. Or had they always been there? "It looks good in here. Did you clean already?"

"Yeah." I had to resist the urge to reach over and smooth his messed-up hair. "I know. I can't believe this is happening. It feels like a bad dream."

He sat on the stool next to me and absently ran his hand over the bar. "Or worse."

"Worse?" The bar smelled of wood polish.

"Did you get the sense that the police chief thought this might be some kind of setup?" He rubbed his temples and ran his fingers through his hair again. *It must be a nervous habit,* I thought.

"I'm sure she's going through every possibility. Chief Meyers is by the book." Then I paused and looked at him. "Why would someone want to set you up?"

He shrugged and pushed back his stool. Then he walked around the bar, grabbed a rag, and began polishing the already shiny keg taps. "I can't sit still. I have to do something."

My question went unanswered. I watched Garrett scrub the platinum tap handles with gusto. "You don't strike me as a sleeping pill kind of guy," I said.

His hand stopped for a second, but then he continued to rub the soft cloth on the tap. "Yeah, well, you should have seen me when I worked in the corporate world."

I waited for him to say more, but he went back to work cleaning. I picked up a salted peanut and cracked the shell, thinking to myself that Garrett was going to be one tough nut to crack. I wasn't used to anyone keeping their feelings and words as buttoned up as me. I found it intriguing and infuriating.

"You want a coffee or something?" Garrett asked as he neatly folded the rag and placed it next to the sink.

"That sounds great."

Garrett had installed a professional coffee system in the bar. It was a smart move, not only for customers looking for something aside from beer to drink, but also to help sober up anyone who had consumed one pint too many. He also stocked a small selection of Yakima Valley wines for people who preferred wine to beer. The Yakima Valley growing region was known throughout the world for producing spectacular and award-winning wines. Once a struggling farming community, the valley had transformed in the last three decades. Thanks to fertile soil and Eastern Washington's abundant sunshine, winemakers began planting cuttings of vines, which quickly put them on the global wine map. The area attracted wine enthusiasts from all over the world with over fifty wineries and vineyards offering artisan wines and a variety of events from harvest celebrations to crush weekends.

While Garrett brewed a pot of coffee, I munched on handfuls of peanuts and Doritos. I wasn't even hungry, but like Garrett, I had to do something to keep my mind off what was happening in the brewery.

"Did you know Eddie well?" Garrett asked.

"Not really." I chewed a salty peanut. "He's been brewing for Bruin for a while, but he wasn't into the Beervaria scene. He rarely came downtown."

Garrett removed a container of cream from the built-in fridge below the bar. "I got that impression last night."

A knock sounded on the front windows. I turned to find April Ablin waving wildly. She wore yet another barmaid costume. This one was black, red, and white. The skirt barely covered her backside, and the red bodice was cut so low that her chest was squished up to her neck. White ruffled thigh-high socks and garish red lipstick completed her outfit.

She caught my eye and pointed to the door. *Open up,* she mouthed.

April Ablin was the last person I wanted to see this morning. I thought about ignoring her, but she continued to bang on the window.

"You don't have to let her in," Garrett said as I moved toward the door.

"I know, but trust me, she's relentless. She'll never go away on her own."

He shrugged and reached for two coffee cups.

I twirled one of my braids and squared my shoulders before facing April. "What do you need, April?" I asked, intentionally opening the door halfway and blocking her from entering.

She stood on her tiptoes and peered over my shoulder. "I saw Chief Meyers's squad car and noticed the county coroner's van parked outside." Then she stared at me. "Oh, Sloan, you're a mess. You look awful. Just awful."

"Thanks." I glanced at my flannel shirt, which was splotched with water and dish soap. I probably was a mess, but I wasn't about to fall victim to April's tactics. I knew that she was trying to get me to talk.

"So is the coroner inside?"

"Yeah." I tried to stay as noncommittal as possible. Once April had word of what had happened to Eddie, the entire town would know.

Her gaudy lipstick made her face appear yellow. "What's going on in there, Sloan?"

"There's been an accident."

She threw her hand over her mouth. "An accident. My God, what kind of accident?"

I stood my ground. "Chief Meyers is taking care of it."

Moving to the left and then right to try and get a look inside, April ducked and then stood on her toes again. "Sloan, you are the most tight-lipped person in this town. This is no time for your private and superior attitude. I know that something is going on in there."

Was that how people saw me? As superior? April's words stung. I knew that I was private, but I'd never considered that anyone would interpret that as having a superior attitude.

"April, I can't let you in. Chief Meyers has instructed us to wait for further details and not to speak to anyone. That's all I can tell you right now."

She glared and made a huffing sound. "Fine, but I'm not done here. It's my duty as Leavenworth's ambassador to know everything—*everything*—that's happening in town." With one final huff, she spun around and stormed across the street.

"That went well," Garrett said, handing me a cup of dark black coffee.

"April likes being in the know."

"Yeah, I got that." He pointed to the cup. "Do you want cream or sugar?"

"No. This is great." I inhaled the scent of the bold coffee and tried to shake off April's comment. Was that why Mac had cheated on me? Did he think I was cold or snobbish?

"Don't let her get to you," Garrett said.

"What?"

"I heard her comment. You're not superior. She's trying to get under your skin."

"Thanks." I took a sip of the coffee.

He walked back around the bar and picked up his cup. "I know the type. Trust me, in the corporate world, that's how most people operate."

I was genuinely touched at his attempt to make me feel better and was surprised that he had picked up so much from my short conversation with April. Before I could ask him more about his time in Seattle, the coroner and his team brought Eddie's body out on a stretcher.

CHAPTER

FOURTEEN

WITHOUT A WORD, GARRETT REACHED across and grabbed my hand. I squeezed his warm and rugged hand back in response and turned my head away as they removed Eddie's body from the bar. My stomach lurched. The coffee tasted bitter in my mouth. I wanted to shut my eyes and make everything that had happened in the last hour disappear.

Garrett must have sensed my discomfort, because he clasped my hand tighter. His touch sent a calming vibe through my body. "It's done," he whispered a minute later and released my hand. I didn't want to let his hand go, but I nodded and swallowed hard.

"All right," Chief Meyers said, lumbering toward us and breaking the silence. "That's taken care of. I want a few minutes with each of you in private." Her walkie-talkie crackled again. She twisted the dial on top and hardened her gaze at Garrett. "Your office, let's go."

Garrett held up the carafe of coffee. "Would you like some, Chief?"

She declined with a brisk shake of her head. "Nope. I want a word in your office—now."

He caught my eye as he followed her. I was used to her abrupt and slightly abrasive style, but I knew that Chief Meyers loved Leavenworth even more than April Ablin did. Garrett shouldn't have anything to worry about—at least I hoped that was the case. Trying to keep my mind off of Eddie, I finished my coffee and tidied up the bar. The chief and Garrett returned a few minutes later.

"Sloan, come with me," Chief Meyers demanded, giving Garrett a nod. "I'll take that coffee now."

Garrett poured her a cup. I wanted to flee to the comfort of the farmhouse and my favorite pair of flannel pajamas, but instead I took a final swig of coffee and headed with her to the office.

She pushed a stack of papers to the side of Garrett's desk, rested the steaming cup, and flipped open her notebook. "Okay, let's get down to business."

I sat and waited for her to ask more.

She stared at me and tapped a pencil on her notebook. "You gonna talk?"

"About what?"

"Sloan, you know what I'm gettin' at." Her sharp, eagle-like eyes seemed to penetrate through me.

"I'm not sure that I do." I stared at Garrett's beer formulas on the wall. That wasn't exactly true. I had a feeling she was hinting at Mac, but I wasn't going to throw him under the bus.

Frowning, she tapped a yellow pencil on her notebook. "Your husband."

"Mac?"

"Look, I know how the rumor mill works around here, and I know it's gotta be tough for you." Her face softened, making her almost attractive. Chief Meyers was Leavenworth's first female police chief, and she had won the respect of her male peers and the community from her no-nonsense attitude and no-frills style. I could relate. Decades of working in a profession dominated by men had made me have to work twice as hard to prove myself. Things were changing in the world of craft beer. For three years in a row, *Beer Magazine* had awarded a woman brewer their highest honor—Brewer of the Year. But I guessed that Chief Meyers, like me, had run into her fair share of doubters and chauvinists over her career.

I winced at the fact that news of Mac's indiscretions had made it to the chief. At least she was kind about it, unlike April. She continued. "Garrett said something about a break-in here and that Mac was hanging around, trying to get him to hand over a recipe. What do you know about that?"

"That's right." I went on to explain how I had bumped into Mac on his way out from offering Garrett cash for his citrus IPA recipe, and then how the office had been ransacked.

She jotted down notes and slurped her coffee while I spoke. When I finished, she reached into her pocket and pulled out the plastic bag with Mac's lighter. "You recognize this?"

I nodded. "That's Mac's lighter."

"Exactly." She made another note.

Her cursive scrawl was too hard to decipher, but I made out the word "suspect" next to Mac's name in her notebook. "You don't think Mac had anything to do with Eddie's death. You've known the Krause family longer than me. Mac and I aren't exactly on the best terms right now, but he's not violent."

She cleared her throat. "Jealousy can make people do crazy things, Sloan."

"Mac's not jealous. He's having a fling with a twentysomething barmaid. If anyone should be jealous, it's me." I tapped my boots on the floor.

"Oh, I don't know about that. I'd say he's been sniffing around here a lot for someone who isn't jealous, and the bad news for him is that right now all the evidence points in his direction."

"You mean the lighter?"

"That and the physical nature of the crime. The coroner thinks that someone bashed Eddie on the head and then dumped him into the fermenter. That had to take some muscles, and Mac has muscles."

I couldn't believe that I was having to defend my cheating husband. "But why would Mac kill Eddie?"

"Not sure. It's my job to find out." She closed the notebook. "I'm off to find that husband of yours and see what he has to say for himself. Do me a favor and keep an eye on that new boss, too."

"Wait, you think Garrett could be involved, too?"

"You tell me. What's a big-city guy from Seattle doing

here? Seems pretty strange that he shows up in town and we have our first murder in decades, doesn't it?"

I'm sure my expression must have given away my shock. I could feel my jaw slacken. "He's a brewer, and he wanted to start his own place. He couldn't do that in Seattle, and he inherited this building from Tess."

She shrugged, obviously not in agreement with my defense of Garrett. Chief Meyers was a fair police officer, even if she was a bit rough around the edges, but I couldn't believe she was including either Mac or Garrett on her suspect list. Then again, as long as I'd lived in Leavenworth, there had never been a murder, so maybe this was standard operating procedure.

"He's an outsider, and he's playing his cards close to the chest. Why does everything have to be locked up? What's his paranoia about his recipes? You're a sharp one, Sloan. Keep your eyes open for me. Once I have a time of death from the coroner, I'll be back in touch."

I agreed and walked with her to the front. She left us with instructions not to touch anything in the brewery until the county crew finished their investigation. "I'll be back in an hour or two. You hold tight. Don't let anyone in unless they have one of these." She tapped her badge.

After she left, I locked the front door behind her. "I may need to rethink your policy on locking front doors," I said to Garrett.

He didn't smile. "I wish I had been wrong about that."

"What did Chief Meyers say to you?"

"She asked a bunch of questions about why I decided to

move to Leavenworth. I got the sense she was hoping that I would confess that I was running from the law or part of the witness protection program." He pushed his dark hair from his eye.

"I guess that means you're not."

He shook his head. "Sadly, no. I'm just a guy who wants to brew."

"And it doesn't look like we're going to be doing that anytime soon," I replied. "Hey, on that note, did she happen to mention what we should do about the tank?"

"Actually, yeah." He handed me a business card. "She told me to call these guys. They specialize in cleanups like this."

I shuddered. What a terrible job. "Do you want me to call them?"

"That would be great. If we can have it drained and scrubbed clean, that would be so much better than having to buy a new one. Honestly, I'm not sure I could swing it. That thing set me back over twenty grand."

I knew he was right. The cost for purchasing commercial brewing equipment was astronomical. "Let me see what I can find out." I went to the office to call the cleaning crew. It took me three attempts to dial their number. My brain seemed to be functioning at half capacity. I was sure that it was due to the stress of finding Eddie and the fact that Chief Meyers had both my husband and my new boss at the top of her suspect list.

CHAPTER
FIFTEEN

AS PROMISED, CHIEF MEYERS RETURNED and instructed Garrett on the next steps in the investigation. She directed him to his office so they could go over everything "in private." Since I wasn't needed, I decided to take a walk around the village. I could use a shot of fresh air, and maybe another shot of espresso.

The early fall sun warmed the brick sidewalks. Soon our little hamlet would transform for Oktoberfest. Giant tents would be erected across from Der Keller, and the village square would fill with garlands of fall foliage, pumpkins, and bales of hay. Oktoberfest wasn't a single weekend in October, but rather a continual party from mid-September through November. We would see thousands of visitors each weekend, who would come for the revelry and beer, and to dance the polka until the wee hours of the morning. Every hotel, lodge, and bed-and-breakfast would be booked for those months. Kegs would flow freely, and weekend

German-style parades complete with old-world barrels and keg-tapping ceremonies would draw everyone into the village square.

For the moment, Leavenworth was mine, and I appreciated the calm before the festive storm. I turned onto Front Street and headed toward the gazebo. Massive purple, pink, red, and white cascading flower baskets hung from the street lamps, along with crimson banners reading WILLKOMMEN.

I passed The Happy Rooster, a kitchen and spice shop, and Das Shoppe of das Sweets, a candy shop with a droolworthy display of caramel apples in the window. The hills to the east were dotted with brilliant fall color. It always felt magical when the wooded mountains surrounding the village began their shift into a new season. The air smelled of baking pretzels and apple cider. At Creekside, a restaurant with a year-round covered outdoor patio, German music was being piped from inside. I paused for a minute to listen to the upbeat sound and then continued on to Strudel.

"Sloan, how are you?" The bakery owner greeted me from behind a long glass case full of German sweets and pastries. "Looks like you're brewing today," she said, taking note of my jeans and work boots.

"I was, but my plans changed," I replied. "I could sure use an espresso and maybe one of your cherry strudels."

"You got it." She fired up the espresso machine while I drooled over the golden strudel that had been dusted with chunky crystals of sugar. There was nothing more delectable than German pastry, in my opinion. Over the years, Ursula had taught me how to make *Gebäck,* or *Kleingebäck,* as she called it. German pastry was known for its flaky crusts and delicious fillings like apples, nuts, and berries. Spending hours in Ursula's cluttered kitchen learning how to bake recipes passed down from her grandmother and hearing stories from her life in Germany had been one of the best parts of being a Krause. If Mac and I split, I couldn't fathom having to give up Ursula. How could he have done this to me? I felt a wave of panic and anger begin to well inside and grabbed the pastry case to steady myself.

"I hear that there's been some trouble at the new brewery this morning," the bakery owner said as she poured a shot of espresso into a paper cup.

"Word travels fast."

She laughed. "You should know that by now, Sloan. There are no secrets in Leavenworth." Handing me my coffee and pastry, she gave me a sympathetic look. "Is there anything I can do?"

"Thanks." I returned her smile and held out my pastry bag and coffee. "I think for the moment, this will do the trick."

"You let me know. I'm only a few shops away," she called as I walked to the door.

I knew that her concern was genuine, and while I didn't want to talk about what had happened to Eddie, I felt warmed by her kind words. As I started back to Nitro, I ran into Mac—*literally*.

"Sloan, baby, slow down. What's your rush?" He caught me by the forearm, jostling my coffee and causing it to splash on my sleeve.

I shook myself free from his grasp and wiped espresso from my fingers.

"Where's your ring?" He caressed my ring finger.

"Off. I took it off," I said, and wiped my hand on my jeans. "What are you doing here?"

He glanced around us. "Here? As in on the sidewalk? Last time I checked, it was a free country." Across Front Street, workers were beginning preparations for Oktoberfest, twisting garlands of leaves around the blue and white striped Maypole in the town square.

"You know what I mean." I furrowed my brow. "Are you following me?"

"No, come on, Sloan. I'm getting a coffee. I can't believe you're not wearing your ring." His ash blue eyes pierced me. But that trick didn't work anymore. He reached for my hand again, and I yanked it away. "Why are you so jumpy?"

I ignored his comment about my wedding ring and stared at his light eyes. "Haven't you heard?"

"Heard what?" He shifted his weight and stuck one hand into the front pocket of his jeans.

"About Eddie." I took a sip of the espresso. It was thick and smooth, without a hint of bitterness.

"What about him? I seem to recall you forcing me out of the pub last night. Did something happen with him after I left? He looked sauced."

Mac, unlike Garrett, was completely transparent. I had no trouble reading him, and could tell that he had no idea what I was talking about. Although staring at his puffy face, from years of overindulging in his product, made me reevaluate everything about our relationship. What if I'd been wrong this entire time? I'd never known Mac to have a violent side—impulsive maybe, but not violent.

"He's dead." I waited for his response.

"What?" Mac took a step back and scowled. "What are you talking about, Sloan?"

"I found him this morning." I squeezed the paper cup and nearly popped the plastic lid off. "He's dead."

"You found him." Mac puffed out his chest and reached for my arm.

I ducked from his attempt to console me. "Haven't you talked to Chief Meyers? She was looking for you."

"No. I just got here, but why would she be looking for me?" Sunlight filtered through an ancient oak tree, making his light hair appear almost white.

A young couple in matching running gear approached us. I grabbed Mac and pulled him around the corner. "She's looking for you because I think you're her top suspect right now."

"What?" Mac's ruddy forehead wrinkled. "Me? Why? I left. You saw me."

"I know, but then what? Where were you last night?"

He kicked a pebble on the sidewalk and stuck both hands into his jean pockets. "At the hotel."

"All night?"

Staring at the ground, he didn't meet my eyes. "Yeah, why?"

"You should talk to Chief Meyers."

"Sloan, baby, it's me. Why are you freaking out?"

"She found your lighter by the fermenter."

"So?"

"So that's where Eddie's body was."

He dug around in his pockets. "No, I've got my lighter right here." His jaw tightened as he took his hands out of his front pockets and checked his back pockets. "It's not on me. I had it last night."

"Did you come back to Nitro last night?"

Mac squinted and then looked at his feet and said, "No." His squint was a telltale sign that he was lying. Had he come back to the brewery after I left? Why?

I sighed. "Mac, you have to go talk to Chief Meyers right now. Did anyone see you go back to the hotel? Did you talk to anyone?" I swallowed hard and then asked the question I was dreading. "Was anyone with you last night?"

"NO! No, baby, I swear. I went back to my hotel and crashed. I was out cold."

I wasn't sure if I believed him or not. He was too quick to respond, but there was a small part of me that almost wished that he had said he was with the beer wench. If he really spent the night alone, that meant he didn't have an alibi.

CHAPTER

SIXTEEN

MAC AND I HAD STARTED to walk toward Nitro when, speak of the devil, the beer wench rounded the corner. She stopped in midstride when she spotted us. Her long hair was twisted in a bun at the top of her head, making her look like a gazelle. She wore a pair of skintight black yoga pants and a low-cut, formfitting tank top that didn't leave anything to the imagination, and she was puffing away at a cigarette. Did she think that practicing yoga would cancel out the nicotine; for that matter, did she even know what yoga was?

I felt sick to my stomach. The image of catching her and Mac was burned into my memory. I wanted to flee, but instead pursed my lips and brushed past her. As I walked by, I caught a huge whiff of her smoke and coughed louder than I needed to. It wasn't my proudest moment, but she didn't have much to be proud of either.

"Uh, Mac, I need to talk to you," I heard her say.

Mac muttered, "Not now." His heavy footsteps thudded behind me. "Sloan, wait up."

I didn't bother to turn around and quickened my pace, which was slightly challenging in rubber boots.

"Sloan, wait," he huffed.

There was no chance that I would stop and risk making a scene in broad daylight. I waved to the owner of the stein shop, who was wiping down his stained-glass window, and sprinted toward Nitro.

Mac caught up to me just as I reached the front door. "Sloan, stop." He grabbed the back of my flannel sleeve. "Hold up. Let me talk."

I whipped around and glared at him. "What?"

"There's nothing between me and Hayley. It was a stupid fling. You have to believe me. It's always been you—only you."

"Only me? Really?" My anger was starting to get the best of me, and I didn't like the feeling.

"Baby, please," he pleaded.

"Stop calling me baby!" I yelled, and threw my hand over my mouth. "Mac, I'm not doing this now," I hissed. "Chief Meyers is inside, and you need to talk to her." I ended the conversation by carefully opening the door and inhaling through my nose. *Keep it together, Sloan,* I told myself.

Inside Nitro there was no sign of Garrett at the bar. *They must still be in the brewery,* I thought as I tossed my empty coffee in the trash, left my strudel on one of the tables, and headed for the back. Mac tagged after me.

To my surprise, the cleaning crew had already arrived. A team of workers wearing bright yellow hazmat suits were assembling hoses and five-gallon buckets of industrial cleaner. Chief Meyers directed her team to snap pictures, dust the tanks for fingerprints, and gather clear bags of hops and other evidence. When she noticed Mac and me, she turned to one of her officers. "That should do it. Get shots of each tank and close-up shots of the office."

Garrett was leaning against the office door. She walked toward him and waved Mac and me over. "We're about done here," she said to Garrett. "As soon as my team clears out, you're good to go ahead with cleaning." To Mac she snapped her fingers and pointed at the office. "A word, right now, Mac." The disdain in her tone was clear.

Mac gave me a squeamish look, which I'm not ashamed to admit made me slightly pleased.

"It's crazy in here," I said to Garrett, who moved out of the way for Chief Meyers and gave Mac a look I couldn't decipher.

He nodded to the crew in hazmat suits. "They showed up about five minutes after you left."

"That's speedy service. They told me they would be out right away, but I can't believe they are that fast."

"I guess it goes with the territory." He sounded dejected.

"Right." I wasn't sure how to console him. I'd never been in a position like this either, but our only option was to forge ahead. "Okay, so now what? They get the tank cleaned. Actually it looks like all the tanks are going to need a good scrubbing. Is that fingerprint dust?"

"It's everywhere." He sighed. "Do you think we should dump everything and start new?"

"What did Chief Meyers say?"

"She said it wasn't necessary, but what if the dust throws off my recipe?"

I walked to the copper mash tun to get a closer look. A fine layer of powder coated parts of the tank. "I can't imagine that this would throw anything off. I'm sure they can wipe it down and it will be fine."

"If you're sure." Garrett hesitated. "My recipes can be sensitive sometimes."

I couldn't help but chuckle. He looked injured. "Sorry. I'm not laughing at you. I've never heard a beer recipe referred to as sensitive. I like it."

He smiled. "It is. Kind of like me."

Was he sensitive? He definitely struck me as cerebral and introspective.

"Why don't we wait and see how everything looks after the cleaning crew finishes, and then we can make a decision," I suggested. "Did Chief Meyers say anything about opening the bar?"

Garrett rubbed his temples. "You know, you're not going to believe this, but she said it was fine to open as planned this afternoon as long as they're finished with their investigation and as long as we don't open this space back here up to the public."

"Really?' I was surprised, since earlier Chief Meyers had made it sound like it might be a few days before we could reopen.

"Yeah, but what do you think? Is it a good idea to open tonight or the worst idea ever? Will it freak people out to drink my beer? Can you imagine going to a brewery after someone found a dead body?

"I'm going to have to defer to your expertise on this one. I don't know Leavenworth well enough to get a sense of whether people will come toast to Eddie's memory with us or revolt and shoo us out of town. To be honest, I don't know how I feel about it myself. This is uncharted territory. Part of me wants to lock the door and run back to Seattle. Even though working in the corporate world was sucking the soul out of me, this is too much."

I didn't know how to respond. He continued.

"At the same time, part of me wonders if we don't owe something to Eddie. Should we open up the taps for him? Is that weird, since I barely know the guy? What do you think?"

I considered his words for a minute. Suddenly, I felt my worth at Nitro, and not just for my nose or cooking abilities. Garrett needed my guidance. I felt responsible for finding Eddie, especially in such an awful way. Eddie might not have been the most beloved brewer in town, but he was part of our community, and he deserved an evening in his honor. Garrett's instinct was right and compassionate. Yet another reason he couldn't be a suspect.

We could host a wake at Nitro tonight and offer a free pint in Eddie's memory. I would check in with Bruin, but I had the sense that he would be relieved. Eddie had been Bruin's head brewer and friend for years. Bruin must be distraught over the loss. Hopefully a wake would help put this morning's terrible events behind us. A pub is supposed to be the center of the community, a place for everyone to come together—to celebrate and to mourn. That's what we would do: mourn Eddie's death and gather to raise a glass in his memory.

CHAPTER

SEVENTEEN

THE MORNING AND EARLY AFTERNOON passed swiftly, between having the cleaners on-site and the constant flood of locals stopping to check in on the activity. I suggested to Garrett that it would be best to let me handle the influx of questions and prying eyes. He quickly agreed. "Sloan, I can't thank you enough for your help. You've handled things so deftly and calmly. I don't know what I would have done if you weren't here. If I didn't know better, I would say that the beer gods sent you to me."

I waved off his thanks, my mind reeling. The only way to keep my emotions in check was to keep moving. I had a feeling when I got home later that night, I would collapse, but for the moment there were plenty of distractions to keep my mind off of Eddie's murder. As I had suspected when I called Bruin, he thanked me profusely for the offer and had to hang up because he could barely speak. Knowing that we were providing some relief for Bruin and his team made me all the more resolved to make sure tonight went off without a hitch.

There wasn't time to prepare a full meal for Eddie's wake, so while Garrett oversaw the rest of the cleaning, I offered to run to the grocery store and pick up some meat and cheese trays and crackers. My cell phone rang as I stepped outside. It was Alex.

"Mom, what's going on?" His voice was frantic.

Panic flooded my body. Had I accidentally forgotten to pick him up from school or soccer practice? As a foster kid, I'd rarely relied on adults. I couldn't begin to tally the number of times I'd been left behind or forgotten at school. When I got pregnant with Alex, I made a vow to never let him experience the feeling of being abandoned.

One memory that stuck in my head was from when I was in fourth grade. My foster mom at the time was a stickler for punctuality (among many other things) and refused to wait for anyone. My teacher asked me to stay after class to talk about a special project she wanted me to participate in. I felt equally elated to be asked to do something by a teacher and filled with dread for the wrath I might face from my foster mom if I wasn't in front of the school standing on the yellow line when her minivan rolled up.

I decided to chance it and bounced nervously while my teacher praised my efforts in class and sent me home with a permission slip to participate in a new creative class that would meet after school once a week. I was five minutes late to the pickup spot on the curb. I'd never forgotten sitting on the yellow line watching as moms and dads greeted their kids with hugs and kisses and as car after car and the buses pulled away. My foster mom was nowhere to be found. I waited on the curb in a drizzly rain until it got dark, shivering and curling into a ball to try and stay warm. Finally the principal spotted me as she walked to her car. She gave me a ride home and even stopped at a drive-through to buy me a hamburger and French fries. The principal's car smelled like tea when she blasted the heat to help warm me up. My memory might have been fuzzy, but I was pretty sure she gave my foster mom a lecture when she delivered me home. It didn't work. My foster mom sent me straight to bed in my wet clothes and refused to sign the permission slip. I'd probably never been late since that day.

"Mom, Mom," Alex's voice called.

"Where are you?" I asked, clutching my jaw and trying to force the painful memory away.

"School."

"Oh no, did your dad forget to pick you up?"

"Mom, chill. It's only two o'clock. I'm in study hall."

Thank God, I thought, allowing myself to breathe more fully.

"Dad texted me, though. He said he can't get me because he's in jail. Is he kidding around or something?"

"What?" My voice reverberated through the quiet square.

"Yeah. I just got it. This has to be some kind of joke, right?"

My stomach sunk. Had Chief Meyers arrested Mac? I couldn't believe it. Sure, finding his lighter near the fermenter and his lack of alibi didn't absolve him, but arrest him? Chief Meyers had known the Krause family for decades. She couldn't really think that Mac had any involvement in Eddie's death.

"Mom, are you there?" Alex asked.

"Sorry." I let out a sigh and went on to explain what had happened. When I finished, Alex echoed my sigh.

"That's terrible, Mom. But what does that have to do with Dad? And why is he in jail?"

"I don't know, honey. Listen, I'm going to run over to Der Keller and talk to Oma and Opa right now. I'll keep you posted. Do you want me to come get you after school?"

"Nah, it's fine. I have weight training for soccer. I'll grab a ride and see you at home later."

"Okay, but I might be late. We're going to have a wake for Eddie at Nitro. Do you want to come?"

"Maybe. I'll text you later. The librarian is glaring at me. I better go."

I started to tell him that I loved him, but he hung up before I had a chance. Mac arrested—not possible. Instead of turning left to go to the grocery store, I made a hard right and sprinted toward Der Keller. A couple of shopkeepers called friendly greetings as I breezed by, but I didn't bother to stop.

Making it to Der Keller in less than two minutes, thanks to my long legs and need for answers, I pushed open the heavy carved front doors and scanned the bar.

"Hey, Sloan. Fancy seeing you here," the bartender called. "I thought you were working for the enemy now." He winked.

"Are the Krauses here?" I asked.

"Nope. You just missed them, but Hans is in the back."

"Great." I hurried to the brewery.

Hans was crouched on his knees examining the base of the hop freezer. In order to extend the life of some of our experimental hops and preserve their aroma, we kept them at a chilly twenty to thirty degrees Fahrenheit. If stored properly in airtight packaging, hops will keep for upwards of two years in the freezer.

"Hans!" I yelled, causing him to flinch and bump his head on the freezer.

He sat up and rubbed the crown of his head. "Sloan, what's going on?" His honey blond hair was darker than Mac's and curled slightly.

"Have you heard about Mac?" I tugged on my braid.

Nodding, he rested his screwdriver on the floor and stood. "I wondered how long it was going to take you to run over here."

"So you know?"

He wiped his hands on his work pants and walked over to me. "Yeah, Mac called me from jail."

I couldn't help but feel slightly wounded that Mac had called Hans instead of me. Things might be rocky between us, but he was still my husband.

Hans must have read my mind, because he put his arm around my shoulders and gave me a half hug. "He asked me not to say anything to you."

"As if I wasn't going to find out. Alex just called me." I didn't like how frantic my voice sounded.

Removing his arm from my shoulders, Hans met my gaze. "I know. I know. He's not thinking straight right now,

Sloan." His kind eyes matched the color of the copper tanks as he held my gaze for a moment.

"Why did Chief Meyers arrest him? Did you talk to her? Did she say anything?"

"Slow down," he said, pointing to the front. "Let's grab a drink, and I'll tell you what I know."

Hans's aura had such a calming effect that I couldn't resist. We went to the front of the pub, where he directed me to a high table in the corner, while he went to get us beers. My foot bounced uncontrollably under the table while I waited. This day was like a waking nightmare—finding Eddie's body and now Mac behind bars. Familiar German music played overhead, and the pub smelled of schnitzel and beer and cheese soup. I breathed in the scent and tried to relax.

"Drink this," he commanded, returning with a frothy pilsner.

"Thanks." I managed a halfhearted smile as I took a drink of the pale beer. Hans had chosen wisely, since anything stronger probably would have sent my head spinning. Pilsners are known for their soft but complex fragrance and for their low alcohol content. They're arguably the most popular style of beer in Germany.

Hans slid into the booth across from me and watched me sip my beer. "Better?"

"I guess. I don't understand how Chief Meyers could think that Mac killed Eddie. What did she say?"

"Nothing. I didn't talk to her. Mac got one call. He called me and told me to call his lawyer."

"Did he say anything else?"

Hans strummed his fingers on the table. "He said they found his lighter at Nitro."

"I knew that." I nodded.

He frowned. "That's not all."

"What?" I took a sip of the pilsner, picking up notes of hay and sweet grass.

"They found his prints on the fermenter."

"At Nitro?" I couldn't believe what I was hearing.

"Yeah." Hans sighed and picked up his beer. "It doesn't look good for him right now. Eddie was killed sometime between midnight and two o'clock, and Mac doesn't have an alibi. He says he went back to the hotel and passed out."

"You're not actually worried, are you?" I asked Hans.

Hans scanned the nearly deserted bar. "No. You and I both know that Mac is an idiot, not a killer. But the evidence is pretty damning. Sloan, can you think of anyone who would want to get Mac in trouble?"

I shook my head. "No. Why?"

Leaning forward and dropping his voice, he said, "Think about it. Mac's fingerprints and lighter are found at Nitro the morning after he shows up for your launch and makes a scene. I usually have a pretty good sense about people, but I'm starting to have a few doubts about Garrett."

My boot slipped off the base of the stool and made me almost lose my balance. "Garrett?" I said too loudly.

Hans held out his hand. "I know. He doesn't seem like the type, does he?"

"What would his motivation be?"

"No idea. To sabotage Mac?" He hesitated. "To protect you," he said, more like a question.

"Protect me?" I reached for my pilsner and took another big swig of the pale ale. "I hardly know him. I've been working for him for less than forty-eight hours."

Hans paused, took a drink of his beer, and nodded. "Yeah, it's a stretch, but he seems like he's already attached to you."

"You think so?"

He rubbed his temples. "I don't know. Something is off about this."

"I agree, but I don't think it was Garrett."

We drank our beers in silence for a moment. I watched the bartender chat with an older couple tasting beers at the bar. He was taking them through a tasting flight, starting with the lightest beers first and working his way toward Der Keller's darkest stout. Hans's theory made sense. I tried to think of anyone who would want to tarnish Mac's reputation—not that he hadn't done a bang-up job of that himself—but no one came to mind.

"Mac was in the brewery yesterday," I said to Hans. "He easily could have touched the fermenter. You know how handsy he can be." *Wrong choice of words, Sloan,* I thought to myself.

Hans ignored the comment. His eyes landed on the Krause family crest that had been carved out of old growth wood and hung above the bar. "That's true. It's a Krause family curse—we can't keep our hands off beer equipment. It's in our blood."

"I thought Mac was there to check up on me, but it turns out he offered Garrett cash for his citrus IPA recipe."

"No way." Hans tilted his head to the side and studied my face. "You've got to be kidding. My brother does not pay for beer."

"I know. That's what I said to Garrett."

"Something doesn't add up." Hans finished his beer.

"Do you think the beer wen . . . uh, Hayley, could be involved?"

"How?" Hans gave me an incredulous look.

"Eddie was pissed that she showed up at the opening. I definitely got the sense that they have some kind of history."

"Sloan, how in the world would she have done it, though?"

"Maybe she had help." As I said it out loud, I became more convinced that it was a possibility. Eddie had made it as clear as one of the crystal steins above the bar that he did not want her anywhere near him. What could her motivation be? Maybe they'd had a fling and a nasty breakup. Or maybe she'd cheated on Eddie with Mac. I'd have to find out everything I could about the beer wench.

Hans picked up our glasses. "I guess it's a possibility, but it's a stretch. I have to get back to the shop. I'll check in with you later. Do you need help with Alex or anything?"

"What would I do without you?"

"That's what the women always say, Sloan." Hans grinned and stood.

He had never been lucky in love, and I had never been able to figure out why. Hans was one of the most solid and hardworking guys that I knew. He was a true Renaissance man, well read, a great cook, and handy. One day he was going to make someone a very happy woman. I had tried to set him up, unsuccessfully, a few times before he begged me to stop. Unlike Mac, Hans tended to be more reserved and introspective. He didn't leap into things without thinking about the consequences.

As we parted ways, I couldn't help but wonder if Mac's affair had gotten him into something much more sinister. Could his relationship with Hayley have made someone want to set him up to look like Eddie's killer?

CHAPTER

EIGHTEEN

I HEADED STRAIGHT FOR THE grocery store and piled a basket with meat, cheese, and veggie trays, crackers, pita chips, and hummus. It might not have been as gourmet as last night's offering, but my assortment of snacks would satisfy the masses and soak up some alcohol if anyone opted to drown their sorrows over Eddie's death.

As I made my way down the aisle toward checkout, I heard a crash behind me and turned to find the beer wench surrounded by a pile of canned green beans. She met my startled gaze with a triumphant smirk. I didn't know if it was finding Eddie's body or my most recent run-in with Mac that made me snap, but without thinking, I stalked toward her, kicking a can out of my way.

"What are you doing here?" I clutched the basket of groceries so tightly that I thought my hand might start to bleed.

She placed one hand on her hip and gave me a challenging stare. "Shopping."

It took every ounce of my self-control not to drop the basket and take a swing at her. She chewed on an unlit cigarette and stepped over the pile of cans. I wanted to scream, but the manager and two customers shopping nearby had heard the commotion of the cans falling and came to see what had happened. The beer wench swung her hips as she walked down the aisle, leaving me to deal with her mess.

You can't let her get under your skin, I told myself as I helped restack the cans and regained my composure. Regardless of what Mac said, there was obviously more to their relationship, and I didn't want any part of it. I ignored my shaky hands, paid for the groceries, and hurried back to the pub. I didn't want to chance another run-in with the beer wench, because I had a feeling that I wouldn't be able to hold back the next time.

When I returned to Nitro, Van and Garrett were standing at the bar sorting through a large box of hops.

"Let me help you with that, Sloan." Van tossed a handful of aromatic hops onto the bar and came over to help carry my grocery bags.

"Did you buy the entire store?" Garrett teased.

"It looks like it, doesn't it?" I rested the other shopping bags on the counter. "Maybe I went overboard, but it will all keep, and if this is a wake, it's better to be prepared."

"A wake?" Van grabbed a hop cone and ran it between his fingers. His fingernails were caked with dirt, and his jeans covered in dust from the farm.

"We're holding a wake for Eddie tonight," I explained.

Van smashed the hop. Immediately, the scent of citrus, pine, and spice permeated the air. "I had no idea that you and Eddie were friends," he said to both of us.

Garrett and I both replied, "We weren't," at the same time.

"I'm confused." Van continued to press the hop in his hand. "You're holding a wake for someone you didn't know?"

"You'll learn this about Leavenworth. Everyone will want to toast to Eddie, and given that I . . . found him, it seemed right to hold the wake here," I explained.

Van swept the hop into his other hand. "Got it."

"What about you?" Garrett asked. "You're in the beer business. You must know all the brewers in town. Did you know Eddie well?"

Van walked around the bar and tossed the hop into the garbage can. "We knew each other." He didn't expand on the sentiment, which I took to mean that he didn't consider Eddie a friend. The brewing community in Leavenworth was small, and Eddie had a reputation for being abrasive and competitive. Then I remembered Eddie's comment about the hops the night he was killed.

"Were you supplying Eddie, too?" I asked.

"No. He didn't think my stuff was good enough. I told him to ask Mac—or anyone at Der Keller—for a reference, they'll tell him how good my stuff is, but he didn't want to hear it."

That surprised me. Hops were hard to come by, and I couldn't imagine Bruin turning down the opportunity to try something new. I also thought that Van had said he didn't know Der Keller. Had he worked a deal with Mac that fast? I was going to have to ask Mac about it.

"What do I owe you for these?" Garrett pointed to the box of hops. The box had been partitioned into four sections. Each section contained a different variety of hop.

Van reached into the back pocket of his jeans and handed Garrett a folded-up sheet of paper. "Here's the contract. It gives you exclusive rights for the next five years. I've got a lot of interest, so I need you to move on this ASAP."

Garrett unfolded the invoice and winced for a second. "Can I have some time to look over the terms?"

"Like I said, man, I've got a lot of interest. This is a good deal." He looked to me for confirmation. I threw my hands up. There was no chance that I was going to weigh in without knowing anything about the terms Garrett and Van had discussed. Van sighed. "Look, I've got two more deliveries to do. I can swing back and pick up the signed contract and check for the deposit in a couple of hours, but after that, I'm moving on to the next brewer on my list."

"Okay." Garrett stared at the contract.

Van trudged to the door in his heavy work boots. Garrett handed me the paperwork once Van had walked around the corner and was out of sight. "Will you look at this? Does that price seem high to you?"

I read over the invoice. "Holy hops! That's a huge number."

Garrett reached into the box and examined one of the hop varieties. "He told me it would be more for these experimental ones, but I wasn't expecting the price to be this high."

"The contract locks you in for five years, right?" Hop

cultivation was a booming business in the Pacific Northwest, particularly in warm sunny climates like the Yakima Valley. As the craft beer movement continued to sweep the nation, the demand for hops had skyrocketed. I'd learned at a beer conference I attended for Der Keller in Seattle last summer that one of the biggest issues facing brewers was access to hops. Macrobrewers, who had financial resources and sway with hop suppliers, had stockpiled the most popular varieties, making it nearly impossible for small breweries to get their hands on any signature hops. Some hop contracts extended decades into the future, creating a shortage and high demand for new varieties. So much so that brewing magazines and even the national media had run front page features with titles like WILL A SHORTAGE OF HOPS KILL CRAFT BEER?

Garrett stuffed the invoice into his pocket. "Yeah. This number is giving me sticker shock, but if I'm going to compete, I don't know what else to do."

He had a point. Der Keller had signed a twenty-five-year contract with our supplier for four styles of hops. Still, it was hard to see the number printed at the bottom of the invoice and not have a panic attack. "Do you want me to talk to Otto and Ursula? I'm sure they'd be more than willing to give you some advice."

"No, don't worry about it. I don't want to put you in a weird position. I'll figure it out. I'll call a couple of beer buddies in Seattle."

"Are you sure? It's no trouble."

Garrett shook his head. "No, I'm good." He picked up a bag of groceries and helped me take the food for the wake to the kitchen. The brewery smelled of industrial cleaner. From the floor to the ceiling, every square inch of space sparkled. "The place looks brand new," I commented.

"They did a thorough job." Garrett held the kitchen door open for me. He hovered for a minute before following me in.

"Did Chief Meyers say anything after I left?" I unloaded the trays into the commercial fridge.

"She cleared us to open today, but doesn't want anyone back here, which is fine. I don't either." He stacked boxes of crackers on the stainless steel island.

"Nothing more about the case?"

"Not to me. She comes across as by the book, as you said."

"True."

I debated whether I should tell him about Mac's arrest, and decided that it would be better if he heard it from me. The rumor mill would surely be in full swing later tonight, and someone was bound to let it slip out.

"She arrested Mac," I said as I closed the heavy stainless steel door.

"What?" Garrett stopped stacking crackers and stared at me. "He doesn't strike me as the violent type."

"He's not." I folded an empty paper bag and avoided his gaze. "She found his lighter and prints on the tank."

"I can explain the prints. When he came by yesterday to ask about my recipe, I gave him a tour. I remember him running his hands over the tanks. He was kind of condescending and pretended to be impressed with my 'amateur' setup."

"That sounds like Mac."

"Don't worry, I'll talk to Chief Meyers."

"You don't need to get in the middle of my personal drama." Garrett's offer made me even surer that there was no way he could have killed Eddie or was trying some kind of an elaborate sabotage as Hans had suggested.

"Sloan, we're talking about murder. I think this is a case where I should get involved, and I don't think it has anything to do with you or personal drama."

I sighed. "There's more. He doesn't have an alibi for last night."

Garrett scrunched his forehead and ruffled his hair. I could tell from the way he kept his eyes on the cement floor and kept shifting his weight from side to side that there was something he wasn't telling me.

"What?"

He walked to the dishwasher and inspected the old dials on the front. "I don't know if I should say this."

"What?" I repeated. "Do you know something about Mac?"

His expression was pained when he nodded and looked up from the dishwasher. "I didn't want to tell you this, but I think that Mac might have an alibi."

My stomach sunk. "Okay."

He looked uncomfortable as he ran his fingers through his unruly hair. "I saw him last night after you left. He and that girl from the bar were walking together. They came in and asked for a growler fill."

"When?" I fought with every muscle to keep my tone neutral.

"I don't know. I was up late. I couldn't sleep after all the excitement and the crowd. It was after midnight, maybe even closer to one o'clock."

A feeling of relief and bitter anger came over me. I knew why Mac had lied to me earlier. It didn't have anything to do with Eddie's murder. It was because he was with the beer wench.

CHAPTER

NINETEEN

WHY HAD I BEEN SO dense? Of course Mac was with the beer wench. His attempts to win me back were a ploy. He didn't have any intention of ending things with Hayley. He wanted his fling and me too. Well, no way. I would help him clear his name—by forcing him to fess up about his extracurricular evening antics with the beer wench—for Alex's sake, but then I was filing for divorce. The man was an egomaniac and incapable of change.

"Sloan, you okay?" Garrett sounded worried.

"I'm fine." I opened the cupboard doors and found a silver platter that I could arrange the crackers on. "What else needs to be done before we open?"

Garrett hesitated for a moment. I could tell he wanted to talk more about Mac, but I appreciated the fact that he picked up on my cue and shifted the conversation back to a topic we were both much more comfortable with—beer. "I think we're ready. Until the kegs run out."

"There could be worse problems."

"True. Any ideas on new recipes?"

"You mean for tonight?"

"No. I mean beer."

I could feel my cheeks warm. Garrett wanted my input on beer. "Actually, I do have an idea. What if we each make our own small batches with the experimental hops you got from Van? We can feature them as limited editions and have customers vote on their favorite. What do you think?"

He smiled. "Yeah, I love it. Do a blind tasting?"

"Exactly. Then we can chart votes on the whiteboard at the bar, and whichever batch wins we can brew in larger quantity. It would give everyone some ownership, and I think that will go a long way in helping us find a following."

"You are a genius, Sloan." Garrett gave me a high five. "I'm going to go sketch out a few ideas right now."

My smile broadened as he left for the office. Otto and Ursula had always encouraged me to brew and experiment with different flavor profiles at Der Keller, but I felt like I was constantly in Mac's shadow. His gregarious personality dominated mine. Garrett genuinely seemed interested in forming a partnership and collaborating with me. It felt good to be appreciated in a new way.

I assembled the evening's snacks and thought about what I might try with Van's hybrid hops. For a lighter offering, I decided I would brew a single hop session ale. Sessions, like pilsners, are smooth light beers with relatively low alcohol content so they can easily be sipped all afternoon. On the other end of the spectrum, I would brew a CDA, a Cascadian dark ale. One of the things that made

CDAs—also known as black IPAs—so unique was their dark color but hoppy finish. With that settled, I put the finishing touches on the food for Eddie's wake and prepared myself for the onslaught of questions that was sure to come. The thought of brewing made me smile. There was something about the methodical process of following each critical step in crafting a beer that was like therapy for me. I could certainly use a healthy dose of therapy right now.

Within a half hour of opening the doors, the bar was bursting at the seams. "Beer is flooding out of the taps, Sloan," Garrett called, as I balanced two empty trays in either hand.

"I know. It's a madhouse." I went to refill the platters. The hum of conversation and banter echoed off the walls. A stranger walking into the pub would have thought that Eddie had been the most beloved member of our small town. Everyone had a story to share, and I had a feeling that as the night went on, the stories were going to become more and more embellished. No one mentioned Eddie's surly attitude or the long list of bar fights that he had been at the center of. Instead, his memory was toasted and his past glossed over. I supposed that was human nature—we tended to hold on to the best pieces of ourselves and let the more unsightly pieces fade away.

Bruin and the rest of his team from Bruin's Brewing had pushed two tables together and shouted a toast to Eddie as I passed by. They wore matching felt green hats and Bruin's Brewing T-shirts with handwritten index cards reading TASTES LIKE MORE pinned to their chests.

"Sloan, come have a pint," Bruin said, with a slight slur

in his speech. Was he already buzzed? I was going to have to keep an eye on him.

"Can't. I have to keep the masses fed." I held the empty platters. "What does 'tastes like more' mean?"

He bent his neck forward as if trying to read the index card. "That was Eddie's motto. Anytime he knocked one back and someone asked how it tasted, he would say . . ."

Bruin turned to his crew, who all raised their glasses and roared, "Tastes like more!" in unison.

I smiled and adjusted the tray. "That's good."

Bruin swayed and stuck a pudgy finger in the air. "You come find me. I gotta talk to you, and we aren't going anywhere, are we, boys?" His crew all shouted no.

I promised to come back after I'd refilled the food platters. There was something about his intensity even under the effects of alcohol that made me wonder what he wanted to talk to me about. Could it be related to Eddie's murder?

I spooked myself in the kitchen. Piling cheese and crackers on the tray, I heard someone moving near the tanks and froze. Garrett had roped off access to the brewery per Chief Meyer's instructions. No one was supposed to be back there other than Garrett and me. I grabbed a cheese knife from the counter and went to see who had followed me.

"Hey, no one is supposed to be back here," I called as I stepped out of the kitchen.

"Mom?" Alex's startled voice stopped me in my tracks. "Why do you have a butter knife?"

"Sorry." I let out a breath and relaxed my arm. "It's a cheese knife."

Alex laughed. "What were you going to do if you ran into

129

someone dangerous? Poke them with that?" He must have come straight from weight training, because he was wearing red and gray nylon gym shorts and a T-shirt with the Kodiak mascot.

"Maybe. I hadn't thought that through yet. I guess I'm more shaken than I realized."

"You found a body this morning, Mom."

"I guess I did." I waved him into the kitchen. "Are you hungry? Do you want a snack? I can make you a sandwich."

"Mom, I know that you like to think that you're Superwoman, but you know you're not, and you don't have to be. I'm fine. I had a couple slices of pizza after practice. I came to check on you."

"What would I do without you?" I reached over to ruffle his hair. He ducked and folded his muscular arms across his chest.

"Don't try to change the subject. You always do that, you know."

How had I managed to raise a teenage son who was so astute and insightful?

"Are you sure you should be working tonight?"

"I'm fine, honey, I promise. It's good to be busy right now." I broke a cracker and popped half of it into my mouth.

He tugged one of my braids. "Nice look, Mom. I didn't think you did the German thing?"

I batted his hand away and glanced at my flannel, jeans, and boots. I must look a mess. "It's been an insane day. I never had a chance to go home and change."

"I'm just kidding."

"Have you talked to your dad?" I asked through a bite of cracker.

"I tried to see him, but the police wouldn't let me. Oma and Opa were there, too. I think they're trying to bail him out." He grabbed a piece of Weisslacker, a traditional German beer cheese. I knew it was Alex's favorite. Ursula used to serve it with paprika and slices of pumpernickel bread. The pungent cheese pairs well with beer, but many people find its strong and salty flavor overpowering. Ursula always took pride in the fact that she was teaching Alex how to appreciate Old World foods.

"They are?" Hans hadn't mentioned anything about Mac posting bail earlier.

Alex shrugged. "Opa told me not to worry and to come check on you, so that's what I'm doing."

That was just like Otto to worry about me at the same time his son had been arrested. Why couldn't Mac be more like his dad?

"As you can see, I'm fine."

"Except for the butter knife you're still clutching in your hand." He reached for another piece of cheese.

I hadn't realized that I still had a hold on the knife. I loosened my grasp and placed it on the counter. "Minor detail."

"You want some help?" Alex asked and nodded at the cheese trays.

"That would be great."

We took the trays out to the front, and I watched with pride as Alex circled the room and chatted easily with everyone. I'm sure that every parent thinks their child is amazing, but he really was an extraordinary kid on every level.

"You don't have to wait around here on my account," I said to him when we met in the middle of the room.

"It's cool. I brought my homework. Opa said they would come here once they're done at the station."

"Honey, are you sure you're okay? This has to be really disturbing to have your dad arrested and behind bars."

"Mom, come on. You know that it's a mistake. Dad would never hurt anyone."

I had to bite the inside of my cheek to keep quiet. Mac had certainly found a way to hurt me, but I knew what Alex meant. "Okay, but if you change your mind, come and grab me and I'll give you a ride home."

Alex agreed and headed with his backpack to the only empty table near the windows. I finished circulating the tray, and when I made it to Bruin's table, he grabbed my arm. "Sloan, sit, sit. Have a pint with us." His voice lost its usually jovial tone.

"Bruin, I'd love to, but I'm on the clock. You know the rules."

He scoffed. "No one cares about liquor control rules, Sloan."

I disagreed. Washington State had stringent laws about serving alcohol, as well as not imbibing while on the clock.

"Sit for a minute." Bruin pushed one of his employees from a chair.

I gave the guy an apologetic look, but he didn't seem to mind. He picked up the pitcher in the middle of the table was on those breasts at once, his hands covering and then squeezing the warm soft skin. He broke away and closed his mouth over one erect nipple.

"We should move to the couch," he muttered against her skin.

"No," Terri murmured—and he felt disappointment shift through him as she suddenly slid away and out of his reach. But it seemed Terri wasn't in the mood for much foreplay, either. Before he could suffer disappointment for long, or even move, she settled back onto his lap, this time straddling him.

"You wore a skirt again," he breathed against her breast, then licked at the erect nipple in his face. He ran one hand lightly up her stockinged thigh. "But these will get in the way."

"No, they won't," she assured him. Terri took his hand and guided it up under her skirt to her hip.

Bastien's eyes widened. Those weren't panty hose, but true stockings. And she wasn't wearing any panties. He groaned against her breast, then caught her nipple in his mouth and slid his hands over her bare bottom, wondering how soon would be too soon to enter her.

Terri answered that question by shifting and reaching between them to undo his pants. "I need you *now*, Bastien."

"Thank God," he muttered, sliding one hand between her legs to caress her. He found that she was indeed warm and wet and ready for him.

The moment Terri freed him from his trousers, she brushed his hand away from between her legs but it wasn't until she sighed into his mouth that Bastien felt passion begin to creep warily into him. He'd missed her. He'd missed touching her, talking to her, just being with her. And he'd missed her sighs, her moans, and the way her body moved against his.

Bastien let a hand slide from her waist up to her breast, and he squeezed gently, a small sigh sliding out as she arched her body and moaned in response. He could almost feel the protective ice that had formed around his heart three weeks ago cracking and crumbling away. It left his chest aching. He now understood the phrase "I love you so much it hurts." His heart did hurt, and only Terri could soothe it.

"Terri," he murmured, breaking their kiss and trailing his lips over her cheek. "I need you."

"I need you, too." There was a catch in her voice as she admitted it, an excited breathless sound. Then she caught her fingers in his hair and forced his mouth to hers, kissing him with the passion he remembered and yearned for. The ache in his heart eased, but now the rest of his body ached in its place.

Bastien wanted her badly, and didn't think he could be gentle and caring and considerate about it. His instincts urged him to rip at her clothes and bury himself deep inside her. The hand at her breast shifted to the buttons down the front of her blouse, working them carelessly and popping several in his impatience to feel her skin. It was a relief to get the top open. Then he found himself frustrated by the black satin bra she wore underneath. Terri immediately reached between them and unsnapped the front hook, allowing the material to gape open. Bastien and headed to the bar for more beer. I wondered if Garrett was going to cut their group off soon.

"Sit," Bruin commanded.

My protests weren't working, so I took the newly vacant stool. "How are you doing?" I asked, with real concern. Eddie had worked for Bruin for years, so I could only imagine how upset Bruin must be.

"Not great." His already ruddy face turned even redder. "Eddie is dead. Can you believe it?"

I placed my arm over his arm, which was almost hot to the touch. "I'm so sorry for your loss. How long had he been working for you?"

"Seven years," Bruin said. He shook his head. "Seven long years. We fought all the time, but that's how it goes. Half the time I wanted to kill him, the other half I wanted to hug him."

"Why is that?" I didn't like the fact that Bruin had referenced wanting to kill Eddie, but I gave him the benefit of the doubt, considering his current inebriated state.

"He drove me crazy. He wanted to do everything his way, but I own the pub and brewery. I told Eddie many times that if he wanted to do things his way, he could start his own operation."

"Had he seriously considered that?"

"No." Bruin swiped at the air. "Noooo." He dragged out the word. "He didn't have any cash. The kid was broke. I paid him well, and he was always asking for more. Wanted a raise every other week. I don't know what he did with his money, but he didn't have a dime to his name. He asked me for a short-term loan last week."

"Did you give it to him?"

Bruin shook his head so hard that it looked like it hurt. "No! I'm not a bank. That's what I told him. He could wait until the next pay period just like everyone else, and I told him exactly that."

My mind wandered. Eddie was strapped for cash. Why? Bruin's Brewing was one of Leavenworth's most well-established and longest-running pubs. I couldn't imagine that Bruin wasn't paying Eddie a fair salary. What was Eddie doing with his money? And could he have borrowed money from someone else? Money was definitely a motive for murder. Maybe Eddie had taken a loan out from some-one else, and when the loan was due, he wasn't able to pay up. Could that have been why he was killed?

Bastien stared at her for a minute, part of him wanting to leap over the desk and take her in his arms and show her how much he still loved her. The other part urged caution. "And what about"—he gestured to his body—"my medical condition?"

Terri gave a laugh. "Medical condition?"

Bastien sighed wearily. "You know what I mean."

She hesitated, then asked, "Do you still love me, Bastien? Or are you so hurt that I needed time to think about this that you aren't sure you want anything to do with me anymore?"

"I still love you," he admitted. "I'll love you forever. Or at least for the next four or five hundred years. After that, we might have to work at it."

Terri grinned and walked around the desk.

Bastien watched her, unable to move, still wary, then gave an "oomph" as she dropped into his lap.

"I can accept your 'medical condition,' " she told him. "And I'd like to spend my life, however long it is, with you. Now, if you wouldn't mind, would you make love to me please?" She slid her arms around his shoulders. "I know we still have talking to do, but I really need to feel close to you again. I've felt so cold and scared inside since you left."

Bastien felt some of the numbness that had claimed him for the last three weeks slip away, and compassion took its place. That was how he'd felt; cold and scared, alone inside. It was like all happiness had gone out of his life along with her. Bastien let his arms slide around her waist, and he dipped his head to kiss her.

She was warm in his arms, and sweet on his lips,

Bastien was confused for a minute; then he reran his last words to himself—"*Meredith, where the hell did I put . . . Terri*." Understanding dawned. "I waited the two days."

"I'm a slow thinker," Terri said apologetically. "And thick sometimes. Kate had to come see me before I got over old presumptions."

"Old presumptions?"

"Well, you know. Thirty-three years of vampire movies can leave an impression," Terri explained with a shrug. "I was stuck on the word, not seeing the man. Or the woman, for that matter." She paused in front of his desk. "I was even afraid of Kate when she first showed up at my office in Leeds."

"Kate came to the University?" Bastien asked.

Terri nodded, a small smile tugging at her lips. "She said she just knew that you'd mess up the explaining part."

"I didn't mess up the explaining part," he snapped.

"'Have you seen the movie *An American Werewolf in London*?'" she quoted back to him. She shook her head and laughed.

Bastien flushed. So, okay—maybe that hadn't been the smoothest opening. Since then, he'd thought of at least a dozen better ways to start.

"I was under a bit of pressure," he excused himself. He gave a weary shrug, then sat back in his seat and eyed her. "Are you going to tell me why you're here? Or are you enjoying torturing me?"

"I'm here because I love you."

That sounded hopeful, he thought, his body tensing.

"And because I hope you still love me."

you all are." One of the things that Kate had explained was that most of the employees at the upper level were vampires as well. There were many employees at Argeneau Enterprises who weren't, but those in important positions were. It eliminated the possibility of a disgruntled employee blabbing about what they were to the rest of the world.

Meredith paused in front of her and nodded. "And now?"

"And now, I'm unemployed, homeless, and here," Terri said wryly. She'd quit her job, and even managed to sell the cottage before leaving. She intended to look for a position in America, or Toronto, or wherever it was that she and Bastien ended up. If he still wanted her.

Smiling, the secretary leaned forward and hugged her. "Welcome to the family," she said. Then turned to gesture to Bastien's office door. "It's not locked. He'll be happy to see you. I'm going to an early lunch."

"Thank you," Terri said quietly. She waited for the older woman to leave the office before she knocked, waited for his "Enter"—which *was* rather snappish, she noticed—then walked in.

"Meredith, where the hell did I put—" His harassed tones died abruptly as he glanced up and spotted her. "Terri."

"You didn't put me anywhere, but you left me in Huddersfield." She closed the door and crossed the room, suddenly unsure that Kate and Meredith were right, and that he would really be happy see her. He didn't look too happy.

Bastien scrubbed his hands through his hair with agitation. Marguerite Argeneau had to be the most annoying, interfering . . . And she was now Vincent's problem. For a while, at least.

"Sorry, Vinny," he muttered under his breath. A small smile plucked at his lips at the idea of the chaos his cousin was about to suffer, but it died quickly. As annoying and persistent as she could be, Marguerite Argeneau often got what she wanted. She had managed to get Kate back for Lucern when the woman had fled him for New York. And she had arranged for Thomas to get Etienne and Rachel back together when they had fallen out. It was just a shame she hadn't set her mind to getting Terri back for him.

Not that he wanted her interference, he assured himself.

Meredith was talking on the phone when Terri walked into her office. The woman stopped dead in the middle of her conversation and gaped at her; then she hung up the phone without a word of good-bye or an explanation to whomever she had been talking to. "Am I glad to see you."

Terri smiled. "Well, it's nice to see you too, Meredith."

"Trust me, not as nice as it is for me to see you, Terri." The secretary stood, collected her purse and jacket, and walked around the desk. "He's been a miserable grouch ever since returning from England. He loves you, you know."

"Yes." Terri smiled. "He told me that in Huddersfield. The problem was whether I could handle what

Bastien perked up at this suggestion. "Perhaps you should. Understanding as you are, you might be able to help him."

"Yes." Marguerite picked up her purse off his desk. "A trip to California would be nice this time of year."

"I hear it's lovely," he agreed encouragingly.

"Yes. I think I will." She slung her purse strap over her shoulder, then paused to peer at him. "You know I love you and wouldn't run off to California to tend Vincent if I didn't already know your little problem was taken care of, don't you?"

Bastien's head jerked slightly. Her comment caught him by surprise. "I don't have a problem," he growled, then added, "And what do you mean it's been taken care of?"

Marguerite ignored the question. Whirling away from the desk, she headed for the door. "Well, I'm off to California. Vincent will no doubt insist I stay with him, so ring me there if you have any . . . news."

"Wait! Mother!" Bastien half rose, then paused and simply sank down in his seat again when the door closed. For a minute, he stared blindly at the closed door, wondering what she had been talking about. Bastien suspected she had meant his broken heart when she spoke of his problem, but he had no idea what she meant when she'd said it was taken care of. The possibilities were endless. No doubt a half-dozen New York psychologists were going to call him over the next couple of days—pretty, single *female* psychologists—all claiming a need to talk to him about his mother.

362

gust. There was no such thing as contagious anemia. Now he knew where Vincent had been doing his feeding since arriving in New York. He shook his head in wonder. "The man ate himself out of his first lead role in a play. Dear Lord! How did he manage that? What was he thinking?"

"I don't think he was," Marguerite said with a sigh. "Thinking, that is. I suspect he was so nervous about his lead role that he just—"

"He didn't seem nervous," Bastien snapped. He had known the man for four hundred years; nothing made him nervous.

"That's true," his mother allowed reluctantly, then her expression cleared. "Well, of course!"

"Of course, what?" Bastien asked, suspecting he didn't want to know.

"Well, it was probably comfort eating."

"Comfort eating?" he repeated incredulously.

"Mmm." Marguerite nodded. "Well, there were Etienne and Lissianna, happy with their life mates, and Lucern marrying his, and you with Terri . . . He was probably lonely, suddenly aware of his solitary status, and overfeeding because of it."

"Dear Lord." Bastien sank back in his seat and shook his head.

"The poor boy," Marguerite murmured.

"Yes, poor boy," Bastien said dryly. He rolled his eyes. His mother had always had a soft spot for Vincent; he was her favorite nephew.

"Perhaps I should go visit him," she murmured thoughtfully.

"Good lord, you really are out of it," Marguerite interrupted. Pausing in front of his desk, she scowled at him over her crossed arms, then heaved a sigh and reminded him, "Vincent is back in California."

"Is he?"

"Yes. He is. He flew home a week ago."

"What about his play?" Bastien asked with a frown. "*Dracula,* the musical?"

She gave a discounting wave and began to pace again. "The production closed down two weeks ago."

"Already?" His eyes widened. "I should have gone to see it on opening night, but I didn't know it had opened. Did I?" he asked, not at all sure that he hadn't been told and either not paid attention or just let it slip his mind. Many things had slipped his mind since Terri left.

Marguerite stopped her pacing to say with exaggerated patience, "It never made it to opening night, Bastien."

His eyebrows rose. "Why?"

"They had to close down. Too many of the cast and crew dropped out due to illness."

"What kind of illness?" Bastien asked, his eyes narrowing.

Marguerite hesitated. "They weren't sure."

He couldn't help noticing that his mother was suddenly avoiding his gaze. "Mother," he said in warning tones.

Sighing, she admitted, "They weren't sure, but apparently it was some sort of contagious anemia."

"Contagious anemia," Bastien echoed with dis-

Chapter Twenty

"Bastien, you aren't listening to me," Marguerite Argeneau accused.

"Yes, I am, mother," Bastien said, a tad impatiently. He didn't bother to lift his eyes from the file he was reading.

"Then what did I say?"

Bastien set down the papers he'd been going through, and sat back in his chair to give her his undivided attention. Not that she noticed; she wasn't looking at him at all, but was pacing back and forth in front of his desk with agitation. Sighing wearily, he recounted, "You said that you received a letter from someone this morn—"

"From Vincent," she cut in.

"Fine, from Vincent," he repeated dutifully, then paused to frown. "Why would Vincent send you a letter? He's staying in the penthouse with us. Why didn't he just—"

minute Marguerite called and told me what happened, I insisted Lucern and I change our original plans to include Huddersfield, England, as part of our tour. Then I left Lucern all alone and lonely in the George Hotel and caught the train here to Leeds to see you, all because I love you. I want you happy. I would never hurt you. If I'd wanted to bite you, I could have done so countless times while you were staying with me in New York, but I didn't. I don't bite. Now, please just come to lunch and let me maybe make more sense of this for you. That way, you can at least make an informed decision."

Terri hesitated then nodded. "All right."

door. "Come on, we're going to Harvey Nichols for lunch."

"Oh, but Harvey Nichols is so expensive," Terri protested, dragging her feet.

Much to her amazement, it didn't even slow Kate down. Terri had to wonder if the added-strength bit in vampire movies was true.

"It is," Kate answered, as if she'd spoken the thought aloud. She grabbed Terri's light spring coat off the rack as she dragged her cousin past it.

"You can read my mind?" Terri asked, shocked.

"Yes. That's true, too," Kate said mildly.

"So, all that time, Bastien could read my mind?" she asked in horror. "He knew what I was thinking?"

"Nope. He couldn't read your mind. Which is why you two are perfect together."

"It is?"

"Uh-huh."

"Kate, I don't think . . ." Terri paused abruptly as her cousin stopped walking and turned to face her, eyes narrowed.

"Terri, I am Kate. The same Kate you've always known. The cousin you love, who loves you. The girl you used to hunt tadpoles with. Nothing has changed. And it upsets me that you would be afraid of me because of a change in my medical condition." She paused, then added, "Especially since I took time out of my *honeymoon* to come here and straighten out what Bastien messed up."

"Your honeymoon?" Terri whispered.

"Yes. My honeymoon," Kate repeated. "The

fice window. Prawn was her favorite, but it didn't taste very good at the moment. Nothing did since she'd left New York. Since leaving Bastien.

Terri grimaced and picked up her sandwich again. It had been almost a week since Bastien had left her cottage. And while she had said she needed time to digest what he'd told her . . . well, she had indigestion. She couldn't quite seem to get a grip on what he was. Terri understood what he had said, and while she knew there was probably a lot more explanation, she could mostly comprehend the nanos and blood bit. But understanding and believing and accepting were vastly different things. Terri *understood* what he claimed to be, she *believed* it was possible, but she was having trouble *accepting* it. Her wonderful, sweet, perfect, fairy-tale romance had turned out to have a twist. Prince Charming was a bloodsucker.

"That looks tasty."

Terri glanced up at that dry comment, then leapt to her feet. "Kate!"

"Hi." Grinning, the other woman removed her sunglasses and started forward, walking around the desk with every intention of hugging her.

Fear shooting through her, Terri instinctively held her hand out to stop her cousin, then blinked at the sandwich she was holding up like some Victorian wench holding up a cross.

"Bite?" she offered lamely.

Kate stared at the sandwich, burst out laughing and took it. She tossed it in the garbage bin under Terri's desk, snatched her hand, and drew her towards the did Rachel," he admitted. "But she was an exception. She was dying, and we had to save her."

"Rachel is a vampire, but wasn't one before?" she asked.

"No."

"And Greg?"

"Your garden variety Canadian psychologist—until he and Lissianna fell in love and she turned him."

Terri nodded slowly. "So, for me to be your mate, you'd have to turn me?"

"Yes. If you were willing."

"And if I wasn't?"

"Then I'd have to watch you age and weaken and die, just as you did Ian and your mother—only over a much longer period of time, of course. I'd do that for you, Terri. And I'd love you till the end. It would kill me, but . . . we mate for life in our family." He opened the door, took a step out, then turned. "I'll be staying at the George Hotel for two nights, then I fly back to America."

Terri nodded slowly, and he nodded back; then he pulled the door closed and walked to his rental car. Bastien didn't know if he'd done the right thing leaving her with this knowledge. He might be risking his entire family. But love was about trust, and he trusted Terri. She loved him, and while she might not be able to accept what he was in the end, she would never set out to hurt him.

Terri unwrapped her prawn sandwich, took a bite, then set it down with a sigh and glanced out her of-need insulin injected because they don't produce enough of their own."

"Atlanteans," Terri muttered. "I went and fell in love with the man from Atlantis." She glanced up sharply. "You don't have webbed fingers and toes, too, or something, do you?"

Bastien sighed, trying to remain patient. There was so much myth around both Atlantis and vampires. None of it ever tied together, however, thank goodness. "Honey, you've seen me naked. All of me. You know I don't have gills and fins."

"Oh, yes." She was silent, then cleared her throat. "Bastien?"

"Yes?" he asked hopefully.

"I think I'd like you to leave. I need some time to . . . er . . . digest this."

He felt his stomach drop. "How much time?"

"I'm not sure," she admitted.

Bastien stared at her for a minute, then stood and moved to the door. He paused, then glanced back to ask, "You won't tell anyone, will you?"

"No, of course not. They'd think I was nuts, anyway."

He nodded. "Good. Because you'd threaten my whole family—including Kate."

"Kate?" Terri's head snapped up.

Bastien nodded. "Lucern turned her. She's his life mate."

"Was she willing?"

"Of course she was," he snapped. "We don't go turning people without their permission. Well, we posed to mortal. Atlantean rather than British. Well, we're Canadian now. At least my family is." He paused and frowned; he was really making a flub of this. "Look, honey, sit down and I'll explain everything. Our vampirism is scientific in basis, not a curse or something. We aren't soulless. That night-walking demon thing everyone thinks vampires are—well, it was all just a big misunderstanding."

Terri didn't sit down; instead she narrowed her eyes. "So vampires can walk in daylight?"

"Yes." He frowned. "Well, the sun does a lot of damage, of course. And going out in it means we have to consume a lot more blood to make up for it, but we can go out in it without bursting into flames or anything."

She seemed to accept that, but then, she had seen him in sunlight. She asked, "How old are you?"

Bastien sighed. "Four hundred and twelve."

"Four hundred and—jeez." She sat, then stiffened. "So, all that stuff you knew when we visited the museum . . ."

"I was there for the stuff I was telling you," he admitted. "Not the medieval stuff, just from the 1600s through now."

"Is that all?" she asked dryly. Then shook her head and muttered, "This is nuts."

"No, it's science," Bastien explained. "See, our Atlantean scientists made nanos that would repair and regenerate the body, but they use blood at an accelerated rate to do so, a rate the body can't keep up with. Thus, we need to ingest more blood to feed them and stay healthy. We drink blood to survive, like diabetics ally, I am a pit peckish right at the moment, but I'd rather not—"

"Uh-huh. Bite me!" she snapped. "If you're a vampire, bite me."

Bastien peered at her arm for a minute, then took it in hand, lifted it up, and bit her.

"Ouch!" Terri leapt off the couch, retrieving her arm as she went. Bastien had to snap his teeth back double quick to keep from ripping her vein and flesh. "You bit me! You've got fangs!"

"Now do you believe me?"

Clutching her arm to her chest, she began to back away.

"Please don't be afraid of me, Terri. I love you," he said softly, taking a step after her and holding out his hand in pleading. He was relieved when she hesitated. "Honey, this is a good thing. Really. You'll never have to worry about my dying a horrible, lingering death," he offered. "I won't die like your mother and Ian. I can't."

She stared at him. "Your father is dead. Was he staked?"

"No. He burned to death. We can burn to death." Then he added quickly, "But that wouldn't be a long lingering illness. None of the ways we can die are long and lingering."

"So, the blood in your fridge . . ."

"Was to feed. We don't bite humans anymore, not unless absolutely necessary."

"You aren't human."

"Yes, of course we are. Sort of. We're just a different nationality, really. We're almost immortal, as op-

"It isn't?"

"No." He glanced around the living room of her cottage, absently noting the comfortable charm as he tried to think of the best way to tell her. "Well," he said finally, "have you ever seen the movie *An American Werewolf in London*?"

She gave a perplexed laugh. "Yes. Hasn't everyone?"

He nodded. "Well, I'm not American, or a werewolf, and we aren't in London."

She blinked several times at his comment. Then she said slowly, "No, this is Huddersfield."

"And I'm Canadian and a vampire," he finished brightly.

"Uh . . . huh," she said slowly. "Bastien, are you feeling well?"

"Terri—"

"Is this your idea of a joke?"

She was getting annoyed, he thought with alarm. How the heck had Etienne and Lucern told Rachel and Kate that they were vampires? "Terri, honey," he began. "It's not a joke. I really am a vampire."

"Oh. I see." She was getting snippy. That was interesting. He'd never seen her snippy before. Well, perhaps with the cashier at Victoria's Secret. No, Bastien decided, Terri had put the clerk in her place, but she had not got snippy with the girl.

"You're a vampire." Her voice was disbelieving, and she was nodding her head up and down in a way that didn't look promising. "Fine. Bite me."

Terri held her arm out in challenge, and Bastien frowned. "Terri, I don't want to bite you," he said. Then he paused and said more honestly, "Well, actu-

"Yes. Lissianna."

"And the blood?" she asked hopefully.

Bastien hesitated. This was where it got tricky.

Terri went on, "And Kate said you had something to tell me that we would have to work out if *we* were going to work out."

"That's true," he admitted, glad to avoid the blood for the time being. "There *is* something that I'll need to discuss with you if you agree to marry me, but it isn't that I'm terminally ill. I'm not ill at all."

"You want to marry me?" Terri asked with pleasure.

Bastien rolled his eyes. "Terri, honey. I just flew two thousand three hundred miles chasing after you. It wasn't to ask you on a date."

"Oh, Bastien!" She launched herself off the couch. Bastien caught her with an, "oomph," then found his face peppered with little butterfly kisses.

"Terri, honey, hang on. We do have to talk."

"Later," she murmured. "I've been so miserable since hearing Lissianna and Kate in the bathroom, I—" She paused and peered at him with question. "What were they talking about—that I should understand, because of Ian? I thought they were saying that you were ill, and I should be able to understand and deal with it because of my experiences with Ian."

"We have to talk," Bastien repeated with a sigh.

"Just tell me," she said.

"It's not something you just blurt out, Terri."

"Now you're making me nervous again."

"I'm sorry, but it's . . ." Taking her hands, he drew her back to the sofa and settled beside her. "It's not bad," he started, hoping she would agree.

"Terri—"

"No, wait. Let me speak," Terri insisted. "I made a mistake. A stupid mistake because I was scared. I . . . I love you, Bastien. I do. And the idea of your being ill and watching you go through what Ian and my mother went through scares the heck out of me, but I'm willing to do it if I can spend however much good time you have left with you. I'll take the bad with the good. I'll—"

"I'm not sick," Bastien interrupted.

Terri paused and stared, uncomprehending. "What?"

"I'm not sick," he repeated firmly.

"But the vials in your fridge."

"The vials?" he asked. Then understanding slowly dawned. "Vincent's serum?"

"*Vincent's* serum?" Terri echoed.

"Yes. You know about his digestive trouble. The lab sent those up for him to try. It's a new serum we hope will help," he answered, couching his words carefully so that he was telling the truth, but not revealing everything. Yet.

Terri sank onto the sofa with a plop. "The serum is Vincent's."

"Yes."

"But what about the blood and the IV stand?"

"The IV stand? In the closet of the master suite?" he asked with surprise.

She nodded.

"That's been there a long time. Lissianna needed it at one time, and we've just never gotten rid of it."

"Lissianna?" Terri's voice was a squeak.

haired man who tugged Terri's suitcase out of the trunk of the black car. *Prematurely* silver-haired, Bastien realized as the fellow closed the trunk and moved toward him, dragging the suitcase on its wheels. He took a step forward.

"Bastien, this is David Simpson, my brother-in-law," she introduced. "Dave and his wife, Sandi, picked me up from the airport yesterday. I fell asleep on their couch last night."

Bastien felt all the hot air flow out of him. Brother-in-law. With a wife. "Oh," he said, then held out his hand in greeting. "Pleased to meet you."

"Pleased to meet you too," Dave said with a grin. He placed the handle of Terri's suitcase in Bastien's hand rather than shaking it.

Bastien stared down at the suitcase as Dave turned and hugged Terri. "I have to go. Sandi will worry. Call and let us know what happens."

Bastien lifted his head to watch the man roar off in his Jaguar. "Nice car."

"It's Dave's pride and joy," Terri said. "Would you like to come in?"

Bastien nodded, then followed her up the sidewalk, only then noticing that she was carrying a grocery bag. Obviously, her brother-in-law had taken her shopping before bringing her home, he realized. He followed Terri into her small cottage, his eyes moving curiously around the place as he closed the door. It was small but cozy and tastefully decorated, he noted; then Terri whirled to face him.

"I'm sorry," she blurted. "I'm so sorry. I shouldn't have run off like that."

"Of course you did," she said with a grin, then waved at Terri and went back inside.

Terri shook her head with amusement as she got into the passenger seat of the Jaguar. "You two were made for each other."

"Yes, we were," Dave agreed. He grinned as he started the car, then sent it racing down the street.

Bastien was dozing in the front seat of his rental car when the car roared up behind him. Blinking his eyes open, he saw a black Jaguar pull to a stop with two passengers inside. It took a moment for his sleep-fogged mind to recognize Terri in the passenger seat, then he spotted the man with her and he woke right up. It was seven o'clock in the morning. She hadn't been in last night when he'd arrived, and he'd sat in the car outside her little cottage waiting, until he'd dozed off. He'd slept fitfully in the car, worried sick, wondering if she'd missed a connection, or run into trouble or what. But here she was returning now . . . and with another man? Bastien thought he might pop the bastard.

Opening the door, he slid out of his car. Propping his hands on his hips, he watched the couple get out of the car behind his.

"Bastien!" Terri sounded more shocked than happy to see him, he decided; and that was irritating to his sleep-deprived mind too. And blood-deprived, he reminded himself. He wasn't sure how long it had been since he fed, but he knew it was too long. Maybe he'd bite the guy with Terri rather than pop him.

"Dave, this is Bastien," she said to the tall, silver-

"Oh." She shook her head as the yawn ended, as if trying to shake herself awake, then glanced at Terri. "I'm sorry about what I said."

"Don't be. You were right."

Sandi shrugged. "I could have said it more diplomatically."

Terri grinned, and hugged her. "I love you."

"You're going to him," Sandi said. There was a sadness in her eyes as they parted. "You should be able to find a teaching position over there in one of the universities. I know you'll be happy. But we'll miss you."

Terri felt a thickness at the back of her throat. She'd depended on this couple as her only nearby family for a long time. She forced a smile. "Well, don't jump the gun. He might not want me."

Sandi snorted. "Yeah, right."

"And if he did, he might not now because I ran out on him."

"He'll forgive you," Sandi predicted. "You'll just have to grovel and admit you've been an idiot."

Terri chuckled, then glanced to the doorway as Dave came jogging back down the stairs. "Right! I'm ready. I'll be back shortly, flower," He gave Sandi a quick kiss, grabbed Terri's suitcase handle, then paused and turned back for another kiss before leading the way out of the cottage.

"Drive carefully," Sandi called from the doorstep.

"I will, flower. Now go back to bed—you were up late working."

"Nag," she muttered affectionately.

"I heard that."

the talk, the working together in a crisis—Terri wanted that. She didn't want to lose it after having it. But, in effect, she already had. Sandi was right, she'd given it up already. As for suffering his illness with him, she had been through it twice before. Terri knew that she would be checking with Kate to see how Bastien was. She wouldn't be able to help herself. The updates she received, along with her past experience and her imagination, were enough for her to know exactly what he was suffering and to suffer with him, whether she was there to see it physically or not.

She *was* a coward and a fool, Terri realized. She'd passed up days, months, maybe even years of happiness by anticipating the bad that would follow. There were no guarantees in life. Even if Bastien were dying, she might—as Dave suggested—beat him to the grave. Standing abruptly, Terri walked back into the cottage and rinsed her cup. Then she wrote a quick note to her friends and picked up the phone to call a cab.

"If you can wait ten minutes while I dress, I'll drive you."

Terri glanced to the doorway where Dave stood in a pair of fleece pants and a top. She'd forgotten he was an early riser. "I could catch a cab. Then you won't have to bother."

"I want to run over to Sainbury's for a couple at things, anyway. And I know you need to stop there before going home. I'll just be a minute." He didn't give her the chance to refuse, simply turned and jogged back upstairs. Two minutes later, Sandi came down in her housecoat, yawning.

her sleep through the night. She woke up at five o'clock the next morning, feeling like a bag of dirt. But a well-rested bag of dirt. Smiling faintly to herself, Terri got up and folded the blanket someone had put on her in the night, then folded the afghan as well. She collected fresh clothes from her suitcase and made her way up the stairs to the bathroom, managing to take a shower without waking the couple asleep just across the hall. Terri dressed, brushed her teeth, and went back downstairs. She fixed herself tea in the kitchen, took it outside, and sat on the picnic table, staring blankly at the wilderness growing there as she considered everything Sandi had said, and everything she herself knew.

In truth, Terri didn't know for sure that Bastien was terminally ill. Yet all the evidence seemed to point that way. She decided that she would go on the premise that she was right and make her decision from there, because she needed to know what she wanted if Bastien was going to die. If he wasn't, the answer was simple; she wanted to be with him. But marriage was about sickness *and* health, better *or* worse—there was no line stating *so long as ye both shall be healthy and happy.* Terri needed to know if she loved him enough to be willing to stand by him through the hard stuff, too. If she could be strong enough to do so.

She stared at the brick wall surrounding Dave and Sandi's little cottage, and imagined the days ahead without him. It seemed a pretty bleak world without Bastien. Then she imagined her time with him, and remembered how it already had been. The laughter, maybe he's got five to ten good years. Do you want to miss those to avoid six months to a year of hard times? I'm not saying it would be easy at the end, but can't you enjoy the time you do have and not worry so much about what you'll lose?" He added, "You know, Sandi's right. She could walk out the door and die tomorrow. So could I. Or even, you. Even if Bastien is terminally ill, he might outlive you. We can't live on *might-be*s. Because nothing is set in stone."

Terri lowered her head, her mind running in circles. Confusion seemed to be the key word for the last day and a half. She was exhausted, and that made it difficult to think.

"You look done in," Dave commented. "Why don't you lie down on the couch and rest a bit? I'll wake you when the tea's ready."

"Yes. I think I'll do that," Terri murmured. "I've been awake for more than twenty-four hours, and more than thirteen of those were spent in airports or airplanes."

"Then you can definitely use the sleep. Have a lie-down." He urged her onto the couch, grabbed one of the fluffy pillows that sat on either end, and settled it under her head. Fetching an afghan off the chair, he laid it over her.

"Thank you," Terri murmured. "Sandi's lucky to have you. And so am I."

"Hmm." Dave cleared his throat and looked uncomfortable. Shrugging, he muttered that she should sleep, and left her alone.

Terri slept. They didn't wake her for tea, but let

dared to be ill, to be human. He's probably hurting right now and not even knowing what he did to make her leave."

"But Dave loves you," Terri pointed out.

"And this Bastien loves you," Sandi said firmly. "Everything you've told me about him tells me that. And here you are, hurting both him and yourself, for no good reason other than you're a coward. It takes courage to live, Terri. To really live. To follow your dreams, to love someone, to face each day. Agoraphobics are trapped in their homes because they are terrified of what *might* happen—but as long as they stay inside, they'll never know what *could* happen. You're an emotional agoraphobic. You've been one since Ian died, avoiding emotional entanglements to avoid getting hurt. Well, it's high time you rejoined the living, my girl, and stopped acting like you're the one in the cold hard grave. I bet Ian would give anything to be alive and in love, yet here you have it and you're throwing it away." Sandi shook her head and stomped out of the room, muttering, "I'm going back to work. Sometimes people make me crazy."

Terri bit her lip and glanced at Dave, who patted her arm reassuringly. "She's just stressed out with this deadline. She loves you. We both do, and we hate to see you unhappy. You've been so unhappy for so long, Terri. And it's upsetting to see you throw something good away."

"But he's *dying*, Dave," Terri complained. "I can't watch that happen again."

"Are you sure he's dying? Do you know for sure? Perhaps it's something chronic, not terminal. Or love, and we all die, and everyone suffers the pain of grieving. The trick is to enjoy what you have *while you have it*. Not run like a bunny from the good things because they might be taken away sooner than you'd like."

"But—"

"Do you regret the time you had with Ian? Would you give that up, have it wiped from your memory to avoid the pain of having lost him?" she asked. "Or your mother? Do you wish she'd died giving birth to you so that you wouldn't have had to suffer losing her at nineteen? Then, as I said, there's Dave and me. If we grow sick, will you stop visiting and shun us? Or if I walk out that door and get hit by a bus, will you regret knowing me because of the pain losing me causes? Will it hurt less today than tomorrow, or next week, or next year?"

"No, of course not."

"That's because you love us, Terri. And you love this Bastien. The only difference is you gave him up before you *had* to. You're suffering *for nothing*. You're causing it yourself. You're being a fool."

"That's a bit harsh, isn't it, flower?" Dave asked mildly.

"Is it?" Sandi turned raised eyebrows on him. "How would you feel if I ran off on you, not because of something you did wrong, or because I didn't love you, but because I *did* love you and you were sick? Because I might hurt later?"

Dave's eyes widened, and Sandi nodded. "Uh huh. Well, that's about how this Bastien feels right now. Terri's punishing him because she loves him and he's left him," Terri admitted slowly. The story poured out of her. She recounted every moment of the last two weeks, without leaving anything out. She didn't even slow down or acknowledge Dave when he came back into the room to join them. It was like a purging of her soul.

The couple sat silent throughout, not saying a word until Terri finished and sat back to await their thoughts. Those thoughts weren't long in coming. Knowing the couple as she did, Terri had expected Sandi to be sympathetic and Dave to perhaps think she was an idiot, so she was taken by surprise when her sister-in-law shook her head and said, "You stupid girl."

Terri stiffened in shock, but Sandi wasn't finished. "You found true love—your perfect match—and allowed fear to make you throw it aside? You *idiot!*"

While Terri was gasping, Sandi slapped her hands on her thighs and sat back to cross her arms over her chest. "That's it, then. I suppose you'll be moving to France next."

"What?" Terri asked, confused.

"Well, I presume you love us."

"Of course, I do," Terri said. "I don't know what I would have done after Ian's death without you two to—"

"So," Sandi interrupted with a shrug, "you'd best move to France and get away from us. The more time you spend around us, the more you'll love us—and you know we'll die someday too."

"It's not the same," Terri protested.

"Certainly, it is. Love is love, and loss is loss. We all

the rearview mirror and nodded. It was more than
fine with her. She really didn't look forward to being
on her own in her little cottage again. Terri knew, the
moment she was alone, all those thoughts and memories she was trying so hard to forget would come
crowding in.

"I'll make the tea while you girls catch up," Dave
offered as he parked the car.

"You're a good man, Dave," Terri said with affection.

"He's better than good," Sandi announced. They
got out. "He's a star."

"So are you, flower," her husband responded, taking her hand and dropping a quick kiss on her forehead before turning toward the house.

Terri smiled as she followed the couple inside, but
her heart was aching a little at their easy affection. It
reminded her of Bastien.

"Well!" Sandi led the way into the living room and
dropped onto the couch with a sigh, then raised her
eyebrows at Terri. "Now that we're alone, would you
care to talk about this Bastien and what he did to
break your heart?"

Terri stiffened, then glanced sharply at her sister-
in-law.

"What makes you think he broke my heart?" she
asked finally. "Or that I love him, for that matter?"

"Oh, please." Sandi gave a laugh. "Every other
word out of your mouth has been 'Bastien.' And you
didn't fly home early, looking like death warmed
over, because things were going well. So, spill it.
What did he do?"

"Actually, he didn't do anything. I'm the one who

she had lived among for ten years, and probably picked up a bit of herself over time—sounded foreign to her ears. The cars they passed as they walked through the parking garage to Dave's black Jaguar seemed oddly shaped, small and strange after two weeks among larger, sleeker North American models. Even riding on the left-hand side of the road no longer seemed normal. In truth, Terri had adjusted so quickly to being back in the States, England now felt as foreign as it had the first time she came.

"So, tell us about the wedding. Did it go off without a hitch?"

A small burst of laughter slipped from Terri's lips.

Sandi, who had asked the question and turned in the front seat to include her in the conversation, raised her eyebrows slightly at Terri's response. "Oh, now you have to explain that reaction," she said. "It sounds like quite the story."

"The wedding," Terri said with a hollow smile; then she launched into a recounting of the calamities that had befallen Kate's wedding and what she and Bastien had done to resolve them. She managed to fill the entire ride back to Huddersfield with the tale, winding down just as they turned onto the street where Dave and Sandi lived.

"We thought you'd like to stop in for tea before we take you home," Dave explained. "We knew you wouldn't have anything at home to eat, and thought this would give you the chance to unwind a bit. We'll take you to Sainsbury's to pick up groceries before we drive you home, too. Is that all right?"

"Yes, that's fine. Thank you." Terri met his gaze in

"Awful?" she suggested helpfully.

"Well, I wouldn't have put it quite so bluntly, but yes, you look awful," he admitted, concern now crowding his eyes.

"Wore herself out with all that partying she did in New York, no doubt. It's a good thing she's home and can rest now."

"Sandi!" Terri turned to embrace the shorter red-head, who had appeared from the crowd. "When I didn't see you, I thought perhaps you were working on a deadline or something."

"She is. But that wouldn't stop her coming to pick up her favorite sister-in-law," Dave said staunchly, slipping his free hand around his wife's shoulder to hug her close.

"No, it wouldn't," Sandi agreed, hugging him back. She smiled, then explained, "I was in the ladies' room . . . as I usually am when the important stuff happens."

Her words made Dave chuckle, and they brought the first sincere smile to Terri's lips since she'd left Kate and Lucern's wedding reception.

"Well, come on," Dave said suddenly. "Let's get you out of here and home."

He ushered the two women to the parking elevators. The couple chatted about the traffic on the ride in, and about what had happened while Terri was away, leaving her to merely listen and absorb the fact that she was home again. The funny thing was, it didn't feel like home anymore. Nothing seemed quite the same as when she'd left. Their accents—accents

Chapter Nineteen

"Ter!"

Terri glanced up and spotted Dave at once. It would be impossible not to spot her brother-in-law. Being tall, prematurely gray, and good-looking made him stand out in most crowds. Forcing a weary smile, she turned in his direction as she came through the arrivals gate. "Dave. Thank you for coming to get me."

"No problem." He gave her a hug in greeting and took the handle of her suitcase in one smooth move. "How was your flight?"

"Long," she said on a sigh.

"Isn't it always?" he asked. "A shame they got rid of the Concorde."

"Yes."

"You look . . ." Her brother-in-law hesitated to say it, but he didn't have to; Terri knew how she looked.

You need to tell her you aren't dying, and that she will never have to watch you die a long lingering death."

"Yes!" Bastien grinned as he realized that, in this instance, his state could be an advantage. Chuckling, he turned and gestured to his driver. Thinking he would need it when Terri arrived, he'd made the man stay here with the car. Now, the engine started and the car moved forward.

"Have a good trip, and give her a hug and a hello for me," Vincent said. He walked with Bastien to the curb, then added seriously, "I'm happy for you, cousin."

"Thanks, Vincent," Bastien said. He slid into the backseat of his car.

"No problem. Just don't mess up, huh? She's perfect for you. Much nicer than that holier-than-though Josephine."

Bastien paused in surprise. He'd been about to pull the door closed. "I thought you liked Josephine."

Vincent wrinkled his nose and shook his head. "None of us did. But you thought you loved her, so we would have put up with her. The good news is, none of us has to pretend to like Terri. She's a sweetheart." Then Vincent slammed the door closed and gave him a thumbs-up. The car pulled away.

"Where is she?" he asked, cutting to the heart of the matter.

"On a plane on her way back to England."

"What?" Vincent couldn't have shocked him more if he'd said she was calling from jail.

His cousin nodded. "I happened to be passing the desk on my way out here to see you when I heard my name mentioned. The clerk was taking a message for me, so I took the phone. It was Terri. She was calling from the plane."

"But, what is she—Why did she—?" Bastien struggled to understand.

"It seems she overheard Kate and Lissianna talking in the ladies' room," Vincent said grimly. "They were discussing your not having told her about your 'state.'"

Bastien's shoulders slumped. She knew what he was. Now she was running from him just as Josephine had done.

"No. Terri misunderstood. She thought they meant you were terminally ill. When I said that wasn't so, she said not to bother lying to her—she'd seen the medicine and blood. She said she knew you were ill. Terri thinks you're dying, like her mother did, like her husband did, and she said she can't watch you die, too. She loves you too much to be able to bear it."

"She loves me?"

Vincent nodded, then grinned. "Well? What are you waiting for? Get in your car and get to the airport. Follow her," he said. "You have to go explain the truth. Tell her everything. She loves you, Bastien.

of her. Just in case Kate's message had gone astray, she would call the hotel and leave a message for Vincent as well. But she wouldn't risk it until the flight was in the air.

"Cousin!"

Bastien stopped his pacing—a pacing he'd been doing for the last hour and a half—and glanced at the man rushing toward him. Vincent. Bastien had returned to the hotel to find that Terri hadn't come back. He'd decided then that her cabbie had probably had a fit when she admitted she couldn't pay, and had refused to return her to the Hilton. He'd imagined her walking the streets of New York, and had made his driver drive him back and forth along the routes she could have taken, but found no sign of her. Then Bastien had resigned himself to pacing here, every moment making him more tense as he imagined all the ways she could be hurt or killed before she made it to the hotel. A beautiful woman, dressed in a long, possibly stained maid-of-honor gown, walking alone down the street? The imaginings he'd come up with were nightmares.

He was actually grateful for the distraction Vincent offered. "Are Kate and Lucern leaving?"

"Actually, they are. But that's not why I'm here. I just got a call from Terri."

Bastien relaxed and tensed all in the same moment. A call from her meant she was all right and able to make the call, but she was probably in trouble somewhere—especially if Vincent's grim expression was anything to go by.

CHAPTER

TWENTY

I GLANCED TO THE BAR, where Garrett was operating taps with both hands.

"I should go help," I said to Bruin.

He yanked my arm. "I still need to talk to you, Sloan."

Garrett had caught my eye and pleaded for help.

"Can it wait? We're slammed."

Bruin eased up his grasp and followed my eyes to the bar. "Okay, okay. But don't leave without talking to me."

"You got it." I stood and went to help Garrett.

"We're going through beer lightning fast," he said, handing me a pint glass.

"Are the kegs running low?"

"I think so. I'll change them out as soon as they blow."

Blowing a keg sounded dramatic, but in reality, it meant that any remaining beer in the bottom of the keg would foam as it fizzled out of the tap.

"How many kegs do we have left?"

Garrett shook his head. "I need to check. If we keep pouring like this, we'll be out of beer by the end of the weekend."

He was right. Garrett had a ten-barrel brewing system. A barrel of beer held approximately thirty-one gallons or two kegs. For each ten-barrel batch that Garrett produced, he yielded twenty kegs. Usually we could get 124 pints per keg. At the rate we'd been selling beer last night and since we'd opened today, I guessed that we'd gone through at least three kegs, maybe four. We'd had to dump the entire batch that was already in process since it had had Eddie's body floating in it. Brewing a new batch would take at least two weeks, so we were going to have to get creative to make the remaining kegs stretch until then.

I didn't say anything to Garrett, but one solution would have been to offer a guest tap. I knew that Der Keller and Bruin's Brewing had ample reserves. It wasn't ideal, but in a pinch, we could purchase some of their beer to keep our doors open—at least temporarily.

As I handed a beer across the bar, I noticed Bruin attempting to climb on top of one of the bar tables. Between his weight and impaired coordination, he slipped. A loud crash thundered through the room. Everyone stopped and turned to see what had caused it.

Bruin brushed himself off and stood. He reminded me of a *matryoshka* nesting doll as he rocked from side to side. "I want a minute of your attention. We're here tonight to celebrate the memory of one damn fine brewer—Eddie." He sloshed a pint glass that someone handed him. "Raise your glasses to Eddie."

"To Eddie." Everyone toasted. Then silence spread through

the bar; it felt heavy and necessary. I watched a woman dab her eyes with a cocktail napkin and one of Bruin's staff members place his arm around the burly owner. The silence lasted for a few moments and was finally broken when Bruin cleared his throat. "Enough. Eddie wouldn't want us to be sad. You know what he would want? He would want us to drink up! So go get yourself another pint and get drinking!"

He was the last person who needed encouragement to drink more, but everyone clapped and cheered in Eddie's honor once more before returning to their normal conversations. Unfortunately I knew I was going to have to cut him off soon, and I had a feeling that might not go over well given Bruin's grieving state.

Garrett returned from the back. "We've gone through four kegs. Can you believe that?"

"You can thank Bruin." I told him what he'd missed, and explained that I would tell Bruin that he had hit his limit.

"I anticipated that we'd maybe go through two kegs, but double? Wow."

"People like your beer."

"Sloan, you know as well as I do that everyone is here tonight for the wake. Not my beer."

"True, but if your beer were bad, they wouldn't be drinking this much of it."

Garrett didn't look convinced. I was about to suggest ordering kegs from Der Keller when I looked up to see Otto and Ursula walking in the front door. Their hands were clasped together as if in a show of solidarity. They were both wearing black and matching somber expressions.

"Hey, do you have this covered for a second?" I asked. The

line had thinned at the bar. There was only one customer studying the menu. "I want to talk to the Krauses for a minute."

"Yeah, go ahead."

I weaved through the crowd and greeted Ursula and Otto, who returned my welcome with warm hugs and kisses on both my cheeks.

"Sloan, you have heard about Mac, *ja*?" The lines in Ursula's forehead appeared more pronounced as she frowned. She had a scalloped triangle shawl around her shoulders that I was sure she had crocheted herself.

"Yes. It's crazy." I pointed to the table where Alex was studying. "Come with me."

They followed me to the table. Alex moved his books and gave his seat to Ursula. "Hi, Oma, hi, Opa," he said, giving them long hugs. Watching Alex's relationship with the Krauses always filled me with a deep sense of pride and relief. I'd been able to give him a solid family foundation, something I had longed for my entire life. Alex would never have to know the feeling of being unwanted—thank goodness.

"Do you want something to drink or a bite to eat?" I asked as the Krauses took a seat.

"No, no, Sloan. Do not go to any trouble." Otto smiled, but his expression was strained. His aging eyes had lost their usual merriment.

"It's no trouble. How about a pint of Garrett's IPA?"

"*Ja*, Sloan, that would be nice," Ursula said, wrapping her shawl tighter.

I left to get them pints. When I returned to the table, Alex

It was a problem, Bastien thought; he didn't know where to go. His first instinct had been the penthouse, because she'd planned to stay there. But her things were all at Kate's. However, Terri didn't have the key to Kate's place—he had it in his tuxedo pocket. She didn't have a key, didn't have a purse, and didn't have money. Of course, she might not have thought of that when she'd set out, not if she was upset about a spill on her dress or something. Terri might have ridden all the way out to Kate's, only to have to turn around and return to the reception.

That was probably it, Bastien thought. Terri was probably already back at the hotel and looking for him to fetch the key. He suddenly grinned to himself. He'd pay the taxi and have his driver take them to Kate's so she could change. Then, if he had it his way, they wouldn't bother returning to the reception. At least not for a while.

"Back to the hotel," he instructed, relaxing back into his seat. Terri was probably in a tizzy right this moment. He'd have to calm her down. Bastien could think of lots of ways to do that. Most of them didn't include clothes.

Terri settled in her seat on the plane, and immediately felt some of the tension leave her. She hadn't been at all sure she'd make it. She'd half feared that Bastien would show up looking for her. Surely, the message she'd left earlier had been given to Kate? If not, then someone would have certainly noticed her missing by now. She hoped no one was too worried.

Terri glanced at the phone set into the seat in front

"That's her," Bastien said with relief. Finally, someone who had seen her.

"Yes, sir. I put her in a taxi about half an hour ago."

"A taxi?" Bastien echoed stupidly.

"Yes, sir."

Bastien stood for a moment, bewildered. Why would she have gone in a taxi? Why would she leave the wedding reception at all? He couldn't imagine anything that would make Terri walk out of her cousin's wedding reception. Especially without telling anyone.

Unless she'd spilled something on her dress and needed to change, he thought suddenly. That thought took hold, and Bastien found himself relaxing again. Of course, that was it. Terri had said herself that she was a bit of a clutz. She'd probably spilled something on her dress and rushed off to change.

"Did you want a taxi, too, sir?" the man asked again, lifting his whistle in preparation for calling one.

"Oh, no, thanks." Bastien pulled his cell phone from his pocket and moved to the side to call for the car he'd reserved for the night. The driver had been waiting around the corner, and pulled up within moments. Bastien slid in, ordering the man to take him home. He was at the penthouse, inserting his key in the elevator, before it occurred to him that Terri didn't have a key. And her things weren't here yet. They'd planned to pick them up after the reception. He walked to the car that still sat waiting and got back in again.

"Where to now, sir?" his driver asked. Bastien just sat there.

some time to adjust to what he told her. It wasn't like he was announcing he was Catholic or something. She would have to adjust her whole way of thinking, her beliefs. He reconsidered: Perhaps he should only tell her the part about his loving her and wanting to marry her here at the hotel. She was staying at the penthouse tonight, since Kate would be off on her honeymoon. He would wait until he had her there, make slow passionate love to her, *then* explain about—

No, the penthouse was no good, Bastien realized suddenly. The entire family would be staying there, and Vincent hadn't been joking when he said that Terri was loud. The woman was as uninhibited in the bedroom as she was everywhere else. Though he suspected she'd try to be quiet in the penthouse with his family there. Especially his mother. Bastien didn't want Terri feeling stifled. He *liked* her passion. Perhaps they could just stay at Kate's apartment.

By this time, Bastien had reached the exit to the Hilton. He pushed through the revolving door, then paused on the sidewalk, his eyes searching for Terri in her pale lavender dress. He frowned when he didn't see her. Where had she gone?

"Would you like a taxi, sir?"

"What?" Bastien glanced at the doorman distractedly. He started to shake his head, then paused to ask, "You haven't seen a woman out here in a long lavender gown, have you?"

The man hesitated. "Pretty? Long brown hair? Big green eyes?"

hall. She *had* to be here somewhere. She couldn't have just disappeared.

"Perhaps she stepped outside for some fresh air," Etienne suggested, joining them with the drinks he'd gone to collect from the bar. "Here you go, darling."

"Thank you." Rachel took the drink her husband held out and took a sip. "Mmmm. A Bloody Mary. My favorite."

Bastien heard the comment, but he was already walking toward the exit. Etienne's suggestion that Terri might have stepped outside for some fresh air was a possibility that he hadn't considered. That was probably where she was, he assured himself. She was no doubt sitting out in front of the Hilton on the marble base—the place where they'd snogged like teenagers the night he'd taken her to *The Phantom of the Opera*.

He smiled to himself, relaxing at the memory. It was just coincidence that the wedding reception was being held at the same place they had enjoyed such a lovely end to a wonderful date. But it was a lovely co-incidence. This was the perfect spot for him to admit his love, and to have the talk he planned to have with her. Bastien was going to tell her he loved her, and ask her to marry him, and if she admitted she loved him back, which he was pretty sure she did—at least, he hoped to God she did—then he would tell her everything. If all went as he hoped, he would take Terri back to the penthouse and turn her tonight. Then they could begin their lives together.

Of course, there was a possibility she would need

that she probably should have left some message for Kate, so her cousin wouldn't waste time worrying about her on her wedding night.

Spotting a row of pay phones, she moved to them. Terri dropped fifty cents in, and dialed the hotel to leave a message with the desk. It was a cheerful, *I'm-fine-and-at-the-airport, just-waiting-for-my-flight, have-a-great-honeymoon-and-I-love-you* type of message. As if she wasn't doing something completely unexpected, leaving so abruptly and ahead of schedule. It was the best Terri could do.

She hung up, then picked up the phone again, only to pause and glance at her watch. It was the middle of the night in England. She couldn't call now; she'd wake Dave and Sandi up. Maybe she should wait and call them from France, she decided. Although that wouldn't give the couple much warning, or time, to get to the airport to meet her. Well, if they couldn't get there in time, she'd take a taxi. She couldn't really afford it, but such was life.

"Was she in there?" Bastien asked Rachel as she came back out of the ladies' room. He'd returned from taking care of Vincent, to find Kate missing. He had walked the reception hall several times in search of her, before giving up and asking Etienne's wife to step into the washroom and see if she was in there.

"No. Sorry, Bastien." His sister-in-law shook her head. "I checked every stall. There's no one in there at the moment at all."

Bastien frowned and turned to look around the

She purchased her new tickets, canceled the old, and handed over her luggage. Terri then went to the washroom to change, only to realize she had handed over her suitcase and only had her hand luggage. It held nothing to wear. She walked right back out of the bathroom and surveyed the fashion stores available in Terminal One: Herme's, Ferragamo's, and American Clothier.

She managed to find a comfortable yet inexpensive outfit in Ferragamo's. After paying for it, she carried the bag with her through security, found her departure gate, went into the nearest washroom, and quickly changed out of her long gown. The pantsuit she'd purchased was nothing special, and Terri put her long, lavender dress in the Ferragamo's bag with relief. She'd drawn attention in the fancy gown, and she didn't really want people staring at her right now.

Stepping out of the stall, she moved to the row of sinks and set her carry-on and purse on the counter, then surveyed herself in the mirror. She looked like hell, of course. And there was very little she could do about it. Terri went through her carry on and applied some makeup, but it didn't hide the empty look in her eyes. She finally pulled out a pair of sunglasses and tried them, then decided they would draw as much attention as her hollow eyes. Taking them off, she dropped them in her bag and headed out to the waiting area.

She had a little less than two hours to wait. That seemed a long time, especially with the worry that someone at the reception might notice her missing and start looking for her. She suddenly considered he hadn't been at all sure she would return, and supposed the only reason for him to have taken a chance on her was how shattered she apparently looked.

Terri thanked him as he carried her case down, then slid into the backseat as he stowed her bag in the trunk.

"Which airport, miss?" he asked the moment he was back behind the wheel.

"JFK," she murmured, then leaned her head back and closed her eyes.

It was a long ride to the airport. Terri didn't sleep, though the taxi driver must have thought she was doing so. She didn't think, either—she lay quiet and still, and merely was. Her mind was blank, her heart empty. Oddly enough, that state made the long journey to JFK pass quickly.

Terri dug the money out of her purse to pay the cabbie as he pulled up to the terminal. She gave it to him as he handed over her luggage; then walked into the airport and straight to the ticket desk.

There was some difficulty getting a flight. All of those leaving New York for England were earlier in the evening. The last to leave for Manchester was departing even as Terri spoke to the ticket agent, but again her pale and shattered look helped; the woman went to herculean efforts to get her out of New York and on her way. Terri ended up with an incredibly long and circuitous route, flying to Detroit, transferring, flying to France, transferring again, then finally flying on to Manchester. Terri didn't care. She just wanted out of New York and to be on her way back home to her little cottage and her safe life.

"Yes, she does," Vincent agreed. "And now that you know the guests are all safe from ol' rabid Vincent, will you go back and enjoy Lucern's wedding?"

"I thought you came for something that little Katie left behind," the landlady said as Terri led the way into the apartment, collected her purse and already packed and waiting suitcase, then immediately turned around with them in hand.

"No." Terri paused in the hall as the woman locked the door behind them. "I'm sorry for the trouble. But I have to get to the airport, and I couldn't go back for the key."

"Oh, it's no trouble, dear. I just misunderstood," the woman assured her as they waited for the elevator. She looked Terri up and down. "Are you going to the airport dressed like that?"

Terri nodded silently.

"Are you all right?" The landlady was staring at her with concern now, and Terri was sure she must look terrible since crying her eyes out at the reception.

"I will be," she assured the woman quietly, though she wasn't at all sure it was true.

"Well, have a safe trip." The old woman said. Her concern was still obvious in her voice.

Terri thanked her, then hurried out as the elevator doors opened.

The cabby hopped from his car as soon as she came out the front door of the building. Terri could tell by his expression, as he hurried up the steps to take her suitcase, that he was relieved to see her. She guessed

"That was an emergency. I don't normally feed in my own home, or in the homes of relatives."

"You bit Chris, too," Bastien reminded him. "And that was *after* biting the housekeeper."

"I had barely sunk my teeth into Mrs. Houlihan when you guys interrupted. I was still weak. I couldn't hunt weak," he explained patiently. Then he added, "And, by the way, you're welcome."

"For what?" Bastien asked.

"For taking care of the housekeeper," he explained. "Meredith called upstairs one day, while you and Terri were off on one of your jaunts that first week, and I took the message. She had the address for where Houlihan was staying. I went and wiped her memory of what happened. And the memories of the two people she talked to. You won't have to worry about her anymore."

"Did you?" Bastien asked with surprise, then realized the matter had completely slipped his mind. He hadn't been worried at all; he'd been too distracted with Terri. That could have been a bad thing. Details like that had to be kept track of and taken care of. It was a good thing Vincent had been on the ball. He was sincere when he said, "Thank you."

His cousin shrugged. "I caused the problem, I took care of it. Now." He glared at them all meaningfully. "Can I get back to my guest? She really is a fascinating woman."

"She certainly seems to have a strong mind," Marguerite commented, glancing curiously over to where Lady Barrow sat.

324

watched them all with growing confusion, Bastien glanced to his mother and shook his head.

"Etienne?" Marguerite asked, and her youngest son tried as well, only to shake his head after a moment.

"You have an . . . interesting family, Vincent," Lady Barrow said politely, and he abruptly stood.

"Please excuse me for a moment, Kathryn. I need a word with them." He excused himself, then took his aunt's arm and led her away from the table. Bastien and Etienne followed. Once they were far enough away to not be overheard, he turned on them with irritation. "I wasn't going to bite her. God, you people act like I'm some rabid dog, likely to go gnawing on every neck that goes by."

"Well, we knew you had to feed, Vincent," Marguerite said. Her tone had changed and become soothing.

"I did that at dinnertime. I came up to the bar for a quick bite, then nipped back." He grinned evilly; then winked.

"Well, then, what are you doing up here now?" Etienne asked.

"What does it look like I'm doing?" he asked in exasperation. "I'm talking to Kathryn. She's a fascinating woman."

"You aren't going to bite her?" Bastien asked suspiciously.

"No, Bastien. I'm not going to bite her. I wouldn't go biting guests at Lucern's wedding."

"Well, how were we to know that?" Bastien snapped. "You bit my housekeeper."

in. Terri knew the landlady could have buzzed her in from her apartment, but she supposed the old woman wanted to be sure it was her. Whatever the case, Terri resigned herself to waiting impatiently.

"There he is."

Bastien followed his mother's gesture to a booth in the back of the bar. Vincent and Lady Barrow sat, heads together, talking.

"Hmm. I wonder if we made it in time," Bastien muttered.

"There's only one way to find out." Marguerite Argeneau strode forward, leaving her sons to follow as she wove through the crowded bar.

"Aunt Marguerite!" Vincent got to his feet at once when she stopped at the table. "What are you do . . ." His voice trailed off and his mouth tightened as he spotted Bastien and Etienne.

"I think Lady Barrow has to go to the ladies' room," Marguerite announced, focusing her penetrating silver-blue eyes on the woman.

Lady Barrow gave a laugh. "Actually, no, I don't."

Marguerite blinked in surprise, then turned a glance on her sons. "Bastien"—she gestured to the woman—"fix it."

Bastien was so surprised that his inestimable mother hadn't been able to control Lady Barrow's mind, as she had so obviously just tried to do, that it took him a minute before he tried to do so himself. And he found it impossible to even read her mind, let alone slip into it. After a moment, trying, as Lady Barrow horror as he turned to tell her the fare, then she suddenly went calm. "Can you drive me from here to the airport after I grab a bag?"

The cabbie looked surprised, then suspicious, then pleased at the large fare to come. He nodded. "Sure, lady."

"Wait for me. I'll just be a minute." She slipped out of the taxi before he could protest. Terri half expected him to jump out of the car and chase her to insist she pay for the fare, but some angel must have been looking out for her—the cabbie remained in his cab as she lifted her skirt and jogged lightly up the steps to the front of Kate's apartment building.

Terri didn't have the key, though. Bastien had it, because he had a pocket in his suit, whereas she didn't have a pocket anywhere on her outfit. The plan had been that, once the reception was over, they would come collect her things, and she would stay with him for this, her last night in New York. He had said they needed to talk, and that he had something to ask her once the wedding was over. Terri, in her heart of hearts, had hoped that talk had something to do with love and their future together. Now she knew it was about death and dying.

With nothing else for it, she buzzed the landlord's apartment, now grateful that Kate had introduced her to the couple. It was the wife who answered, and Terri quickly explained that she had rushed back to the apartment to get something she'd left behind, but had thoughtlessly left her key at the wedding reception. The woman said she'd be right down to let her problem. She'd have to slip away. She felt bad about it, but it seemed the only option. She didn't want to ruin the day for her cousin and Lucern.

She dried her hands off, wiped the tears from her face, then moved to the door and slid out. Noise and color assaulted her at once. The reception was in full swing. No one noticed her standing by the bathroom door. Terri quickly judged the fastest and easiest route out of the hall, and then took it. Much to her amazement, she managed to escape without running into anyone who might have stopped her; and the few she passed whom she knew didn't seem to notice her.

Terri walked straight out of the reception hall and to the escalators rather than risk having to wait for the elevators. The moving stairs had been turned off for the night, but she walked down them quickly, crossed into and out of the lobby, and rushed straight out the front door of the hotel.

"Taxi, miss?" the doorman asked. Terri nodded. He blew his whistle, bringing the first waiting cab squealing into the driveway. It came to a halt in front of her, and the doorman opened the door. Terri murmured a thank you as she got in.

"Where to, miss?"

Terri gave Kate's address and sat silent in the backseat, her mind blank. It stayed that way for the entire ride. It wasn't until the taxi pulled up in front of Kate's apartment building that Terri realized she didn't have a purse. It hadn't been necessary. Transportation had all been taken care of for the wedding, the meal was paid for, so there had been no cause for her purse. Terri stared at the cabbie with a sort of denly angry. So terribly angry. How dare he let her fall in love with him, knowing that he was dying? How dare he not tell her about his condition from the start, so that she might have guarded her heart and saved herself all the coming trauma? How dare he be sick on her? How dare he even consider dying? How dare he?

The bathroom filled with music and laughter as several women entered. Terri was aware of their chatter, but didn't really hear it as her mind whirled under what she had just learned. She waited where she was until they left and silence filled the room again; then she let her feet back down, straightened her clothes and let herself out of the stall. She moved to the sink and stared at her reflection as she washed her hands, but didn't really see herself at first. Her mind was caught up in memories of Ian. But now, when she recalled how Ian had lain moaning in bed at night, he had Bastien's face. When Ian begged her to end it all, it was Bastien speaking.

Movement drew her attention to her reflection, and Terri stared blankly at the tears running down her cheeks. She was crying, which seemed odd because she wasn't aware of feeling anything. In fact, her mind seemed rather numb. Yet there they were: tears leaking out of hollow eyes and coursing down her cheeks in little rivulets. She turned her attention to her face and noted that she was blanched of all color.

She couldn't go back to the wedding reception like this. She couldn't even allow anyone to see her this way. Turning the taps off, Terri contemplated the was loading an app onto Ursula's smartphone. "See, Oma, you just click here, and the word pops up in English."

Ursula took the pint that I offered her and met my eyes from under her reading glasses. "He is so smart, like his mother."

"What are you doing?" I asked, as I scooted an empty chair up to the table.

"It's an app that translates German to English."

"But your English is flawless," I said to Ursula.

"You are too nice." She smiled. "But I do need help to remember words in English sometimes."

I was surprised to hear that. Ursula and Otto had been in Leavenworth for nearly four decades. I'd never noticed her having any difficulty mastering English.

"Have you talked to Mac?" I asked, changing the subject.

Otto nodded. "*Ja*, he is out on bail."

"He is? That's great news." I looked at Alex and squeezed his hand.

"But he is not free. He is to stay in town, and the police will have many more questions for him." Otto's voice sounded shaky.

"Has Chief Meyers officially charged him with Eddie's murder?" I bit my fingernail.

Ursula cradled her beer in her aging hands. "I think it sounds that way, but I do not exactly know."

"So now what?"

"He is meeting with ze lawyer now," Otto replied. He ran a wrinkled finger around the rim of his pint glass.

"That's good, right?"

"*Ja*, but the police they said he cannot go anywhere and must stay in touch for now." Ursula sighed. "I cannot believe they think that Mac could do anything so terrible."

"He didn't." I placed my hand over hers. "We all know that, and I think I know a way that he can prove it."

"How?" Otto's eyes widened.

I didn't want to say anything about the beer wench in front of Alex. It was important to make sure that he maintained a healthy relationship with his father even if things were quickly going downhill between us. "I think there's a witness who will come forward."

"Zis is wonderful news, Sloan." Ursula clapped her hand over her heart. "Wonderful."

"Yeah, as soon as we close tonight, I'll go see Mac."

"Thank you." Otto's eyes revealed his understanding. "Zis must be difficult for you."

"I'm fine." I gave him a nod and stood. "On that note, I should get back to work."

"Ze beer is good, Sloan. Please tell Garrett how much we enjoy it," Ursula said.

"He'll be thrilled to hear that." I thought for a second and then forged ahead with my question. "Hey, have either of you met Van, the new hop farmer in town?"

"Hop farmer?" Otto narrowed his eyes. "What is zis hop farmer? I do not know zis name."

"He's new. He said something about working with Mac."

Otto thought for a moment. "No, I am sure I do not know of a new hop farmer."

I shrugged. "Well, Garrett's talking about signing a five-year contract with him and has a few questions. Would you wanted to end it, why had he waited until he couldn't do it himself? Why wait until the weight rested on her shoulders, and she had to carry the guilt of not being able to do it for him? For Terri had borne a mountain of guilt. She'd felt guilty that it was he and not she, that she was healthy while he suffered; that she couldn't save him; and ultimately, that she couldn't even end his suffering when he asked it of her.

More understanding, Kate had said? Yes, Terri understood. She knew exactly what Bastien would go through with whatever terminal illness he had, because it seemed to her that this was what they had been speaking of. The medicine, the blood, the IV stand, and the secrets all suddenly made sense. As did the medication that caused photosensitivity, and the fact that Bastien merely picked at his food most of the time, seeming to have no appetite. It was all so obvious now: Strong, handsome Bastien had a terminal illness. Terri understood. She understood how it would go, and it was always the same. Death was death, whether by Hodgkin's disease, breast cancer, or whatever Bastien was suffering. Terri knew this, and she hated the fact that he was going to suffer.

But she couldn't, she wouldn't go through it with him. It was impossible. She had thought suffering with her mother and Ian was bad. But Bastien? Watching that vital, strong, and handsome man fade to skin and bones? To see him become weak and lost to horrible pain? Having him beg her to end it for him as his body rotted away? It would kill her. Terri could not handle it. She knew she couldn't. And she was sud-

Chapter Eighteen

Terri's thoughts were in an uproar. *"Terri is different, she'll be more understanding, especially after what she went through with Ian."* Kate's words brought a myriad of memories floating through her mind: sobbing into her pillow at night as she listened helplessly to Ian's moans of pain, a pain that no amount of morphine would ease; the sickly sweet smell of death in the house that had seemed to cling to everything, including Terri herself, for months afterward; Ian's loss of dignity as he grew so weak he had to have every little thing done for him, down to the most personal and humiliating task.

It had been torturous for Terri. But she knew it had been a thousand times worse for him, and she'd had to carry that burden too. She'd known that Ian wished it would all just end. He'd begged her many times to finish it for him, once he was too weak to manage it himself. Terri had resented that. If he had follow her back to England. Either way, he has to tell her. It wouldn't be a good thing for her to find out on her own."

"No," Lissianna agreed. "It's better he tell her than she find out by accident."

Find out what? Terri wanted to scream with frustration. Not to mention pain—her legs were now absolutely killing her.

"I don't know why he's delaying," Kate fretted.

Lissianna gave a short laugh. "That's easy enough to answer. It's because he loves her just as much as she loves him. I've never seen him like this. The man is always smiling, or whistling, or—I wasn't yet around when Josephine was in his life, but Lucern says Bastien wasn't even this happy when he thought he loved *her*."

Terri almost sighed out loud at this news. His family thought Bastien loved her. And she made him happier than Josephine—whoever that was. Her legs were suddenly forgotten. She could take a little pain.

"Well, then, why is he risking things working out with Terri by keeping quiet?" Kate asked. She sounded frustrated.

"As I said, because he loves her," Lissianna repeated. "Haven't you heard about Josephine?"

"Yes, of course. But Terri is different. She'll be more understanding. Especially after what she went through with Ian. She—"

Whatever came next was lost to Terri, for music briefly swept into the room as the door was opened, then receded to silence again as it closed. Lissianna and Kate were gone.

empty stall. Well, this was embarrassing. What should she do? Lower her feet and cough or something, to let the two women know that they weren't alone? Or should she keep her mouth shut and avoid embarrassing herself or the others? She'd also learn what they were talking about.

"Oh." Kate sighed. "No, Bastien hasn't told her yet, and I wish he would. He won't be able to keep it a secret for long. She's *bound* to find out."

Find out what? Terri wondered, prickly heat running down her neck.

"She leaves soon, though, doesn't she?" Lissianna asked.

"And do you think he won't follow? Or that she won't come back?"

"You think it's that serious?" Bastien's sister asked with interest.

"Yes. And you do, too, or you wouldn't be asking if he'd told her," Kate said dryly. "It's hardly something you tell just any gal you're dating."

Told me what? Terri repeated in her head. Damn, she wished they'd get more specific. And hurry. Her muscles were starting to burn from holding her legs up. She didn't know how much longer she could keep them raised.

"Yes, it's serious," Kate went on with a sigh. "I know Terri. She loves him with all her heart. Being just as much in love with Lucern I recognize the signs," she added dryly. "The way they feel about each other, they won't be apart for any longer than necessary. *If* she even goes home, or he doesn't just done today—first at the ceremony, then on the church steps in the receiving line, and finally while posing for the endless wedding pictures. The reception had offered the first real chance she'd had to sit down, but it had been endlessly interrupted by standing as one guest or another made a toast to the bride and groom. Now the meal was over and the dancing had started. Terri wasn't too sure her feet were up to that. At least, not in these shoes. Her feet felt swollen and chafed in the satin bridesmaid slippers.

She lifted her feet, holding them straight out to examine them. The shoes were pretty enough, but damned uncomfortable. Terri briefly considered whether it would be bad form to take the darn things off and run around in stockinged feet for the rest of the night. She thought she might get away with it—the skirt was long; it might hide her bare feet—but her stockings would no doubt be ruined by night's end.

Stockings or feet? Which should she sacrifice? she pondered, staring at her raised shoes.

"Has Bastien told Terri yet?"

Terri stiffened inside her stall, her feet still straight out in the air.

"Shh, Lissianna." She recognized Kate's voice. "Someone could be in here."

"I checked first. The stalls are empty," Bastien's sister said reassuringly.

Terri glanced from her raised feet to the floor where they should have been. Having them up as she did, Lissianna had seen only what appeared to be an

"I'm glad you think I'm nice, Mrs. Leever," Lucern interjected. "I hope that means you'll consent to dance with your new son-in-law?"

"Call me Mom, Lucern. You're family now," Aunt Lydia said. Lucern led her out onto the dance floor.

Kate smiled at Terri, as John Leever, her father, stood to take his turn on the dance floor with her as well. Terri watched them go, her thoughts drifting back to Bastien now that she was alone and no longer distracted. He had told her in the car on the way to the reception hall that he had something he wanted to discuss with her. Those solemn words had been bothering her ever since. They had immediately brought several things to mind: the vials, the blood bags, the iv stand, and Kate saying there was something that Bastien needed to tell her. Terri had been worrying over the topic ever since.

What was he going to tell her? How bad was it going to be? She hoped it wasn't too horrible, but she supposed she'd have to wait and see.

Terri shifted restlessly on her feet, then set her empty glass down on the nearest table and made her way to the ladies' room. Two ladies were leaving as she entered. Terri didn't recognize either woman, so she assumed they were either friends of Kate's from the city or relatives from the Argeneau side. She smiled and nodded politely as they passed, then walked along the stalls to the end.

Terri went in, locked the stall door behind her, pulled her skirt up and her panties down, and released a sigh of relief as she sat down. Her feet were a bit sore from her new shoes and all the standing she had corner. Come along, then. Let's find the boy before he gets himself in trouble."

"We can take care of this, Mother," Bastien said quickly. "Why don't you—?"

"Miss all the fun?" she asked. "I don't think so."

When Bastien and Etienne exchanged wry looks, she added, "Just thank me for deciding not to interfere with you and Terri."

"You won't?" Bastien eyed her with a combination of hope and wariness. He found it difficult to believe she meant that.

"I won't," Marguerite assured him. "You seem to be doing well enough on your own. Mind you, should you mess things up I may change my mind." On that note, she turned to lead the way out of the room.

Terri watched Bastien, Etienne and their mother leave the hall in search of Vincent as she listened idly to her aunt raving about this "perfectly lovely man" that she thought Terri should meet. It was sweet of the woman, really, but Terri wasn't looking for a man. She had one. Well, sort of. Her gaze slid back to the door through which Bastien had exited.

"Terri doesn't need a man, Mom. She already has one," Kate announced as Lucern led her over.

"She does?" Lydia Leever asked avidly. "You didn't say anything, dear. Who is he?"

"Lucern's brother Bastien," Kate answered.

"Oh!" Aunt Lydia was obviously pleased at the news, for she hugged Terri. "Well, that's wonderful. He's such a handsome man, and if he's half as nice as Lucern, the two of you should be very happy."

things from me. One would think at your age you would know better than to even waste your time trying. I am your mother. I see, hear, and know *everything*."

"Is that right?" Bastien asked.

"That's right," she said firmly. "And perhaps you will realize it in another two hundred years. It only took Lucern until he was six hundred to figure it out. Honestly. Boys are so much harder to raise than girls." Marguerite scowled at her sons for grinning at this oft-heard complaint, then sighed. "So, no doubt you don't want Etienne to tell me that you love Katie's little cousin Terri?"

Etienne burst out laughing at Bastien's grimace.

"Well, you didn't think it had slipped my notice, did you?" their mother asked with amusement. "After four hundred years, one would expect me to know and understood my boy enough to recognize when he is in love." She sighed, then nodded. "I approve, by the way. She's a lovely girl. And it will ease some of Kate's feelings of loss when she has to give up the rest of her family. Not to mention that having Katie in the family will make it easier on Terri as well. Actually, this will all work quite nicely."

"I hadn't thought of that," Bastien said with surprise. "I mean; them making it easier for each other."

"Well, that's why you have a mother." Marguerite patted his shoulder, then glanced around. "Have you tried looking out in the hallway, or the bars on the main floor?" When her two sons exchanged glances, she rolled her eyes. "Well, you didn't expect Vincent to bite her right here, did you? He'll use a nice dark

Bastien nodded, then glanced around. "Vincent was headed in this direction when last I saw him. I thought to search this area first, then make a sweep of the rest of the hall."

"Good thinking." Etienne fell into step as he started to walk again. After a few minutes, he said, "So, a little birdie tells me Terri is . . . important to you."

"A little birdie, huh?" Bastien asked dryly.

"Yeah." When Bastien didn't either agree or disagree, Etienne added, "I was talking to Terri at the party last night. She seems nice. Actually, she *is* nice," he said, collecting himself. He explained, "I read her mind."

"I can't do that, so it's good to know my instincts about her are correct." Bastien said.

"Well, I can read her, and I can tell you that I like her. She's like my Rachel—something special."

"Yes, she is," Bastien agreed. "She's sweet and beautiful and smart and—"

"And you can't read her," Etienne repeated. "And you love her. You've obviously found your life mate. Congratulations, brother! I'm very happy for you."

"Yes. Well, don't tell Mother that." Bastien shook his head as Etienne clapped a hand on his back. He didn't need any interference.

"Don't tell me what?"

Both brothers turned, groaning as Marguerite Argeneau joined them.

"Mother." Bastien kissed her cheek dutifully. Etienne followed suit.

"I don't know why you boys keep trying to hide

"I'll take care of it," Bastien said. "You two continue your dances. You have a lot of people to go."

The newlyweds nodded and thanked him. They moved off to find the next couple from the wedding party to dance with, and Bastien glanced at Terri.

"Go ahead, I'll be fine," she assured him, though she really didn't know what there was for him to take care of. The family all seemed to be overreacting a bit. "I'll fetch myself a drink and sit, give my feet a rest," she assured him when Bastien didn't look happy. "Go on. Kate and Lucern will obviously just worry, and they shouldn't have to worry about anything on their wedding day."

"I agree. You're a special woman, Terri." Bastien caught her by the chin and gave her a quick kiss. "I won't be long."

He straightened from kissing Terri and swung around to see where his cousin had got to. Unfortunately, the man was no longer in sight. Frowning, Bastien headed in the direction he had last seen Vincent leading Lady Barrow. His eyes scanned the people in front of him worriedly. He understood that Vincent was probably hungry about now; it was around this hour that he usually went out to hunt. But they couldn't have him running around feeding off the guests!

"Brother!"

Bastien slowed his steps and turned as Etienne hurried to join him.

"Lucern and Kate told me what was up, and asked me to help you."

He shrugged. "She was a good friend to me that day, and we've kept up the friendship since. I've agreed to attend the next Romantic Times conference as a favor to her."

Terri knew that was saying something. According to Kate, Lucern refused to do any of the conferences as an attendee. Even at the one he'd gone to last week, he hadn't gone as Luke Amirault the author, but Lucern Argeneau, Kate's fiance.

Noting the man's sudden frown, she glanced back toward the table. Vincent was holding Lady Barrow's hand and carrying it to his mouth to kiss. Terri could almost hear his sexy, trademark "Enchantée," from where she stood. The man was an incorrigible flirt, she thought with vague amusement.

Lucern didn't appear amused. When Vincent led the woman onto the dance floor and buried his face in her neck, Lucern's gaze sliced to where Bastien and Kate danced. Bastien turned, as if his brother had spoken his name. Their eyes met briefly; then Lucern glanced toward Vincent and Bastien's gaze followed. Bastien murmured something to Kate, and she looked to see what Vincent was up to as well. Not one of them seemed too pleased to see Vinnie with Lady Barrow. Terri didn't understand why. He was just dancing with the woman. A little too close, perhaps; but just the same, they were only dancing.

All four of them watched the couple dance. When the music ended and Vincent began to lead the woman off the dance floor, Lucern led Terri to Bastien.

An elegantly clad woman approached the table to speak to Chris, and Terri tilted her head to stare. The woman looked terribly familiar, and Terri was sure that Kate had introduced her at some point, but she'd met so many people today that it was hard to put names to faces.

Terri was sure the woman worked in the publishing industry somewhere, though, and judging by the way C.K. straightened in his seat as the woman addressed him, she'd guess that the lady had some influence.

"Lucern?" Terri glanced at her dance partner curiously.

"Hmm?"

"Who is that woman?"

He followed her pointing finger. "Kathryn Falk."

"Ah." Terri nodded. "Lady Barrow."

"Yes. She's a nice woman. Smart and savvy. Kathryn was very helpful to me at the first romance conference Kate dragged me to."

Terri bit her lip to keep from laughing. It was a bit of an understatement. Kate had told her all about Lucern's codpiece getting caught on the tablecloth at the medieval feast, and how Lady Barrow had climbed right under the table with Kate to help her unhook him. She'd apparently held a flashlight or something while Terri's cousin worked to free Lucern. It had sounded like a hilarious tale.

"She did more than help Kate unhook my codpiece," he announced, and Terri guessed she hadn't hidden her amusement very well. He'd obviously guessed what she was thinking. "She also gave me a ride back from the airport, and some advice, and . . ."

working on a book, but that he could occasionally come out of his shell. It seemed tonight he had. He seemed very happy.

"Yes, it did," she agreed, then qualified herself with, "Well, except for C.K.'s sneezing."

They both grinned at the memory. The poor editor had been mortified: standing at the front of the church with the other groomsmen, sneezing every few minutes. The worst part was that he had apparently warned Kate and Lucern that he was allergic to certain flowers when they'd asked him to stand up in the wedding, and they had both assured him that they would see to it that none of those flowers made it into the wedding arrangements. They had been careful when choosing the first arrangements; but both had forgotten all about his allergy when the tragic floral crisis had occurred, and they had unintentionally chosen unfortunate arrangements the second time around. The editor had been having a miserable time of it all day.

Her gaze sought Chris out. The editor couldn't dance with his cast, but he wasn't at the head table where he, as a member of the wedding party, had been seated for the meal. That table was now empty, most of its inhabitants on the dance floor. Abandoned, Chris had chosen to join the table where his coworkers from Roundhouse Publishing were seated. Vincent was standing behind the editor's chair, one hand patting his shoulder soothingly, no doubt sympathizing over his floral misery.

Terri really hoped the editor's luck changed soon. He seemed too nice a guy to suffer so.

Chapter Seventeen

"Well, it's done. You're now a married man," Terri said lightly to Lucern as he whirled her around the dance floor. The ceremony and feast were over, and he and Kate had done the traditional bridal dance. Now Lucern was making his way through the females in the wedding party, while Kate danced with each of the males. Then they would move on to the other important guests. As maid of honor and best man, Terri and Bastien had been the first approached. "How does it feel?"

"Good." Lucern grinned, then added, "I'm just grateful the ceremony went off without a hitch. After all the calamities that plagued the arranging of this wedding, I thought for sure there would be some crisis. But it's all gone as smooth as silk."

Terri smiled at the man. She hadn't found him very talkative until tonight. Kate had explained one evening that he always got that way when he was

Guilt immediately ran through Terri. She wasn't really tired, just confused. And she felt bad for letting it come between them when they had so little time left to enjoy each other. There was probably a simple explanation for all of what she had seen, and the easiest way to hear that explanation was to ask. She would, she decided; but first she wanted to eliminate his uncertainty. Leaning up, she pressed her lips to his and kissed him. Bastien remained still for a moment, then kissed her back gently, his mouth moving over hers with infinite care, a warm caress that slowly became warmer.

Terri moaned, her arms sliding around his neck and holding on as her body arched and stretched against his. This was Bastien, the man she loved. Did anything else matter?

The opening of the office door made them freeze, then turn toward the door.

"Sorry for interrupting." Lissianna offered them an apologetic smile. "But the first of the cars have returned, and Kate's parents and sisters are leaving. Mother thought Terri would wish to say good-bye."

"Of course!" Bastien slipped an arm around Terri as they walked the door. "We'll come say good-bye."

know the number and can't find a phone book," Terri blurted.

"I know. He told me. You don't have to call, though. I arranged for several company cars to take everyone back to their homes and hotels. I already sent Chris back in one." He was around the desk by this time, and he paused before her to take her face in his hands. He smiled down into her eyes. "In fact, I sent a lot of people on their way. The rest are waiting for the cars to return, so . . . we have a few minutes before we have to go play host and hostess again."

"Oh." She smiled, but confusion was still reigning in her mind. The blood, the medical vials in both Bastien's office refrigerator and the penthouse office, the IV stand she'd found while rudely snooping her first day here, and a secret that Kate had mentioned— one Bastien would have to tell her and they would have to work out: these things were all running through her mind, round and round, like a rat on a wheel. Blood, medicine, IV stand, secrets?

Bastien's mouth covering hers was distracting, and Terri tried to force her fears from her mind. But her brain kept running. Blood, medicine, IV stand, secrets.

"Terri?" Bastien murmured, pulling back when she didn't respond. "Are you okay?"

She opened her eyes and forced a smile. "I'm just a little tired."

He caressed her cheek with one thumb. "It's late."

"Yes," she whispered.

Bastien nodded, but there was a flicker of uncertainty on his face.

Closing the door behind her, Terri moved to the desk and sat down. She pulled the phone closer to her, then realized she didn't have a clue what the number would be to call for a car service in New York. Or if it was even possible. She supposed it must be, or Chris wouldn't have agreed to her calling. Biting her lip, she glanced over the desk for a phone book, but of course there was none. Terri turned her attention to the drawers. Her eyes landed on the large bottom left drawer first. It was large enough to hold a telephone book. It was also not quite closed. Reaching down, Terri pulled it open, then simply stared. What looked like a desk drawer was not a drawer at all. It didn't pull out, but swung open revealing a mini refrigerator. That was a bit startling in itself, but what was in the little refrigerator was even more so.

Terri stared at the contents: two vials similar to the ones she had found in Bastien's office on Monday morning. And there were also at least a dozen bags of blood. She stared at them uncomprehending for a moment, completely bewildered as to why these things should be in Bastien's desk drawer. She knew medical research was a part of Argeneau Industries, and she *had* heard of people bringing their work home with them, but this was a bit much.

A sound made her start with guilt, slam the refrigerator door closed and jump to her feet.

"Oh, there you," Bastien said, appearing from the hallway and crossing the room. He smiled.

"I came to call a car service for Chris, but I don't

and yelled, "Please. But how will you do that with all this noise?"

Terri hesitated. She hadn't thought of that. Then she knew the answer. "I'll use the phone in the office!"

"Oh!" He nodded. "Okay."

"I'll be right back," she yelled. "Just sit tight!"

Leaving him there, in the middle of Kate and Lucern's stag and doe party, Terri wove her way through the guests to the entry, then hurried down the hall to the office. She'd noticed that the editor seemed tired when he arrived. When she'd asked, C.K. explained that he'd been working overtime for the past week; trying to catch up with work. He'd managed to perk up a bit and have some fun, but it was getting late and Terri had noticed that he was starting to yawn and look exhausted. When she'd seen him take his jacket off the back of his chair and put it on, she went over to see if he wanted her to call him a car.

The office was empty when she entered; not that Terri had expected it to be otherwise. The guests at the party were all family and friends, all of them either from the city or having shown up yesterday or today for the wedding tomorrow. But it was possible that Kate and Lucern or someone else had sought out a quiet place to be alone for a bit: something she'd considered suggesting to Bastien at least half a dozen times. But, as the maid of honor and best man, they were the hosts of this party and simply hadn't been able to slip away. She was glad the room was empty. It might have been embarrassing to walk in on an amorous couple.

She arched her eyebrows. "What are you going to have in the Jacuzzi?"

"I'm going to have *you*."

"Mmm," Terri murmured, unable to control an excited shiver.

"Mmm," Bastien murmured back. He pressed a kiss to her lips. "God, I love it when you do that."

"What?" She asked huskily, planting a kiss by his ear.

"Shiver with excitement. Or moan, groan, writhe, or arch. I just love it when you're excited," he admitted.

Terri laughed. "You're the one who does it to me. I'm beginning to think that you're something of a magician. In fact, right this minute I'm sure of it."

"Oh? Why is that?"

"Because, we're nowhere near the Jacuzzi, yet I'm already wet."

Bastien nearly tripped over his own feet at that admission. His eyes jerked to her face and hunger immediately flared in him as he took in her wicked smile. "Damn," he muttered. "Maybe we'll leave the Jacuzzi for another time."

Terri laughed as he began to walk faster.

"Do you want me to call you a cab?"

"What!" Chris yelled over the surrounding noise.

Terri shook her head. The editor hadn't heard her over the loud throbbing music. She leaned closer until her mouth was almost touching his ear. "Do you want me to call you a car service? It can't be easy taking the subway with that cast."

C.K. hesitated, debating the matter, then nodded

solemnly as they reached the entry. "And a good friend."

"I'll remind you of that the next time I need a favor," his cousin said lightly.

"You do that," Bastien agreed. The elevator arrived and the doors slid open.

"Hello, beautiful," Vincent greeted Terri as he swapped places with her, taking her spot on the elevator. "Don't do anything I wouldn't do," he added as the doors started to close. "And since there isn't much that I wouldn't do, that means the two of you should have lots of fun."

Terri glanced from the closed elevator doors to Bastien with a grin. "My arrival didn't scare him off, did it?"

"No. He's gone to get his date and take her to dinner," Bastien explained. Then he stepped forward and scooped Terri into his arms.

"Bastien!" She squealed in combined surprise and alarm, her hands clutching instinctively at his shoulders.

"Have you ever had a glass of champagne in a Jacuzzi?" He started up the hall toward the master suite.

"No, I don't believe I have," Terri admitted. She unclenched her hands to slip them around his shoulders and relaxed against his chest. "I take it we're going to have champagne in the Jacuzzi before we set up for the party?"

"No," he said promptly. "*You're* going to have champagne in the Jacuzzi."

"Yeah?" He glanced up as Vincent opened the office door.

"Terri just buzzed. She's on her way up in the elevator."

Smiling, Bastien tossed the now empty blood bag into the waste basket under the desk and gave the fridge door a push to close it. He stood and hurried around the desk.

Today was the only day he hadn't managed to book a free hour to see her. And while Kate would be here soon for the stag and doe party, helping to set up for it was a perfectly legitimate reason for Terri to come early. He hadn't expected to be so lucky as to have her show up this early though.

"I thought that news would cheer you up," Vincent said. His amusement was apparent as Bastien approached the door.

"You thought right, cousin." He slapped Vinny on the shoulder and moved past him into the hall. "You thought right."

"Well then, this news might make you even happier." His cousin followed him.

"What's that?" Bastien asked with distraction.

"I have to pick up my date and take her to dinner before the party, so you'll have this place to yourself until the guests start arriving. Or at least until Aunt Marguerite, Rachel, and Etienne come back from collecting Lissianna and Greg from the airport. That should give you about two hours. You'll have to set up for the party on your own, but—"

"You're a good cousin, Vincent," Bastien said

she had come to be with her cousin before the wedding and didn't feel right about abandoning her at a time when she was so excited and nervous about the up coming nuptials.

Bastien understood. Besides, they spent time together. It was just that, in the evenings, they only managed to see each other on double dates with Lucern and Kate. The other couple didn't wish to go without seeing each other, but insisted on chaperones when they did. In an effort to make sure their wedding night was special, Kate refused to be alone with Lucern until then. And, as long as Kate and Lucern couldn't be alone together, neither could Terri and Bastien. Which meant, to spend any time on his own with Terri, Bastien had to arrange to see her while Kate was at work. While he himself should be working.

After taking off the first week of Terri's stay here in New York, Bastien was swamped trying to catch up with everything he'd neglected. But he had still managed to make time to be alone with her for at least an hour every day. He had made it a point to be sure they went places, too. After that first lunch in the office, Bastien hadn't wanted her to think that his only interest in her was sexual. But, somehow, no matter where they went or what he had planned, they always ended up making love. They'd made love in some interesting and unexpected places this week, and it wasn't always he who initiated it. Terri was turning out to be as insatiable as he had found himself becoming. She was doing a good job of making up for the years of abstinence since her husband died.

"Bastien?"

the requirements for a true test of the enzyme—Vincent had to refrain from feeding off living donors while taking it, and he would need to be tested daily to see if it was working, as well as to be sure he wasn't suffering any damaging side effects—Bastien was running really late. He'd thanked the fellow and merely tossed the vials in the large unlocked fridge, rather than waste time on the locked one. Then he'd rushed off to his meeting.

But of course he'd forgotten the vials that night when he'd gone up to the penthouse. In fact, Bastien had forgotten them repeatedly until today, but he hadn't forgotten to bring the matter up with Vincent. His cousin had agreed to try the serum, and to switch to bagged blood, but refused to do so until the weekend following the wedding. He didn't want it to interfere with his play rehearsals, or with Lucern and Kate's wedding if there did happen to be side effects.

Bastien understood. He'd checked with James to be sure that the vials of serum wouldn't expire, but had only finally remembered to bring them upstairs with him tonight. He would keep them in the penthouse office refrigerator until Vincent was ready for them.

That chore out of the way, Bastien grabbed a bag of blood from the now restocked shelves of the fridge. Thankfully, he'd at least remembered to have that done. Although he was surprised he had even managed that. He'd been a tad distracted all week, what with finding ways and times to squeeze in visits with Terri. She wouldn't go out with him alone when Kate was free, explaining apologetically that

Chapter Sixteen

Bastien unlocked the refrigerator in his desk and set the two small vials inside. He'd finally remembered to bring them up to the penthouse. They'd been in his office all week, since the day Terri had come for lunch, Monday. He had just been getting ready to leave for his appointed meeting with the lab guys that morning, when James came into his office to give him the new synthetic enzymes for Vincent to test. They were the latest effort to treat the condition that forced Bastien's cousin and uncle to feed from living donors. Life would be much easier for both men if they could survive off of bagged blood as most of the rest of the clan did. Vincent was usually the one who tested each new serum and, knowing that he was staying in the penthouse at the moment, James had brought the serum to Bastien.

By the time the scientist had finished explaining

"Oh!" Terri gasped as he filled her, then moaned as he withdrew.

Bastien turned his head and caught her next moan in his mouth, kissing her, his hands sliding beneath her bottom to hold her still as he drove back into her. Terri clutched her hands in his hair, her fingers curling and unintentionally tugging as her mouth became more demanding. Then she wrapped her legs around his hips, and held on for dear life.

It was fast and hard, neither of them either willing or able to go slow to drag out the pleasure. Within moments it was over, both of them crying out together as release overtook them. Then they stayed, leaning weakly against each other, trying to catch their breath.

"Well," Bastien murmured after a moment. Taking his weight off her, he caught her face in his hands and kissed her forehead. "Hello." He next kissed Terri's nose as it wrinkled with perplexity, and explained, "I might have forgotten to say that when I came in."

"Oh. I think I may have, too." Terri gave a breathless laugh. "Hello."

Bastien kissed her mouth again, not urging it open this time, but simply moving his lips over hers. Then he had a quick nibble at her plump lower lip, but was interrupted when a knock sounded at the door. He pulled back slightly and glanced over his shoulder toward the sound. When a second knock came, he turned back and smiled at her wryly. "I think our lunch is here."

blinked her eyes open, staring blindly at the office beyond his shoulders. Bastien continued to caress her. Her stunned mind grappled with her feelings, trying to wrap itself around them. *Did* she love Bastien?

The question was pushed from her mind as he slid one hand up along the top of her leg, pushing the skirt before it. When his hand shifted, slipping between her legs, Terri released a groan. It was cut off by Bastien's mouth as he freed the nipple he was suckling and raised his lips to claim hers. She kissed him frantically, gasping into his mouth and arching on the desktop as his fingers slid beneath the edge of her panties.

Bastien was moving so quickly it was leaving her dizzy, but dizzy with want. How had he done this to her so fast? she wondered faintly, but in the next moment she didn't care. He slid one finger into her. Terri sucked on his tongue desperately as he slid the finger out, then in again. Then he brushed the nub that was the center of her excitement with his thumb, and she nearly leapt off the desk in reaction, her body jolting under the sudden shot of pleasure that radiated from that one small spot. Tearing her mouth away, Terri leaned her head back, gasping for air. Bastien's mouth worked its way along her throat and his fingers continued to caress and excite her.

"Bastien. Please," she said at last, straightening to clutch his shoulders. "I need you."

It was all she had to say. Bastien grasped her hips and slid her to the edge of the desk, even as he reached for the zipper of his pants. In the next moment, he had them undone and was sliding into her.

their business clothes. She'd also borrowed a matching blue silk blouse. Bastien reached between them and set to work on the buttons.

He was very good with them, Terri noted absently as he undid the last reachable button and tugged the top out of her skirt to get the remaining few. Once that was done, he pulled the shirt open and broke their kiss to look at what he had revealed. His fingers immediately moved to run lightly over the upper curve of her breast and the top of her white satin bra.

"Beautiful," he murmured, and Terri glanced down. Her breasts rose pale and round from the white material, framed on either side by the edges of her blue top. Then Bastien pushed the top off of her shoulders, and reached behind her to unsnap her bra. It too slipped away.

Terri groaned as his hands replaced the lacy cups, her eyes dropping half closed as he caressed her breasts. She watched for a moment, her breath coming faster with every passing second, then she reached for the buttons of his shirt. She wasn't as practiced as Bastien apparently was. Terri was also slightly distracted by what he was doing to her, but she managed to undo his shirt. She let her hands slide over his skin, shifting them around to his back, when he suddenly knelt to first lick and then suckle at one of her breasts.

"Bastien," she breathed, arching into his attention. Terri loved the things he did to her. She loved how he made her feel. She loved the way he made her laugh, the way he made her feel safe. She loved *him*.

The thought caught her by surprise, and Terri

worry, she raised a hand to caress his cheek. "Are you all right, Bastien? Is something wrong?"

He blinked, as if coming out of a trance or back from deep thought, but rather than answer her, Bastien kissed her again. This time it wasn't the gentle coaxing kiss of a moment before, it was desperate and a little rough. Caught by surprise, Terri fell back a step, coming up against the edge of the desk. Bastien immediately eased up slightly, but didn't stop kissing. Not that she wanted him to. After a week of having him at her side every waking moment, the last two days had been distressing. Terri had missed him—his company, his laugh, the way he gestured with one hand when emphasizing something, the way his eyes sparkled when he was teasing, the half grin he always got on his face upon first spotting her. She'd missed talking to him, and listening to him. And though it had only been two days, it felt like forever since they had been together like this, in each other's arms, bodies pressed close together, mouths meshing.

Bastien thrust his tongue into her mouth, and Terri eagerly devoured it, her arms twining around his neck. She arched into him. She felt his hands slide down her back, but was startled when he caught her behind the thighs and lifted her up to sit on the desk.

Except for those evenings in nice restaurants, jeans and casual tops had been her uniform for the majority of this trip, but today was an exception. Knowing they were eating in the office, Terri had borrowed a dark blue skirt from Kate. She hadn't wanted to look like a bum among all the Argeneau employees in

"A distraction?" She seemed perplexed.

"Mmmm. And I decided that I would just have to sacrifice myself to the cause."

Terri blinked at that announcement, and at the cheeky way he said it; then her lips twitched with the beginnings of amusement. "You're 'willing to sacrifice yourself to the cause,' are you?"

Bastien congratulated himself. His distraction was already working. Easing closer, he raised his hands to either side of her waist. "Yeah. I'm willing to go all the way, if necessary, to accomplish the task."

"All the way?" Terri was definitely distracted now, and amused.

"All the way," he assured her, leaning in to kiss her cheek by her ear.

"That's pretty selfless of you," she breathed. He moved to kiss her other cheek.

"Mmmm," Bastien murmured. "I'm a selfless kind of guy." Then he kissed her properly, covering her mouth with his. Terri opened to him, a little sigh slipping out and rolling lightly across his lips. He loved it when she did that. Bastien loved it when she sighed, and when she moaned. He loved it when she shifted, or arched, or writhed against him. He loved how he affected her, and he loved the effect she never failed to have on him. Heck, he just plain loved her.

That thought made Bastien pause. He loved Terri. It was a wonderful thing. If she didn't turn from him as Josephine had.

Terri pulled back as Bastien suddenly stilled. She peered at him quizzically, wondering at the expression on his face. It looked pained. Beginning to purse and fell and spilled my Coke all over your lovely carpet. I—"

"Shh, shh, shh. It's all right," he interrupted. Moving forward, he took her arm and urged her to her feet.

"No, it's not all right. Just look at it. I've—"

"It will clean," Bastien assured her, taking her towel away and dropping it on the stain without even really a glance. "You didn't hurt yourself when you fell, did you?"

"No. But I—I don't know if Coke stains, but if it does, I think I've ruined your rug."

"Terri, it's just a carpet. A thing. Things are replaceable. As long as you're okay, that's all that matters."

"But—"

When her gaze dropped to the stain again, he took her arm and urged her away from the couch. He moved her toward his desk to keep her from looking.

"Don't worry about it," Bastien said again, but he knew his telling her wasn't going to accomplish the task. Terri would worry; she couldn't seem to help herself. It was as much her nature to be responsible for her own actions and worry about things as it was his. If he gave her half a chance, she'd be insisting on paying for cleaning or replacing the carpet. He wasn't going to give her the chance. A distraction was needed, and Bastien decided that, if he had to sacrifice himself to the cause, he was more than willing to do so.

"Why are you grinning?" Terri asked.

"I was just thinking a distraction is the only thing that will keep you from worrying about spilling that pop."

ening his tie. He hated wearing the bloody things, and he took them off every chance he got. He'd undo it now and not put it back on until necessary.

"No, sir, but Terr—I mean, Miss Simpson arrived a bit early. She's in your office, sir."

"Is she?" Bastien smiled at the news, then added, "If she's told you to call her Terri, then you're welcome to do so, Meredith. There's no need to call her Miss Simpson on my account."

"Yes, sir." His secretary smiled. "I'll be heading to lunch in a minute. Shall I switch the lines over to the receptionist's desk so that she can take messages?"

"Yes, please," he said. "Have a good lunch."

"You too, sir."

Bastien nodded as he walked to his office door, but waited there for Meredith to collect her purse and leave the office before he opened it and stepped inside. The sight that met his gaze made him pause in the doorway and stare. Terri was on her hands and knees, her behind barely covered by a dark blue skirt, wagging from side to side as she scrubbed a towel over the carpet. His entrance didn't faze her. She hadn't heard the door open, because she was muttering.

Bastien was so distracted by the view, it took a moment for her words to register. She was mumbling something about what an idiot she was. That was enough to make him tear his eyes away from her behind, close the door quietly, and move forward.

"Terri? What happened?"

She stiffened, her body stilling, then she glanced sharply over her shoulder at him and groaned. "Oh, Bastien, I'm sorry. I'm such a clutz. I tripped over my medical labs were specialties of Argeneau Enterprises. In fact, Meredith had said Bastien was at a meeting right now with lab guys. This was probably something to do with that.

Satisfied, Terri set the vials back in the refrigerator and surveyed the beverages. She settled on a Diet Coke, grabbed a glass from the collection under the bar and poured her drink, then carried it back to the couch. Of course, Terri forgot all about her purse, which she'd set on the floor out of the way. But not out of the way enough. She tripped over the darn thing, and stumbled forward.

She managed to save herself from falling any farther than to her knees by catching herself on the couch, but she had to let go of the pop to do it.

"Darn," she breathed, staring at the puddle of liquid on the carpet. She followed that with a stronger curse and leapt into action. Pushing herself to her feet, she whirled back the way she'd come and hurried behind the bar in search of a towel or rag. But, of course, there was nothing. Terri turned back to the room, her gaze shooting around until it landed on a door on the opposite wall.

"Please be a bathroom," Terri prayed as she hurried in that direction. She could have cried with relief when she saw that it was. And there were towels. Expensive, fluffy white ones. She'd replace them if she had to. It seemed better to ruin the towels than the carpet.

"Are the caterers here with lunch yet, Meredith?" Bastien asked as he walked into the outer office, loosried the magazine with her to collect it, then carried her purse back to the couch, set it out of the way by her feet, and started to leaf through the magazine again. Terri had only turned a couple of pages when she became aware that she was thirsty. It must have been all that walking. Lifting her head, she glanced toward the bar and hesitated. Meredith *had* said to help herself.

Setting the magazine down on the coffee table, Terri stood and moved behind the bar. There were countless bottles of liquor on a triple set of shelves with a mirror backing on the wall. It almost looked like a professional bar. But she wasn't interested in alcohol. Turning, she surveyed the area behind the bar, noting that there were two refrigerators. One was small, and one large. Terri tried the small one first and found it locked. She tried the larger one and it opened at once. This fridge was packed with liquid refreshments of every variety. Juices, pops, even milk made up its contents. But there were also two small vials of a clear liquid.

Terri picked up the small containers curiously. She recognized the vials. She'd seen enough of them—first, when her mother had been ill, then when Ian had been dying. They were medical vials, and both had the same long incomprehensible term and medical symbol on them.

Terri set them back, confusion reigning in her. Why would Bastien have medical vials in his refrigerator? It only took her a moment to come up with the answer. Medical laboratories were one of his company's interests. Blood banks, medical research, and farther inside. A huge desk the size of a double bed sat in front of a wall of windows with an awesome view of the city. There was the bar Meredith had pointed out in the corner, a black leather overstuffed couch, two matching chairs . . .

Cripes! Half the office was a bachelor's living room, with an entertainment console and a bar, and the other half was business-related with a desk, computer, fax machine, filing cabinets, and a large table for meetings.

"Jeez," Terri murmured, then gave her head a shake. She really shouldn't be impressed. After all, the penthouse was rather impressive too. Still, to work in an office like this? Man, she wished her own was half as nice. Or even a quarter. Her office at the university wasn't much larger than a closet. There was barely room for her desk and a chair for visitors.

Terri moved to the chair in front of Bastien's desk and sat down, setting her purse on the floor as she did. After sitting there, staring for a moment, she shifted restlessly, stood, and walked to the bookshelf Meredith had pointed out. Terri scanned the book titles with interest, noting that—as in most things—Bastien's taste didn't vary much from hers. But starting a book that she was only going to have fifteen minutes to read seemed a bit silly. Turning away, she crossed the room to the coffee table in front of the couch to go through the magazines lying there. There was quite a selection: women's magazines, men's magazines, business, fashion, celebrity gossip.

Terri picked up one of the women's magazines and sank onto the couch, then recalled her purse. She car-stepped to the side to allow Terri to enter. "He had a meeting with lab guys from Clinical Testing on the third floor, but said he'd be back by noon. He should be along shortly. In the meantime, you're welcome to wait in his office."

"I'm a little early," Terri apologized as she stepped into the office. In truth, she was fifteen minutes early. Not that she was eager or anything, Terri thought dryly. She'd actually got out of the cab in front of the building more than half an hour ago, but, knowing it was way too early, she'd window-shopped a bit and popped into a Starbucks for one of their iced drinks before making her way back to the office building.

"Sit wherever you'd like," Meredith said. "There are magazines on the table. Books on the shelf. There's even a television and stereo in that console there if you'd like. Can I get you a drink while you wait?" the secretary offered. Then, when she got no response, she said, "Terri? Can I get you a drink?"

"Oh." Terri closed her gaping mouth. She turned to blink at the woman. "No, thank you."

"Okay." Meredith grinned. "Well, if you change your mind, there's a fridge full of them behind that bar. Of course, there's alcohol as well. Help yourself. And if you need anything else, just let me know. I'll be out here until Mr. Argeneau returns."

"Thank you," Terri called as the woman stepped out of the room and closed the door. Then she turned back to gape at the office again. Dear God, she'd never seen anything like it! Bastien's office was bigger than the whole of her little cottage in Huddersfield. Eyes wide, she peered around as she moved tended on setting to work on that the moment she arrived, and holding it whenever was possible. She'd known it would be last-minute, but being from England made it difficult to arrange, and she'd hoped Kate's friends would understand. However, the chaos that had ensued after she arrived had driven the thought from her mind. Now she was reminded. A stag and doe party would eliminate the need for a bridal shower, which was great. It would be more fun. The guys could be there. *Bastien* could be there.

"Yes. We'll have to get together. I could come to your office and meet you for lunch," she suggested.

"Perfect." Bastien kissed her again, then they walked into the restaurant.

"Hi." Terri paused before the desk in the outer office and smiled widely. "Meredith? I'm Terri."

"Oh." The woman was on her feet at once and taking the hand Terri held out. "Miss Simpson, what a pleasure to meet you in person."

"Terri," she repeated firmly. "And it's a pleasure to meet you, too. Thanks so much for all the help you gave us with the florists and caterers. Really, you were wonderful."

"Oh." Meredith flushed and waved a hand in dismissal. She started around the desk. "It was nothing. Just doing my job."

The secretary gestured for Terri to follow as she moved toward the door to Bastien's office. "Mr. Argeneau said you were coming. The caterers haven't arrived yet, but they should be here soon. As should he," she added. Meredith opened the door and

"Be good," she muttered against his mouth, trying to sound firm.

"I'd rather be bad," he whispered, trailing his lips to her neck.

Very aware of the driver, Terri caught back the moan that threatened to slip from her lips. Excitement raced through her, brought on both by Bastien's words and what he was doing. Bastien had already managed—with just a kiss—to make desire unfurl inside her. She was so glad that she had spoken up. Silence might be golden, but good communication was priceless.

Terri was really wishing they could skip the rehearsal dinner and go back to the penthouse for a quick refresher course on Bastien and Terri 101. Or a long refresher course. Possibly a really long one. Several days would have been good. But, of course, that wasn't possible. Bastien wasn't the only one sighing with regret when they arrived at the restaurant and had to untangle from each other's arms.

"I know we aren't going to get any time alone tonight," he said as he slid out of the car. He took her hand to help her out. "But it's occurred to me that we really have to get together tomorrow for a meeting."

"A meeting, huh?" Terri asked with amusement. She straightened on the pavement beside him.

"Yes. To discuss the stag and doe."

Terri blinked. Bastien had a wicked grin that told her he wanted to do more than just discuss something. But his mention of "stag and doe" made her realize that she had forgotten all about her intention of arranging a bridal shower for Kate. Terri had in-

"I'm looking forward to it," the editor admitted.

"Well, let's get this party moving," Kate said, gesturing toward the church doors.

"Good thinking." Bastien was much more relaxed now that he knew that he wouldn't have company in the car. "Come on, baby."

Terri blushed at the affectionate endearment as he steered her toward the exit. He'd called her baby! Right there in front of everyone! He wasn't trying to hide their relationship at all. Man, she was going to get so hurt if this went wrong.

Grimacing at her thoughts, Terri slid her arm around Bastien's waist and concentrated on matching her step to his. "I missed you last night," he said, quietly pulling her into his arms as soon as they were in the backseat of the chauffeured car. Then he added, "When I wasn't worrying."

"Worrying?" Terri pulled back in surprise as he tried to kiss her. "Why were you worrying?"

He hesitated. "Well, you seemed to change once Kate and Lucern arrived. I was . . ." He shrugged. "Just worried that maybe you didn't want them to know about us, or something."

"Oh," she said softly, then smiled. "I was worried *you* might feel that way."

"I'm glad we were both wrong," Bastien said. He kissed her as the driver began to back the car out of its parking spot.

Terri sighed and leaned into him. A moment later, she caught his hand with a choked laugh. It had gone wandering down her upper leg, then tried to wander back up under the skirt of her baby-blue dress.

"So, when's the wedding? And am I invited?" Chris Keyes asked.

Terri blushed scarlet and turned to make a face at the editor. He had been released today, just in time for the wedding rehearsal. Lucern had chosen the man as his third groomsman, to make up the numbers needed to match Kate's bridesmaids. Etienne and Thomas were the other two. Bastien was, of course, the best man, and Terri was maid of honor. And Kate's two sisters and her friend and coworker Leah made up the bridesmaids. Leah, Terri, Chris, and Bastien were the only members of the wedding party in town for the rehearsal, though. The others wouldn't show up till the end of the week.

"If you two are done, maybe we can go to the restaurant now," Lucern said, preventing any further embarrassment from the editor.

"Okay," Bastien agreed. "Lucern, you're riding with Kate. Terri's with me." He paused and eyed Chris and Leah with what might have been dread. "How did you two get here?"

"I had a car pick them up, just like with us and the girls," Lucern announced. He added, "The driver will take them to the restaurant too, then drive each of them home afterward."

Terri glanced at C.K. with surprise. "Are you back in your own apartment then?"

"Yes." C.K. grinned. "They finished the painting, which was the last of the repairs, last night. Tonight will be my first night home."

"Oh, good!" Terri exclaimed. "I'm sure it will be a relief for you to be back in your own bed."

table. It was better that way and, while it could be painful at times, at least it prevented misunderstandings. Terri decided this case was no exception; she wanted to know where she stood. Last night she'd thought waiting to see what he did would be the smart move, but now that he was being so polite and she still didn't have a clue, Terri decided she was damned well going to find out.

Taking a deep breath, she turned to him and blurted, "I like you. I don't know how you feel about me, or what what we've done means to you, but I like you. If it was just good fun, and you don't want Kate and Lucern to know about it, or if it—"

Terri's opening gambit came to an abrupt halt as Bastien suddenly took her face in his hands and pulled her forward to cover her mouth with his. She sighed into his mouth with relief as he kissed her, uncaring that they were standing in the middle of the church. He snogged her senseless, actually, she decided a moment later as her arms slipped around his waist. The man wasn't just giving her a hello kiss.

"Okay, you two, cut it out. The minister's getting nervous."

Bastien ended the kiss at Lucern's words, but not quickly. He eased the kiss, then turned to nibbling Terri's lip. Once, then twice, then he straightened with a grin.

"Hi," he said with the sexiest grin Terri had ever seen.

She smiled and covered the hands still cupping her face. "Hi, back," she whispered.

the words almost desperately. The tension was just killing her. She and Kate had arrived at the church at the same time as the car had brought Bastien and Lucern. The men and women had met on the sidewalk, and Kate and Lucern had kissed and hugged each other as if they'd been apart forever. Terri had watched them with a small smile, then glanced to Bastien to see him watching too. Then, as if sensing her eyes on him, he'd turned her way, waited a moment as if expecting her to say something, then had nodded and murmured a polite hello.

Terri had felt disappointment drop over her, but had tried to hide it, merely nodding in return. And they had been like that ever since. All through the ceremony rehearsal, they'd been stiff and polite. Yet Terri had caught Bastien glancing at her a time or two, with a look of hunger he'd quickly veil whenever she caught his eye. Once, she'd caught him looking at her with an expression she thought might be longing, but Terri couldn't be sure. He'd cloaked that as soon as she glanced his way, too.

"There's no need to thank me. You are more than welcome in my home. And I enjoy your company."

Terri considered his words: *You are more than welcome. I enjoy your company.* Both were in the present tense, not the past tense as if whatever they had were over. She wasn't sure what to make of it, or how Bastien was feeling. And all of it made her really wish they'd had the chance to talk. The uncertainty was killing her. Terri had no patience for games, no wish to waste time guessing at what people thought or felt. She had always preferred to have the cards on the

"You're darned right I have. Terri's as close-mouthed as a clam. If I didn't read her mind, I wouldn't have a clue of what was going on between those two." Kate watched her cousin and Bastien unhappily. "I don't know why he doesn't just grab her and kiss her. That's what she wants."

"He probably wants it, too, but I think Bastien thinks Terri wouldn't welcome it because of how she acted when she was with you yesterday," Lucern explained, finding himself also watching. The couple was studiously ignoring each other.

"What?" Kate glanced at him. "How did she act with me yesterday? And what has how she acts around me to do with Bastien thinking she doesn't want him to kiss her?"

"Well, she paid a lot of attention to you the moment we arrived, and pretty much ignored him."

"And he's jealous? Of me?" Kate asked with disbelief.

"No. Not jealous. But Bastien said she hardly even looked at him. I think he's worried that maybe he was just . . . well, sort of fill-in entertainment while you were gone."

"Oh, for heaven's sake. Terri isn't like that."

"Perhaps not. But Bastien doesn't know that. Or at least, he can't be sure of it. They only met a little more than a week ago," Lucern pointed out, then his eyes narrowed. "Look. They're talking. Maybe they'll work it out now."

Across the room, Terri said, "I should thank you for allowing me to stay in the penthouse." She spoke

Chapter Fifteen

"What is Bastien *doing?*" Kate asked. The minister had just finished giving his last-minute words of advice, wished them good evening, and moved off to speak to the wedding coordinator.

Lucern glanced down at her, then followed her gaze to where his brother stood silent and grim-faced beside Terri. "Standing there," he said.

"Well, I can *see* that. Why isn't he talking to Terri?" Kate shook her head in exasperation. "He didn't even smile at her when we arrived today, he just nodded."

"So? That's all she did, too," Luc pointed out.

"Only because that's what *he* did. Terri wasn't sure how to greet him, and she waited for his greeting to see how she should act. He was cool, so she was cool."

"You've been reading her mind," he accused. There was amusement in his tone, however.

Bastien nodded, but wasn't sure he believed the prediction. He understood that Terri hadn't seen Kate in a while, but she hadn't even *looked* at him tonight. What if she regretted what they'd done? Or what if she didn't want Kate to know about it? Maybe she was thinking of this as just some vacation fling and wanted to keep it secret to avoid pressure from Kate. He really didn't think Terri was the type—he was almost positive she wasn't—but then again, he never would have predicted that once Kate and Lucern showed up, she'd avoid touching or even looking at him.

Bastien supposed he'd have to wait until the rehearsal to get a better idea of what was going on. He'd wait to see how Terri greeted him and go from there. If she acted like her normal cheerful and affectionate self, he'd know it was all going to be okay. But if she acted reserved and avoided eye contact, he'd know something wasn't as it should be.

Personally, Bastien hoped Terri would just walk up and either take his hand in hers or slip her arm through his, or even kiss him hello. He preferred the last option, though if she did walk up and kiss him, he couldn't promise he wouldn't kiss her senseless on the spot. But he didn't really expect that to happen— they'd be in a church after all. Still, Terri was naturally affectionate, and if she liked him as he hoped, she would greet him with some outward show of affection. That would free Bastien to be openly affectionate back. The ball was in her court.

tastes good. I can hardly believe now that I actually got bored with doing so in the past."

Lucern grinned. "That's pretty serious."

"Yeah." He nodded enthusiastically. "And every time we kiss? Pow!" Bastien slammed the palm of one hand against the other. "We have a sexual chemistry like I've never experienced. And it isn't just sexual. I mean, I want her all the time—but it isn't just wanting sex. I want to . . ." He paused, searching for the words to explain. "I want to give her pleasure. I want to hold her while she finds her pleasure. I want to take her inside me, my heart, and keep her there warm and safe and always a part of me."

"Yeah. That's how I feel about Kate," Luc said softly. "Have you tried to read her yet?"

"Yes, I have. And no, I can't."

"It's sounding pretty good then."

"Yeah."

"But?" Luc asked when Bastien sighed.

"But I don't know how *she* feels," he said miserably. "I just assumed that she felt the same, but then you guys showed up and she hardly looked at me after that."

"Oh, well, I wouldn't worry. She was probably just happy to see Kate. They're pretty close and—other than those few minutes last Friday when Kate dropped off Chris and grabbed me to go to that conference—they haven't seen each other in over six months." Luc clapped a reassuring hand on his shoulder. "They'll talk up a storm tonight and get all that girl stuff out of the way. Then, tomorrow at the rehearsal, she'll be all over you."

though. She'd rather be able to be herself; but she didn't want him feeling uncomfortable. Terri decided she would just play it by ear. If he greeted her tomorrow as just the cousin of his soon to be sister-in-law, she would respond accordingly. If Bastien greeted her with a kiss and hug or something like that, Terri would respond in kind. The ball was in his court.

"Thanks, brother."

Lucern grimaced. "I don't want this any more than you do."

"Yeah, but *you* agreed to it. I didn't get a vote," Bastien muttered, walking around the bar with a glass of blood in hand. That was about the only nice thing about Terri being at Kate's; he didn't have to drink out of a bag anymore, grabbing a quick fix behind closed doors. But that was the only nice thing. And he'd gladly ingest bagged blood forever to have her back. He dropped onto the couch with a sigh.

"So?" Lucern peered at him curiously. "How is it going between you two?"

Bastien frowned, then admitted, "I don't know."

Luc's eyebrows rose. "You don't know?"

He shrugged. "Yeah. I don't know." Sighing, he sat forward and set his glass on the coffee table and ran a frustrated hand through his hair. "I thought things were going great. I mean, Luc, you wouldn't believe how well we get along. Even I don't even believe it. It's all so perfect and natural and easy. We talk all the time, finish each other's sentences, we just . . . I don't know. Click. It's like she was made for me." Bastien shook his head, then added, "I'm even eating. And it to our family farmhouse. Every time I approached the driveway that led to our restored turn-of-the-century home and hop farm, I said a silent thanks. Never could I have imagined living in the clapboard house with its wraparound front porch and acres of organic land when I was growing up. However, today, a wave of sadness came over me as I parked in front of the mailbox. Thanks to Mac's indiscretions, the farmhouse and the stable life I had worked so hard to carve out were in jeopardy.

I pushed the thought away and focused on the task at hand—food. If I was going to survive the destruction of my marriage (and I had every intention of surviving), I would have to put one foot in front of the other, like I always had. I swung open the unlocked front door and stepped inside to a deafening silence. *Focus, Sloan,* I reminded myself as I scanned the antique pie safe where I kept my cookbooks. My collection of cookbooks could qualify me for an episode of *Hoarders.*

Citrus, I thought as I flipped through recipe after recipe at the kitchen island. *What will pair with a citrus IPA?* Then inspiration struck. I wouldn't make appetizers to simply complement the beer. I'd make them *with* the beer.

I tugged off the skirt I'd worn to make a professional first impression. Given Garrett's nerdy attire, I figured I was safe to change. I pulled on a pair of jeans and my favorite T-shirt, which read REAL WOMEN DRINK BEER.

Next, I checked the industrial fridge and freezer that Mac had insisted we install in the garage. Mac liked to entertain, so we kept it stocked. I never knew when I would have to whip something together at the last minute after he'd called to say he was bringing regional distributors or a new vendor partner home for dinner.

I grabbed a bag of oranges, a bunch of fresh cilantro, a couple of red onions, and organic chicken breasts. That should make a nice skewer. Now I needed the beer. I grabbed an empty Der Keller growler, slipped on a pair of flip-flops, and headed back to the car.

The drive back to town took less than five minutes. The afternoon sun glimmered on the smooth surface of the Wenatchee River as I drove along its banks. We were between festivals in Leavenworth, which meant that Commercial Street had ample parking. Living in a small town that relied on tourism to fund the economy had its fair share of trade-offs. During Oktoberfest, Leavenworth's population tripled. Having beer lovers pack into tents in the square and stumble into the pubs and shops was great for business, but it made going about day-to-day life nearly impossible for locals. In a few weeks, finding a parking space within a mile of the village square and beer hall would take an act of God.

Enjoy it while you can, I told myself as I pulled into a parking space in front of Nitro. Steering the car into the curb, I noticed Mac's bumblebee yellow Hummer parked nearby. My stomach flipped. *What the hell is he doing here?*

Since I'd caught Mac with the beer wench, he'd been making unimaginative attempts at an apology, from flowers to chocolates and notes left on my front doorstep. All of them ended up in the trash. So far I'd been quite successful at avoiding him, which was a major feat in this town.

Why he was at Nitro was beyond me. I had to get rid of him fast.

be willing to talk to him about your suppliers? Maybe even take a quick look at the contract?" I knew that Garrett had said he had brewer friends in Seattle, but the Krauses were the best in the business. Hopefully, he hadn't already signed the contract. I never saw Van come back by, but then again I'd been in the kitchen most of the afternoon.

"*Ja*, of course, Sloan," Ursula replied. "We would love to help."

"Thanks." I stood and kissed her and Otto on the cheek. Then I turned to Alex. "Are you going to hang out longer?"

"We will take him home. Do not worry about it," Otto said, resting his hand on Alex's shoulder.

"Are you sure?"

"Sloan, we will do zis for our girl." Otto winked.

I swallowed back my emotion as I thanked them and walked away. Otto had called me his girl ever since I married Mac.

Mac hadn't only ruined our marriage by cheating on me, but he was taking away the only family I'd ever known. I didn't know what I would do without Otto and Ursula in my life. The thought of losing them made me even angrier at Mac.

CHAPTER

TWENTY-ONE

BY THE TIME WE CLOSED two hours later, we'd gone through every pint glass in the pub. I took a crate of glasses to the kitchen and started the industrial dishwasher. Garrett wiped down the tables and bar. The town had polished off every last crumb of cracker and slice of cheese. Good thing I had gone overboard on the appetizers.

"Well, that was rough, but I think it was exactly what we all needed," I said to Garrett as he brought in the last of the pint glasses.

"Agreed, but do you think I should hire more help?"

"Can you afford more help?"

"Not really, but I don't know about you—I'm beat."

I rubbed the base of my neck. The last two days had taken a toll on my muscles and my mental health. "It's been busy, that's for sure, but I don't think you need to rush out and hire extra help. This is an anomaly. Two back-to-back big nights like this don't happen in Leavenworth. I expected opening to be busy, and of course everyone came out for Eddie tonight, but I'm sure it's going to slow down."

"You think?"

"Trust me, Leavenworth isn't that big. When the crowds begin to come in for Oktoberfest, we'll definitely have to have a plan and more help, but I think things are going to settle down."

"You haven't steered me wrong yet." He wiped his hands on a dish towel. "In that case, I'm going to start brewing."

"Now?" I glanced at the kitchen cuckoo clock. It was after ten o'clock.

"Yeah. When I was working in the corporate world, me and a few of my buddies would have midnight brewing clubs."

"I'm familiar with midnight brewing." Like Garrett, Mac was more inclined to sleep until lunchtime and brew into the wee hours of the night.

"I'm not a morning person. I tend to hit my stride after the sun goes down. Brewing at night is the best." He ran his hands through his hair and arched his back. I couldn't help but notice how muscular his chest was.

"Cool," I said, turning away. What was I doing staring at his chest? "Speaking of your friends. Did you have a chance to talk to them about Van's contract?"

Garrett tossed the towel in the sink. "No, not yet, and luckily Van never came back by. Thanks for reminding me. I'll call them now. They're probably brewing as we speak—you want to stick around and help?"

I considered it, as like Garrett, I was antsy to get back to brewing, but I had to go confront Mac. "Thanks, but I'll take a rain check."

"See you tomorrow, then."

"What time do you want me here?"

He shrugged. "Whenever. I probably won't be up and moving until after ten or eleven, but you can let yourself in."

"Sounds good." I gathered my coat and bag, and headed for the front door. The air was crisp and smelled like fall outside. I took a second to inhale and shake off the craziness of the evening. I had learned from Alex that Mac was staying at The Rheinlander, a hotel across the street from the village square. Mac had complained to Hans about being cooped up in a hotel room. Hans, like me, had no sympathy for him and told him to suck it up.

The Rheinlander was a stunning display of German architecture and looked like it belonged tucked in the Alps, with its wrought-iron balconies and striking white plaster walls with contrasting dark wood trim.

I cut through the square, meandering past the gazebo, and climbed a set of steps. The hotel was lit up with softly glowing antique lights and strands of twinkle lights wrapped around a row of potted plants that lined the entrance. I didn't bother to check in at the reception desk, but rather walked straight to the elevator and punched the button for the fifth floor. When I'd kicked him out of the farmhouse, Mac had rented a suite on the hotel's top floor.

You can do this, Sloan. I gave myself a pep talk as the elevator dinged and stopped on Mac's floor. *Think about Alex.*

The thought of my son's father going to jail was enough to spur me to move forward and knock on his door.

My hands felt tingly as I waited for him to answer. Why did it have to be me? He had gotten himself into this predicament, and I was the person who had to bail him out. It wasn't fair. I was about to turn around when the door opened a crack and the beer wench, wearing nothing but a plush bathrobe, gasped at the sight of me.

Classic. *Keep it in control, Sloan.* I dug my fingernails into my thigh and forced myself to speak. "Where's Mac?"

Her face turned as white as her robe. "Uh, um . . ." She stuffed her hands into the front pockets of the robe and called behind her. "Mac, uh . . ."

Obviously, she's extremely bright and articulate, I thought as I watched her squirm. I didn't typically think of myself as catty, but she brought out the worst and most insecure parts of me.

"Who's that?" Mac called. "Room service? Send them on in."

Hayley looked like she might be sick. "Uh, Mac, come out here."

I hated how much I was enjoying watching her look so miserable, and I was also surprised by her shift in attitude. When I had run into her at the grocery store, she had seemed so smug, and now she was acting like she was terrified of me.

"Uh, um, uh, do you want to come in?" she mumbled, and opened the door wider.

"Just put it on my tab," Mac called.

Irritation flashed on her tanned face. "Mac, come out here!"

I almost felt sorry for her, but as I got a closer look at her youthful skin, I realized she was closer to Alex's age than mine. God, he was such an idiot.

Mac huffed as he entered the living room area of the large suite. "What is it?" Then he froze in midstride when he met my eyes. "Sloan, what are you doing here?" He strolled over and tried to kiss my cheek. I moved my head to the side just in time. I also caught sight of Hayley's envious gaze.

For a minute, Mac didn't know what to do. He looked at the beer wench and then me. "Hey, give us a minute," he said to Hayley, and nodded to the bedroom.

She slunk away and shut the bedroom door with gusto. Apparently, Mac was going to have some making up to do after I left.

"Baby, this isn't what you think," Mac said, sitting on the leather couch and patting the spot next to him.

"It never is, is it?" I sat in the chair farthest away from him with a glass coffee table blocking the space between us.

"No, really. She came over because she's upset. That's all. I swear."

"I don't care." I folded my arms across my chest.

"Baby, Sloan, you have to believe me. It's over. She's upset about Eddie, and I was consoling her—that's all."

"*Consoling* her by taking off her clothes?"

"What? No! No, it's not like that. She's upset, like I said, about Eddie. She wouldn't stop crying, and I didn't know what to do, so I told her to take a bath. You always liked baths when you were upset. I thought maybe it would calm her down. Baby, I swear I didn't touch her."

"Don't talk to me about what I like and don't like, and stop calling me baby! I never liked it when we were together, and I certainly don't like it now."

"Sorry. Sloan, you have to believe me."

"I know this is going to be a shocker, but I don't believe much of what comes out of your mouth right now."

He hung his head. "I know. I'm sorry."

"Look, I didn't come to fight. I came to talk to you about Eddie's murder."

"What about it?"

"You." I sat up and squared my shoulders. "Mac, you're in a lot of trouble, and I know that you're lying to protect me."

He didn't respond. He kept his eyes on his expensive argyle socks.

"I know that you were with her when Eddie was killed. Garrett told me. I just don't understand why you didn't tell Chief Meyers the truth. Everyone is worried about you—your parents, Hans, Alex. You can't lie about being with her. This is a murder investigation, Mac."

His voice was almost inaudible as he whispered, "I know."

"Then tell the chief. If not for me, then for Alex. You could end up going to jail for something you didn't do."

"I know."

Mac was never this subdued.

"You know, in a strange way, I guess I appreciate that you're trying to keep your affair secret from me, but you've gone too far this time. This is serious stuff."

"I know."

147

"Is that all you're going to say?"

He started to speak, but Hayley opened the bedroom door. She was fully clothed and looked like she was fuming. "I'm outta here," she said, power walking to the door. I expected Mac to jump up and chase after her, but instead he sat unmoving and let her leave.

After she had slammed the door, I studied his face. "Mac, what is going on? You're not acting like yourself."

He cracked his knuckles. "I know. I messed up in this, and I don't know what to do."

"What's the question? You tell Chief Meyers that you were with your girlfriend last night. End of story."

"No, no, not the end of the story, and Hayley is not my girlfriend. I made a stupid mistake, once—one time, Sloan. I'm an idiot. I don't know what I was thinking, and I know you don't believe me, and I get it, but she's nothing to me."

"You don't have to lie to protect me, Mac."

He sighed. "That's not the only reason."

"What?"

"I was with Hayley last night. After the scene at Nitro, we left and I brought her to Der Keller. I thought we could have a beer and talk like rational adults."

"Ha! Adults?" I couldn't contain my anger.

"Right. That became apparent. She's not exactly mature."

"Because she's a child."

"She's not a child, Sloan. She's twenty-four."

"Oh, and that's supposed to make me feel better? You could almost be her dad."

"I know." He got up and started pacing. "I admit it. I'm

an idiot. She seduced me, and I should have said no. I screwed up, and I'm going to do everything I can to prove that to you and win you back."

"By taking the fall for a murder you didn't commit?"

"No." He picked up a fake apple and tossed it in the air. "I thought having a drink would calm her down, but she was fired up about Eddie and then insisted we go back to Nitro. She said she left something there. When we went back, everyone was gone. Your new brewing buddy filled a growler for us. I was planning to tell her last night that I had made a mistake and she had to back off. She's latched on to me and doesn't seem to understand that I'm not interested in a relationship."

"Okay. I still don't understand why you haven't said all of this to Chief Meyers."

"Because I'm worried about Hayley."

"Why?"

"We came back here, and she broke down when I told her there was no future for us. She didn't stay very long, but when she left, she took my lighter. She told me she was going out for a smoke."

My mind raced to keep up with everything Mac was saying.

"Are you saying you think Hayley had something to do with Eddie's death?"

Mac tossed the apple again and frowned. "I don't know how she could have done it, but she hated Eddie."

"She did?"

He nodded. "They broke up last month."

"She and Eddie were a couple?"

"They dated for almost a year. I guess it turned nasty at the end."

I couldn't believe what Mac was saying. Hayley and Eddie had a history, she hated him, and she had left with his lighter right around the time Eddie had been killed. Maybe she wasn't just a beer wench. Maybe she was a killer after all.

CHAPTER

TWENTY-TWO

"MAC, YOU DON'T HAVE A choice. You have to tell Chief Meyers this."

He set the plastic apple back in the basket of fake fruit resting on the coffee table. "It doesn't look good for Hayley."

"It doesn't look good for you!" I couldn't stop myself from shouting. The man was infuriating sometimes. "Hayley is going to have to figure this out for herself. She's a big girl, and you have a son to consider, Mac Krause."

"I know."

"Do you? Because you're not acting like you understand the severity of this situation. Mac, your parents bailed you out of jail—jail!"

"Sloan, calm down. I'll talk to the chief. I've got everything under control."

I wanted to scream that he had nothing in control, but fighting with Mac was only going to make me feel worse.

"Promise me you'll talk to her first thing tomorrow," I said, standing up.

"Yeah, like I said, I've got it under control."

Lying came naturally to Mac. I could tell by the fact that he wasn't making eye contact that he wasn't being entirely truthful with me. "First thing tomorrow," I repeated, with one hand on the door. "You're going to talk to Chief Meyers tomorrow."

I didn't wait for him to respond. Mac was covering for the beer wench. I couldn't believe it. How could he be so dumb? I walked to the elevators and punched the button to the lobby. He'd brought this on himself, and once again, I had to play the role of being the mature adult in our relationship.

When I stepped out of the elevator, something caught my eye. It was a security camera strategically positioned behind a potted plant. Cameras. Of course, the hotel must have security cameras throughout the lobby and probably on each floor. The footage would be able to pinpoint when Mac had arrived at the hotel last night and when Hayley left. I wondered if Chief Meyers had asked anyone for the video. The thought of facing Mac again was too daunting, so I plopped into one of the comfortable plush chairs in front of the fireplace and sent him a text about the cameras. Hopefully, he would come to his senses with a good night's sleep and pass this on to Chief Meyers in the morning.

After I texted Mac, I sent Alex a message letting him know that I was on my way home and asking if he needed anything. Since our farmhouse was on the outskirts of town, I tried to consolidate trips to the grocery store and post office.

He responded right away to let me know that he was fine and to "come home already!"

I grinned as I stepped outside. Mac might be harboring guilt over his fling—or whatever was going on between him and the beer wench—but I didn't share his sentiments. My duty was to Alex, and I was going to see to it that Mac followed through on talking to Chief Meyers. Alex was at a crucial stage of his development, and he needed a dad around to help guide him through these formative teenage years.

My car was parked four blocks away on Commercial Street, so I retraced my steps through the village. The village was like a ghost town. The shops and restaurants had closed for the night and sat in a gloomy slumber. A shiver ran up my arm as a smattering of dried leaves whipped in the wind behind me.

It's just a few leaves, Sloan, I told myself as I sped up. It was probably due to Eddie's murder, but a strange and uncomfortable feeling invaded my body. I felt like I was being watched or followed. I stopped and checked behind me. For a minute I thought I caught a whiff of smoke. Maybe someone had a fire burning. Evenings were turning cool again—a sure sign that fall was right around the corner.

The street was dark and void of movement. At the edge of the shops, one restaurant, The Organ Grinder, was lit up. It stayed open after everyone else closed, mainly to serve waitstaff and bartenders who didn't start their evenings until most people in Leavenworth were heading to bed. I let out a sigh of relief. No one was following me, and worst case scenario, if someone was, I could easily sprint up the street to The Organ Grinder. This was a time when having long legs was an asset.

I continued on, but didn't get far before the tiny hairs on my arms stood at attention. The sound of footsteps approaching made me stop in my tracks. I whipped around and scanned the square.

"Hey, who's here?" I called, trying to sound confident.

No one answered.

"I have pepper spray, and I'm not afraid to use it." That was true. Mac had bought me pepper spray and made me swear that I would keep it in my purse. I'd thought it was ridiculous. Why would I need pepper spray in Leavenworth? He claimed that I might bump into a drunk college student or a vagrant passing through town. I disagreed. Nothing dangerous or sinister happened in our remote village, but I didn't want to argue with him, so I stuck it in the bottom of my purse and forgot about it.

Now I fumbled through my purse trying to find it and trying to stay as calm as possible. My fingers landed on the small tube, and I yanked it out of my purse.

Something rustled in the gazebo. I held the pepper spray in one hand and repeated, "I'll use this if I have to."

Although I had no idea how. I'd never bothered to read the instructions because I never thought I would actually have a need for it.

I waited and listened.

The wind kicked up leaves and made the branches on the oak trees sway and quiver. What was wrong with me? Why would someone follow me? *It's just the wind, Sloan,* I told myself, and raced on to my car. I kept the pepper spray clutched in my hand until I unlocked the front door, then quickly locked it again once I was safely inside.

Usually, I prided myself on being self-sufficient. I didn't like feeling vulnerable and on edge like this. Alex was probably right. Hopefully, once I was home, I could relax, put this insane day behind me, and get some much needed sleep.

I pulled out onto Front Street. *Relax, Sloan. You're fine.*

As I navigated out of downtown, I noticed a single headlight in my rearview mirror. At first I couldn't decide if someone had a headlight out, but then I heard the sound of a motorcycle revving its engine. I didn't think much of it until I turned onto the highway and the motorcycle swerved to the side and zoomed up to my window.

My heart lurched. The rider was dressed in a black leather jacket and matching black leather pants, and had a black motorcycle helmet shielding their face. I tightened my grip on the steering wheel and eased off the gas.

The motorcycle didn't pass me. Instead it slowed and kept pace with my speed.

Keeping a firm grasp on the wheel, I turned to face the driver. Was something wrong? Could my brake lights be out? Was the rider trying to get my attention?

The driver pointed at me and then made a slicing motion across their neck.

What the hell?

My pulse pounded.

I wondered if I should pull over or slow down, but before I could decide what to do next, the cyclist revved their engine and sped off.

Maybe it hadn't been the wind when I was walking

through town. Maybe I had been followed. Could the motorcycle rider have followed me through the square and to my car? Why the slicing of the throat?

I couldn't shake the feeling that I'd just been warned. But why and about what?

CHAPTER

TWENTY-THREE

WHEN I GOT HOME, ALEX stared at me with concern. "Mom, are you okay? You look pretty messed up."

"I do?" I stared at my jeans.

"Your braids look like Pippi Longstocking, and you look like you just saw a ghost or something."

Why did he have to be so astute when it came to reading me? "I'm fine, bud. Tired, that's all." I kicked off my shoes and smoothed my hair. "Did you eat?"

"I had some soup. I saved you some."

"You're the best." We went into the kitchen, and I warmed up a bowl of chicken corn chowder in the microwave.

Whenever I make a pot of soup, I double the recipe and freeze half of it. That way, when I'm in need of a quick and easy meal, I can grab a container of soup from the freezer and have dinner ready in a matter of minutes. The creamy steaming chowder smelled delicious as I removed it from the microwave and added a healthy dose of fresh ground pepper to the top. To make the chowder, I sauté onions, celery, garlic, carrots, and russet potatoes in bacon fat. Then I cover the veggies in homemade chicken stock, add shredded chicken, and frozen corn. I let it simmer on low for an hour until the potatoes are soft. When it's time to serve, I purée corn in the blender and add it in, along with heavy cream. Then I finish it with bacon and shredded Irish cheddar cheese. It's Alex's favorite soup—it's like comfort in a bowl.

Alex poured himself a glass of chocolate milk and opened a bag of peanut butter pretzels. He pulled out a barstool and sat next to me as I ate my soup. "Did you talk to Dad?"

I blew on the spoon and took a bite of the savory soup.

"I went to see him before I came home," I said to Alex, and took another bite of the corn chowder.

"How's he doing?"

"He's fine. You don't need to worry. I'm sure that Chief Meyers is going to drop the charges tomorrow."

"That's good news, right?" He stuffed a handful of crunchy peanut butter pretzels into his mouth. The kid could eat around the clock and never gain an ounce of fat.

"Right. And, seriously, I know that things are crazy right now. I want to try and keep things as normal as possible for you." I choked back a sob. "On that note, how's your homework situation?"

"Mom, you've already said that, like, a million times, but I'm not a kid anymore. I can handle it."

I reached over and ruffled his hair. "I know you're not a kid, but it's still my job to look out for you."

He chugged his chocolate milk. "You're such a *mom*."

"Guilty as charged." I scarfed down the rest of my soup, finally realizing how hungry I had been.

"My Xbox is calling," Alex said, putting his glass in the sink. "See you in the morning, Mom."

As I watched him lope down the hallway, I felt even more frustrated with Mac. Why would Mac risk our family's stability for the beer wench? What did he know about her other than that she had the body of a twenty-year-old? The fact that she and Eddie had been a couple and had had a nasty breakup made me wonder if she could have decided to off him. But how? Eddie wasn't a huge guy, but he must have weighed close to one hundred and seventy pounds. How could Hayley have moved him?

Or what if Eddie was already on the landing? Maybe she seized the opportunity and bashed his head in. The access hatch was at waist level, so if she clubbed Eddie on the back of the head, he could have fallen in. All she would have had to do at that point was stuff his legs inside.

That made logical sense. The question was what was Eddie doing with Garrett's fermenter? Could he have been trying to sabotage the beer?

Questions ran through my head as I walked to the bathroom. What I needed at the moment was a long hot bath and to put everything else out of my mind. I filled the tub with blistering water, added a handful of lavender and rosemary sea salts, and lit a collection of fragrant candles lining the windowsill. Then I cracked the window and slid into the foamy water. Living in the country allowed me the luxury of bathing with the window open. I loved the feeling of cool fresh air funneling in from outside while I was soaking.

I let the tension and stress of the day melt away as I breathed in the steamy, herbed air. At some point I must have dozed off, because I startled awake when a gust of cold air blew out one of the candles. *That's your cue to get out, Sloan,* I told myself as I drained the tub and dried off with a towel. I checked on Alex—some habits died hard—before I headed to bed. The intensity of the day must have taken a toll on him, too. He had fallen asleep on the couch with his Xbox game still playing on the TV and his controller tucked under his arm. I shut off the TV, moved the controller to the coffee table, and covered him with a fleece blanket. I couldn't resist planting a soft kiss on his forehead.

Since I had kicked Mac out, I hadn't been sleeping well, but with the day's events, I had no trouble falling asleep. The minute my head hit the pillow, I was fast asleep. I woke the next morning to the sound of Alex moving around in the kitchen. Tying on a soft cotton bathrobe, I padded down the hallway to find him making eggs and toast.

"Morning, Mom." He greeted me with a wide smile.

"Someone is up early and chipper. What time is it?"

He scrambled eggs on the open flame like a pro. "Not that early. You slept in."

I glanced at the clock on the coffeepot. It was after seven thirty. "I did!"

"It's good, Mom." Reaching for a plate, he scooped eggs onto it and passed it to me. "You need to eat. I'm forcing breakfast on you whether you want it or not."

"I want it. It looks and smells incredible. Thanks." I took the plate and kissed the top of his head. "How did you sleep?"

"Fine. I got a text from Dad this morning."

"Already?" Waking up at seven thirty might have been sleeping in for me, but Mac would have considered it an ungodly hour. He preferred to start his day once the sun was fully overhead. It was a brewer thing. Most brewers tended to work late nights since pubs didn't open until the afternoon.

"He said he has an early meeting with the police chief and wondered if I wanted a ride to school."

Thank goodness. Mac had listened for once and was taking my advice.

"What did you say?" I asked.

"I told him that would be great. I thought maybe you would sleep later."

"That's sweet, and these are fantastic." I pointed to my plate of eggs. Alex was a natural cook. It was in his DNA, plus he had also benefited from many cooking lessons with Ursula. His eggs were light and fluffy, and scrambled with spicy Italian sausage and red peppers.

The toaster dinged. That was another luxury item that Mac had insisted on purchasing for the kitchen, not that he ever used it. It was a top-of-the-line model with a shiny butter-yellow finish and more settings and dials than a small airplane. It could bake a pizza or simply brown toast.

"You want some?" Alex asked as he removed two slices of bread and began liberally slathering them with lemon curd.

"I'll stick with your eggs." To prove my point, I stabbed the eggs and took another bite. "Delicious. When is your dad coming?"

Alex looked at his cell phone. "Soon. I better get moving." He folded a slice of toast in half. Lemon curd oozed out of the sides. He licked his hand and consumed the entire piece of toast in one bite. Then he inhaled eggs and gulped two glasses of orange juice.

"Do you need a lunch?" I asked, standing to put my plate in the sink.

"Nah, it's Thursday, and that means pizza party in math class."

For Alex a pizza party in class was a bonus day of fun, but growing up in the foster care system had meant that class parties were often the only kind of party I had experienced as a kid. The first time I ever had a birthday party was when I turned thirteen. The foster family I was staying with then had eight other kids, but my foster mom made sure that everyone's birthday was recognized with a family dinner and a birthday cake. She even asked me what kind of cake I wanted. I was so floored by her kindness that I couldn't answer. I'll never forget that meal. It wasn't fancy, and quite honestly she wasn't the best cook, but that birthday meal was the best thing I had ever tasted. We had tacos with gobs of nacho cheese and beans out of a can, and she made me a pink strawberry layer cake with strawberry jam and marshmallow cream frosting. It was the most beautiful cake I'd ever seen, with mounds of cloud-like frosting and pink sprinkles. When I learned from my social worker a few weeks later that I'd been placed in a new foster home, I cried for two days.

"Pizza party, that's fun," I said to Alex, shoving my memories back inside.

"It's better than a test," he replied with a grin.

A honk sounded outside.

"That's Dad, I gotta run. See you tonight." He kissed my cheek, grabbed his backpack, and ran for the door.

I was both relieved and irritated that Mac had blared the horn instead of coming inside. It was probably better. I didn't want to get in any kind of a disagreement in front of Alex. After I put our breakfast dishes in the dishwasher and got dressed, I decided to head to Nitro. Garrett wouldn't be moving yet, which would give me time to work on my test batches and clear my head. Today was a new day, and I couldn't wait to start steeping grains and boiling hops.

CHAPTER

TWENTY-FOUR

I FELT A STRANGE SENSE of déjà vu when I arrived at Nitro and unlocked the brewery doors. The space was quiet and still, with no signs of a break-in or a dead body, but I couldn't shake the feeling that something was off. Before I got to work, I checked behind the shiny tanks, in the kitchen pantry, and in the office closet. Not sure that Mac would actually follow through, I left Chief Meyers a message asking about the hotel video footage and mentioning the motorcycle last night.

For my first batch of beer, I started boiling water in the small tanks that Garrett had brought with him from Seattle. Most home brewers had pieced-together systems made from recycled kegs or large stainless steel pots. Garrett's home brew system was top of the line. I'd seen a prototype of the self-contained system at a craft beer convention, but I'd never used something so small. I could do five-gallon batches, which was great for experimentation, because no one wanted to dump gallons and gallons of beer if they ended up with a bad batch.

After the water had reached the right temperature, I added twelve pounds of a grain mixture that I had selected. Soon the kitchen was filled with steam and smelled like a real brewery. Mashing (or steeping) the grains would take about an hour. So while I waited for the first step, I began slicing white peaches. In order to pull out the flavor of the Cascade hops I planned to add, I wanted to use a sweet yet delicate fruit, like the peaches. I drizzled them with some honey; sprinkled them with cinnamon, nutmeg, and a dash of cloves; and slid them into the oven. I would broil them to enhance the candy flavor and add them to the boil later. The fall-inspired scent made my stomach rumble, despite the fact that I had devoured Alex's eggs.

While the grains were steeping, I took stock of the inventory in the kitchen. I wondered if Garrett had thought about a food budget long term. That would have to be one of our discussion points later today. I was happy to take charge of food for the front, but I needed some direction and a plan. We couldn't keep running to the store or my home kitchen every day, and having a small menu would be essential in building a loyal customer base.

Garrett wandered into the kitchen wearing jeans and a Seattle Sounders T-shirt as I started the final step in the brewing process. "I thought I smelled grains." His hair stuck out in every direction, and his T-shirt was wrinkled from sleep.

"Did I wake you?"

"No. I should have been up a while ago. That was brutal last night. I guess it caught up with me." He walked to the far counter and carefully measured level tablespoons of coffee into the pot. "What are you brewing?"

"I'm doing my first taster batch. I'm almost done if you want in on this." I pointed to the stove.

"That's okay." The way he poured water into the coffee carafe reminded me of my high school chemistry teacher when he demonstrated a chemical reaction in test tubes and beakers. Garrett carefully poured the liquid from a height of nearly a half foot above the carafe and watched it swirl in the bottom. "I want to start on the main fermenter."

"Have you given any thought to a food budget?"

He squinted and rubbed his temples. "Food budget?"

"For the front. I don't think it will be very cost-effective to be running back and forth to the grocery store every day. Plus, if we have a standard menu, then customers will come knowing they can get small bites with their pints."

"Man, no one told me how expensive running a brewery was going to be." He reached for a coffee cup. "That makes sense, though. How much do you think it's going to cost?"

I could tell he was stressed about cash. "I don't think you need to worry about cost in that the goal will be not only to cover our food cost, but give you another revenue stream. We should be able to set up terms with some local vendors so your upfront costs aren't too high."

He stared at the coffeepot as if willing it to brew faster. "That would be great."

"Do you want me to sketch out a menu and make a few calls?" I turned the heat to low and checked the temperature to make sure that the beer was cooling properly. "I guess the only question is whether you're thinking of hiring a chef. Right now it's just me and you, right?"

"Hiring a chef would be awesome in the future, but I don't have that kind of cash now."

The more Garrett spoke of his financial situation, the more worried I became. How strapped was he? What if he didn't have enough to pay me? I would do whatever it took not to have to rely on Mac for a single cent, even if that meant going back to bartending or working another job.

"We'll keep it simple. I can do a daily rotating soup. That's easy. All we have to do is ladle it up when customers order. We can do meat, cheese, and veggie trays. I can make them in the morning and wrap them in plastic so they stay fresh in the fridge."

He poured himself a cup of coffee. "Do you want some?"

"No, I'm fine."

"What are the other pubs in town doing?"

"It depends on who you're talking about. We can't compete with Der Keller when it comes to food. They have an entire kitchen staff, head chef, line cooks, and waitstaff. They run a full restaurant with lunch, dinner, and a Sunday German brunch."

Garrett frowned as he opened the fridge and poured three separate spoonfuls of cream into his coffee.

"If you want, I'm sure Bruin would let us look over his menu. I can head over that way and grab one of his menus for you. They serve simple pub fare, which is much more in line with what I think we can accomplish here. I'm thinking simple and easy pub snacks. At least until we build our customer base."

"That's a good idea." Garrett stirred his coffee and stared at a spot on the counter. "Have I mentioned how much I appreciate you?"

"Nope." I grinned. "That's why you're paying me the big bucks, right?"

He nearly spit his coffee on the counter. "Ha! Big bucks. Don't I wish."

I turned off the brewing machine and turned to him. "This has to cool. Let me run over and chat with Bruin. Then we can take a look at his menu and I'll sketch out some options for you. We can print them up here. It doesn't have to be anything fancy. In fact, I think it would be great if we continue your science and chemistry theme in the front. I can have Alex design a menu to look like a chart of the elements or something."

Garrett took a drink from his mug. "I wanted to have shirts made with beer as an element."

"I can look into that, too. Selling growlers, hats, and T-shirts is another excellent way to bring in some extra cash."

"Add it to the list." Garrett attempted a smile.

"Drink your coffee. I'll be back in an hour or so." With that, I grabbed my purse and headed for the front. Garrett definitely needed nudging and coaching on running a small brewpub. As intelligent as he was, I was surprised that he knew so little about managing a business. How could he have not thought about things like food and swag? Hans had warned me that Garrett was in his head, but I hadn't expected him to be quite this clueless. Maybe that was the thing about people who were really smart. I remembered one of my professors in community college who said he could complete any math problem in ten minutes or less, but could never find his keys and got lost going to the grocery store. Maybe that was Garrett's problem—he was book smart but not street smart, or beer smart.

My motivation for stopping by Bruin's Brewing was twofold. I did think it would help Garrett to see Bruin's menu, but I also wanted to follow up with Bruin about last night. He had mentioned wanting to talk to me about something, and I wondered if it was connected to Eddie's murder.

Bruin's Brewing was located on the east side of town, about a ten-minute drive from the village square. The brewery was half the size of Der Keller, but had gained a loyal following since it opened ten years ago. Since it wasn't in the heart of Beervaria, it didn't have to adhere to the same design aesthetic. Instead it was built to resemble a mountain cabin. The A-frame exterior was built from old-growth logs. Massive ten- to fifteen-foot wood-carved animal sculptures lined the front walk and wraparound porch. There was a grizzly bear, moose, bobcat, and Sasquatch. On the porch, pine Adirondack chairs were gathered in small groups so people could have a pint while they waited for a table inside.

The brewery didn't open for another hour, but I figured Bruin and some of his staff would be in the back. I walked past the sculptures to the employee entrance and knocked on the door. Bruin answered it almost immediately.

"Sloan, to what do I owe this pleasure?" He wrapped me in a hearty hug and squeezed my shoulder so tight I thought it might pop out of its socket. I could smell stale booze on his breath and, like Garrett, he had slept in his clothes. The felt hat was gone, but his TASTES LIKE MORE index card was still pinned to his chest.

"I was hoping to steal one of your menus for Garrett."

He released me from his grasp. "Stealing from the enemy. I didn't know you had it in you. Those big brown eyes look innocent, but apparently you have a dark side."

"Don't we all?" I joked, but Bruin scowled and muttered something that sounded like "Yes, we do" under his breath.

"Come on in, I'll get you a menu," he said, trying to recover his jovial tone. "How did the rest of the night go?"

"Not bad." I followed him through the kitchen and to the knotty pine dining room. Deer antlers and antique hunting rifles were hung on the walls. Each table was carved from wood, and an oversized chandelier in the middle of the room had been made from elk antlers. Bruin's Brewing felt more like a hunting lodge than a pub.

He walked behind the bar, poured two pints of stout, and slid one my way. "Oh, no, thanks—it's too early for me." I waved off his offer of the pint. The thick chocolate-colored beer looked like molasses.

"Sloan, if you want to consider yourself a brewer, you're going to have to learn how to drink in the morning." He gulped down the pint he'd poured for himself and then reached for mine and chugged it, too.

The guy had a problem. I wondered if anyone had confronted him about it. Most brewers were connoisseurs of craft beer, but very rarely did that translate into a drinking problem. Brewers were known to imbibe slowly, in small quantities, to taste their creations throughout the day. Chugging two pints before noon was a different story. As much as I didn't want to, I would have to talk to Mac about Bruin. They had been friends and friendly rivals for years, and if anyone could get through to Bruin, it was Mac.

He poured himself another pint, reached under the counter, and handed me a menu. The menus were printed on plain paper and laminated. This one had seen plenty of use, as it stuck to my hands when I picked it up.

"What's Garrett thinking of serving?" he said as he gulped half of the pint in two large swigs.

"That's what I'm trying to help him with. We're pretty bare-bones at this point, so I want to keep it simple. I think he's worried about competing with Der Keller, since we're right around the corner."

"Nah!" Bruin nearly fell over as he swiped the air with one hand. "You'll be fine. If you listened to what Eddie had to say, he thought there was enough room in this town for more breweries. I agree, but I told him he was stuck with me and not to get any ideas."

"What do you mean?"

"Huh?" He swayed slightly and caught himself on the counter.

"Was Eddie thinking of starting up a new brewery?"

"Huh? Nah, he'd never do that to me. I gave him his start. We had a good thing going here, and he wouldn't do anything like that."

Or would he? I wondered.

"What do you think?" Bruin waved a fat finger at the beer-splattered menu.

I glanced over it. They featured four kinds of burgers—beef, elk, buffalo, and a mixture of all three—along with an elk stew, a steak and baked potato plate, and a daily chili. It was a meat-lover's dream and required much more prep and grilling time than we had at Nitro. Since we didn't have a cook, anything we served would need to be prepared in advance and ready to grab and go.

"It definitely matches the vibe in here," I said, pointing to the antlers mounted above the bar.

"That's what I told April. She can take her German village and shove it where the sun don't shine, if you get my drift."

I understood his sentiment and had to agree with him. April wasn't high on my list of favorite people, but I wondered what she had to do with his hunting theme. "I take it April is still after you to turn this place into Beervaria, too?"

Bruin's meaty cheeks bulked out as he replied. "She can shove it. I've told her a hundred times she's not in charge and I'm not in the village. I don't have to put up with any cuckoo clock or nutcracker crap. This is a man's bar. No offense or anything—women can come in and drink my beer, too—but I'm not putting up tourist crap for April."

"April wants you to change the look?"

He scowled. "She can try, but she's not going to make me change a thing. She can come around here with her petitions and try to tell me that Eddie was a thug who ought to cover up his tattoos to protect the town's reputation, but she's nothing more than talk."

"She wanted Eddie to cover up his tattoos?"

"That nosy woman wants to control everyone in town. If she had it her way, we'd all be wearing lederhosen and prancing around, but I bought this building so I didn't have to do any of that crap, and I like your guy Garrett. I can tell he thinks like me."

I couldn't believe that April had asked Eddie to cover his tattoos or pressured Bruin to change the look of his manly pub, and yet at the same time, it made perfect sense. That sounded like April.

"I should get back. Do you care if I take this? I'll be sure to return it later this afternoon," I said to Bruin.

"Keep it. It's yours." He turned to the taps. "You sure you don't want a pint?"

"No, thanks. I've got a new batch brewing back at Nitro that I need to go check on. I'll bring this over later." I left before he could try to pressure me into having a breakfast beer with him. In the short time we'd been talking, he had consumed three pints. I wondered how many he'd had before I arrived, and how many he could finish before noon. I also stewed on what Bruin had said about April. She was annoying and a gossip, but could she have harmed Eddie because he threatened to taint her perfect image of Leavenworth? That seemed like something out of a movie, but then again, I wouldn't have put it past her.

CHAPTER

TWENTY-FIVE

SPEAK OF THE DEVIL, I thought as I pulled into a parking space across the street from Waterfront Park and watched April Ablin curtsey out Nitro's front door. She must have spent thousands of dollars on her German-inspired wardrobe. Today she was dressed in yet another ruffled plaid costume and knee-high tights. Even during the height of tourist season, I refused to dress like April. Not that I didn't appreciate the fact that people from all around the world flocked to our small town to celebrate Oktoberfest, but there were plenty of other ways to celebrate our German heritage and plenty of other people in town who enjoyed dressing up for the monthlong party.

"Sloan!" April called in her fake singsong voice. "Over here."

Just my luck. I considered pretending not to hear her and sneaking around the block, but she targeted her eyes on me and waved with both hands.

"What's up, April?" I asked, crossing the street.

"I was checking in on that handsome hunk of a brewer you're working for. I'm sure that with everything that's happened over the last few days, things must be terribly dramatic for you, Sloan." She fanned her face. "Speaking of Garrett, do you know if he's given any thought to my suggestions to make Nitro more in line with the aesthetic we all strive to maintain in Leavenworth?"

"I'm fine, and you'll have to talk to Garrett yourself."

She reached for my arm with her fake nails and feigned concern. "Everyone is so worried about you. I had to check in and see how you're holding up." She took a quick breath and continued. "Mac arrested? I absolutely couldn't believe it when I heard the news. Although given his recent indiscretions, perhaps he's been hiding a side that none of us knew about."

"Mac's fine."

"Sloan, you don't have to put on a brave face for me." She tapped her nail on my forearm. Her index fingers were painted with the German flag and then each nail alternated red, yellow, and black. I had to give her credit for being fully committed to her self-prescribed role as Leavenworth's German ambassador. "I can only imagine what you must be going through. First learning that your husband has been cheating, then a murder, and now his arrest." Her breathless tone made it clear that her words were nothing more than lip service. She was loving this.

"Really, April, I'm fine." I tried to move closer to the door, but she stopped me.

"What about Garrett? Such a terrible first impression for

him to have of our town. Have you assured him that this is completely unprecedented? He isn't thinking of letting you go, is he? I mean, you know, having so much drama surrounding his only staff member is a bit of scandal for a new business." She gave me a sugary smile that made me want to punch her in the face.

"He seems to be holding up just fine." I spotted Van unloading his rusty pickup across the street and waved in hopes that he would come over and rescue me from April's clutches. Instead, he shot me a quick nod of acknowledgment and booked it in the opposite direction. Apparently, he'd already had the pleasure of meeting April.

"Who's that?" April snapped.

"Van?" I asked, pointing my thumb in his direction. "You haven't met Van?" I couldn't believe there was a single person in the greater Leavenworth area that April hadn't forced herself upon.

"No. Who is he?" She drummed her fingers together.

"He's a hop farmer."

Glaring at me through her clumpy mascara, she scowled. "Since when?"

"Since I don't know. A while, I guess, because Garrett's been using his hops."

"Impossible." April's jaw tightened. "I know every business in Chelan County. I've never heard of him."

I shifted Bruin's menu into my right hand. "I don't know what to tell you, April, but he's been around town for the last few days. Did you need something?"

Without answering, she glanced at the menu. "What do you have there?"

"Nothing. It's a menu."

"That looks like Bruin's menu. Are you planning something with him? Is he thinking of joining forces with Garrett? Oh my goodness, please tell me that he's finally going to do something with that eyesore he calls a pub. I told him a million times that Eddie was terrible for business—all of those hideous tattoos. You know he wanted Bruin to turn the place into a hipster joint. Isn't that what they call them? Seattle is crawling with them. Can you imagine? Here in Leavenworth?" Her words were so rapid, I could barely distinguish them.

"Chill." I gave her a hard look. "I borrowed a menu, that's all."

"That's not all!" She pursed her lips and stared at me as if willing me to divulge some deep dark secret. "What is going on? Why do you have his menu?"

"April, seriously, nothing. I wanted to look over his menu. That's it." She was exhausting when I was at my best, and this wasn't a good time. I wanted nothing more than to tell her off, but I knew that antagonizing her would only make things worse.

"You're up to something, Sloan, I can tell. And I'll have you know that it's my duty and responsibility to this community to keep everyone informed of what's going on in town."

"That's great, but unfortunately, there's nothing going on."

She pursed her lips together so tightly it made my mouth hurt. "This isn't over, Sloan. I'm going to find out what you're up to one way or another."

"Go for it." I shrugged. "I need to get to work."

"I know you're lying," she called as I flung open the front door.

The woman was maddening. No one—other than Mac—could get under my skin like April Ablin.

Garrett threw his hands up in surrender as I stomped inside. "Easy, what's wrong?"

"Sorry." I blew out a long breath of anger. "I bumped into April outside."

"Yeah. She was here." He turned and pointed with his thumb to a basket sitting on the bar. It was packed with kitschy German trinkets and tied with a gaudy red, yellow, and black plaid bow. "A gift from the welcome wagon."

"There's a sweet group of ladies who volunteer to welcome people to town. Der Keller has donated coupons for a free beer tasting for years. In fact, it would be a good marketing opportunity for us. We can print up tickets for a tasting or free appetizer to include in the welcome packages. It's a good way to get exposure and new people through the door."

"I didn't see any coupons in the basket," Garrett said.

"That's because April is her own welcome wagon. She brought that for you to try to get the *scoop* on what's going on. Seriously, she is the biggest gossip around, and I'm sure that's a not-so-subtle hint that she wants you to German up this place."

"Ha!" Garrett laughed. "Don't worry, she didn't get any gossip from me."

"Thanks," I said with a smile. "Sorry. I don't know why she bugs me so much. Usually, I can get along with anyone."

"I know the type." Garrett walked to the bar and untied the bow. "Want to see what she brought us?"

"Not us. That's all you." I followed him to the bar.

The basket contained German mustard, sausages, pretzels, jam, a green felt hat, a beer stein, a nutcracker, and dozens of other local items. It looked as if April had bought one of everything from each store in town. She was really trying to impress Garrett.

"Nice." I grinned and picked up a bottle opener in the shape of a nutcracker. "This will come in handy."

He laughed. "I've always wanted one of those."

"Leave it to April. She has a way of knowing exactly what everyone in town wants, or at least what she thinks they want." I could hear the bitterness in my tone.

"Don't let her get under your skin," Garrett said, tossing the bottle opener back into the basket. "Do you think we can regift this stuff? We could give it away as brewery prizes."

I raised one eyebrow. "I love it, and if word gets to April that you're giving away her German basket, I'll love it even more."

"Let's do it." He picked up the felt hat. "I think this should be the first thing to go."

"Agreed." I joined him at the bar and handed him Bruin's menu.

"Whoa, I wouldn't want to be a vegetarian here. He likes his red meat, doesn't he?"

"I don't think he gets many vegetarians through his doors, at least not for the food." I picked up a notepad and pencil behind the bar. "As you can see, his menu is still more involved than what I'm thinking. What if we do hummus and veggies, cheese and meat, a daily soup, and a rotating dessert? Does that sound good for the short term? I can price everything out and then we can get rolling on a menu."

"Works for me." Garrett gave me a thumbs-up.

"Is there anything else that needs to be done before we open?"

"Can you speed up the brewing process by a couple of weeks?"

"I wish." I tapped the pencil on the notebook. "What are you thinking about guest taps? Do you want me to run over to Der Keller and see what they have?"

He frowned. "I don't want to, but I don't think we have a choice."

"Okay. Let me price out the menu, and then I'll go talk to Otto or Ursula. I'm sure they'll cut you a deal. They might even comp you a keg."

"You don't need to do that. I don't want to put you in a weird position."

"Trust me, you're not. That's the kind of people the Krauses are. I don't have to ask them for a special favor, they'll want to help you. Actually, I mentioned your contract with Van to them last night and they said they'd be happy to look it over with you if you want."

"No, I talked to my buddy in Seattle late last night. He's on it." Garrett reached for the pencil and scribbled something in the notebook. "Nuts. We need nuts. Doesn't every pub need nuts?"

"Given the circumstances the past couple of days, I would say we have plenty of nuts running around town, but you're right. Do you want those as a menu item or something we offer as a complimentary bar snack?"

"People can pay a few bucks for a bowl of peanuts, can't they?"

"Sure." I made a note to research peanut vendors. If we were going to charge for nuts, we needed to make sure that they were high quality. "I'm on it."

Garrett took April's basket to the office while I penciled out Nitro's menu. I was excited about getting to put my culinary training to use. I had a great fail-safe recipe for hummus that was simple to make in large batches and that I could tweak every few days. From sun-dried tomatoes to fire-roasted red peppers and pesto, we could experiment with different flavor combinations. Another way to elevate a hummus plate was to marinate the vegetables, and I knew exactly what I would marinate them in—a beer vinaigrette. The meat and cheese plate would feature whatever was fresh at the butcher shop and bakery. I made a note to stop by both. The only thing left to figure out was the daily soup and dessert.

To keep things as streamlined as possible, I decided to feature a soup and dessert pairing for each day of the week with the exception of Sundays. On Sundays we could get creative and bake whatever we were in the mood for—or use whatever we had left over. Chili was an obvious choice, as were seafood chowder and tomato bisque. I could do creamy potato, beer and cheese, and chicken and rice soups. That would get us through the week. In terms of dessert, I had to do a chocolate stout brownie. We could also do beer floats and my cupcakes.

With the menu roughed out, the next thing I needed to do was talk to vendors to see what our hard food costs would be. I tucked the notebook under my arm and called to Garrett to let him know that I'd be back in a while.

My first stop was the bakery. I wanted to serve fresh bread with the meat and cheese plates, and pita bread with the hummus. Once I had ordered bread and worked out a delivery schedule at the bakery, I continued on to the German deli to talk to the butcher.

The German deli was like a candy store for foodies, although it also housed two full rows of imported German candy so, technically speaking, I guess it was a candy store. The deli smoked and cured all of its meats and sausages, and made traditional German side dishes like sauerkraut, pickled red cabbage, potato salad, and schnitzel. My mouth watered when I stepped inside and surveyed the twenty-foot display of sausages. The owner reminded me of Otto. He had the same thick accent and bushy white eyebrows, and expertly sliced sample after sample of his homemade delicacies for me to taste. I opted for an assortment of meats—beer-cured salami; veal loaf; Black Forest ham; and *Bierschinken,* a pork and beef bologna with chunks of marinated ham, cardamom seeds, and white pepper. It was a favorite in the Krause household and something that most tourists had probably never had a chance to taste. The meats would keep for up to a week—if not longer—and would allow us to gauge sales and whether there were particular things that were a hit with our customers.

I turned down the deli owner's offer of a frankfurter and continued on to Der Keller with a full belly. It felt good to have product ordered and a menu finalized. Now I needed to scrounge up an extra keg or two of beer.

My stomach flopped as I entered the brewery where I had worked for almost two decades. It had nothing to do with sampling too many sausages at the deli and everything to do with the anticipation of running into the beer wench or my husband. I scanned the dining room and spotted Otto at a booth. He had a stack of paperwork piled on the table and a half of a pint glass resting next to him.

I made my way toward the booth, not bothering to make eye contact or check in with the bartender or waitstaff. It was after noon, and the lunch crowd was humming. Otto looked up and greeted me with a wide grin. "Sloan, how nice to see you. Sit. Sit."

"Am I interrupting you?" I asked, acknowledging the stack of papers in front of him. "You look busy."

"No, no, never. I always have time for my girl."

My throat tightened. "What are you working on?"

He removed his wire-framed glasses and pressed his veined fingers on the bridge of his nose. "Ze books, Sloan. It's always something, you know. We have more money going out than coming in these days."

This shocked me. Der Keller had always been one of the most solid and stable businesses in town when it came to finances. Otto and Ursula had been savvy yet cautious entrepreneurs. They hadn't fallen into the trap that so many other start-ups had of expanding too rapidly and purchasing unnecessary expensive equipment.

"Really?" I said to Otto. "But this place is always buzzing." Right now the toasty pub was packed with regulars drinking pints and noshing on steaming plates of sauerbraten.

"*Ja,* I know, but the money it is going out to so many places. I cannot keep up anymore."

"Do you need help?"

He smiled at me, but his eyes looked weary. "No—thank you, Sloan, but this is not a problem for you to concern about."

I couldn't help but return his smile at his grammar. It was one of the many things I loved about Otto and Ursula. Their nuances of speech cracked me up. When Alex was young, he used to mimic their speech patterns. Neither Mac nor I had bothered to correct him, since we both thought it was adorable.

"Would you like a drink or some lunch?" Otto offered. He fit the space perfectly. Der Keller was a testament to his tireless efforts and love for his homeland. It came through in every detail from the carved tap handles behind the bar to the rustic décor and the menu inspired by old family recipes.

"No, thanks. I'm here on official business, actually."

His glossy eyes twinkled. "Oh, business. *Ja,* what can I do for you?"

I told him about our dilemma at Nitro, how we were low on beer with having to dump the tank where I'd discovered Eddie's body.

"Zis is no good—no good. Of course we will help with this. How much do you want? I will have the boys send it over right now." He started to move.

"No, no, you don't need to rush. We're okay for today, but if you'd let us offer a guest tap, we'd be more than willing to pay for it."

"Never, Sloan, not for my girl. Zis is compliment for you."

"Otto, this isn't for me, and you don't owe me any favors. This is business."

"*Ja,* and zis is how I do business with you." He refused to let me say more and stood. "We go to the back, and you tell me what you want me to send over."

I agreed and followed him into the brewery. Anger bubbled within me as I watched his hunched shoulders and lumbering gate. How had Mac taken him away from me?

CHAPTER

TWENTY-SIX

I BUMPED INTO HANS ON my way out of Der Keller. Otto had promised to send over four kegs of beer and refused payment. "Zis is for the village," he insisted. "You tell Garrett that we welcome him to our beer Bavaria."

Hans stepped backward and widened his eyes when he saw me. His tool belt was slung around his waist, and a pencil was tucked behind his ear. "Hey, Sloan, you're the last person I expected to see here."

"I was meeting with your dad," I said.

"About Mac?"

"No, about beer. Why? Has something else happened?"

He shrugged. "Not as far as I know."

"Alex told me that he was going to talk to Chief Meyers this morning, but I haven't heard anything since." Then I realized that I hadn't spoken to Hans since I'd last seen Mac. I filled him in on our conversation from the night before and confessed that I suspected Hayley might be involved.

He listened intently and, when I finished, stuffed his hands into his work overalls. "I'm impressed, Sloan."

"With what?"

"You. After what Mac did, most women would kick him to the curb and let him sit in jail. You are a rare breed."

"Well, thanks, but to be honest, part of me wanted to let him sit in jail. I couldn't do that to Alex, though. He needs his dad."

"My point exactly." Hans glanced at Der Keller's large front windows. "What did you need with Dad?"

I told him about our beer dilemma and how I was working on a pub menu for Garrett, too.

"He called me last night."

"Who?"

"Garrett." Hans removed his screwdriver from his tool belt and tightened a loose screw on the windowsill. "He thinks you're some kind of magician or beer goddess. He thanked me profusely for tossing out your name. I guess things are going well with him." It wasn't a question, but more of a confirmation.

"That's me, beer goddess." I winked. "And like Garrett, you have my thanks as well."

"I had a feeling you two would hit it off." He gave me a sly smile. "Professionally speaking, of course."

"Given that the last time I checked I was still married to your brother, I would hope so."

Hans examined the string of hops twisted around the front entrance. "Have you given any thought to what you're going to do next?"

"You mean with Mac?"

He nodded but kept his face turned away from me. "I don't want to be in the middle, but he asked me to tell you that he'll do anything to save your marriage."

"I don't want to put you in the middle either, Hans, but he sure has a funny way of showing his commitment to our marriage, since every time I've seen him in the last forty-eight hours, the beer wench has been at his side."

Hans sighed and removed a dead hop from the vine. I changed the subject. "Hey, did you know that she dated Eddie?"

"Hayley?" Hans returned his attention to me and brushed his hands together. The scent of the lemony hop filled the air.

"Yeah. I don't know any details, but apparently they had a nasty breakup pretty recently."

"Hmm." He glanced across the street to the Christmas shop. Despite the fact that it wasn't even officially fall yet, the shop had a huge Christmas tree and life-sized Santa on display in its front window. Christmas was a big deal in Leavenworth, and there were multiple shops in town that dedicated their inventory to the holiday year-round. "I hadn't heard that, but you know me, I try to stay out of the gossip loop. Although I did hear a rumor that things weren't going well with Eddie and Bruin. Maybe Eddie let his personal problems spill into work."

"What did you hear about them?" My curiosity was on high alert. Bruin hadn't mentioned anything about the fact that he and Eddie weren't getting along. Which might mean nothing. Or it might be connected to Eddie's murder.

"Bruin put an ask out around town for a new brewer. He made it sound like he was planning on cutting Eddie loose."

"Really? Who did you hear that from?"

Hans folded his chiseled arms across his chest and gave me a knowing look.

"April?"

"Who else?" he confirmed with a nod. "You know April; she likes to stir things up, so it could be gossip, but when I saw Bruin at the Nitro launch, he asked me if I had any interest in getting back in the beer business. He was sloshed but I didn't get the sense that he was kidding."

"Bruin made it sound like he was broken up about Eddie's death. I wonder what was going on between the two of them. Did April give any specifics?"

"Nope. Just that."

"I wonder if she told Chief Meyers." The sound of a truck backing up made me turn around. We don't get many semis on Front Street. This one contained the massive white tents that would be erected for Oktoberfest.

Hans watched as a crew began unloading the tents, temporary gates, and ten-foot tables. "April loves to hear herself talk and isn't exactly a shrinking wallflower, so I would put my money on the fact that she's told everyone in town."

He was probably right, but I wanted to hear it from the source's mouth. As much as I didn't want to have another conversation with April, this information could help clear Mac.

"Things are going to get crazy around here soon. I can't believe they're already setting up for Oktoberfest." Leaning in to give him a kiss on the cheek, I said, "I should get back."

To my surprise, he pulled me into a hug and whispered, "Sloan, you know you can call on me or Mama and Papa anytime. We all love you."

I fought back tears and leaned my head on his shoulder. "I love you guys, too."

"You know that you'll always be my sis, no matter what happens with you and Mac, right?"

"Stop." I punched him gently on the shoulder. "You're going to make me cry and ruin my reputation as a hard-nosed brewer."

His golden brown eyes looked misty, too. "Sorry, but it's true."

"Let's go out for a pint later," I called as I quickly whipped around in the opposite direction and started walking down the sidewalk.

The sweet moment with Hans had made my self-doubt and fear of abandonment well to the surface. I blinked as hard as I could and willed myself not to cry. Part of me wondered if Mac and I would have ever gotten married if it hadn't been for the Krause family. Sure, I'd been pregnant, but I could have raised Alex on my own.

Don't think about that now, Sloan, I told myself as I crossed the street and headed for April's office. Now was as good a time as any to have a conversation with her.

In addition to her duty as Leavenworth's welcome woman, April worked as a real estate agent. Her office was located in a warehouse that had been refurbished to look like a German beer hall. The flags of Germany, the United States, and Leavenworth city flew on poles outside, and flyers for lakefront cabins and mountain getaways were taped to the windows.

When I stepped inside, the space smelled like cheap perfume and stale coffee.

"Is April in?" I asked the receptionist.

She chomped a wad of gum and held up a finger. "I'll check. Who is asking?"

"Tell her that Sloan Krause is here." I took a seat in an uncomfortable faux leather chair and thumbed through a Leavenworth brochure.

I could hear April's shrill pitch on the other end of the phone when the receptionist called her. "Be right up," she screeched and then appeared around the corner before the receptionist had even had a chance to hang up the phone.

"Sloan, what a delight." She clapped her hands together. "I had a feeling I would be seeing you, but I didn't think it would be this soon. You are much more pulled together than I realized." Her glaring red lipstick looked as if it had been applied by a toddler.

"What are you talking about?"

"Property, of course." She glanced at the receptionist, covered her mouth with one hand, and then spoke loudly enough for everyone within a mile radius to hear her. "The divorce. I'm guessing you want to get a head start on securing property, and I don't blame you, dear. In fact, I'm very impressed that you're thinking so strategically."

"Can we go talk in your office?" I asked, with a nod to the receptionist.

"Of course. I'm so sorry. I should have thought you would want privacy at a time like this. I mean, a cheating husband." She made a *tsk*ing sound. "It must be so terribly embarrassing for you."

If I could have kicked myself without looking ridiculous, I would have. It was my own doing. As curious as I was about the rift between Eddie and Bruin, no amount of time spent with April Ablin was worth it.

"Hold all of my calls," April said to the receptionist with a dramatic flip of her wrist. "And bring us some coffee, or maybe tea. Yes, I think a delicate situation like this requires tea."

The receptionist gave me a sympathetic smile as I followed April to her office. I felt sorry for her. Spending five minutes with April was punishment enough; I couldn't imagine working for the woman.

April's office was an extension of her obsession with all things German. Every square inch of wall space was taken over with Oktoberfest and Maifest posters, photos of German chalets, and cuckoo clocks. I counted at least thirty. They all ticked in a weird rhythm together. I wondered what it sounded like in the small square office when they all cuckooed on the hour.

"Have a seat," April said, motioning to the red love seat with throw pillows arranged to look like the German flag.

I tossed a lederhosen-clad teddy bear to the side and sat on the soft couch. My body sunk into the oversized pillows, making April tower over me from behind her ornate baroque desk. I wondered if she'd stolen the desk and matching chair from Ludwig's castle.

"Sloan, I cannot tell you how happy I am that you've come to me for help. I wanted to mention it earlier, but didn't want to overstep my bounds, you know." She put her hand over her heart. "I've been wanting to reach out, but didn't want to pressure you. I've lost sleep over this. I'm just so worried about you."

Her concern was about as genuine as her fake barmaid costume.

I clenched my teeth. "Thanks." I started to explain that I hadn't come for help or real estate advice, but she interrupted.

"I mean it's such a scandal. Everyone is shocked. I suppose we shouldn't be. After all, the man did enjoy chasing skirts, but I thought that was in fun. My heart is absolutely broken for you."

The receptionist arrived with a tray of tea and a plastic plate with store-bought gingerbread that looked like cardboard.

"Put that right here," April said, clearing a space on the desk. "And be sure to shut the door behind you. We're having a very private conversation, and you know how important discretion is to me."

I had to bite the inside of my cheek to keep from laughing.

April poured us both a cup of tea, and I had to stand up to reach mine across the intimidating desk. "Do drink something. I'm sure it will make you feel better and then we can get down to business. Mac will never know what hit him. You've spoken to a lawyer already, right? I should probably get their name so we can coordinate our attack."

"I'm not here about an attack, April." The teacup was scalding. I carefully balanced it on my knees. It smelled weak.

"However you want to term it is fine with me. Just know that I'm behind you one hundred percent."

"I'm not here to talk about property or anything about Mac for that matter."

Her face dropped. "Oh."

The tea was burning my knees, so I sat up and rested it on the edge of the desk.

"Why are you here?" Her voice couldn't conceal her disappointment.

"I wanted to ask you about Eddie and Bruin."

She perked up and gave me a cunning smile. "Do tell."

"I heard that there might have been tension between them?"

"More than tension. In fact, I would call their relationship contentious. Bruin was about to fire Eddie."

"Are you sure?"

"Sloan, as I'm sure you know, one of my roles as Leavenworth's ambassador is to keep my finger on the pulse of everything going on in town."

That was an interesting spin on being a gossip, but I nodded politely and waited for April to continue.

"I spend a good amount of time making sure I know exactly who is up to what around here." She plucked two cubes of sugar from a crystal bowl and dropped them in her tea. "Bruin had had it with Eddie's behavior, and between you and me, I don't blame him. Those ugly tattoos and surly attitude have no place in our village. It's our duty as patrons of America's Bavaria to uphold the standards of our German ancestors."

I wanted to ask her if Ablin was a German surname, but decided against it. She was talking, and I wanted to keep it that way.

"Bruin put up with Eddie for too long, if you ask me. He has finally been coming around to understanding his role in keeping Leavenworth on the map as the premier German destination in the United States. We all have a responsibility to uphold. If we let our standards slip, imagine what could happen."

"What do you mean, Bruin was coming around?" He hadn't sounded like he was coming around to anything involving April when I'd spoken to him earlier.

"You've seen his place. It does not fit the vision that we have for expansion."

"Expansion?"

"Yes, haven't you read the town council meeting notes? You should really come to the monthly meetings, you know. As a citizen, you have an obligation to."

"I've been pretty busy."

"That's no excuse, Sloan. I'll give you a pass this month, what with the scandal and all, but I expect to see you there next month." She stared at me, waiting to pounce if I protested. "We've outgrown the village square and need to push outside of downtown. Bruin's property is one of the first places visitors see when they arrive at the train station, and it simply won't do to have their initial impression of our town be a grungy hunting lodge."

"And Bruin is okay with changing the look of the brewery?"

"Well, I'm working on it, and I'm confident he's starting to see things my way. I think Eddie was a terrible influence on him." She shuddered as she spoke. "He wanted to make Leavenworth feel like Seattle or—worse—Portland. We can't let that happen. With him gone, Bruin is warming to the idea of making Bruin's Brewing more in line with Beervaria."

That wasn't what he had said to me, but I kept quiet. "You think that Eddie and Bruin were fighting over changing the design of the pub?"

"No, no, they were fighting about everything. Bruin didn't elaborate, but he was going to fire Eddie, and from what I heard, it sounded like soon."

"And you're sure this wasn't a rumor?"

"Positive." She reached for another cube of sugar. "He was already on the hunt for a new brewer. In fact, he e-mailed me and asked me to post something on the community pages board."

"Really?"

She looked smug. "Yes, Eddie's days at Bruin's Brewing were numbered."

"I wouldn't have guessed that," I said almost to myself.

April wrapped her hands around her teacup. "Now, about you. Are you sure you don't want to talk about property?"

"Thanks, April, but I need some time."

She opened a drawer on the desk and pressed her business card into my hand. "This has my cell in case you don't have it. Call me anytime. I'm here for you, and I will make sure you get a great deal."

I stood and tucked the card into my bag. "Will do. Thanks for the tea."

"Anytime," she called in her sugary voice. "You take care of yourself. I'll be keeping an eye on Mac for you."

Great. Just what I needed, April Ablin keeping an eye on my private life. I made my way to the reception desk and outside before she could stop me. What I really I needed was some fresh air. April's overpowering perfume had given me a headache. I also wanted to think about what she'd just revealed. If Bruin and Eddie were fighting, could Bruin have decided to end their battle with murder?

CHAPTER

TWENTY-SEVEN

I DIDN'T HAVE TIME TO dwell on my conversation with April or consider Bruin as a suspect, because when I pushed open the front door at Nitro, I was greeted with a line of a dozen or more people waiting for drinks at the bar.

Garrett towered over the line and gave me a shrug of surprise. I hurried to drop my things off in the office and tie an apron around my waist.

"When did you open?" I asked, squeezing behind the bar and reaching for a clean pint glass.

"Ten minutes ago. I was going to wait until four, but there was a line."

"That's a good sign," I said as I poured a frothy pint of Pucker Up and handed it across the bar to one of the waiting customers. "See? I told you that people like your beer. There's no other excuse this afternoon."

He furrowed his brow. "I don't know about that."

"What?"

He leaned closer and whispered, "Look to your left."

I stood on my tiptoes and peered around him. Chief Meyers was seated at the table in front of the window and appeared to be canvassing the pub. Her steely eyes caught mine, and she gave me a nod of acknowledgment. "What is she doing here?"

Garrett wiped foam from the side of a pint glass. "She didn't say. She showed up right after you left and said that she was here to observe."

"Observe? Observe what?"

"No idea." He held the full pint glass to the light. "This doesn't look cloudy to you, does it?"

The golden beer looked like glass. I could see Garrett's smoky brown eyes through it. "Not at all."

"Good. There's nothing worse than unfiltered beer in my opinion."

I agreed with him. Like anything else, craft brewing went through trends, and one of the current trends was to skip the filtration process. Filtering ensured that a beer would be bright and clean. Without filtering, beers ended up cloudy with chunks of yeast and hops that settled to the bottom of the glass. I didn't want my beers to be chunky and couldn't wrap my head around why brewers were so enamored with the trend.

Once we'd poured pints for the line, I went over to check in with Chief Meyers. Her bulky frame took up the entire stool. She was writing on a carbon paper form when I approached the high-top table. I didn't even know that anyone used carbon copies anymore.

"Sloan." She didn't look up from her notes.

"Can I get you anything? A beer?"

"I'm on duty."

"Right. A soda? Water?"

She shook her head and clicked her ballpoint pen. "I'm fine. Sit."

I slid out the stool opposite from her and sat down. I had to place one hand on my knee to stop it from bouncing. It's a nervous habit I picked up as a kid.

"Did you find anything on the hotel's surveillance camera?" I asked.

"They're sending it over. Haven't seen it yet." Her uniform was rumpled, and her short-cropped hair was greasy. I wondered if she had slept since Eddie had been killed. Things like this didn't happen in Leavenworth, and I knew that Chief Meyers saw it as her personal responsibility to bring Eddie's killer to justice.

"How's the rest of the investigation going?" I asked Chief Meyers.

She studied me for a moment. Her eyes were piercing and made me feel like I was in trouble. "I was about to ask you the same question."

"Me?"

"I told you to keep an eye open, Sloan, not interrogate everyone in town." She stared at me with her dark, steely eyes as if daring me to lie.

"I guess I've asked around a little. I feel responsible, given that I found Eddie's body and that he was killed here."

She watched someone behind me for a moment and then focused back on me. "I get it. But if our perp has killed once, there's good chance he or she could kill again if antagonized."

"Wait, are you saying that Eddie's death might have been random? Not personal?"

"I didn't say that. I'm warning you to watch your back."

My foot bounced on the cement floor. Had I unintentionally put myself—or worse, Alex—in danger by trying to make sure that Mac didn't get sent to jail permanently? "Do you have any leads?"

"None that I can share with you." She clicked the pen in a steady rhythm.

"But you're not suggesting that we have a serial killer on the loose in Leavenworth or anything?"

"I'm not suggesting or denying anything. Can't." She tapped her badge. "Duty." Her eyes wandered to the bar. "What else can you tell me about your business partner?" she asked, tilting her head to one side.

"Probably not more than what you've already heard from the gossip mill around here." I glanced behind me. Garrett's elbows were resting on the bar as he chatted with a guy holding a taster of beer. I bit back a smile when he caught my eye and held up a Dorito. "He came from Seattle, where he worked in technology, and decided to open Nitro after his aunt Tess died."

"Yep." Chief Meyers wrote something in the margin of the carbon paper.

I'd thought we were past her considering Garrett a suspect, too. Mac had finally been cleared, and now she was focusing her attention on my boss.

"What about this alleged break-in?"

"Alleged?"

"We only have Garrett's word."

"I saw the office. It was trashed. Someone definitely broke in."

"Or someone made it look like a break-in." She gave me a hard look. "It's not a coincidence, if you ask me, that Nitro had a break-in and a murder in the span of a few hours."

Chief Meyers gave me a knowing look and then shifted her body weight. I almost thought she might lose her balance and topple off the stool, but she caught herself at the last moment and tugged at her belt. "Civilians trust you, Sloan. Keep an eye out for me and report back any strange behavior immediately. I'm relying on you, and like I said, be careful. Be smart."

She didn't say anything more, but her tone made it clear that I was being dismissed. I returned to the bar wondering why she had turned her attention to Garrett. Was that why she was camped out here? Was she watching him for suspicious behavior or activity?

"Well, what did she say?" Garrett asked.

"Nothing," I lied. There was no need to worry him. I trusted my instincts, and my instincts told me that Garrett was no killer.

"You look worried, Sloan." He handed me the bowl. "Dorito?"

"No thanks."

He whistled. "Turning down Doritos. That's bad. She's watching me, isn't she?"

"No," I lied again. "I was thinking about our keg situation."

"Yeah, right. Good try." He smiled.

I hadn't gotten used to the fact that Garrett was astute at reading people, including me.

"Hey, she can camp out as long as she wants. I think it's pretty funny, actually. You know the joke is always cops hanging around doughnut shops, but here in Leavenworth, the cops hang out at my pub. I'm good with that." He sounded sincere, and nothing about his body language made him appear worried.

I hoped that my people skills weren't fading. If I was wrong about Garrett, that meant I could be working side by side with a killer.

CHAPTER

TWENTY-EIGHT

THE REST OF THE AFTERNOON and evening passed with ease. Chief Meyers stuck around longer than I'd expected, but finally left shortly before we closed up for the night. I took my notes on the menu home with me and told Garrett that I would have Alex design something for him to approve tomorrow. We had explained to everyone that our pub menu would be coming soon, and not only did I want to fulfill that promise, but both Garrett and I agreed that having the food situation sorted out was a top priority.

As usual, Alex was waiting up for me when I got home. He wore a pair of tapered soccer warm-ups and a hooded black sweatshirt.

"Hey, Mom," he called from the living room. "I'm in here."

He was stretched out on the couch with his iPad on his lap, his phone on the coffee table, and his video game playing on the big screen.

"It looks like you're going for the trifecta of digital devices," I commented, and kissed the top of his head.

Pausing his game, he sat up and turned off the iPad. "Me and some of the guys have a group game going. It's pretty cool. I'm air playing my game on the big screen and chatting on my phone."

"You've lost me," I said with a grin, and took a seat on the far end of the couch.

He rested his legs on my lap, and instinctively I began rubbing his feet. When he was little, we would curl up on the couch like this and watch *Wallace & Gromit* while I massaged his legs. He used to suffer from terrible growing pains in his preteen years. Massaging his legs was the only thing that relieved the tension.

"See, I'm playing this on my iPad but also on the TV." He showed me how he had connected his devices. I listened with genuine interest, but was secretly thrilled that he had a natural inclination toward technology. I was perfectly happy to let him take the lead on digitalizing our house.

"Speaking of technology," I said after he finished, "do you have any interest in a project? I'll pay you."

Alex had been saving up for a 3D printer. Mac had wanted to buy one for him for Christmas, but I stood my ground and insisted that such a big-ticket item should be earned. Alex was a great kid, who fortunately had a good work ethic, but Mac was too quick to give him spending money and an allowance. I wanted to instill the value of saving. Having grown up with nothing, I knew how important it was to be self-sufficient.

"How much does it pay?" Alex's eyes lit up.

"Don't get too excited. Not that much." I showed him my notes on the menu for Nitro. "We were hoping you could design a menu."

"Sure. That would be fun." He wiggled his feet free and sat up. "And since you're family, I'll cut you a deal. How about a hundred bucks?"

I raised one brow.

"What? That's a steal. Do you know how much design firms charge? Plus I'm saving up for the new FIFA game for my Xbox."

"I thought you were kidding. You're serious?" I dropped his legs and stood up.

"What's the big deal? Don't freak out, Mom."

I knew it wasn't entirely Alex's fault, but his sense of entitlement reminded me too much of Mac. I had worked for every penny I had ever earned, and as difficult as my early years were, they'd taught me resilience. I wanted that for Alex, too.

"How long is this going to take you?"

He shrugged. "I don't know. A few hours."

"Right. And how much is minimum wage?

"I don't know, Mom. Seriously, you are freaking." He fiddled with his controller.

"No, I'm trying to make a point. You're fifteen years old, and you think for a couple hours of work you deserve one hundred dollars?"

He threw his hands in the air. "Fine. I get it. How about twenty-five bucks?" He winked.

"That sounds more like it." I folded my arms across my chest.

He turned off his devices and took the notebook. "I'll go work on this now." Starting down the hallway, he stopped in midstride. "I forgot to tell you there was a black car parked in the driveway when I got home."

"Really?" My mind flashed to my conversation with Chief Meyers.

"Yeah, it's probably no big deal. They drove off when I got here, but it was kind of creepy. No one ever comes out here, you know?"

The hair on my arms stood at attention. Was someone watching us? Last night the motorcycle. Tonight a strange car in our driveway.

"I'm sure it's nothing, honey," I said to Alex, with a calm I didn't feel. "Do me a favor and turn on the alarm system when you're home by yourself. Just until everything settles down."

Mac had installed a security system when we bought the farmhouse that had never been used. At the time, I thought it was ridiculous. Mac knew that Leavenworth wasn't the kind of place where anyone had alarms. He'd agreed, but had it put in anyway. "You never know—maybe one day our hops will be so popular people will kill for them," he had teased. I figured the system had been another status symbol for Mac, but tonight I was thankful that he'd ignored me.

"Whatever you say, Mom." Alex saluted and continued to his bedroom.

"Don't stay up too late," I called after him.

My mind wouldn't rest. I couldn't stop thinking about Bruin and Eddie. Instead of heading for the bath or trying to sleep, I decided to play around with a couple of dessert options for Nitro. I was in the mood for chocolate and needed something to get my mind off Eddie's murder.

Chocolate stout brownies were a classic choice for pub fare. I happened to have a bottle of dark stout in the fridge and always kept a stock of imported German chocolate on hand for Mac. For the batter, I melted salted butter on the stove and slowly incorporated chunks of German chocolate. Once the chocolate had melted, I removed the mixture from the stove and cracked in eggs, and added flour, sugar, vanilla, and extra cocoa powder. Then I slowly poured in a quarter cup of the dark frothy beer. It should give the brownies an intense chocolate flavor with a hint of malt.

I preheated the oven and slid the pan of brownies in to bake. While I waited for them, I took a quick shower and pulled on my favorite pair of pajamas. The entire house smelled of chocolate, which enticed Alex from his room. "What smells so good, Mom?"

"Brownies. You want one?"

"I want the whole pan." He followed me to the kitchen and waited impatiently while I removed the pan from the oven and sliced into the brownies. I really should have let them cool for at least thirty minutes before cutting them, but I was with Alex—they smelled too good to wait.

"Careful, they're super hot," I cautioned as I handed him a gooey brownie on a plate.

He broke off a piece and blew on it. "Yum."

I followed suit and tasted my creation. There was no mistaking the chocolate flavor, and my palate picked up the subtle beer flavor, too.

"What do you really think?" I asked Alex.

"Awesome." He ate another chunk.

"You don't have to be nice."

"Mom, they are awesome. I'm serious—if you'd let me, I'd eat the whole pan."

"Not the whole pan this late, but you can have another." I smiled at his praise. The brownies tasted rich and chocolaty to me, but it was good to have Alex confirm that they had turned out okay. I have a serious chocolate problem, so I'm not necessarily the best judge. After I cut him another brownie, he returned to his room to work on the menu, and I decided to call it a night. I felt good to have the menu in the works and one of the dessert recipes nailed down. If only I could have felt the same way about Eddie's murder. Baking the brownies had been a happy, but brief, distraction. As I walked down the hallway and flipped off the lights, I couldn't help but wonder if I was missing something critical about the case. Had Chief Meyers been trying to hint at that?

Stop, Sloan; let it go and go to bed.

I tried to follow my own advice but found myself tossing and turning for most of the night. Having a murderer in our midst was unsettling, but being mixed up in the middle of it was alarming. The thought of a killer on the loose made sleep nearly impossible.

CHAPTER

TWENTY-NINE

AFTER A RESTLESS NIGHT, I finally gave up the battle at five thirty and stumbled down the hall to make a pot of coffee. Alex was crashed in his room. I smiled at the sight of him curled up in the fetal position with a contented look on his face. He'd slept in the same position since he was an infant. Some things never changed.

The coffee took forever to brew. Or maybe it was that I was barely functional after tossing and turning all night. I guzzled two cups in a matter of a few minutes. It wasn't until I started in on my third cup that everything seemed to come into focus. It was way too early to go into work, and I had to take Alex to school. I might as well make use of the time, so I pulled out two of my favorite dessert cookbooks and flipped through the pages for inspiration.

I wanted both of the dessert options to include beer. We were running a brewery, and it made sense to feature our beer in as many ways as we could. The beer cupcakes for opening night had been a hit, but the more I thought about it the more I was worried about how much time they would take to bake and frost each day and how they would hold up. No one likes a stale, dry cupcake. Cupcakes are really made to be consumed immediately, and since I wasn't sure what the demand for desserts was going to be, I didn't want to make something that couldn't keep. The stout brownies would do well for a few days as long as I kept them in an airtight container.

After much debate, and looking at at least thirty different recipes, I finally decided on a citrus-infused shortbread. I would use the same ingredients I had in the cupcakes but make a shortbread instead. It should hold up well, and we could serve it with a scoop of vanilla or lemon ice cream.

I started by creaming together butter and sugar in the mixer. Then I added vanilla, grated lemon and orange rind, and a couple of healthy glugs of Pucker Up. The citrus scent perked up my senses along with my third cup of rich coffee. I squeezed fresh lemon and orange juice into the batter and then sifted in the dry ingredients. The batter was thick, with a gorgeous lemon yellow color. I spread it into a glass baking pan and placed it in the oven.

When Alex woke up an hour and a half later, I had warm slices of shortbread to share with him. He devoured the cookies and helped himself to a brownie.

"Breakfast brownie—it's a thing, right?" He grinned.

"Where do you put it?" I waved my hand over his lanky frame. He shrugged and headed to the shower. While Alex got his stuff ready for school, I sliced the remaining brownies and shortbread and packed them in a Tupperware to bring to Garrett. Obviously, he would have the last word when it came to dessert.

On our way to the car, Alex handed me a mock-up of the menu he had created. He'd done a great job. The design was clean and simple but perfectly captured Nitro's chemistry lab vibe. Alex had used the elements as his inspiration and spelled out *Be (beryllium) Er (erbium)* on a chart with the tagline *Beer, the essential element*. I knew that Garrett would love it and could already see Alex's design on T-shirts and growlers.

"This is perfect," I said, studying the sketch.

"You like it?"

"I love it." I tucked it into my bag. "I'll have Garrett take a look at it today and, as soon as we finalize the menu, have you add in the desserts and prices."

"Cool." His cheeks warmed slightly, but he blew off my compliment and hopped into the passenger seat.

He clicked on the radio and hummed along to a song I didn't recognize. We drove in contented silence. As I turned onto the highway, the sound of a car revving its engine blasted behind us. Alex shouted and pointed to the car that sped by us, leaving a trail of smoke and skid marks on the road. "That's it! That's the car that was in our driveway last night."

My heart raced. We were being followed? I didn't recognize the car. It was black with tinted black windows and a personalized license plate that I couldn't make out. I tried to remember every detail I could before it disappeared. It had to have been going close to ninety, and the speed limit on the highway was only fifty-five.

Alex's eyes were wide. I could tell that he was nervous, so

I did my best to keep my composure. "It's probably some dude with a big ego," I said, reaching over and patting his knee.

"Mom, I'm sure that was the car at our house last night."

"I believe you." I kept my tone light. "But I'm sure it's nothing."

He shook his head. "Mom, this could be serious, you know?"

I took my eyes off the road for a second and gave him a reassuring look. "I know, and I promise I'll talk to Chief Meyers about it today, but I don't want you to worry. I'm sure there's a logical explanation."

"Maybe Dad should move back home for a while," he said, turning his head and staring out the window. "You know, to have a man in the house."

"Alex, look at me. It's fine. We're fine. I'm a capable adult, and we don't need your dad to move back in. I'll take care of it, okay?"

"Okay." He didn't sound convinced, and I prayed that he wouldn't talk to Mac about this. Knowing Mac, he would be at my door in a matter of seconds.

When we arrived at school, I repeated the sentiment as Alex jumped out of the car and headed into the building. Was he right? Did we need someone to protect us? Who was the mysterious driver in the black car? I didn't recognize it from town, but then again, I didn't spend a lot of time looking at cars. Why would someone come to the house? And had they really been following us this morning, or was it a random coincidence? There weren't that many roads to town. It was completely possible that the driver of the black car had gotten lost last night and pulled into our driveway to turn around. Maybe they were staying nearby and we happened to hit the highway at the same time.

Even as I thought about it, that sounded much less plausible than I wanted it to be. What were the odds that the same car had appeared at our house and then sped past us on the highway less than twenty-four hours later? But then, why would someone be following me?

I let out a long sigh and continued on to Nitro. My promise to Alex wasn't lip service; I planned to find Chief Meyers later this morning and let her know about being followed. Maybe she was already familiar with the car. I could ask around town, too. There weren't very many cars with tinted windows in Leavenworth. Someone must know who the black sedan belonged to.

You're probably worrying over nothing, I told myself as I pulled into a space in front of Nitro, grabbed the Tupperware of desserts, and headed inside. To my surprise, Garrett was already awake and brewing. He wore black rubber boots and had his chemistry goggles covering the top half of his face.

"Morning," I called over the hum of grains being fed into the mash tun.

He flinched at the sound of my voice. "Oh, it's you."

"You're up early."

Shutting off the grain feeder, Garrett tugged off his goggles and offered me a hand. "Do you need help with any of that?"

I gave him the Tupperware. "Actually these are for you."

He peeled open the lid and grinned. "Breakfast."

"You sound like my son." I shook my head. "Dessert."

"What's the difference?" Garrett reached in and took out a brownie. "When I would come visit Aunt Tess, she always served me dessert for breakfast. You must be channeling her spirit." He bit into the brownie and gave a nod to the heavens.

"I couldn't sleep last night so I decided to test out a couple of dessert options."

"This. Definitely this," Garrett said with a mouthful of brownie. Then he removed a slice of the citrus shortbread. After he'd tasted it he nodded enthusiastically. "And this, too."

"It's just a first try—" I started to say.

He held out his palm. "Nope. Consider dessert done."

"If you're sure?"

Devouring another slice of shortbread, he gave me a thumbs-up. "I'm sure."

"Random question, but you don't happen to have a black sedan, do you?"

"No. Why?"

"I don't know. I'm sure it's nothing, but I've seen a black sedan around town."

"Around town?"

"Alex thought he saw it at our house last night and then it was on the highway this morning. It's probably nothing. I'm probably imagining things."

Garrett frowned. "Sloan, you don't strike me as the type of woman who imagines things."

What did he mean by that? My heart thumped in response to his intense stare. The guy had a way of throwing me off-center. "I'm not usually, but I think everyone in town is on high alert right now."

"You should talk to the police chief."

"Now you really sound like my son."

"That's because you have a smart kid." He held up the Tupperware. "Are these for me?"

"Sure. Knock yourself out." I patted my bag. "I have menus for you to look at, too."

He followed me to the office, eating another brownie as he walked. "You don't mess around, do you?"

I placed my bag on the far chair, found Alex's mock-up menu, and handed it to Garrett. "What do you mean?"

"This." He waved the menu. "All of it. Dessert, menu, guest taps. Is there anything you can't do?"

Laughing, I waved his kind words away. "Where do you want me to start? The list of things I'm not good at is pretty lengthy."

"Right." He looked over the menu. "This is perfect. I guess Alex takes after you."

"He's an amazing kid. I wish I could take credit, but I swear he was born that way." Had I been too hard on him last night? I felt a wave of regret for getting on his case about money, but Mac wasn't exactly the best role model when it came to money management.

"Would it kill you to say thanks?" Garrett had removed his goggles and tossed them on the desk.

"What?"

He shook his head. "Never mind."

I started to apologize. I knew he was right. Accepting praise had always been difficult for me, but before I could say anything more, the sound of a voice in the front made us both turn around.

"Hello, is anyone here?" a man's voice called.

Garrett looked at me. I shrugged as we both headed for the front.

Van was standing near the front door holding a huge box in his arms. I knew without looking that the box contained hops; their smell permeated the space. "Good, someone is here. I took a chance. I know it's early, but I have to be over at Bruin's this morning, so I thought I would stop by and drop off your order, and get that contract."

"Did we order more hops?" Garrett asked.

Van shifted the box in his arms. "I got a call for double your initial order. In fact, I've got three more boxes in the truck."

"You got a call?" Garrett shot me a puzzled look. "Did you order more hops?"

I shook my head. "No."

Van's expression was equally dumbfounded. "I don't know, but I got a call from someone at Nitro yesterday who said that you needed double the order on my hybrid line. I hand-picked these this morning so they would be fresh."

"It's just the two of us," Garrett said, tousling his hair. "Who called you?"

Van shrugged. "I don't know, I assumed it was you. A guy who said he was from Nitro."

"Well, it wasn't me."

"So you don't want these?" Van scowled. "They are fresh and, to be honest, they're going fast, so if I were you, I would get them while you can. These suckers aren't going to stick around for long."

I could tell that Garrett was still puzzling through who

would have called to order hops for us. Van raised his brows. "Hello?"

Garrett cleared his throat and gave his body a little shake. "Huh, uh, yeah, I guess I'll take them. I have to replace an entire batch anyway."

Van set the box on a table and pointed behind him. "I'll grab the rest of the boxes."

After he left, Garrett turned to me. "You didn't order the hops?"

"No. Why would I?"

He sighed. "Do you get the feeling that someone isn't happy to have Nitro on the beer scene?"

I hadn't, but he did kind of have a point. First the missing recipe, then Eddie's murder and the ruined beer, and now someone ordering expensive hops. "You think so?"

He scratched his head. "Something's up. That's all I know." He glanced out the window where Van was stacking two boxes of hops. "Can you finish with him? I want to go check something."

"Sure," I agreed, watching his shoulders slump slightly as he walked back toward the office. Could Garrett have been right? Was someone trying to sabotage him? Who wouldn't want him to succeed? Bruin? Or worse . . . Mac? What if this was Mac's doing?

CHAPTER

THIRTY

ONCE VAN HAD UNLOADED THE boxes of hops, he handed me a dusty invoice. "Is something going on with Garrett?"

"Why?"

"Whoever called me sounded exactly like him."

"You're sure?"

"Positive."

I didn't say anything about Garrett's suspicion that someone was trying to sabotage him, but I also wondered why Van was convinced that Garrett had been the person who called him yesterday. Garrett didn't have a particularly distinct voice, and Van didn't know him that well. How could he be so sure?

To Van, I asked, "Are you delivering to Bruin next?"

He stuffed his hands in the front pockets of his well-worn jeans. "Sort of. I've got some stuff to deliver, but he wants to talk to me." He leaned to one side and peered over my left shoulder. "I don't know if you've heard or not, but Bruin's been on the hunt for a new brewer for a while."

"Really?" I pretended this was news to me.

"Yeah. Things were tense with him and Eddie."

"They were? I thought they had a good thing going over at the brewery. It's been around forever and always seems to be busy."

Van picked up a hop and ran it between his hands. "The pub is doing great, but those two hated each other. I'm surprised you didn't know that. They almost came to blows here."

I thought back to opening night. Had I interpreted Bruin and Eddie's interaction the wrong way? I'd thought that Bruin had been trying to calm Eddie down, and while Eddie may have been irritated that Bruin was drunk, I didn't remember them almost coming to blows, in Van's words.

He continued. "Eddie was going rogue, and Bruin was tired of having to reel him back in. You know the recipes at Bruin's Brewing are Bruin's, not Eddie's."

"Really?" I'd always been under the impression that Bruin was the cash behind the pub and that Eddie was responsible for the beer.

"Yeah. Bruin is an old home brewer like your boss. The name says it all. He didn't need Eddie, but brewing is a young man's game. You know how physically exhausting it can be. He's been looking to hire someone to take over."

Suddenly, I realized what he was hinting at. "You mean you? You want to brew?"

"Don't look so surprised. I brew."

"But what about the hops and the farm?"

"I'll still do that, too, but I told Bruin I was hoping to have a chance to at least throw my hat in the ring. No one ever thinks of the hop guy as being able to brew, but if I didn't know how to brew, I couldn't produce such good hops, you know?"

"Of course." I nodded, but I was struck by Van's frankness. I was also surprised that he was interested in brewing, but I didn't say that to him, since it sounded like that was everyone's take.

"I don't know if I really have a shot, but I'm glad Bruin is at least going to give me a chance to show him what I can do."

"So this is an interview this morning?"

"I guess. You know Bruin. He's pretty chill." He looked at his tattered jeans and mud-caked boots. "It's not like a suit-and-tie kind of interview or anything, but I'm bringing him a few bottles of my home brew, and he told me to be ready to walk through the brewery so that he can make sure I know what all the equipment is."

"How's the home brewing going?"

He chucked the hop on the floor and perked up. "You want to try it? I've got a case in the truck. I figured it was better to bring extra."

"Sure, if you have enough, I'd love to try it."

Without a moment of pause, he ran out to his truck and returned with four bottles of home brew. Each had a plain white label with the beer name written by hand. Van reminded me of Alex when he used to come home from elementary school with an art project for me. He thrust the bottles at me and waited with an expectant look.

"You want me to taste this now?"

"Yeah, go for it. Let me know what you think. I've heard that you're the best brewer in town."

It was pretty early in the morning to sample beer, but I didn't want to let Van down. He seemed strangely anxious for my input, so I walked to the bar and cracked each beer open. Then I poured an inch of Van's creations into four tasters.

Starting with the lightest beer, I picked up the first taster. According to Van's handwritten label, this was his lager. I held it to the light. The beer was cloudy, impossible to see through, and had bits of yeast floating in it. This wasn't a good sign. Van either needed to improve his filtration process or was intentionally going for an unfiltered beer.

I didn't want to offend him, so chose my words carefully. "Tell me about the lager," I said, swirling the beer in the taster. "How did you brew it? Is it fresh hopped? And tell me about the filtration process."

Van launched into an explanation of his process while I smelled the beer. There was a slight bitter scent, but I hoped that was due to the type of hop he had used. He explained that this was a single-hop lager and he'd done two rounds of filtration. Uh-oh. That definitely didn't bode well. Taste is subjective when it comes to beer, but a well-brewed pint should never give off an unpleasant odor. When I gave brewery tours at Der Keller I loved getting to educate beer fans on how and why a beer can go bad.

Van's description of the brewing processes sounded like he was quoting directly from *The Beginner's Guide to Brewing*. I took a taste. The lager lacked flavor and had a terribly bitter finish. Some bitterness was important in brewing a perfect pint, but Van's lager was excessively bitter and hit the back of my palate. It also had a hint of a butterscotch, which I knew was diacetyl flavor resulting from using a bad yeast or a problem with the fermentation process. I swallowed and plastered on a smile. "Very interesting." That wasn't a lie, the beer was interesting, but it certainly wasn't good. If this was the beer he planned to have Bruin taste, I knew that it would be back to the hop farm for Van.

"What hops did you use in this?"

Van's eyes darted to Garrett's beer taps. "My hops. You like it? It's good stuff, isn't it? That's my hybrid batch." He pointed to the box sitting on the table. "If it's as good as I'm thinking it is, maybe I shouldn't sell this strand of hops and keep it proprietary, you know?"

He wasn't exactly asking me, so I gave him a slight nod and moved on to the next taster. Like the lager, the beer had some serious filtration issues, but had a nice almost-copper color. I was surprised that the label listed this beer as an IPA; it looked more like a red to me.

Van drummed his dirt-caked nails on the bar. "You're making me nervous. How is it?"

Holding the murky amber beer to the light, I acknowledged his anxiety. "It's part of a tasting. If you're going to brew professionally, you'll have to get used to it—and remember, taste is subjective. What one person loves someone else may hate."

"You hate it?" His lip curled.

"No, I haven't even tried it yet." I tasted the beer and immediately picked up a husky astringent flavor. Another bad sign. The astringent taste most likely came from overboiling the grains.

When brewing, it's critical to start with low heat and slowly bring the water to a rolling boil. One of the most common mistakes that new brewers make is dumping grains straight into a scalding pot of water, which strips their flavor and leaves an unpleasant aftertaste.

Having Van stare me down while I sampled his beer was unnerving, especially because I didn't get the sense that he would welcome constructive feedback.

"This is an IPA?" I asked.

He nodded and reached for the glass. "What do you think of the color? I went for a half red, half IPA. I'm not sure what to call it, but I think this one is my favorite."

I didn't want to crush his enthusiasm, but someone really needed to bring him back to earth. There are two types of home brewers in the world: those who constantly educate themselves and seek feedback to improve their brewing process and quality, and home brewers like Van, who think because they've taken one workshop or brewed one batch of beer, they are going to hit it big without doing any of the work required to improve their craft.

Again I considered how to frame my question. "How long did you steep the grains?"

Scratching his head as if I had asked him to solve a math equation, he squinted at the beer. "Uh. The standard amount of time."

I wanted to tell him there wasn't a standard. Steeping times depended on the type and style of beer.

"How long have you been brewing?" I asked, picking up the third taster of beer.

"A long time. At least six months. I brewed with a buddy for a while, but we parted ways. It was messed up. He wanted to take the brewing equipment that I bought. That stuff isn't cheap."

"No, it's not."

"That's a nut brown ale." He twisted the bottle around. "I used real hazelnuts."

I could tell because there was nut and grain residue at the bottom of the tasting glass. It reminded me of sludge. This beer had a decent malty profile, but was lacking body and any depth. I didn't pick up any nut undertones, but I did get a chunk of a nut in my mouth. Yuck. I regretted offering to taste Van's beer, and knew without a doubt that there was no chance that Bruin would hire him based on what he'd produced so far. He needed a mentor and many more brew hours under his belt before he would be ready to brew on the scale of Bruin's setup.

"It's good, isn't it?"

I put down the nearly untouched taster of the nut brown ale. Professional brewers rarely boasted about their own product.

The last beer was a dark stout. It was thick and the color of night. I smelled the taster and picked up a smoky, almost plastic scent. The harsh smell made me want to dump the taster in the sink, but I took a sip. The beer was almost undrinkable due to intense phenolic flavor. It tasted medicinal.

"Well?" Van looked at me expectantly.

"Have you tasted this one?"

He nodded. "It's really good, right?"

"I think it's contaminated."

His jaw tightened. "What?"

I handed him the taster. "Smell it. What do you smell?"

"A campfire?"

"Right. That burning smoky, clove-like smell is called phenolic flavor, which develops when a beer has been contaminated."

"How would it get contaminated?" Van sounded angry.

"Bacteria can get in many ways—through a leaky valve, if your equipment hasn't been sanitized properly, or even from using tap water."

"Tap water?"

I nodded. "If there's too much chlorine in the water, it can cause phenolic flavors."

His eyes widened.

"I wouldn't recommend serving this beer."

"Really?"

"No one wants to drink contaminated beer."

"But what did you think of the flavor?"

"To be honest, I couldn't taste anything over the phenolic flavor."

He flinched, but recovered quickly. "There's coffee in that one. You don't taste it?"

I couldn't tell if he was asking because he actually wanted to know or if his ego was really that inflated. But before I could craft my response, he looked at the clock and bolted for the front door.

"I'm late. Thanks for tasting my beer. Tell Garrett I need

that contract and his check—like, yesterday." With that, he took off.

Garrett appeared behind me as the door banged shut.

"How long have you been standing there?" I asked.

"Long enough." He made a face and pointed at the tasters. "Phenolic flavors, contamination, and cloudy beer. Sounds like you've had a mouthful."

I stuck out my tongue. "That was seriously some of the worst beer I've ever tasted."

"He doesn't seem to think so."

"I know. I tried to insert some constructive feedback, but I don't think he heard it. I think Alex could brew a better beer."

"No, he only heard what he wanted to hear." Garrett picked up the nut brown ale and scowled. "This looks like he scooped sand from the ocean into the bottom of the glass."

Despite the fact that I don't typically drink this early, I poured myself a taster of our Pucker Up and drank it in one shot.

"Whoa, that must have been a rough tasting." Garrett chuckled. "Knocking them down, huh?"

"I had to get that terrible taste out of my mouth." My tongue was dry. "Did you hear? He wants a signed contract and a check today."

"That's what I heard, but I'm not sure that's going to happen."

"Did you hear back from your friend in Seattle?" I swallowed twice to get the taste of Van's beer out of my mouth.

"I did." Garrett didn't elaborate; instead he dumped the nut brown ale in the sink.

Did Garrett not want me involved in making decisions for Nitro? His tendency to be less than forthcoming when I asked questions was unnerving.

"Van is on his way to an interview with that beer," I said, changing the subject.

Garrett scowled. "Oh, that's not going to go well for him."

"No."

"Where is he interviewing?"

"With Bruin."

"Bruin?" A look flashed across Garrett's face that I couldn't read. "Are you sure?"

"Yeah, why?"

He shook his head. "No reason. I guess I didn't think that Bruin would hire someone so fast."

Garrett wasn't telling me something. Was he worried that Van would give his hop contract to Bruin? Or was it something else?

CHAPTER

THIRTY-ONE

GARRETT AND I SPENT THE remainder of the morning working in the brewery. It felt good to get back in the familiar rhythm of brewing, and despite the fact that we were still getting to know one another, we easily settled into a seamless routine.

"Do you have any music preference?" Garrett asked when we started the first batch of Pucker Up. He held his smartphone in one hand and some kind of futuristic speaker in the other.

"I'm up for anything."

"Awesome." He plugged his phone into the speaker, which pulsated with neon blue, yellow, and green, and blasted Nirvana. That made sense, given his age and Seattle roots. The grunge music scene had started there in the nineties. I couldn't imagine Garrett banging his head to "Smells Like Teen Spirit" in a mosh pit, but stranger things had happened, I supposed.

We had decided to brew a batch of each beer together. That way I could watch Garrett's process from start to finish. Not only would brewing together ensure that I had all the steps down, but Garrett (unlike Van) had specifically asked me to give him feedback and offer any input or suggestions that I had along the way.

The brewery quickly became a sensory delight—my nostrils flared happily with the scent of hot grains and boiling hops. Steam opened my pores and revitalized my senses. The familiar process of brewing offered me a momentary reprieve from Eddie's murder and centered me in the experience. Garrett was a great partner. He knew when to hand me a paddle to stir the grains and gave me space to experiment with my own take on the beer. The morning blew by, and before I knew it, we had two batches of beer ready to add to the fermenters, and growling stomachs.

"What do you say, time for a lunch break?" Garrett asked, wiping his hands on a dish towel hanging over his shoulder.

"Sounds great. Suddenly I'm starving."

"The beer will do it to you."

I laughed and was about to head to the office to grab some cash. Since I'd spent my early morning baking the citrus shortbread, I had forgotten to pack a lunch. I could run down the street to the German deli and grab a sandwich or splurge for a bratwurst.

"Where are you heading?" Garrett asked.

"Lunch. I'm going to run down to the German deli. Do you want anything?"

"I was hoping to take you out to lunch. My treat, as a small token of my thanks."

"You don't have to do that," I protested.

"I didn't say I *had* to. I want to." He looked down at his boots. "Give me a minute to change into shoes and then we can go."

It was silly, but my stomach fluttered at the thought of having lunch with Garrett. I knew it was a business lunch, but I couldn't help feeling like it was a date. That was probably because I'd never had lunch with other men while Mac and I were together—not counting Hans, of course.

Garrett returned a few minutes later wearing an entirely new outfit—a clean pair of jeans, a beer T-shirt, and flip-flops. The man was a conundrum. I didn't peg him as a flip-flop kind of guy. I also felt self-conscious about my appearance. My jeans were splattered with water from the brewing process, and I was sure that my hair must be a mess from the steam and sweat. My hair has a slight natural wave, and it has a tendency to curl and frizz with heat and the water vapors from brewing. *Nice first impression for your not-really-a-date lunch, Sloan,* I said to myself as I followed Garrett outside.

"It's gorgeous, so I thought we could take advantage of the sun and eat outside on the patio," Garrett said, pointing to The Carriage House, Leavenworth's most expensive restaurant. It had an outdoor patio complete with humungous hanging baskets, potted trees with twinkle lights, and a gas fireplace. Part of the charm of The Carriage House was that they featured horse-drawn carriage rides during each festival and for special occasions.

Now I really felt self-conscious about how I looked. I freed my hair from its ponytail and tried to smooth it down. "We don't have to go anywhere fancy," I said. "I'm happy with a

German sausage with a huge pickle on the side." In addition to being worried about how I looked, I knew that cash was tight for Garrett. I didn't want him to feel like he had to spend extra money on me. He might be thankful for my help, but I was equally thankful for the job.

"That's not lunch. That's a glorified food cart." He continued on toward The Carriage House. "When I lived in Seattle, I ate at food carts or the Market every day. Lunch and dinner."

"Dinner, too?" I asked, following after him. "Did you work that late?"

"Always. Working in a cube crushes your soul. I don't care if I go broke; it's worth saving my sanity."

I'd never worked anywhere but restaurants and pubs, so it was hard to imagine what Garrett's office life must have been like when he was in Seattle. He wasn't exactly forthcoming about his past. I studied his comfortable stride as we walked toward the restaurant. He didn't appear tense, but I knew all too well that outward appearances could be deceiving.

We arrived at the restaurant, and he held the front door open for me. A waiter dressed in a crisp white shirt and black slacks led us to an outdoor table. He slid out my chair and waited at rigid attention for me to sit. Once he'd poured water in our glasses and reviewed the daily specials, he returned inside.

Garrett winked. "See, classy, right?"

I laughed. "Classy."

Bees hummed in the hanging baskets surrounding the patio. I couldn't blame them; the scent of jasmine was intoxicating. No wonder Garrett had given up his Seattle job for this. Even with the distraction of Eddie's murder and everything with Mac and me, it was hard to argue that there was any place more relaxing or idyllic than Leavenworth in the late summer. From this vantage point, the town square looked like something out of a movie set. The hills surrounding us were ablaze with color. I breathed it in and smiled.

"Kidding aside, I can't thank you enough, Sloan. You've been a godsend." There was something about the intensity of his stare that made me feel wobbly.

"You said that already, and there's no need to thank me." I fiddled with my hair.

He sighed. "But there is. My job was killing me. A slow death by Excel spreadsheets. I didn't know what I was getting into by coming here, but I knew I had to do something. I didn't want to wake up one day and be fifty and have spent my best years stuck in a cube, you know?"

I nodded in agreement. While I didn't know how it felt to be stuck in a cubicle, I knew how it felt to be stuck. I was coming to realize that maybe I had stayed with Mac because it was the easy thing to do, not because of love. I wished that I had Garrett's ability to pack up his life and start fresh, regardless of the risk. If I hadn't caught Mac cheating, would I have stayed forever?

"I get that I have a long way to go to prove myself around here, but without you, I might have had to close the doors before they even opened."

"That's an exaggeration, to say the least," I said, taking a drink of my ice water.

Garrett shook his head dramatically. "I'm serious. I can't believe I never thought about things like food. I've been so wrapped up in my beer. I thought I was smarter than that."

"You've had a lot to think about. Starting up a pub is no small feat. That's why so many home brewers never make the switch. Don't beat yourself up."

He started to reply, but our waiter returned with a loaf of steaming hot French bread and two ramekins of salted butter. "Something to drink?"

Garrett looked to me.

"What do you have on draft?"

The waiter listed off four Der Keller beers, two of Bruin's beers, and a special tap they just got on from Seattle.

"Try that, Sloan," Garrett said. "He's a buddy of mine."

"Sounds good to me," I said to the waiter.

"Two CDAs," he confirmed. "And something for lunch?"

I ordered a summer spinach salad with shredded chicken, hard-boiled eggs, fresh strawberries, and candied pecans, tossed with a strawberry balsamic dressing. Suddenly, I was famished. Garrett ordered a blackened salmon salad. I chided myself for constantly comparing him to Mac, but I couldn't help it. Mac would never order a salad and usually teased me about my affinity for fresh greens. He always ordered greasy burgers or heavy steaks. Bruin's meat-inspired menu was definitely more Mac's style.

Stop, Sloan, I told myself as the waiter left to get our beers. There was something about Garrett that I couldn't define. I wanted to blame my fluttery stomach on the fact that I was hungry, but I knew it was also due to Garrett's intense gaze.

We chatted easily about the pub and our new menu until our beers arrived. Garrett's friend was definitely talented. We geeked out over how pristine the Cascadian dark ale was. Despite its nearly black color, we could see through it, and there wasn't a trace of sediment in the glass. It was the exact opposite of Van's beers.

"I can see the other side of town," Garrett said as he peered through his glass.

I smelled the beer and swished a taste on my tongue. It tasted equally clean. "This is awesome."

"Yeah." Garrett nodded enthusiastically as he drank. "I told you."

I was about to change the subject and ask him his thoughts about beers for Oktoberfest when his face turned serious.

He took another drink of his beer and placed it on the table. Then he leaned forward and frowned. "Look, Sloan, there's something I think you should know. I've been debating about telling you, but I think you need to know."

I gulped. "Okay." What else could be wrong? I braced myself for whatever Garrett had to say.

"It's about your husband."

"Mac?" I clutched my pint glass to keep my hands from shaking.

He glanced up at one of the hanging baskets. I got the sense that he was trying to choose his words carefully. "This could be talk. You know how it is with brewers. It's a brotherhood—in the best and worst sense. We want to support each other, but it's also a competition, you know?"

I almost said something about it being a sisterhood, too,

but I let it go because I didn't trust myself to speak. Had Mac been cheating on me with other women, too? What did Garrett know?

"I'm the new guy in town, so I know everyone is trying to establish their turf and figure out where I fit in." He brushed away a bee that had flown close to his beer. "You can take this information with a grain of salt, okay, but I think you should know what the other brewers are saying. Or maybe you already know, and it's gossip."

My heart was thumping. What was Garrett getting at?

Garrett studied my face before he continued. I had no idea if my nerves were betraying me. I tried to keep my expression neutral, but I had such a tight grip on my pint glass that I was worried I might crush it and cut open my hand.

"Like I said, this could be a rumor, but a couple of guys have said that Der Keller isn't doing well."

"What?" I furrowed my brow and released my grip on the glass. I thought back to my conversation with Otto. He had mentioned that things were tight.

Garrett nodded. "They're saying that Mac made bad investments and overextended himself. I heard they took a huge loss."

I felt a slight sense of relief that the gossip Garrett had heard wasn't about me, but I was perplexed by this news. Ursula and Otto had been very lean when it came to unnecessary spending. They were good to their employees and maintained the restaurant and brewing operation, but they had never been extravagant spenders. Mac, on the other hand, liked everything flashy. Maybe it was the result of growing up with immigrant parents who had skimped and saved every penny to make a fresh start here. One of our recurring arguments had centered on Mac's spending, but I couldn't imagine it affecting Der Keller. Mac didn't have that much control . . . unless something had changed that I didn't know about.

"They're even saying that Der Keller might have to declare bankruptcy."

"What?" I couldn't help yelping. "Who? Who's saying that?"

"Everyone. Bruin, Van, even Eddie mentioned it to me before he died. I know I should have said something to you earlier, but I knew that things were . . ." He trailed off for a moment. "Things were tense with you and Mac, and I didn't want to make it worse."

"That doesn't make any sense," I protested. "Otto and Ursula hold the majority of the shares in the company. Mac and Hans both have smaller stakes. The long-term plan has always been that when they retire, they'll hand over their shares, but as far as I know, there hasn't been any talk of them retiring in the near future."

Garrett shrugged and picked up his beer. "I don't know. You're right. No one has said anything about them retiring. The only thing that I've heard is that Mac is in over his head and has been trying to sell off some of his shares."

"What?" I was incredulous. "He can't do that. He can't sell any shares without Otto and Ursula's permission."

"I don't know. I'm just telling you what I've heard."

"Sorry." I rubbed my temples and tried to regain my composure. What was Mac up to? "And you've heard this from multiple sources."

Garrett scowled and nodded. "I'm afraid so." He waved a bee from his face. Down below us, an accordion player tested his instrument. The sound was so familiar in Leavenworth that I barely noticed, but Garrett sat up to get a better glimpse at where the music was coming from.

I reached for my beer and took a big swig. "But that doesn't make sense. Why would Mac offer you cash for your recipe if he didn't have any cash?"

"That's something I wondered about, too. Unless it was a ploy. Maybe he wanted me to think that he was swimming in cash, and then was going to offer me shares?"

It was a possibility and sounded slimy enough to be something that Mac might try. I had questioned why Mac had offered to pay Garrett for his recipe. That was totally out of character. At the time I'd thought it was because of me, and that Mac was trying to make a point, but now I wondered if I'd been wrong. Maybe Garrett was on to something.

I wasn't surprised to hear a rumor that Mac had invested poorly. That was completely in character. He was always looking for ways to flaunt his success and looking for the next big trend in the beer industry, but what I couldn't understand was Ursula and Otto's involvement. I had suspected that part of the reason they kept their purse strings so tight was because they recognized Mac's lack of self-control. I couldn't believe that they would have handed power or financial control of Der Keller over to Mac, but maybe I was wrong.

Our food arrived at that moment. We ate in silence. My salad was a colorful melody of succulent strawberries and smoky roasted chicken. The sweet berry balsamic blended the flavors beautifully, but I barely tasted it. I was consumed completely by the horrible thought of Der Keller being in trouble. Cheating on me was one thing, but if Mac had done anything to put his parents—the only real parents I'd ever known—in financial risk, I might kill him.

CHAPTER

THIRTY-TWO

AS SOON AS GARRETT AND I finished our salads, I jumped to my feet. "Listen, I need to go talk to Hans right now," I said to Garrett.

He nodded. "I get it."

"Thanks for lunch," I said before I headed for the door.

"I'm sure it's nothing, Sloan." He offered me a half wave as I walked away.

I hoped he was right, but I had a bad feeling it was something—something big. What would Ursula and Otto do if they had to declare bankruptcy? They were too old to start over, and they had poured everything they had into making Der Keller a success.

Heat burned in my cheeks as I power walked to Hans's workshop. I knew that I'd been out of the loop with the Krause family for a few weeks, but I couldn't believe that Otto and Ursula would have given Mac control of the brewery. I had to talk to Hans.

Hans had made it clear many years ago that he wasn't interested in running the brewery. His passion was working with his hands. He had taken over an old pottery studio and turned it into his workshop. The small space smelled of cut wood, and the floor was always coated in sawdust. Hans was content to craft a custom picnic table or build intricate lattices for Der Keller's patio hops. He was handy and would often be called in to fix brewery equipment. Once when the night crew accidentally ran the forklift into a wall, Hans showed up at midnight to repair the Sheetrock. He gladly offered his services in exchange for his stock in the company, but that was the extent of his involvement, and I knew there was no way that had changed. I would start with him first.

The sound of his table saw running greeted me when I pushed open the door to his wood workshop. As always, a cloud of sawdust enveloped me as I stepped inside. I coughed and brushed the grainy particles floating in the air away from my face.

"Hans!" I shouted over the sound of the table saw.

He didn't respond. His safety glasses were focused on the two-by-four he was feeding through the saw.

I yelled again and waved. "Hans!"

The movement must have caught his eye because he shut off the saw and brushed sawdust from his face. He removed his safety glasses and walked over to me. "Sloan, what are you doing here?"

Without giving him a chance to breathe, I launched into the speech that I'd practiced in my head on the walk over. "Your brother. Do you know what he's done? Have you heard the rumors going around?"

"Slow down, slow down." Hans tucked his safety glasses into his overalls and gave me a concerned look. "What's going on?"

"Mac! Have you heard?"

"Heard what?"

"He's trying to sell his shares. Apparently, he made some bad investments and is out of cash?"

Hans scratched his head. "Are you serious?"

"That's it?"

"What's it?"

"You're not acting like you're surprised."

He squinted at me. "This is *my* brother we're talking about."

"I know, you don't have to tell me—but your parents. Did they give up their shares? How has this happened? People are saying the brewery might go bankrupt."

Hans shook his head. "Der Keller isn't going bankrupt. Mama and Papa made sure of that."

"What do you mean?"

"When was the last time you checked your mail?"

"I don't know." I shrugged. We rarely got mail at the farmhouse. Mac had our personal bills sent to the brewery. He thought it was safer that way. Although, come to think of it, maybe it was just because he didn't want me to see them. And I never got any personal mail, and Alex texted his friends. The only things that ever showed up in our mailbox were junk mail or catalogs.

"Sloan, you should check your mail."

"What are you talking about?"

He tried to brush off his coveralls, but there was so much sawdust that he managed to clear only one streak. "Let's go sit in my office."

"Why?"

"Come with me." He didn't wait for me to protest.

His "office" was located in the back of his woodshop. He had built a pergola outside with two handmade rocking chairs and a side table that faced a small rock garden. Hans's craftsmanship extended to the garden. Huge cedar pots contained red-leafed Japanese maples and fragrant jasmine. There was a bubbling fountain in the far corner and cedar boxes overflowing with late summer herbs.

"Have a lemonade." He tossed me a bottle of lemonade and pointed to the rocker.

I followed his command and sat. "Hans, what is going on, and why are you asking me about my mail?"

He took his time to open his lemonade and then took a long, slow sip. Then he sighed and met my expectant gaze. My feet bounced on the asphalt. "I thought my parents were going to talk to you directly about this, but I guess they didn't."

"About what?"

"About Der Keller."

"Oh no, is it really in trouble? What has Mac done?"

"Sloan, relax. It's okay." He took another sip. "They decided after everything that's happened recently that it's time for them to scale back a bit. They think that what's happened between you and Mac is their fault."

"What?"

"I know. Trust me, I've told them everything you're thinking a thousand times, but they won't hear it. They feel responsible."

"I'll talk to them."

"You should, but it's not going to change anything. You know how stubborn they can be."

I smiled at the thought of sweet and kind Otto and Ursula, and how right Hans was about their stubborn streak. It was one of the reasons they had succeeded in Leavenworth. They refused not to.

"That's why they didn't tell you. They were worried that you would refuse."

My mind spun. What would I refuse?

Hans flipped the cap to his lemonade in one hand. "They decided that the timing was right to restructure the company."

I held my breath. Why was Hans so calm? If Ursula and Otto had restructured the company, that had to mean that they had given Mac more control. The entire time Mac and I had been together, Otto and Ursula controlled 70 percent of Der Keller's shares. The other 30 percent was divided equally between Mac and Hans—a substantial piece when it came to pulling profit shares but not enough to give them any authority in decision making. Additionally Mac, like other employees, pulled a salary in his role as brewery manager.

"But Mama and Papa are smart. They know that Mac can be impulsive. They kept ten percent, they gave me thirty percent."

I cut him off. "But that gives Mac a giant share!"

"Hold up, Sloan. I wasn't done."

"Sorry."

"They gave Mac thirty percent."

My confusion must have been evident on my face, because he rocked back in his chair and grinned. "I don't understand."

"That's why you should check your mailbox. They gave the remaining thirty percent of the shares to you."

"Me?" I must have heard Hans wrong.

His smile broadened. "You. They gave you thirty percent of the company, Sloan. You deserve it. You've worked as hard—if not harder—than anyone else."

"No! No, they can't give me that many shares. I don't even want shares."

"That's exactly why they gave them to you and why they didn't want to tell you."

"Wait, no. This isn't right." Was this really happening? Why would Otto and Ursula give me that kind of stock in Der Keller? "This is your family business."

"Sloan, you are family."

"You know what I mean."

"Is your last name Krause?" Hans raised his brows.

"For the moment, but probably not for long."

"Sloan, my parents love you. You are their daughter, no matter what happens with Mac. They want you involved in Der Keller's future. Actually, I think Dad's exact words were something like 'there is no future without Sloan.'"

"I never imagined they would give me part of the company."

"I know, which is why you're the perfect person to control the remaining shares. Mac would run the company into the ground. Not intentionally, but because he has a tendency to leap without a net. Mama and Papa are astute businesspeople. They didn't make this decision lightly. It's been in the works for years. They talked to me about it, and I gave them one hundred percent approval. The timing got bumped up."

"Why? Why now?"

"Like I said, they feel guilty. Giving you your stake in Der Keller now frees you up. You won't have to work at Nitro, unless you want to, and I think quite honestly it's a brilliant power play on their part. You and Mac are going to have to work together to make decisions for the company. They're holding out hope that you'll get back together."

"That's not likely."

"Yeah, but they can hope. Plus, Mac has to come to you. He can't make decisions without one or both of us signing off." He winked. "Like I said, Mama and Papa might look like frail, little old grandparents, but Der Keller is where it is today because of their shrewd business decisions."

My throat felt like sandpaper, and not because I was thirsty. I couldn't believe it. The Krauses had given me nearly a third of their multimillion-dollar operation. I was flattered and flattened by the news.

CHAPTER
THIRTY-THREE

"HANS, I CAN'T ACCEPT THIRTY percent of Der Keller," I said, standing up. "Don't get me wrong, that's the nicest gift anyone has ever given me, but I can't take it."

He twisted the cap on his lemonade. "You don't have a choice, Sloan. The paperwork is done."

"I'm sure I have a choice. You can't just give someone shares in a company."

"You've met my parents, right?"

"You know what I mean. I can refuse."

"Go ahead and try." Dimples formed in his cheeks as he smiled. "Good luck with that. If you want, we can walk over there now. I'd like to see how this goes."

He had a point. I couldn't refuse Ursula's offers for Sunday night dinners or Otto when he insisted on paying for Alex's summer camp. How was I going to refuse this?

"What do you know about Mac making investments and borrowing against his shares?" I asked, changing the subject.

Hans's dimples disappeared as he answered. "Not much, but Mac plays his cards pretty close to his chest when it comes to me. He's smart enough to know that I'll push back."

"Do you have any idea what he might have invested in?"

"He mentioned hop farms a few times, but he could have just been talking. You know Mac."

It was true—Mac was a big talker. When I first met him, I was dazzled by his larger-than-life dreams and personality. The reality of living with him day to day had tempered my enthusiasm. It was a rare occasion when he actually followed through on one of his ideas. I had learned to filter his plans and brainstorms. Usually, he'd get fired up about a new inspiration for a day or two before he lost interest. Maybe this was one of those times. It wouldn't have been out of character for him to talk about investing and never actually follow through.

"Sloan, don't look so worried. Even if—worst case scenario—Mac has overinvested, you and I hold majority control of Der Keller. It's going to be fine."

His confidence was inspiring, but I wasn't as easily convinced. A buzzer vibrated on Hans's tool belt. He pushed it off. "Time to stain." Wrapping one arm around my shoulders, he walked me inside. "Sloan, I promise everything is going to work out."

"I hope so." I gave him a weak smile and headed for the door.

"Are you going to talk to Mama and Papa?" he called, shaking a quart of wood stain.

"Yeah."

I had prided myself on living a quiet and calm life. I'd experienced enough change in my young years to last a lifetime. Up until a few weeks ago, my days had been uneventful. My routine involved working at Der Keller and making dinner for Alex and Mac. Suddenly, however, I'd been bombarded by change, and I wasn't sure how I felt about it.

The sky felt heavy as I walked to Der Keller. Rain was in the forecast, and the clouds looked like they were ready to burst. I had a feeling I was, too. I wasn't sure how much more I could take or if I could maintain my composure much longer.

Otto spotted me first. He was watering the hops and flower boxes in the front of the restaurant with a stainless steel watering can. "Sloan, hello, hello! Zis is a happy surprise."

Placing the watering can on a chair, he leaned in and kissed both of my cheeks. My throat tightened. I didn't want to have to turn down his offer, but I had to.

"Is Ursula here?" I asked.

He nodded toward the back patio. "*Ja,* she is cleaning the tables."

That sounded like Ursula. She easily could have tasked any of the staff with cleaning the outdoor furniture, but she claimed that scrubbing and polishing the wood kept her young. Again, I wondered why Mac hadn't inherited his parents' work ethic.

"Can I talk to you two for a minute?"

Otto's wide smile turned solemn. "Of course, but your face is so long."

I nodded. "I'm fine, but I need to talk to you and Ursula."

"Come, come, we will find her." He moved with ease through the pub, giving a slight nod to a waiter who sprang into action when he realized that someone's pint glass was nearly empty. There wasn't anything that Otto missed. He knew each customer by name and waved friendly greetings as we weaved our way through the tables and outside.

"Sloan!" Ursula's face lit up when she saw me. She wore a pair of thick yellow rubber gloves that would have come up to most people's elbows. On Ursula's petite frame, they nearly came up to her shoulders. She squeezed her sponge into a bucket and tugged off the gloves. "How are you?" She embraced me in a long hug and then touched my hair. "I like your hair long like this. It is soft on your face, *ja*."

"Thanks. I'm good." I returned the hug, not wanting to let go. I knew that turning down their offer would be a disappointment, but I felt weird about accepting it.

"Sit, sit," Ursula commanded, motioning to a table a few feet away that she'd already cleaned. "It looks like rain— maybe we should sit inside?"

"No, it's fine," I said. I didn't want to have this conversation in front of half the town.

They exchanged a knowing look and sat across the table from me.

"I just talked to Hans," I started.

Otto raised one bushy white eyebrow. "Hans?"

"He told me about Der Keller."

"*Ja*, and you are happy, no?" Ursula studied my face and smiled brightly.

"It's such a wonderful gesture. I can't thank you enough." I noticed I was winding a strand of hair around my finger.

Otto interrupted. "No, you don't thank us. You have made this a success. We want you to have part of it."

"That is so kind of you, but I can't accept. It's too much."

"I told you zis is what she would say." Ursula punched Otto in the shoulder.

Otto shook his head. "No, zis is what we want for you, Sloan. It is not a gift. It is what you are due."

"But, I can't take a third of the company. It's not right."

Ursula sat up. "No, it is right. You must accept."

This was going to be even harder than I had imagined.

"Really, I can't. I wouldn't feel right about it."

Ursula gave Otto another nudge in the arm. "See? I told you zis would happen. You tell her."

Otto nodded at her and then stared at me. "Sloan, you are our daughter. We always wanted a little girl and then you came along. We are so lucky to have you, and you are our best brewer. You have ze nose, as we say here. Zis is what we want, but it is also what is right for Der Keller. Ursula and I are slowing now, and we know it is much to ask of you, but we need your help. Our knees and backs need a rest." His eyes twinkled. "Would you do that for us? Would you help us?"

His words melted me. I blinked back tears as I met their sincere gazes. How could I say no to that?

"But what about Mac? I don't think it's a great idea for us to be working together. And then there's Garrett. I made a commitment and promise to him. I can't leave him stranded."

Ursula knew she had won. She clapped her hands together. "Zis is no problem. We have already talked about it. Mac will run the day-to-day operations. You can oversee the brewing and attend board meetings for now. We will start to back away slowly. Not all at once. You can take your time and work with Garrett. It is perfect, right? We talked it through and want it to be the very best for you."

"That's so kind of you. I can't thank you both enough, but I'm still not sure. I don't know what's going to happen with Mac and me, and . . ." I didn't want to mention anything about the company's financial position. I wanted confirmation that Mac was really in too deep before I worried them.

"*Ja, ja,* we understand," Otto replied. "You do not need to worry about Mac. We will talk to him. Hans agrees. We talked to him, and he also wants you as part of the company. You are family, Sloan, and we want to keep Der Keller in the family."

Ursula reached across the table and placed her aging arm over mine. "*Ja,* family. It is right, don't you see?"

I nodded and wiped a tear from my eye. "Thank you."

Otto called for a round of celebratory beers. I didn't feel exactly like celebrating, and yet I felt completely supported and surrounded by love. Otto and Ursula were like parents to me, and as much as I wanted to decline their generous offer, I couldn't. I knew they had played me. They knew exactly what to say to get me to stay. Whether they really needed my help or not was a moot point. I was now a partial owner in Leavenworth's largest brewery.

CHAPTER

THIRTY-FOUR

I LEFT OTTO AND URSULA, and returned to Nitro, where Garrett had already opened the bar. Had I been gone that long?

Mouthing an apology to Garrett, I hurried to the kitchen to assemble small plates for the evening. We had decided to roll out the new menu the next week, so in the interim I planned to pull together whatever we had on hand. Tonight that meant crackers, nuts, and a plate of the desserts I'd made that morning.

We would offer complimentary bar snacks until we had finalized the menu, so I didn't have to worry about pricing each platter. Once I'd assembled the food on trays, I circulated them around the room. It wasn't very crowded yet. A handful of people had gathered at the bar, and three of our twelve tables were occupied.

I wound my way back to the bar. "Sorry I'm late. I lost track of time," I said to Garrett, placing the trays behind the bar. I knew if I put them front and center, the regular drinkers would devour them in a matter of minutes.

"You have a lot on your mind," Garrett replied, pouring a pint.

Did he know that I was now a part owner in Der Keller?

"Are you okay?" He wrinkled his forehead.

"What?"

"You're acting kind of weird. Is everything okay? You're not mad about what I told you?"

"No, I'm fine, and I'm glad you told me." I rubbed my temples. "Anything you need from me?"

He handed me a tray with four beers. "Can you take this to table two?"

"For sure." I balanced the tray of beers on one arm and slid away, thankful for a chance to pull my thoughts together.

Table two was a group of business travelers in town for a conference at the Sleeping Lady resort on the outskirts of town. It was a gem of a place and attracted visitors from all over for winter skiing, summer hiking, family vacations, weddings, and business retreats.

I delivered their beers and gave them some suggestions for local hikes. I was about to return to the bar when I noticed Mac and April talking outside. With a quick glance to make sure that Garrett didn't need me, I tucked the tray under my arm and opened the door halfway.

"What's going on?" I didn't trust April for a second. I could only imagine the tale she would be spinning about how I was ready to list the farmhouse. The last thing I needed was for April to inflame an already fiery situation between Mac and me.

"Sloan, there you are, dear. We were just talking about you, weren't we, Mac?" April batted her fake lashes at my husband and linked her arm through his. "Your ears must be burning."

Mac looked like he was burning. His eyes were so intense I almost lifted the empty beer tray to shield myself from his gaze.

"Oh, yeah?" I tried to sound casual, but Mac was obviously fuming about something. Either April had gotten to him or he had learned that I now owned a sizable chunk of his brewery. Mac's vision when Otto and Ursula retired had always been to retain sole ownership of the company. He knew that Hans didn't share his passion for beer, and frankly, I think he liked it that way. When his parents finally handed over the reins, Mac would be in control—and the man liked to be in control. Them giving me a piece of the business had thrown a giant wrench in his plans.

"Are you guys coming in for a pint?" I asked, keeping my tone light.

"No, I'm on my way to meet with some very important businessmen in town." April smoothed her ruffled barmaid skirt. I wondered if her outfit was considered appropriate business attire.

"Mac?"

He glared at me. "Nope."

Without another word, he and April sauntered away. He was pissed, and I loved it. *Thank you, Ursula and Otto,* I said to myself as I practically danced inside.

"Someone's had a change of attitude," Garrett noted.

I stacked the tray with the others and took an empty pint

glass from one of the customers at the bar to refill. "Is it that obvious?"

He handed another customer a taster tray. "Yes. Although I saw you talking to your husband, so to tell you the truth, this is not the reaction I was expecting you to have."

I had to pinch the top of my thigh to stop myself from saying anything about Otto and Ursula's offer. It also didn't go unnoticed that Garrett had been watching me. Was he simply showing concern as my new boss, or could it be that he felt something magnetic between us, too?

I smiled. "Honestly, neither was I."

Business picked up over the next hour. I didn't have time to dwell on Mac, or on Otto and Ursula's offer, for that matter. Garrett and I poured pint after pint. I enjoyed the easy rhythm we'd fallen into, and it was obvious that the town had fallen for his beer. When it was time to head for home a few hours later, I had so many thoughts running through my mind that I thought it might explode.

CHAPTER

THIRTY-FIVE

MY EXCITEMENT VANISHED WHEN I pulled into our driveway and spotted Mac's Hummer parked in front of the house.

Time to face the music, I told myself as I took my time gathering my things and walked as slowly as possible to the front door.

"Sloan, we need to talk." Mac's arms were folded across his chest, and he stood blocking the entryway.

"What are you doing here?" I stood on my toes to see over him. Was Alex home? I didn't want to hash things out in front of him.

"He's not here. He's at practice," Mac snarled. "They have daily doubles tonight, remember?"

"How did you get in?"

Holding up his key chain, he gave me an exasperated look. "Key. I own this place, remember?"

"Are you going to let me in or just stand there?" I shifted my bag on my shoulder.

Mac sighed and moved to let me pass. He stayed right on my heels and followed me to the kitchen.

"You didn't answer my question. What are you doing here?" I repeated, trying to keep my tone even. One trick I had learned from my social worker was to focus on a singular thing when feeling anxious. It could be as simple as looking for every yellow object in a room or turning my attention to my breath. With Mac staring me down, I shifted my thoughts to the pings of rain above. The rhythmic sound of rain splattering on the roof brought a smile to my face. I was ready for fall—soup season.

"Why are you smiling?" Mac yanked a stool from the counter and sat down. He didn't take his eyes off of me. They reminded me of crystal blue lasers.

"The rain." I pointed to the open-beam ceiling above us.

His face softened for a moment. "You always did love the rain." He scoffed and shook his head. "I never could get you to close the windows at night even in the middle of a torrential downpour."

"It's good for you." To prove my point, I dropped my bag on the counter and walked to open the barn door and windows. The sound of rain hitting the porch and the smell of damp fall air rushed in.

"Classic Sloan." Mac reached for an orange in the fruit bowl and began peeling it. Then his eyes drifted to the fireplace in the dining room. "When did you take our wedding picture down?"

"What?" I followed his gaze to the mantel, which had been carved from a reclaimed barn door. He was right;

our wedding picture was missing. "That's weird. I didn't move it."

He scowled. "Right. Like you didn't take off your ring either."

A shiver ran down my spine, and not from the breezy air blowing in from outside. I hadn't touched the picture. Could Alex have taken it down? It didn't seem like something he would do, but then again, I knew this was a rough time for him. Maybe our wedding picture was an unhappy reminder. I didn't want to say anything to Mac, but I thought back to the motorcycle and strange car in our driveway. Was there a chance that someone had been in the house? Why would they take our wedding picture and leave the expensive antique beer steins and crystal stemware? I was probably making something out of nothing.

"Why are you here?" I poured myself a glass of water, changing the subject and bracing myself for his response.

"You know why I'm here." His expression was challenging.

"I take it that you talked to your parents."

"My parents? What do they have to do with this?"

Did he think that I had coerced Otto and Ursula into giving me shares? "Everything. This was their idea. Not mine."

"My parents want you to sell the house?" Mac looked confused.

"What?"

"The house." He waved his arm around the room. "This. Our house. They want you to sell?"

I quickly realized that Mac and I were talking about two different things. "No. Of course not." I gulped water. "What did April say to you?"

"She said you went to see her today and that you're looking to sell—fast."

So much for having my back. April had gone straight to Mac. I wanted to strangle her. "Mac, you know April as well as everyone else in town. I didn't tell her I wanted to sell; that was her idea."

He studied my face as if he was trying to decide whether I was lying. "You don't want to sell?"

"No. I mean, I don't know, but not yet anyway. We have a lot to work out."

He sat up. "So I have a chance? Sloan, baby, that's the best news I've heard in days."

"Slow down. I didn't say that. I said we have a lot to work out."

"Hey, if you're willing to work on things, I am, too. I told you, I'll do anything to get you back. Anything."

"Mac, don't." Clouds rolled across the sky. Thunder rumbled in the distance. It was as if the weather gods were responding to our exchange.

"You don't have to believe me, but I'm going to prove it to you, baby."

"You don't have to prove anything, and please stop calling me baby."

He swept his orange rinds into a neat pile. "But you're not going to sell?"

"No, I promise. I have no intention of selling the farmhouse—for now."

For a moment I thought I had dodged a bullet and that Mac had forgotten my reference to his parents, but the man was smart and smooth—that was one of the things that I'd first found attractive about him. After the news that I wasn't selling the farmhouse settled in, he scowled and asked, "Why did you think I was here about my parents?"

I considered my options. *I could lie, but he's going to find out sooner or later, so I might as well rip the Band-Aid off and get it over with.* "You haven't talked to them about Der Keller?"

"No. Why?"

"Have you talked to Hans?"

"Sloan, don't do this to me. I haven't talked to anyone in my family about Der Keller. What's going on?" He removed an apple from the fruit bowl and juggled it with one hand.

"Do you want a beer or something?" I sighed.

"No, especially because I bet my fridge is full of that guy's beer." He said "that guy" with venom.

"Suit yourself." I opened the fridge and poured myself a pint of Pucker Up from the growler I'd brought home the other day.

"What's the deal with Der Keller? Does this have something to do with Eddie's murder?"

"No. Not at all."

"Then what?"

I took a deep breath. "Your parents have restructured the company." A gust of wind hit the side of the house, causing the red gingham curtains in the dining room to blow toward the farm-style table.

"Oh, that. They mentioned that was going to happen.

They want to scale back. It's a good thing. They've put in their time. I want them to retire."

"But have you seen the new paperwork?"

He shook his head. "No."

"Wait here." I left the kitchen and found the mail key on a hook by the front door. I didn't bother with a raincoat. Fat wet drops hit my face as I walked out to the mailbox. They felt refreshing. Sure enough, inside the mailbox was a large manila envelope addressed to me and with a return address of Der Keller's law firm.

Once I was back inside, I slid the envelope, which was dotted with raindrops, to Mac. "Read this."

Then I clutched the edge of the counter and held my breath waiting for him to explode.

CHAPTER
THIRTY-SIX

MAC DIDN'T SPEAK AS HE looked through the paperwork. He turned over page after page, reading every word of the legal documents that I had yet to see. His expression was impossible to decipher. He was so focused on the papers that he barely glanced up.

I paced back and forth in the kitchen, busying myself by emptying the dishwasher and taking inventory of the fridge. I couldn't believe Mac was reading each line on the inch-thick contract. He had to be fuming. He was never quiet for this long. Actually, he was never quiet period.

When he finally finished, he stacked the papers, folded his arms across his chest, and tipped back on his stool. "I didn't see that coming."

"Neither did I. Don't look at me like that. I didn't have anything to do with this. I only found out about it this afternoon." I clutched my pint glass and took a sip.

"I didn't say that you did." Mac's lips had flattened into a thin line. "This has my parents written all over it—literally."

I wiped the already spotless counter for the third time. "Don't be mad at them. They're trying to do what they think is right for Der Keller's future, but I tried to tell them that I couldn't accept."

"What? What are you talking about?" Mac jumped from the stool. "You're going to accept. Of course you're going to accept. You don't refuse an offer like this, especially not from my parents."

"You're not mad?"

"Oh, I'm mad, but not because they gave you what's due. I'm mad because, obviously, they don't have much faith in me. What, did they think I was going to freak out or something?"

"Probably. That's what I thought you would do."

He closed his eyes and rested his head in his hands for a moment. "Sloan, look, I know I screwed up—big time. I get it, you're pissed at me. My entire family is—Hans, my parents, hell, I'm probably public enemy number one around town."

I started to talk, but he cut me off.

"No, I'm not done. It's fair. I deserve that. I screwed up. I screwed up the best thing that's ever happened to me." His eyes were intense and penetrating. He almost made me want to believe him. "I'm going to take everything that I have coming to me like a man. I told my parents that, you know? I apologized to them, too."

"Okay."

"Don't look like that. I know it's going to take a lot of

work to prove to you that I'm sorry and that I'm going to change. I have nothing but time, Sloan, and I'm going to make it my mission to show you."

I wanted to tell him not to bother.

"I'm going to own my mistakes and make it better, baby. But I didn't think that screwing up with you would make my parents lose all of their trust in me." His voice cracked a little.

I had to stop myself from going over to comfort him. He was right. He had made choices that put him in this position, and it wasn't my responsibility to make him feel better.

"Hans knew about this, too?" He stared at the billowy curtains.

I nodded.

Turning back to face me, he couldn't mask the hurt in his eyes. "Got it."

"Are you sure this isn't about me?"

"What do you mean?"

"I mean me having an equal piece of the business."

His expression looked even more pained. "Sloan, you deserve it. Had anyone in my family bothered to ask me, I would have agreed and told them to go for it."

I wasn't sure I believed him. He was too agreeable. I had the sense that his response was all part of his attempt to win me back.

"Well, I haven't even looked at the contract," I said, nodding at the paperwork on the counter between us.

"Give it a look. You're not getting out of this. You know my parents better than anyone. It's ironclad. Like it or not, you and I are Der Keller's future."

I hadn't thought of it in those terms, and I wasn't sure I did like the thought. If I was going to carve out my own life, how could I do it if I was still tied to Mac?

"You have to give them credit, though," Mac said, tapping the stack of paper. "They've still got some tricks up their sleeves." He shook his head and chuckled. "I bet they had a good laugh at that."

"I don't think they did anything to be intentionally spiteful." I took another taste of the beer. It had gone slightly flat.

"You wouldn't."

Given that our conversation was going so well, I decided to ask him about what Garrett had told me. "Mac, is everything okay with you? I heard a rumor that money is . . . tight."

His cheeks flamed. "Who told you?"

"It doesn't matter. What's going on?"

"Nothing. A couple bad investments. No need to worry, baby."

I wanted to press him, but my cell phone rang and vibrated on the counter. It was Alex. He needed a ride home from practice.

"I'll go," Mac said. "I had better give him the lowdown before he hears April's rumor that his childhood home is on the market."

"I can't believe that woman," I said, feeling my anger return.

"She's something."

Mac and I finally had something to agree on: our mutual dislike for April. He grabbed his car keys and started for the front door. "Hey, did you know that she and Eddie had a fling?" he asked casually as he turned the handle.

"What?"

"Yeah. Can you believe it? Eddie and April. I thought she hated the guy because he didn't fit her perfect image of Beervaria. Way too many tattoos, for starters."

"Wait, are you serious? April and Eddie were an item?"

"Dead serious. She didn't want anyone to know. That's probably why she made such a big deal of acting like she hated him. From what I heard, they dated for a while. Eddie broke it off with her, and she was not happy about being dumped."

"April and Eddie?" I repeated again. "You're sure?"

"Yes. Why are you freaking out?"

"No reason. I can't picture Eddie and April together, that's all."

"Why would you want to?" Mac made a face and left to pick up Alex.

Thoughts of my future at Der Keller and my future with Mac faded away as I considered what he'd just revealed. I wouldn't have wanted to be on April's bad side, and if Eddie had left her a woman scorned, could she have killed him?

CHAPTER

THIRTY-SEVEN

FOR THE NEXT WEEK, I was so busy rolling out our new menu and brewing at Nitro, shuttling Alex between school activities and soccer matches, and meeting with Der Keller's lawyers that I didn't have a free minute to focus on anything else. Even Eddie's murder slipped to the background. I tried to keep my ears open, as Chief Meyers had asked, but no one was talking, and there had been no new arrests or developments in the case—at least none that were public knowledge.

I had been dreading the official meeting with Otto, Ursula, Hans, and Mac for days. After I signed the final paperwork for my percentage in the company, we were due to meet to discuss how to roll out the reorganization. I still hadn't mentioned anything about it to Garrett. I didn't want to worry him unnecessarily. If Otto and Ursula stayed true to their word—and I had no reason to think that they wouldn't—my stake in Der Keller shouldn't affect my position at Nitro. At least, I hoped it wouldn't.

When the day arrived, my stomach churned with nerves. We were meeting at Der Keller before it opened. Otto didn't want to share the news with staff yet, and I agreed with him. Hans was the only one at the pub when I tentatively opened the front door and stepped inside.

The scent of strong coffee and spiced apple coffee cake greeted me.

"Morning, Sloan," Hans said as he held up an oversized coffee mug in a toast. "Mama made a pan of her German coffee cake. She thought it might get everyone in the right mood."

"And you made coffee," I noted. "I could kiss you."

"Go right ahead." He stretched his neck out.

I planted a kiss on his cheek and poured myself a cup of coffee. "Thank God you made the coffee." Hans and I shared an affinity for dark, strong brew, both in beer and java. "Where is everyone?"

He sliced me a large piece of Ursula's coffee cake as I took a seat. "No idea. Mama had me come by to pick up her coffee cake. I thought they were right behind me, but I've been here for ten minutes."

"And Mac?" I glanced around the dark pub.

"No sign of the scoundrel yet." Hans winked.

I warmed my hands on the coffee mug. "Have you talked to him more about his investments?"

Hans shook his head. "I haven't had a chance, but don't worry, I've got your back. I'll bring it up this morning. It's on my list."

"You have a list?" I smiled.

He reached into the pocket of his Carhartt rugged jeans

and set a tape measure and a small number two yellow pencil on the table. He dug deeper in the pocket and removed a crumpled scrap of graph paper. "I have a list."

"I was kidding." I sipped the dark coffee and felt a familiar calm come over my body. "This is perfect."

"Thanks." Hans gave me a nod of acknowledgment. "What else do you think we should discuss this morning?"

"Where do I start?" I stuck my fork into the moist coffee cake. The aroma of apples, cinnamon, ginger, and cloves was familiar. Ursula made coffee cake at least once a week for the staff. Her apple coffee cake was my favorite. The slightly sour Washington Granny Smith apples made the cake moist and gave it a tang that balanced beautifully with the aromatic spices. This didn't disappoint. I quickly devoured half of the slice that Hans had cut for me.

"Have you thought about day-to-day operations?" Hans asked, watching me eat.

"No, I mean, I've thought about them, but I don't want be here every day. I'm not ready for that, and I don't want to leave Garrett in the lurch. I made a commitment to him to stay for six months, and I'm not willing to break that."

Hans nodded. "I don't want to be here either. I know my parents want to support me in whatever I do, but I think there's a part of them hoping that woodworking will become a hobby."

"Yeah." Hans was right. Otto and Ursula loved their boys, but they loved Der Keller, too. I knew they wanted to keep the family business strong and the family together.

Mac showed up before we could continue our plan of attack. "Hey." He gave Hans a curt nod. "You two look like you're plotting against me." His cheeks were scruffy with blond fuzz, and his hair looked frazzled. *Must have been a late night,* I thought.

"Having our morning coffee." Hans sounded irritated.

"Where are Mama and Papa?" Mac asked, pulling out a chair and sitting on the opposite side of the table from Hans and me.

"I was going to ask you that," Hans replied, glancing at the digital watch on his wrist. "I thought they were right behind me."

Mac cut himself a giant hunk of the coffee cake. When he caught me staring at him, he shot me a dazzling smile. "Don't worry. I'll share, baby."

I rolled my eyes and scooted my chair closer to Hans.

Hans said something under his breath that I couldn't quite make out but knew was a jab at his brother. We drank more coffee, and I picked at my remaining slice of cake in silence.

Twenty or thirty minutes later, Hans pushed back his chair, walked over, and peered out the windows. "This isn't like them." He turned to Mac. "Do you have your phone? I left mine at the workshop."

Mac whipped out his cell. "Always."

"Give them a call," Hans said. He looked worried. Hans never looked worried. I could feel my pulse start to pound in my fingertips.

Mac shrugged and dialed his parents. While he was waiting for them to pick up, he said, "You know what the odds are of them actually answering?"

It was a running joke amongst us. Otto and Ursula had

finally caved in to relentless pressure and purchased a shared cell phone. Thanks to Alex, they'd quickly learned the new technology and had even started texting. Every time I got a beer emoji from Ursula and Otto, I would break out in a grin.

"Papa?" Mac's voice matched Hans's look of concern. "Papa, slow down. I can't hear you."

I clutched my fork so tightly that it left an imprint in my skin. Hans moved away from the window and stood behind Mac.

"What?" Mac shot a look at me and then shook his head when I started to ask what was wrong. "Okay, wait there. We're on our way."

He clicked off the phone. His tone was serious. "Mama fell."

"Is she okay? What happened?" I dropped the fork.

"I don't know. I could barely hear him over the siren."

Siren.

Hans must have read my mind. "Siren?"

"Papa called for an ambulance. They're transporting her to the hospital."

"What are we waiting for? Let's go." Hans was already halfway to the door. Mac and I raced after him. *Please, let Ursula be okay,* I prayed silently as I ran to the car.

CHAPTER
THIRTY-EIGHT

THE TIRES SQUEALED AS MAC took every turn at three times the posted speed. When we'd been together, one of our recurring fights was about how fast he drove. Today, I found myself grateful for his adrenaline-junkie tendencies. We couldn't get to the hospital fast enough.

Everything happened in a blur. Mac dropped Hans and me off at the entrance to the emergency room and sped off to find a parking space. We found Otto right away. He was sitting in a chair near the nurses' station with his head between his hands.

"Dad, what happened?" Hans knelt next to him.

Otto looked up at us with wet eyes. Tear streaks stained the sides of his cheeks. "She fell."

"I heard that much." Hans met my eyes and nodded to the empty chair next to his father.

I took the cue and sat next to Otto, placing my hand on his knee.

Otto gave me a pained smile and then let out a long sigh. "I should have helped her down ze steps, but she would not hear of it."

"So she fell on the steps?" Hans tried to pry more details from his father, while not overwhelming him.

"*Ja*. She missed da last step and took a nasty fall." He shuddered.

I squeezed his knee tighter.

"And you called the ambulance?" Hans asked. "Did she hit her head?"

"No." Otto rubbed his temples. "I don't think so. She fell on her side. They think that she shattered her hip."

I put my other hand to my heart. That was terrible news. Fracturing a hip at her age would not only be painful, but I had a feeling it would be a long recovery.

"Where is she now?" Hans asked. I was so impressed with his calm composure.

"They are taking her in for X-rays. If it is broken, they will do surgery."

"Now?"

"That's what they said in the ambulance."

I knew without having to look up that Mac had arrived. One of the nurses nudged her friend and pointed to the door. Then she gave Mac a half wave and flirty smile. Classic. Only my husband would find a way to flirt in the midst of an emergency.

"Dad, what's going on?" Mac's approach was the opposite of Hans's. He paced in front of us and spoke loud enough for the entire waiting room to hear.

Hans got up from his knees and put his arm around Mac's

shoulders. "They think that Mama broke her hip. She's having X-rays done right now."

Mac either wasn't satisfied with Hans's answer or he couldn't handle that his brother knew more about what was going on than him. He sidled up to the nurses' desk as if it were a bar and rested one arm on the counter. The nurses smiled up at him, completely taken in by his suave moves. I wanted to throw up. I was sick with worry over Ursula and disgusted by Mac's overt behavior.

He returned with the same information that Hans had told him, but proceeded to repeat everything he'd learned from the nurses anyway. It wasn't much longer until a surgeon wearing mint green scrubs and a face mask came to speak to us. He explained that Ursula had indeed broken her hip. They would have to do surgery to repair it.

Ursula was strong, but any surgery came with risk. The surgeon wasn't sure how long it would take. He estimated two to three hours, but warned us that it could be longer. All we could do was wait. Mac paced the perimeter of the waiting room, Hans went to find coffee for Otto, and I sat next to Otto, holding his hand.

"She's going to be fine," I assured Otto. "She's strong."

"*Ja*, Sloan, thank you. I know." He didn't sound convinced but put on a brave face.

In the frenzy of the morning, I'd forgotten about Alex. When Hans returned with a Styrofoam cup of hospital cafeteria coffee, I walked outside to call Alex. He picked up on the first ring.

"Mom, you're not supposed to call me at school."

"Honey, I know, but there's been an accident."

"What?" His voice got higher.

"It's Oma. She fell this morning and is in the hospital. They're doing surgery now."

"What happened?" he asked.

"She broke her hip. She's going to be okay, but I wanted you to know. Do you want me to come get you?"

"Yeah. Of course I want you to come get me."

"Okay. Hang tight. I'll be there in five minutes."

I hung up and asked Mac for his car keys. "I'm going to go get Alex."

Mac reached for my hand. "I'll drive."

I didn't protest. This was no time to fight. Mac's palm was sweaty as we walked hand in hand to the parking lot. "She's going to be okay," I said, not only for his sake but for my own. "She's one tough cookie."

He squeezed my hand. "She's a fighter. You know when I was a kid, I was never afraid of Papa, but Mama, man, she would give me *the look,* and I would cower in the corner. That's all she had to do—give me one look."

I chuckled.

"She's been giving me the look a lot lately." His voice was thick with regret and emotion. "I've let her down. I don't know what's wrong with me."

"She loves you, Mac. You'll make it up to her."

We made it to the car. He dropped my hand and unlocked the passenger door for me.

He started the engine and navigated past a group of nurses out for a midmorning walk. "I've screwed up with you, Sloan. Big time. And I'm going to find a way to make it right."

"Mac, I can't do this now."

He started to say something, but stopped himself and focused on the road.

We made it to the school, where Alex was waiting near the front. He hopped into the backseat and asked for an update on his grandmother. I let Mac explain what had happened. Alex seemed to take it in stride. He massaged my shoulder from the backseat. "She'll be okay, Mom. She's got German steel running through her blood—right, Dad?"

Mac agreed. "Strongest woman on the planet. There's no doubt about that."

I knew they were right, but was worried about Ursula. Regardless of what the future held for me and Mac, I couldn't fathom the idea of anything happening to her.

CHAPTER

THIRTY-NINE

IT FELT LIKE HOURS UNTIL we finally received word from the surgeon that Ursula's surgery had been a success. They had repaired the fractures, and she had come out of it with flying colors. She was in the recovery room, so it would still be a while before we could see her, but the news that the surgery was over lightened the mood.

The waiting room had become like a party. Word of Ursula's accident had quickly spread around town, and business owners, friends, and neighbors arrived with cookies, sandwiches, flowers, and balloons. Even Garrett showed up. I spotted him hanging near the sliding doors looking uncomfortable.

I excused myself and walked over to him. "Hey, I guess you heard the news."

He gave me a quizzical look. "You called me, remember?"

"Oh, right." I'd completely forgotten that I'd left him a

message earlier when we were en route to the hospital. "Sorry, it's been a crazy few hours."

"No problem." Garrett reached for a paper bag at his feet. "I brought this for you. It's not much, but it was all I could think of in the moment."

"Thanks. You didn't have to bring me anything."

"I know."

Was it my imagination, or was he blushing? He glanced to the front of the waiting room where Mac, Alex, Hans, and Otto were chatting with friends and munching on snacks. "Listen, I've got to get back to the brewery. I just wanted to make sure you were okay and didn't need anything."

"That's so thoughtful. You didn't need to come by, but thanks."

He pushed the bag at me.

"I'll check in later, once we know how Ursula is doing."

"You don't have to come in today." He started backing out the door. "Be with your family."

My family. I picked up the bag and peeked inside. Garrett had filled it with Cool Ranch Doritos. There had to be at least eight bags of chips. I wondered if he'd bought every bag of Cool Ranch Doritos in the supermarket. I couldn't hide my smile as I walked over to join everyone.

Otto's smile was equally wide when the surgeon announced that Ursula was awake and ready for visitors. Everyone in the waiting room let out a cheer. The Krauses were beloved, and the town had come to show their support. I knew that there was going to be a long recovery ahead for Ursula, but if the crowd in the packed waiting room was any indication, she was going to have lots and lots of help.

When it was my turn to go back, I straightened my shoulders and prepared myself for the worst. She didn't look as bad as I expected. She didn't look good either. Her face was ashen, and her normally bright eyes were hazy.

When she saw it was me, they cleared a bit, but I could tell she was in a daze. The effects of the anesthesia hadn't worn off completely. "Sloan, my dear, come in. Come sit."

I sat next to the bed. Ursula was hooked up to a variety of machines and IVs. I tried to steady my breathing. I didn't want her to know that I was worried.

She reached a shaky hand out. I covered her small and bony fingers with mine. "How are you feeling?"

"I am fine. Nothing to worry about. I needed a new hip anyway. Zis one, it is too old, like me," she kidded.

"You gave us a scare."

"It is nothing. Do not worry about me. I worry about you, my dear."

"That's ridiculous. You can't worry about me. You have to take care of yourself right now."

"*Ja, ja.* I will be fine. I will be up and moving in no time, see."

"You will follow the doctor's orders." I gave her a firm look.

She laughed. Seeing her smile made me feel better. "I will. I know you will force me to rest." Then she narrowed her glazed eyes. "Sloan, I do worry about you, you know. You keep things too tight." She tapped her heart. "In here, you know."

I didn't trust myself to speak. Tears pooled behind my eyes.

"It is okay for you to let people take care of you."

Blinking back tears, I wiped them away with my free hand.

"It was a hard life for you, I know, but you are a Krause now, and that will never change. No matter what."

Her words cut through me. I couldn't hold back my emotions. Sobs escaped from my lungs as the tears I'd been trying to contain spilled from my eyes.

She held my hand tighter and let me cry. "Zis is good."

When I finally paused to catch my breath, she let go of my hand and pointed to a box of tissues resting on her nightstand. I reached for the tissues and dabbed my eyes. "Sorry, I didn't mean to do that. I just don't know what I would do without you."

She smiled softly. "I feel the same. You are my daughter, Sloan."

I gulped and felt my throat start to tighten again. *Enough with the tears,* I told myself. "Can I get you anything?"

"No." She kept her head still as she answered. I could tell she was trying to move as little as possible. "I will sleep again soon, I think."

"I'll let you rest," I said, pushing back the chair.

She nodded. "*Ja.* I will see you soon."

I wondered if my eyes were red and puffy as I walked down the sterile hallway to the waiting room. I hadn't expected to have a sobfest; I had wanted to be strong for her. Instead, she'd been strong for me. How had I gotten so lucky to find a mother like her?

Alex was waiting to see her next. "How is she, Mom?"

"She is her same feisty self, a little subdued. They have her on some pretty heavy medication. I think she's getting tired, so it might be a quick visit."

"That's okay. I just want to see her, you know?"

I kissed the top of his head. "I know." I wanted to grab him, hold him tight, and never let him go, but instead I watched him walk down the hallway. I didn't even realize that Mac had come up beside me until I heard him whisper in my ear.

"We made a cool kid."

I looked at him and nodded. "Yes, we did."

"She seems good, don't you think?"

"She seems great," I agreed.

"I guess this is going to change their plan to scale back slowly." Mac glanced behind us to his dad, who was talking to a nurse.

I hadn't even thought of Der Keller and how Ursula's injury might affect operations. "Have you heard anything about when she'll get out and what the follow-up is?"

"Dad's talking to the nurse about that now. It sounds like she'll stay in here for at least three or four days. Then she'll need around-the-clock care once she's home. She can't do stairs."

The Krauses owned a three-story Victorian, and their bedroom was on the third floor.

"Hans and I are going to head back to the brewery soon to talk about hiring someone to come in and help with her care. Dad won't hear of it, but I don't think he can do it alone."

"No, no way. He can't do it alone. Imagine things like lifting her into the shower—and what about their bedroom?"

He nodded. "Exactly. Hans and I are going to move their bed down to the den on the main floor."

"I'll help."

"You don't have to, Sloan." His eyes searched mine. "I know this has to be hard for you . . . because of me."

"Mac, stop. I love your mom. I love your parents. Regardless of how I feel about you right now, I'm going to do everything I can to help."

"If you're sure?"

"I'm sure."

Alex came back from his time with Ursula a few minutes later. We piled into Mac's truck and headed for Otto and Ursula's house. While the guys moved heavy furniture from the third floor to the first, I made a pot of chicken noodle soup and a double batch of peanut butter cookies (Otto's favorite). Mac must have thanked me twenty times for helping. This was what family did for each other. And like it or not, he was my family.

CHAPTER

FORTY

THE GUYS CLEARED OUT THE den and moved Otto and Ursula's bed and dressers downstairs while I put the finishing touches on dinner. The kitchen smelled of garlic and fresh herbs. I wanted everything to be hot and ready to serve once Otto came home.

Mac came in as I placed a lid on the soup. He grabbed a bottle of seltzer from the fridge and leaned against the tile countertop. "I really think we need to get them in-home nursing care right away."

"It's probably a good idea." I turned the heat to low.

He twisted off the cap to the seltzer. "Want one?"

I declined.

"Sloan, like I said earlier, I don't know what I would do right now without you." He paused and chugged the water. "I've screwed up with everyone, and I know that I don't deserve your help."

"Everyone?"

His tone had changed. I had a feeling I knew what he meant, but I wanted to hear him say it.

"Don't play dumb. I know that you know."

"You mean about your investments."

He stared at Ursula's collection of German china for a minute and then met my gaze. "How did you find out?"

"This is Leavenworth."

"Mama heard, too. She wasn't happy."

"What did you invest in?"

"Hops. It sounded like a sure thing. Van was convincing. He said he already had five years of solid orders for his hybrid hops." He polished off the seltzer.

"That's what I heard, too."

"He doesn't. He doesn't have any hops. There's nothing out there on the land. It was a scam. We have more hops at the farmhouse than he does."

"What?"

Mac sighed. "Yeah. I got hosed."

"But he brought in boxes of hops to Nitro. Garrett and I created new beers specifically around those hops. I don't understand."

"I don't know where he got those, but they're not from his land. I went out there last week. It was a stupid move to invest without seeing the farm, but it sounded like a sure thing."

I tried to make sense of what Mac was saying, but I couldn't. "Wait, you're serious. Van doesn't have a hop farm?"

"Nope. It's a dust bowl."

"Maybe he hasn't started planting yet?"

"No. He left town."

"What?"

Mac nodded. "He left town with my money, and I have nothing to show for it."

"And your mom knows?"

"I had to tell them. They weren't happy. They told me that they'd taught me better when it came to business. The look of disappointment on their faces was worse than losing the money. Mama was going to talk to Der Keller's lawyer today. If they can track Van down, we should be able to get our money back—if he hasn't spent it."

"But I thought Van wanted to brew? He had me taste his home brew. He said he was interviewing with Bruin."

"I don't know. That was probably a scam, too. The guy is no brewer. I can't believe I got taken so easily."

I'd been so focused on April, maybe in part because I wanted her to be the killer, that I had overlooked Van. He was running a scam. What if he had pulled off the biggest scam of all? My mind began to spin with possibilities. What if Van had killed Eddie?

Alex interrupted my thoughts. "Hey, Hans and I are done upstairs. Opa called and said he might just stay the night."

Mac shook his head. "I don't know if that's a good idea. Maybe we should go try to strong-arm him." He winked at Alex.

We decided to part ways. Mac and Alex would go back to the hospital and try to convince Otto to come home for the night. I had a sneaking suspicion that he wouldn't leave Ursula's side, so I packaged up a container of hot soup and a bag of peanut butter cookies just in case. Hans would go to Der Keller and give the staff an update. I wanted to at least check in with Garrett.

Downtown was a short walk from the Krauses' house. It felt good to be outside and breathe in fresh air. It was after seven, but the sky was already beginning to darken. In the next month, it would be dark by six. I turned the corner onto Main Street and ran right into April.

"Sloan, darling, how are you? I heard the terrible news that Ursula took a little tumble." April had on yet another gaudy costume. This time it was orange and black plaid, with matching tangerine lipstick. She reminded me of a pumpkin.

"More than a little tumble. She broke her hip in three places."

April fanned her face with her hand. "Oh, no! So terrible, and to such a sweet lady."

Her sincerity was about as genuine as her fake lashes. Maybe it was because I was on edge and feeling particularly protective of Ursula, but I couldn't take one more minute of her fake attitude.

"Hey, I've been meaning to talk to you," I said, plastering on a smile.

"Yes? About your house?"

"No, about Eddie, actually."

A look of panic flashed on her face. She blinked rapidly. "What about Eddie?"

"Well, it's interesting. Rumor has it that you two had a fling."

April's face lost its color, making her makeup look even more garish. "What?"

"That's the word around town. You and Eddie, I would have never guessed." It wasn't my proudest moment, but it did feel good to give April a taste of her own medicine.

She stepped back. "It was nothing. Really. I can't believe how gossipy people can be around here."

I had to hold back a laugh. Sucks to be on the other side, doesn't it?

"I think everyone is surprised because you made it seem like you and Eddie weren't exactly friends."

"We weren't." She rolled her eyes. "It was a fling. Nothing more. I tried to tell Eddie that, but he wouldn't let go. He was absolutely obsessed after I broke it off."

"*You* broke it off?"

"It was never going to work. He refused to listen to my advice about blending in more around here, so I told him we were through."

"And then what happened?"

"Nothing." She shrugged. "He wrote me a stack of love letters, kept sending flowers, candy, but I told him I wasn't interested anymore. Poor thing. I think I broke his heart."

I wasn't sure that I believed her. I wouldn't have put it past April to claim that she was the one to break it off just to save face. Then again, after Mac's revelation about Van's scam, I had no idea who to believe at the moment. Was everyone in Leavenworth lying?

"What about Hayley?" I asked. "I heard they were dating, too."

"Yes, that's true. I think she was a rebound for him. He was trying to make me jealous, but of course it didn't work."

"With Hayley?"

"Exactly. I think he figured that if he pranced around town with a young piece of eye candy, it would get under my skin, but I told him to go for it. Of course, as you know, his eye candy only had eyes for your husband."

Only April could find a way to work in a dig at me in the middle of a conversation about her secret affair.

"Did you tell this to Chief Meyers?"

"Of course. I gave her Eddie's love letters. I bet they had a laugh over that at headquarters. Let's just say that the man did *not* have a way with words."

I couldn't picture tattooed Eddie pouring his love for April out on paper. For that matter, I couldn't picture Eddie and April. I guessed the old adage about opposites attracting was true in their case.

"You're not implying that you think *I* had something to do with Eddie's death, are you?"

"Not necessarily, but as you know, everyone is a suspect."

April shook her head. "Not me. Police Chief Meyers took me off her list very early on in her investigation. Now, if you want to talk suspects, I have some ideas."

"Who?"

"You know that supposed hop farmer you pointed out a while ago? What do you know about him?"

"Not much. He's a hop farmer and home brewer, but otherwise nothing." I wasn't about to share what I had learned about Van from Mac with April.

She moved closer and lowered her voice. "I have it on good authority that he's not who he says he is, and I think Eddie realized that." I thought back to opening night at Nitro and how Eddie had started to confront Van about the hops being his. How had I been so blind? Van must have been stealing hops from Bruin. Everything was beginning to make sense. Hops were hard to come by. With no hop farm, Van must have been skimming from Bruin's reserve.

For a moment, April actually sounded sincere, but then she slipped back into her singsong fake voice. "It's tragic. I think it got him killed." April and I agreed on something.

"I told Chief Meyers, and while she's unable to disclose details of the case to the general public, I believe that, due to my high status in the community, she made an exception."

"How so?"

"Well." April paused and looked around us as if to make sure that no one was listening. "She clearly hinted that she was on to Van as well. If you ask me, there's going to be an arrest in the case soon and Van will be behind bars."

A group of tourists with Leavenworth maps and matching German hats appeared across the street. April smoothed her skirt and dashed away. "Sorry, duty calls."

I felt sorry for the travelers, but not sorry enough to try and rescue them from April's clutches. I continued on to Nitro, more convinced than ever that Van had killed Eddie.

CHAPTER

FORTY-ONE

GARRETT LOOKED SHOCKED WHEN I showed up at Nitro. "Sloan, you didn't need to come in."

"I couldn't stay away. The beer was calling me." I winked. "Ursula is doing fine. There's nothing I can do for her right now, so I'd rather stay busy if that's okay with you."

"It's great," Garrett said, nodding to the crowded pub. "I've been pouring pints with both hands for the last hour."

"Let me give you one of mine." I grabbed an apron and tied it around my waist, feeling a sense of relief knowing that Ursula was well cared for and that I was back where I was supposed to be.

"Garrett, you never signed that contract with Van, did you?"

He shook his head. "No. Why?"

I told him everything I had heard from Mac and April. Garrett listened with an expression I couldn't read. When I finished, he rested his chin in his hands. "I was leery of the guy from the first time I met him. Who gives a business owner a contract for that kind of cash on a dusty piece of paper? I scanned it and sent a copy to my friend in Seattle, he said it was bunk. But, I knew for sure Van was up to something the day that he had you taste his home brew. And God, that beer. That was the worst home brew I've ever tasted." He shuddered. "That tipped me off. Not that every hop farmer is a brewer, but a hop grower is going to understand basic flavors and how to bring that out in a beer."

"Why didn't you say anything?"

"Chief Meyers asked me not to." Garrett's face was glum.

"What?"

"I'm sorry, Sloan. She was tracking him and asked me for my help. The deal was that no one—even you—could know. I've felt terrible having to keep this from you." He twisted a bar napkin in his hands. "You have no idea."

My head hurt trying to make sense of what Garrett was saying. "What? You've been working with Chief Meyers?"

"Yeah, since before we opened. She and Aunt Tess were close, and Chief Meyers had gotten a call from a colleague in Wenatchee. Van had tried a similar scam there, but was working under a different name. She thought it was a prime opportunity to 'bust him,' in her words. I had strict orders to play along. That was fine when I didn't know anyone here. I was the new guy in town, so it made sense. But then I met you, and you've been so helpful and great." His voice caught. "Knowing that you and Der Keller could be hurt by Van's scam and not being able to say anything has been terrible."

I thought about our lunch at The Carriage House and how many times Garrett had seemed distant when I had asked him questions. It all was beginning to make sense. "So there was no rumor in the beer world about Mac's investments. You knew the whole time?"

He swallowed and ran his hands through his hair. "Yeah. Can you forgive me?"

What was it with men lying to me? I had trusted Garrett, and while I knew that his reasons were different than Mac's, it still stung to know that he'd kept so much from me. "But Chief Meyers kept asking me about you—I don't understand."

"I think that was a test for me. She hammered it home that if anyone knew, I could blow the whole thing."

That was fair. I considered it for a moment and thought back through every interaction I had had with Van. Why hadn't I put the clues together earlier? Everything he had said had been a lie, from his nonexistent hop farm to his horrible home brew. He had to be the killer. But why? I voiced my questions aloud. "So did you and Chief Meyers suspect Van all along? Why did Van kill Eddie?"

"No, no!" Garrett tossed the napkin on the counter. "I had no idea. The only thing the chief and I were working on was Van's scam."

"But you must have wondered."

He picked the napkin back up and folded it into a square. "To be honest, Sloan, at first I thought maybe Mac did it."

"Me too." I frowned.

"Yeah, well, you don't have to worry about that anymore. It had to be Van, and as for why, well, until the police find him, it will be hard to know." He traced the outline of the napkin with his index finger. "My guess is money. Greed.

Eddie must have figured out his scam. Caught him stealing hops. Van snapped. You'll have to talk to Chief Meyers. I'm sure she has other theories in the works."

I had a million more questions, but the sound of a pint glass banging on the bar shook me back to the present. A thirsty customer winked and pointed to the empty glass. I plastered on a smile and took my place behind the bar.

Throughout the night, Garrett caught my eye. Each time he would shoot me a look of apology. I wasn't exactly angry with him—more hurt—but I wasn't ready to talk either.

After we closed, Garrett tried again. He poured us both pints. "A peace offering?" He raised one glass in the air.

At that moment, I spotted a man peering in the windows, and my heart froze. I recognized the overalls right away. Was that Van? It couldn't be, could it? The man made eye contact and flew past the window. "That's Van!" I shouted to Garrett and, without thinking, grabbed his arm and ran toward the door. The pint glass Garrett was holding shattered on the floor and sent beer spraying.

"Sloan, wait!" Garrett yelled, but he followed after me.

Van, or someone who bore a remarkable resemblance to him, took off down Commercial Street toward Waterfront Park. I called after him, but he didn't stop. I ran track in high school and still have a decent stride. I took off after him at a full sprint. I didn't have a plan in mind; I just knew that I had to catch him. Garrett huffed behind me. "Sloan, slow down. Let's call Chief Meyers."

The man sprinted down the hill and headed toward the entrance to Blackbird Island, a grassy park in the middle of the Wenatchee River. I hesitated for a second and followed after him. My lungs burned, and I had to breathe through my nose to keep oxygen flowing.

"How did you learn to run like this?" Garrett gasped between words. He had a size advantage over me, but was struggling to keep pace.

"He's getting away."

We crossed over the footbridge. The smell of dank fall was everywhere in the leaves rotting on the side of the bridge, the slippery moss snaking up the trees, and the crisp air.

"Sloan," Garrett puffed. "Stop. This is crazy."

He was right. What was I doing? Maybe my stress level had finally reached its boiling point. This was stupid. Instead of chasing after Van, I should stop and call the police. Slowing my pace, I stopped under an antique streetlamp and reached in my jeans pocket for my phone. Only, in my hurry to chase after Van, I had left my phone and everything else at Nitro.

Damn.

Garrett caught up and came to a stop. He hunched over and placed his hands on his knees. "Thank God. Seriously, are you a closet marathon runner or something?"

"Do you have your phone?" I ignored his question and the chill settling in my body.

"Huh?" He pondered my question for a minute, still trying to steady his breathing. "No."

I considered our options. We could continue after Van on the wooded island and risk him attacking, or we could return to town to call for help and risk him getting away. Neither sounded great, but I decided the wiser plan would be to return to town for reinforcements. Chief Meyers could have her team surround the island and block the exits going out of town.

"Come on," I urged Garrett, as I turned around and started up the hill. It was only about a quarter of a mile back to the nearest shop. Of course, not many of the shops on this end of town were open late.

We had just started up the slick sidewalk when I thought I heard footsteps behind me. I stopped and spun around. "Did you hear that?"

There was no sign of movement nearby and no other sounds.

"No." Garrett followed my eyes to the foggy lamppost.

I must be jumpy, I thought, and picked up the pace. Again, I heard the sound of thudding feet behind me. My pulse quickened. This had been a dumb move. What if Van had a weapon? He'd killed once. What would stop him from doing it again?

In the distance, through the misty fog, I could see the glow of the streetlights along Front Street. Every muscle in my body ached as I crested the hill and raced toward the closest shop.

I sprinted to the door and tugged on it. Locked.

Damn. I shivered in response to the cool air and the adrenaline pumping through my body. Why had fall decided to descend in all its gloomy glory tonight?

"Sloan, this way!" Garrett yelled and pointed to Brat Haus, a dive bar. I sprinted toward the bar and thrust open the doors. A wave of stale smoke assaulted my face. Washington State hadn't allowed smoking indoors for years, but the residual smell of cigarettes was layered on the pub's dingy walls.

A few heads turned when I stumbled inside, but mainly everyone was focused on a woman in a miniskirt and tube top singing karaoke on a small stage.

"I need a phone!" I shouted over her off-key voice to the bartender. At the same time, Garrett asked a man nursing something on the rocks for his phone. The bartender handed me a cell phone.

I punched in 911, and the minute the operator answered, I launched into an explanation of chasing after a fugitive. I'm sure they thought I was crazy, so I had to repeat the story three times and beg to talk to Police Chief Meyers before they finally got her on the line.

"Chief Meyers here," she said in her gruff voice.

"Chief Meyers, it's Sloan Krause. I know where Van is. He's on Blackbird Island. Garrett and I followed him."

She perked up at this news and asked me a few brief questions about the direction I'd last seen him running and how long ago I left him. I gave her as many details as I could remember. A few seconds later, the sound of shrill sirens wailed past Brat Haus and the blue, red, and white lights of the squad cars lit up the karaoke stage.

I probably should have stayed where I was, but I had to see if they caught him, so I headed back down the hill, completely unaware that I'd left Garrett behind. Every police car in Leavenworth must have been called out to the scene. They blocked the top and bottom of the hill. There were police officers on the footbridge. Flashlights danced off trees, and the sound of barking dogs filled the empty evening air.

Someone came up next to me as I watched from a safe

distance. It was Garrett. "You're fearless, Sloan. Crazy, but fearless."

"Ha!" I wished I were fearless. Was that how Garrett saw me?

We watched as a helicopter arrived on the scene and directed a spotlight on the island. It whipped the leaves on the tops of the trees, and the light was so bright that I'd have sworn I could make out pinecones on the forest floor.

"Are you still upset?" Garrett asked. I was acutely aware of the fluttery feeling in my chest.

"I just wish you could have trusted me. I wouldn't have said anything."

"I know, I wanted to tell you. I tried to at lunch the other day, but things have been . . ." He paused and searched for the right word. "Eventful since you started at Nitro." Were his eyes misty, or was that from the reflection of the street-lamp?

"That's a nice way to put it. You know what's ironic?"

He shook his head and moved closer to me. Our shoulders touched, making my heart reel.

"I've always prided myself on not attracting drama."

"What are you talking about? You didn't attract any of this."

"That's kind, but I think the last few weeks would show otherwise."

Sweat glistened on Garrett's forehead. "I can't believe he came back to town."

We turned our attention to shouting down below. Had they found him? Shrill whistles sounded from the police team on the ground. The helicopter darted near the bridge and illuminated the banks of the water. Sure enough, huddled under the bridge was a man's figure. It had to be Van.

Garrett and I watched as the team surrounded him and Chief Meyers belted out orders on a bullhorn. Van had to come out with his arms up in the air; otherwise they would move in.

At first I thought maybe he was going to resist arrest, or try to wait it out, but after two more warnings from the police chief, Van emerged from under the bridge with both hands in the air like goalposts.

They got him. In a spontaneous moment of relief, I hugged Garrett, who stood rigid, not returning my embrace.

"Sorry," I mumbled. "I'm so relieved that they caught him."

Garrett started to say something, but stopped and offered me his coat. "You look cold. Should we walk back?"

I nodded, knowing that there was much more to discuss, but for the moment, I wanted to be safe inside Nitro.

CHAPTER

FORTY-TWO

AS DESERTED AS DOWNTOWN HAD been an hour ago, it had now become a street party. The commotion and sound of sirens had brought the entire town out. I lost Garrett in the mix.

I wrapped his coat tighter against my body and weaved through the growing crowd. People stopped me to ask if I was okay and what had happened, but the reality of the situation had begun to sink in. My teeth chattered, and I couldn't stop shivering.

"Sloan!" Mac plucked me from the crowd and threw his arms around me. "I heard you were involved."

"No, not really." My voice sounded weak and quaky.

"You don't look so good." He scanned the street. Shops and restaurants that had closed hours ago had reopened their doors. The owner of the bakery circled with a tray of coffee and cookies, one of the restaurant owners stood in front of his shop with a wagon full of water and sodas, and another had set up a small table with snacks and hot tea. Tears welled in my eyes. This was how my village responded to a crisis.

Mac motioned to the bakery owner and handed me a paper cup. "Drink this. You need to warm up."

My hands trembled as I took the cup.

"Did he come after you?" Mac puffed out his chest. "If he did, I'll kill him."

"Mac, stop. He didn't come after me. I went after him."

"What? Why would you do something like that?"

I sipped the coffee, thankful for its warmth and strong flavor. "I don't know."

"Sloan, you scared me." Mac's tone was so sincere that I almost considered forgiving him.

"I'm fine." I wanted to find Garrett and sit down, but the crowd around us had doubled. *There must be three hundred people jammed into Front Street,* I thought. Farther down the sidewalk near Der Keller, I spotted Hayley, who was draped over one of the brewery's bartenders. Mac saw her, too. I waited for him to say something, but he just shrugged.

"Baby, I know you don't believe me, but she was a fling—a stupid fling—nothing more."

He ushered me underneath an awning. His eyes were almost frantic. "Sloan, I promise—it's done. She's crazy."

"I bet." I laughed.

"No, I mean crazy—like stalker crazy. I caught her parked by the house."

"What?" I finished the coffee, wishing there were more.

"She's been following me." He kicked a leaf at his feet.

"Does she drive a black sedan?"

"No, she rides a motorcycle."

Of course. Hayley had been following me, not Van.

Mac continued. "But her mom has a black sedan."

I crumpled the empty coffee cup. "She's been following me, too, Mac. And Alex."

He hung his head. "I'm sorry." The breeze picked up, sending a few leaves swirling in the wind and making me shiver again. Mac leaned closer and rubbed my arm. I stepped away and hugged Garrett's coat around me. It smelled faintly of hops and whiteboard pens. "I think she might have been in the house. Someone slipped our wedding photo under the door at my hotel room last night. Our faces are both scratched out."

"Geez, Mac." I shuddered. "That's crazy."

"I know." He tried to console me, but I pushed him off.

"Did he really do it—Van?" Mac asked, taking my cue and moving to my side. "Everyone is saying he killed Eddie."

I nodded. "I think so." Then I thought about Mac's lighter. It had been bugging me how his lighter had ended up by Nitro's fermenting tanks since the day I'd found it. "How did your lighter get back there, Mac?"

He pointed up the street where Hayley and the bartender were now locked in a passionate kiss. "Hayley."

"How? She never came past the bar."

"You're not going to like this." Scuffing the sidewalk with his expensive leather shoes, he tensed and glanced back up the street at Hayley. "She broke in to Nitro and stole a recipe for me."

"What?" I responded loudly enough to make a group of people nearby stop their conversation and turn in our direction. "Are you kidding me, Mac?" I huffed. "You had her steal for you?"

He held his arms up in a surrender. "No! I had no idea that she was going to do that. I mentioned something about Garrett's beer in passing. I admit it, I've been jealous. Watching you with him is ripping my heart out."

Mac has a tendency to be melodramatic.

"She wanted to impress me, so she snuck in and swiped the recipe. That's when I realized that she was nuts. I fired her, Sloan. I'm done with her, and she's done at Der Keller."

The crowd parted as two police cars rolled up Front Street. Their lights were still flashing, but the sirens had been turned off. I took that as a positive sign that the scene was winding down.

"I need to go," I said, stuffing the coffee cup into Garrett's coat pocket.

Mac stopped me. His voice became tender. "Sloan, I know I have a lot to prove to you, but I'm going to spend every hour of every day showing you that I've changed. We have suitcases of memories that we can't toss away. We're good together—you know that—and I'm lost without you."

The regret was apparent in his tearful plea. Gone were his sappy puppy dog eyes. Instead, they held a sadness I'd never seen. Once again he reached for my arm, but in a flash I was tugged the opposite direction.

"Yoo-hoo! Sloan, there you are." April exclaimed. "Come with me. They need you at Nitro." She whisked me away from Mac and around the corner.

"You can thank me later," she whispered.

"For what?"

"Saving you from that snake, honey." April bulldozed through the busy sidewalk and shoved me through the door when we made it to Nitro. "Chief Meyers needs you, and, Sloan, don't be stingy with details. I want *all* the gossip when you're done." She placed her hands on her hips and waited by the door.

Garrett and Chief Meyers sat at the bar when I stumbled into Nitro. I smelled coffee and noticed their conversation come to an abrupt halt.

"Sloan," Garrett said, pushing back his barstool and getting to his feet. "You disappeared." Without asking, he poured me a cup of coffee and placed it at the open seat next to Chief Meyers.

I took that as my cue and sat.

"Garrett informed me that he gave you background on our investigation." She removed a walkie-talkie from her belt, turned it off, and set it on the counter.

"He did." I cradled the ceramic cup. The heat warmed my hands.

She sounded almost apologetic as she explained that not only had Van been arrested and taken into custody, but he'd also confessed to killing Eddie. "He realized that Eddie was on to him," she said, drinking the scalding coffee like a shot of whiskey. "Eddie came here the night he was killed to talk to Garrett. He had a feeling that Garrett didn't trust Van either, but Van was already one step ahead. He followed Eddie here, knocked him out, and tossed him in the tank."

My body shuddered at the memory. "Why did he come back?"

Chief Meyers's eyes lit up. "That's where our perp went wrong. He stashed cash on Blackbird Island. Came back to get it. Not sure why he was sniffing around here. Maybe he hid something in the back." She looked at Garrett. "I'll have my guys give this place a thorough sweep. If he left a crumb, we'll find it."

Garrett gave her a half smile. "Thanks, Chief."

Her stool scraped on the floor as she pushed to her feet. "I've got a pile of paperwork waiting for me. Good work, both of you. Leavenworth can sleep tight tonight knowing that Van is behind bars." She reached into her pocket, pulled out two police badge stickers, and slapped them on the counter. "Usually I save these for the kids at Oktoberfest, but I'd make you both official deputies if I were authorized. Couldn't have done this without you," she said to Garrett.

Garrett laughed. "I think I'll stick to beer."

Chief Meyers turned to face me. "One sharp guy you're working with here, Sloan."

"Yeah." I wanted to ask her why she was including me. I hadn't done anything. In fact, I'd missed the most obvious detail of her entire investigation—that Garrett was working with her.

She clapped me on the shoulder. "Stop by headquarters tomorrow. I have a few follow-up questions for you, but they can wait."

Garrett watched her saunter out, then immediately shoo April and everyone else who had gathered to watch the commotion away. *Thank God for small miracles,* I thought.

"Do you want a ride home?" Garrett asked, as he cleared the coffee cups.

"I'm fine." I shook my head and removed his coat. "Thanks for this."

"Don't give it a thought." He waved me off. "You're sure you're okay?"

"Sure." I nodded. "I need to go check on Alex. I'm sure he's oblivious to everything that happened tonight, but still . . ." I trailed off.

Garrett came around the bar. "Listen, Sloan, I'm sorry that I couldn't tell you."

"It's fine. I get it." Tonight had been filled with too many apologies. My head pounded. I couldn't process one more. I needed to be home and to hug my son. "See you tomorrow," I said as breezily as possible, and walked to the door. Thoughts of Van, Hayley, Eddie, and Mac evaporated on the drive home. I was safe, Leavenworth was safe, and despite the many questions I had about my future, I was headed to the sanctuary I had created at the farmhouse and to hold Alex as tightly as I could. For now that was all I needed.

Garrett, probably in his late teens, sat at one of the old vinyl booths across from his aunt Tess. He hadn't changed much in the last twenty years. He had filled out and his hair was a touch darker, but otherwise I would have recognized him right away.

He watched as I thumbed through a handful of photos. Then his face clouded. "Remember how I thought you looked familiar when we met?"

"Yeah." I looked up at him.

He slid a picture facedown across the table. "Look at this."

I turned the photo over and staring back at me was a picture of a woman who looked exactly like me swinging a young girl with olive skin and dark black hair in front of the Maypole.

"Who is this?"

Garrett shook his head. "I don't know. I was up in my aunt's room yesterday, and it was in a frame on her dresser. That's why I thought you looked familiar. I've seen the picture hundreds of times but never paid attention to it before."

I studied the picture. The resemblance between me and the woman was undeniable. I felt like I was staring into a mirror. And the girl. The young girl. My breath caught.

"Sloan, do you think that's you and your mom?"

My heart dropped along with the photo. I'd often wondered about my parents and had even made a couple of attempts in my late teens and early twenties to find them, but once I'd met Mac and become part of the Krause family, tracing my roots became less important. The Krauses adopted me, and I adopted them back. Their family story became my story.

"Are you okay?" Garrett looked at me with concern.

I couldn't force my jaw to close. "We could be twins, couldn't we?"

He held up the picture, then studied me and the woman. "Yeah." Handing me the picture, he repeated his question. "You're sure you're okay?"

"Yeah, but I don't understand. I have no memory of ever being in Leavenworth until I met the Krauses." One of the things that I had learned from my caseworker was that kids in crisis had a tendency to block out memories. It was a form of self-protection. But wouldn't some memory have been triggered when I moved here? I must have passed the Maypole thousands of times, but I had no memory of dancing around it in my youth.

The picture felt weighty in my hand, not because I was worried or scared about what it might mean, but because it held the promise of my past. How could I dream of a different future without understanding where I'd come from? The Krauses would always be my family, no matter what happened between me and Mac, but I had another story to find—my own. Garrett had given me hope. An excitement I didn't even know existed began to build in me. This was my time. I knew exactly what I was going to do with the photo: I would use it to trace my lineage, and wherever that led me, I would be able to close a lingering hole in my heart— and make room for something new.

Read on for an excerpt of

The Pint of No Return

Ellie Alexander

Now available from St. Martin's Paperbacks

THE SOUND OF ACCORDIONS PLAYING the Chicken Dance, Leavenworth's most popular polka during Oktoberfest, filled the bustling square. All around me city crews, dressed in matching baby blue T-shirts with this year's Bavarian crest— two pewter beer steins, a pretzel, a black bear, and a German sausage—were setting up for the weekend festivities. The town gazebo had been decked out in strands of fall foliage wound together with yellow, orange, and white twinkle lights. Hay bales and pumpkins flanked the cement steps. Navy blue banners with golden leaves and the word: *Willkommen* hung from the lampposts that lined Front Street. Even the trees burst with welcoming fall color. It was no wonder that Leavenworth had become one of the most popular places to visit during Oktoberfest.

I smiled and waved to a worker inflating a bouncy house on the grassy area near the gazebo. Front Street would soon be filled with vendor tents, arts and crafts booths, and an entire kid zone (known as the Kinderplatz) with a climbing wall, clowns, and tons of games and activities to keep our youngest guests entertained while their parents imbibed dozens of imported German beers that would soon be tapped. Over the next three weekends, thousands of visitors would make the trek through Washington's breathtaking mountain passes and winding roads to join in the revelry.

When Oktoberfest first began in 1989 four-hundred people raised a pint glass in a toast to Germany's famed beer celebration. Through the years the festival had grown exponentially. Now events stretch over multiple weekends and draw crowds, brewers, performers, and beer lovers from all over the world.

It was impossible not to get caught up in the excitement, especially with every shop in the village getting in the spirit with elaborate fall displays. Collections of nutcrackers wearing lederhosen and baskets of apple strudel and kuchen (sweet cake topped with powdered sugar and toasted nuts) tempted passersby in the front windows of the square where each storefront was designed to resemble chalets in the German Alps. From half-timbered structures with ornate window carvings, balconies lush with blooming geraniums, and white stucco siding framed with dark trim, every shop looked like a cottage from the Germany countryside.

Despite the craziness that had surrounded my life the past few weeks, I felt a sense of calm watching the familiar bustle that accompanied fall's biggest bash. Oktoberfest brought out the best in our remote village. Preparations had begun months in advance with shopkeepers ordering cases of

German flags and spending weeks washing their front windows and sweeping their sidewalks. The fact that the annual festival coincided with the official start of fall made it that much more spectacular. Our little Bavaria looked like a movie set. If I didn't live here, I might not believe that our pristine cobblestone streets and sunlit title rooftops were real.

Could there be any place more beautiful? I thought as I stopped to admire a leafy oak tree, glowing gold with sun.

Alas, that thought quickly evaporated when I heard someone call my name in a nauseating sing-song tone.

"You-hoo! Sloan."

My stomach sunk. I knew the nasal voice all too well. Play nice, I reminded myself and turned to see April Ablin racing toward me. April was Leavenworth's self-proclaimed town ambassador and my nemesis. As always she was dressed in a bar-maid costume that squished her ample bosom up to her neck.

I thought about making a run for it, but I knew that it wouldn't do any good. April was persistent.

"Morning," I said, trying not to stare at her garish makeup.

"Oh, Sloan, I've been looking everywhere for you." She gasped for breath. "Have you heard the news?"

"No. What news?"

Her face, which was caked in three layers of foundation in an attempt to hide the winkles creasing her brow, gleamed with delight. "Oh my goodness, I can't believe you haven't heard. I was under the impression that the Krause family knew everything there was to know about beer." She gave me a look of pity and fluffed her white ruffled apron tied over a red and white gingham skirt. "How rude of me. I'd forgotten that you're not exactly part of the Krause family anymore, are you? I suppose that means you're out of the *beer* loop."

I didn't bother to acknowledge her dig. "What's the news, April?"

"Right." She twirled her fingers together. They were painted red, white, yellow, and black with the German flag adorning her thumbnails. Like everything else on April from her hair extensions to her gaudy lashes, they were fake. "It's incredible. We are about to be movie stars."

"Movie stars?" I frowned.

"Yes! Can you believe it? A documentary film crew is arriving later this afternoon. They're shooting their film here. Right here in Leavenworth! Our little Leavenworth or as we natives like to say—*haus*." She butchered an attempt at an accent. "And during Oktoberfest nonetheless. This is going be huge for us—huge. This is going to put us on the map."

"Aren't we already on the map?" April brought out the worst in me. I thought about pointing out the fact that Leavenworth attracted thousands and thousands of visitors each year. It was hardly as if we were struggling to get people to come to our version of beertopia. Actually the opposite was true. Hotels, bed and breakfasts, and rental properties had been sold out for months. Oktoberfest was so popular that tourists who had booked late had to stay in nearby Wenatchee or Cle Elum (a thirty minute or hour long drive respectively) and get shuttled in for the day. The same was true for the Christmas markets. Families reserved hotel rooms and airbnbs over a year in advance. Every season brought a new festival— the winter lights, maifest, fall foliage, and many more. There wasn't a moment that went by when our village wasn't brimming with out-of-town guests.

"Sloan, you know what I mean. Having a major film shot here is going to elevate us even higher on a national and international level." To emphasize the word elevate she placed both hands under her chest and shoved her cleavage up towards her neck.

"That's great," I said, starting to back away.

"Not so fast." April reached for my arm to stop me. She appraised me from head to toe and scowled. Then she leaned in. I could smell stale coffee that she had attempted to mask with a breath mint. "I've been meaning to talk to you about your . . ." she paused and gave me a once over. "Attire."

My eyes betrayed me and followed April's gaze to my jeans.

"We need everyone in town on board for this film," April continued. "And those ratty jeans, ugly yellow boots, and beer T-shirt are not going to cut it. I've sold the film crew on the fact that we are the next best thing to being in Munich at Oktoberfest."

That was a slogan I had heard repeated many times. Villagers prided themselves on Leavenworth's famed festivals. Rightly so. Attracting visitors to the Northern Cascades had been a community effort. If it hadn't been for a small group of residents who banded together to transform their beloved town into the German mecca it is today, Leavenworth might not exist. The town had been on the brink of collapse after major mining and logging industries departed in the 1960s. Given its remote location in the Washington Alps, Leavenworth could have become a ghost town, but thanks to a resourceful and creative community, the town rebranded itself.

Every shop and business had been spruced up and given a Bavarian facelift. The community embraced the idea of modeling itself after a quaint German alpine village, as did tourists. Hence, Leavenworth as we know and love it today, was born.

"What does that have to do with my outfit?" I asked April. In my work at Nitro, a new startup brewery, jeans and a T-shirt was standard attire. Not to mention, every self-respecting brewer owned a sturdy pair of rubber boots. Waterproof, slip-resistant footwear is essential in the brewing process. My bright yellow boots had been special ordered from a brewing supply company in Wisconsin. They had reinforced steel toes and thick soles. When carrying or cleaning heavy kegs and equipment you could never be too careful.

April rolled her eyes which were outlined in black and coated in emerald green eye shadow. "Sloan, we have to show them that we're a real German village and that means that *all* of us need to dress for the part." She did a twirl in the middle of the sidewalk to show off her dress. "As they say in the motherland it is *witchtig* that we all embrace our heritage and duty. That's important, in case you didn't know."

I wanted to remind her that in reality we weren't a German village and that I was pretty sure no one in modern Germany dressed in April's outlandish costumes. Of course, there were a handful of shop owners in town who outfitted their staff in German costumes as a marketing tool to attract more customers, but April was the only resident I knew who embraced the idea of dressing like a barmaid on a daily basis.

"Thanks, I'm good," I declined.

April's pumpkin orange lips thinned into a hard, narrow

line. "As Leavenworth's official ambassador I must insist that you rethink your anti-beervaria stance."

"I don't have anti-beervaria anything. I'm just not going to dress up. That's all."

Her cheeks burned with anger. "You haven't heard the last from me, Sloan Krause." With that she stormed away on strappy high-heeled sandals that caught on the cobblestones and nearly made her topple over.

April wasn't going to ruin my morning. I crossed the street and rounded the corner to Commercial Street. Nitro, the small pub where I had recently been hired to help with brew operations as well as manage the bar and food service, sat just two blocks off the main strip near Waterfront Park. Garrett Strong, a homebrewer and former engineer from Seattle, had inherited the building from his aunt Tess. When Tess died she left what had originally been a brothel in the late 1880s during the height of the Great Northern Railroad expansion to Garrett—her only nephew. The two-story chalet-style building had served as a diner and bed and breakfast for years. Tess had been a fixture in the village and one of the driving forces behind Leavenworth's transformation from a rundown mill town to a thriving Bavaria. Garret had made the space his own by tearing out the dingy vinyl booths and tossing his aunt's huge collection of German kitsch. The main floor had high ceilings and exposed beams. In the front, there was a collection of high bar tables and stools where customers could leisurely sip a pint. A twenty-foot distressed wood bar separated the dining area from the brewery equipment, kitchen, and office in the back.

Garrett's esthetic was sparse and sterile. The walls had been painted a stark white which made the brewery feel open, but also gave it a clinical feel. I had wrapped the exposed beams in twinkle lights and arranged vintage black and white photos along the walls to give Nitro a touch of home. So many of Leavenworth's shops and restaurants were packed with nutcrackers, cuckoo clocks, glockenspiels, and German souvenirs that I appreciated Garrett's clean, industrial vibe.

He was also extremely tidy. Cleanliness is close to godliness when it comes to brewing. There are so many things that can taint a beer or make it go bad. Good brewers know that keeping fermenting tanks and wart chillers in tip-top shape ensure a high-quality craft beer. Garrett was no exception. Nitro's shiny steel tanks sparkled like new due to our regimented cleaning schedule. As did the cement floors, that we mopped down every night.

I opened the front door and weaved through the bar. Garrett tended to be a late sleeper so I wasn't surprised to find the brewery quiet. I left my coat and purse in the office and went to check the tanks. We had been perfecting a new beer that we would be debuting just in time for Oktoberfest—Cherry Weizen. Leavenworth's proximity to the lush organic orchards of the Yakima Valley meant that we had an abundance of scrumptious handpick produce at our fingertips. For the Cherry Weizen we had ordered twenty pounds of bright, tangy Washington Bing cherries. I removed a taster from the tank with a turkey baster. Then I siphoned the Weizen into a tasting glass and took a sip. The beer was a gorgeous amber color with a touch of pink.

I swirled the liquid on my tongue. The Weizen had a perfect balance. It wasn't too sweet or tart. The refreshing summer flavor of sun-ripened cherries came through without being overpowering. I could already picture tourists sipping a cold pint of the picnic-worthy brew on our front patio.

One of my favorite parts of the brewing process was seeing a beer come to life. After fermenting for weeks in our tanks, this beauty was ready to carbonate and tap. I had a feeling that it was going to be a hit and sell out fast. Garrett and I planned to keg the Cherry Weizen this morning. As long as everything went according to plan, it would be ready later this evening, and would be flowing out of our taps by the time the crowds descended for Oktoberfest.

In addition to the fruity wheat beer, we would be pouring our regular line up of brews—our signature Pucker Up IPA, a Bottle Blonde, a light wheat beer, and a Perk Me Up Porter, a chocolate coffee stout. Unlike Der Keller, Leavenworth's oldest and largest brewery, Garrett preferred Northwest style beers. Der Keller was one of the featured brewers at Oktoberfest and would be showcasing their signature German beers, like Kolsch, Hefeweizen, Dopplebock, and Dunkel. My in-laws, Otto and Ursula Krause, had brought their native beers to Leavenworth when they immigrated to the United States. It happened to be at the same time that the town was going through a major re-branding. They'd jumped on board with the idea of creating a Bavarian village and within a few years Der Keller had become one of the largest producers of craft beers in the state.

Without the Krause family, I would probably be waitressing or bartending somewhere—if I was lucky. I grew up in the foster care system which meant that I never had permanent roots. My early and teen years were spent bouncing between homes—some were kind and welcoming and many were worse than being abandoned. Once I finished high school, I paid for community college by working at a farmer's market and waiting tables. A twist of fate changed my future when Otto and Ursula happened upon my farm stand one day. They were regulars at the market, coming each weekend to source local produce for their new brewery Der Keller. We got to talking about baking, and Ursula's eyes would light up. She regaled me with tales of sweet twisted bread brushed with butter and hand-spun honey from her homeland. Their enthusiasm for baking, beer, and life was contagious. I began to bake test batches of cookies and cakes and ask for their feedback. Their big-hearted personalities made me long for a family like theirs.

The Krauses offered me a job at the brewery and to set me up with their oldest son, Mac. At first I declined, but they were relentless in their quest. Not that they were pushy. Rather, Ursula would take my hand, and pierce my soul with her kind eyes. "Sloan, the brewing world it is changing. It needs a woman's touch. You will be perfect. Tell her, Otto."

Otto was equally insistent. "Ja, it will be good. You have the nose. It is a gift that not many people have. I will teach you how to use it. You will become a legend. Sloan, the pretty female brewer with the super sniffer." His eyes twinkled when he spoke.

How could I resist? I dove into craft brewing with Otto and Ursula as my mentors. Then they introduced me to Mac. It didn't take long for him to charm me, or for me to end up pregnant. In hindsight it might have been a mistake to marry him, but I didn't regret becoming an official member of the Krause family. For the first time in my life I had a place and a home to call my own. Otto and Ursula taught me everything they knew about craft brewing, German-style baking, and how to be a parent. I couldn't imagine my life without them. Or without Alex, my teenage son, and Hans, my surrogate brother. Sometimes I wondered if I would have fallen so hard and so fast for Mac if it hadn't been for his family.

When I had caught Mac cheating with one of Der Keller's youngest bar maids a few weeks ago, I had thought my life was over. All of the years we had spent together carving out a home, raising Alex, working side by side in the brewing—were they a waste? I blamed myself. I'd been too lonely and let my heart loose. Growing up alone had taught me to stay guarded and closed. But once I met the Krause family they cracked me open. I never should have allowed myself to love them.

Mac's cheating hadn't just been the end of our marriage—I feared it might mean that I was going to have to give up the only family I had ever known. Not that Otto, Ursula, or Hans felt that way. In fact, Otto and Ursula had recently given me a huge stake in Der Keller. They were preparing to retire soon and wanted to begin stepping back a bit. However they were concerned about leaving the company in Mac's capable, but impulsive hands, so had outlined a deal that gave Mac, myself, and Hans each an equal share of ownership. They both had insisted that I was like a daughter to them and that no matter what transpired between me and Mac, I always had a place at Der Keller. I believed them, but

I had been tossing and turning trying to figure out what was next for me. Part of me wanted to sever ties with the brewery, but I couldn't do that to Otto and Ursula.

The sound of movement upstairs shook me from my thoughts.

Garret was awake. Time to focus on brewing and shelve my worries about my personal life and future for the moment. A minute later, he appeared in the brewery looking bleary eyed. "You're here early, per usual." He winked. "Please tell me we have coffee."

I glanced toward the bar. "I'm pretty sure we have a fresh bag of beans. You want me to make a pot?"

"Good God, yes." He ran his hands through his dark and disheveled hair and followed me into the front.

We kept an assortment of soft drinks along with coffee and tea at the bar for anyone who wasn't a beer fan and for designated drivers who can drink unlimited non-alcoholic beverages on the house. I found the bag of beans in one of the cupboards beneath the bar and poured them into the coffee maker. The scent of nutty beans made Garrett inhale deeply.

"How late were you up?" I asked filling the carafe with cold water.

He blinked twice and stretched. Garrett was tall and thin with a casual style typical of brewers in the Pacific Northwest. This morning he wore a pair of jeans and a light gray T-shirt that read: *Talk Nerdy To Me.* He was the exact opposite of Mac in almost every way. Mac was shorter and stout with ruddy cheeks and blond hair. He could talk to a stranger for hours and talk them into doing anything for him. Garrett on the other hand, was quiet and almost pensive. He chose his words carefully and tended to listen rather than join in a conversation.

"I can't remember," he replied brushing a strand of hair from his brown eyes that reminded me of warm sand. "Maybe around one-thirty or two? I wasn't keeping track of time."

"Were you brewing?" Many pub owners, especially those who owned nano breweries like Nitro, would brew at midnight after last call.

"I was playing around with a couple small batches of a pumpkin ale, but I'm not really feeling it." Garrett leaned over the bar to catch a whiff of the brewing coffee. "That smells so good. Why does it have to take so long?"

I laughed and glanced at the pot. Dark coffee dripped slowly into the glass carafe. "It's been brewing for two minutes."

"Exactly." Garrett pulled out a bar stool and sat. "What do you think of pumpkin? Is it too much? I know that it's a huge trend in Seattle and Portland right now. But do we want to be trend followers or trend setters?"

"Good questions."

He sighed. "Yeah, and getting the balance right is going to be tricky. The first batch I brewed was way too heavy. It looks like sludge in the carboy." The carboy that Garrett referred to was a five-gallon glass tank used in the secondary fermenting process when we tested small batches. We brewed our signature beer on a larger scale in the stainless steel tanks in the brewery, but when experimenting with new recipes we used Garrett's old homebrewing set-up in the kitchen.

"I think the second one is going to be too weak," he continued. "You'll have to give them a try."

He was right about beer trends. Pumpkin had been hot for quite a few years with brewers offering seasonal holiday pumpkin ales in time for Halloween and Thanksgiving. Even though it was only the end of September we were already planning and preparing our holiday line. Craft beer took a minimum of two weeks to three weeks to brew which meant that we had to get started on our next batch as soon as we kegged the Cherry Weizen and cleaned the tanks.

"Hmm," I said, reaching for two coffee mugs. "Personally I'm not a huge pumpkin fan, but could we do something in its place? I think having a late fall seasonal would be good, and then we can release our winter ales in time for the Christmas markets."

Garrett massaged his temples. "Yeah, a fall beer that would pair well with turkey."

I thought about it for a minute while I grabbed cream, sugar, and a stirring spoon. The coffee pot was nearly full. I poured a splash of cream into the bottom of one of the glasses, hit the pause button on the machine, and poured a cup for Garrett.

He clutched the mug with both hands. I offered him the sugar. "No thanks. This is perfect. Thank you."

"No worries." I filled my cup and added a half teaspoon of sugar and a healthy glug of the cream. "What about cranberries?" I asked, stirring the latte colored coffee.

"Cranberries?" Garrett wrinkled his forehead.

"Yeah, what if we do an IRA with fresh cranberries? They would give the beer a nice bite and probably a gorgeous red color." IRAs or Indian Red Ales are a great choice for beer drinkers who like a malty finish with a touch of hops. The popular Northwest style ale pulls a ruby color and has a slight bitterness married with notes of caramel and toffee.

Garrett nursed his coffee. "I like it." He nodded. "Cranberries are very fallish, right? And they go well with turkey, yeah?"

"Right." I took a sip of the coffee and tried to think if anyone around had done a cranberry beer lately. Nothing came to mind. "Sour beers are super popular right now, so it could almost be a mashup of an IRA meets a sour."

"Yeah, let's try it. Can you get your hands on some cranberries?"

"I've got a guy." I chuckled.

"Of course you do." Garrett grinned. "Sloan, you have 'a guy' for everything, don't you?"

"Call it the curse of living in Leavenworth forever," I kidded. Although there was truth behind my words. In a town this size it was impossible to go through a day without bumping into a friend or neighbor at the grocery store or post office. Living somewhere where everyone knows your name has its perks, and also a unique set of drawbacks. Like the fact that everyone in town knew exactly what had gone down between Mac and me.

We mapped out our plan for the day over coffee. The first order of business was kegging the Cherry Weizen. Then we would clean the clarifying tanks. I agreed to hunt down some cranberries for our test beer. When working on a new recipe we only brewed five gallon batches. I was confident that the grocery store would have enough cranberries in stock for that. After that I would finish food for the tapping party, and we would open the tasting room by four. It sounded doable, and like we had a full day ahead of us.

I finished off my coffee, happy to have the distraction of Nitro to keep me from my thoughts.

CHAPTER

FORTY-THREE

THINGS RETURNED TO NORMAL OVER the next few days. With Van locked away, I could focus on things like welcoming Ursula home from the hospital and figuring out how I was going to balance working at not one, but two pubs. Garrett was supportive and flexible. We agreed that I would work mornings at Der Keller until we figured out a more permanent solution or until Otto and Ursula returned to work. I had a feeling that her injury might be the end of their reign at Der Keller, but it looked like things were going to work out okay.

Mac, Hans, and I had begun sifting through résumés. We had some hiring to do—especially when it came to barmaids. I agreed to oversee brewing operations, but wanted to keep the job at Nitro, too. Hans agreed that he would help in the evening until we hired someone. Mac would manage daily operations and was under house arrest when it came to spending. We worked up a contract that stipulated that he needed both Hans and me to sign off on any expenditures over five hundred dollars. He balked at the new agreement, but after his disastrous investment in Van's nonexistent hop farm, he didn't have any room to negotiate.

Fortunately, Chief Meyers had caught Van before he'd cashed in on Der Keller's investment. She couldn't make any promises, but thought there was a chance Mac might get some of his money back. Van had already spent the rest, and Chief Meyers suggested it was better to write it off as a loss and move on. Van was going to prison for a long, long time, and the odds of us recovering any cash from him weren't in our favor.

Garrett and I continued to expand our offerings at Nitro, especially as we prepared for Oktoberfest. I perfected a batch of cherry Weizen, and Garrett experimented with a pumpkin stout and a fresh hopped pale ale. The new beers were a hit, but would be short-lived successes because we had no idea where Van had gotten the hops.

One night about a week after Van's arrest, I was wiping down the bar after the last customer had left and I had just flipped the sign on the front door to CLOSED.

"Sloan, do you have a minute?" Garrett asked, holding a shoe box in his arms. "I want to show you something."

"Sure." I tossed the rag in the sink and joined him at a high-top table.

He opened the shoe box, which was filled with old photos. "I found another box of photos last night and started going through them to see if there were any more we could use for the collage."

I picked up a photo that had yellowed edges. In it, a young

no," she murmured. "I know what you want. I know what I feel."

"Stop, Jillian. Stop!" Marius begged. He forced himself to ignore the pulsing of his erection in her hand and grabbed the ends of her shirt, tying them together as best he could. Without thought, he closed his eyes and pressed his mouth to the crown of her head. "Please," he whispered. "I never meant to hurt you, and—"

"'Hurt me . . . ,'" Jillian echoed.

She reached into her pocket and pulled out a switchblade. Flicking it expertly open she said, "Hayden gave this to me. Hayden, your worst enemy. At the time I thought it was a really shitty birthday present, but it always seems to come in handy." Transfixing Marius with her stare, she held the knife to her neck. "Could you resist me if I made myself bleed for you? I know what it's like when you smell blood. That means my blood will make you insane, if you feel half of what I think you do for me. You won't be able to stop yourself, and it won't be your fault." She swallowed hard. "I'm not afraid."

"Enough!" Marius roared, baring his fangs. The switchblade clattered to the pavement. "Enough." He took her face in his hands. "This isn't you. This is not who you are."

Jillian slowly pulled free and backed up, collecting her weapon.

"Do you think this helps?" Marius continued, unable to contain himself any longer. "Do you think I feel no pain? I watch you run around with Hayden Wilks, and you think it doesn't kill me? He gets to have you in every way that I cannot. It makes no difference that I understand why you're with him, that I know you don't love him. It doesn't matter, because . . . yes." His hands dug into Jill's shoulders as he struggled to stay in control. "I can feel you. Do you understand? I can sense you. I know

So you like vampires? You're not alone.

Don't miss the part steampunk Victorian
historical, part futuristic thriller

Crimson & Steam

by

Liz Maverick

Coming January 2010

. . . He found her on a stretch of Santa Monica Boule-
vard, just inside an alcove. She stood frozen, silent, her
face obscured by shadow. He grabbed her by the shoulders and spun her toward some dull light oozing from a
nearby store's half-broken bulb.

"Coward," she spat. "Do I have to make it really easy
for you, so you can't refuse? Should I just rip my clothes
off and beg?" She pulled the tie holding together her
wrap blouse, and the fabric cascaded away. "Do it. Here
in this alley, Marius. Please."

"Jillian, don't!" Marius's blood raced. Exposed neck,
pale shoulders, pink-tipped breasts—all delicate flesh and
the black lace of her transparent bra. He'd never seen Jill
this way. He'd only dreamed of it.

"I will. I'll beg," she continued. "I'll do whatever you
need to make this okay. I'm not afraid of what we have.
Why the hell are you?"

She pulled the hem of her skirt up and leaned back
against the brick wall. Marius tried to wrench her skirt
down, but she was pulling out all the stops and rudely
pressed her palm against his groin. "Don't try to tell me

Bastien let his breath out on a sigh and hugged her tight. "Damn, woman. I love you."

Terri laughed as tears pooled in her eyes. "And I love you."

"Come on." Jumping up, he tugged her to her feet and began straightening her clothes.

"Where are we going?" Terri asked as he pulled her out of his office.

"To the penthouse," he explained, pausing at the elevator to push the button. The doors opened at once and he tugged her inside. "There's champagne and the Jacuzzi, and . . . I want to turn you now and start our lives together."

He pushed the button for the penthouse, then leaned back against the wall and pulled her into his arms. The doors closed, sealing them in. "I can't wait. I suspect that, with you, life is going to be one hell of an adventure."

Bastien bent to kiss her, and Terri sighed into his mouth. She somehow knew he was right. There would be good times and bad, but life together would always be an adventure.

And speaking of adventures; now *she and Bastien* had a wedding to plan.

"I know. I understand," Terri assured him. She eased up into a sitting position. She was surprisingly light-headed.

"In my excitement, I got a little carried away," Bastien told her apologetically. "It won't happen again."

"Are you kidding?" she cried. "I sincerely hope it does. That was . . ." Terri shook her head. It was mind-blowing.

Bastien smiled slightly, but said, "Terri, I do love you. But I'm not perfect, and I've made mistakes, and will make lots more over the years. I'm sorry I—"

"Shh." She hushed him and took his face between her hands. "No one's perfect, I'm not perfect, and you're not perfect, Bastien. But you're perfect for me."

They kissed gently, and Bastien pulled back and eyed her. "So, what are you doing for the next forty to fifty years?"

"Hmm." Terri smiled. "Actually, I don't have any plans at the moment. I just quit my job and sold my cottage, so I'm rather at loose ends."

"Yeah?" He grinned. "Would you care to spend them with me?"

"I thought you'd never ask," Terri said with a smile.

"Hmm." His expression turned solemn, telling her what was coming was important to him. Bastien brushed one finger down her cheek, then asked, "Would you care to make it four to five hundred years or more? There's a lot to do in this world, and it would be nice to do it all together."

Terri raised a hand to caress his cheek in return, and nodded. "I think I'd like that."

her until Terri didn't think she could stand it anymore, then darkness crowded in.

"You fainted."

Terri blinked her eyes open at those words and stared up at Bastien, then glanced around. He'd moved her to the couch. She was lying on it, her clothing in disarray, while he sat on the edge brushing the hair back from her face with his gentle fingers.

"You bit me," she said with disbelief.

He grimaced. "I'm sorry, I tried not to, but you forced my head back to your neck and I—"

"It's okay," she said quickly to stop his apology. Then she sighed. "Jeez. Kate said it was something, but that was an understatement."

"Are you all right?" he asked with concern.

Terri nodded slowly. She felt all right. She felt better than all right. She felt excellent. Her eyes sought his. "I love you, Bastien. I'm sorry for the last three weeks, but I needed time to accept. It was all so easy, so natural from the start. Like some sort of fairy-tale romance."

"Then it turned into a horror," he said.

"No. Not a horror," Terri said, then admitted, "Well, okay, maybe a little horrorish, but that was only because your explanation—"

"I'm sorry," he interrupted. He gave a slight laugh and ran one hand through his hair. "Can you believe I had to explain it to Rachel for Etienne, because he was flubbing it? Then I turned around and flubbed it with you. I guess it's harder to be smart when it really matters. And it did—*does*—matter to me."

and moved, repositioning herself so that she could guide herself onto him.

"Terri . . ." Bastien groaned as she sank slowly down to take him into her. Her wet heat closed around him.

"Yes," she breathed, lifting herself off and sliding back down.

"Damn." His mouth fastened on her neck and he sucked urgently; then he felt his teeth try to slip out to bite her. He forced them back and turned his mouth to her lips instead. Terri kissed back just as hungrily, her body sliding against his as she raised and lowered herself. Her languid rhythm was driving him crazy. He needed fast and hard after so long without her.

Pushing her skirt farther upward and out of the way, he fastened his hands on her hips and urged her on.

Astride him, Terri broke the kiss on a gasp and caught her hand at the back of Bastien's head, urging his mouth against her skin. The tension inside her was building to unbearable levels.

"Bastien, please!" she gasped, begging for release. He almost had her there. Then she felt his teeth sink into her, and she stiffened in surprise.

Terri stopped moving, her body gone taut as she trembled on the knife edge of excitement, but he continued to pump into her as he sucked at her neck. Suddenly, pleasure exploded through her. Wondrous, ecstatic pleasure. Terri cried out, her arms clenching around his neck and shoulders, and her whole body jerking in his arms. Wave after wave of release rode

when he's with you, when he's touching you, when . . ."
He had to look away. "Knowing I could make you feel so
much more, that my feelings for you go so much deeper,
that you've given yourself to someone who doesn't deserve you because I'm not allowed to have the life I want
to live . . . It makes me feel like dying sometimes. You
must understand how much I care about you. But—"

"But not enough," she interrupted. Then, with a hitch
in her voice she added, "Soul mates aren't supposed to
end like this."

Marius dropped his hands. "I'm sorry."

CRIMSON & STEAM
by
LIZ MAVERICK